Major Bruton's A

By

Michael Fitzalan

Copyright © 2020 by Michael Fitzalan

Dedication

To my travelling companions in Uganda – you know who you are – and my travelling companions in life; we've come so far.

With thanks to all the family for a wonderful trip.

Dedicated to the memory of the Major, he made it all possible.

After my mother died, the family adopted me, and I was invited on to their holiday.

Like all good fiction I have exaggerated, transposed and transformed events to make for an entertaining read.

None of this is real or true except in my head.

Their humour and patience speaks volumes about their strong characters and their warm hearts.

Finally, to the people who made us so welcome in Uganda, I say thank you for your kindness to all of us.

Contents

Chapter 1

The Hotel Reste Corner – Day 1

I woke up in the room, which I shared with Major Bruton, to find the first rays of sunshine struggling through the slats of the wooden shutters outside the window. The single bed was far too small for me and I found myself enviously eyeing the Major's large double bed, which lay between the window and me. His bed was empty and my back ached.

Perhaps, I could lie on that commodious expanse for a short while just to stretch out. Surely, I reasoned, he would not mind if I slipped between the sheets and unfurled myself for an hour or so? I had been curled up like a cat all night and my spine was suffering, there was no way that I could stretch my legs out fully without them dangling over the end of my small bed.

The Major had arrived two days before me and had bagged the biggest bed; in fact, he had booked the hotel and the room next door had two equally small beds. The only other option was an old sofa in the sitting room, which I had found uncomfortable to sit on the previous evening. I was so exhausted that I could not be bothered to move. It was warm in the room, a sheet and blanket covered me, it was cosy and despite my foetal position and the dull ache at the base of my spine, I was very comfortable.

The mattress was too soft, but I enjoyed being prone. I had already had more of my share of sleeping slumped in a chair to know that I was comparatively well off. An eight-hour flight from London to Entebbe followed by a late night drinking whisky left me with little strength. I rolled over and faced the cupboards where my paltry possessions lay hung on wire hangers or still in my flight bag.

Bruton was older and larger than I and deserved the bed; Cambridge educated; he was also wiser. I was going to be relying on him an awful lot over the next month, if I made it through the month. Intelligence deserves a certain privilege of its own.

Tempting as his empty bed was, I could not steel myself to crawl across the room and lie down on that inviting expanse of cotton sheets and well-sprung mattress. The boss was awake and up, I reasoned, so I should be, but I was too tired to care about that.

I could have dozed all day to recover from the flight, but for the pang of hunger deep in the pit of my stomach; the last meal had been lunch, the previous day. I hurled my sheet back; the room was warm, although the source of heat lay behind the horizontal slats of the wooden blinds; the sun made the room bright giving me further compulsion and compunction to leave my cramped corner.

The windows were pinned back to the outside wall and yet there was no breeze, the air was warm and still. I wondered idly what time it was as I struggled out of bed and pulled on yesterday's clothes, a pair of jeans and a dark blue, short-sleeved linen shirt, enough to cover my modesty with the roommates. My underwear had already been secreted into a duty-free plastic bag for boil-wash on my return home.

It was breakfast time in my stomach and night-time in my head, the fogginess of jet lag meant that I walked as if still in a dream. I knew there was a towel for me in the bathroom and an invigorating shower was top priority even before food to ease my tired muscles and to wake my soporific brain.

I had learnt years ago that hot coffee and a sleepy disposition did not mix and nor did tongue and teeth while eating when half asleep. I had no desire to bite my tongue at this stage; I should have done that before I had agreed to join the safari.

Nicotine withdrawal was also kicking in, the desire for a cigarette was growing and that I knew I could manage even before shower and breakfast, but I still preferred to wait for the first cigarette of the day. In the cupboard I found a pair of clean jeans, socks, underpants and a polo shirt to wear after I had bathed.

On opening the door, the sound of the shower greeted me. I had been 'Pip'-ed to the post. There was nothing for it but to walk into the living space and have that cigarette. A pack of Prince Filters lay where I had left it, enough cigarettes inside to reassure me. It was always a problem, running out of cigarettes. I wasn't sure but I thought I could hear singing coming from the bathroom. The malt bottle and empty glasses also lay on the table along with the ashtray full of Marlboro, Prince and cigar butts.

The window had been left open to let the stale air out and a warm, crisp, clean breeze blew in. The faint smell of stale cigars filled my nostrils, but it was infinitely preferable to the smell of stale cigarettes that it obscured.

I tossed my clean clothes on the empty chair next to the sofa and sprawled out across the cushioned armchair by the window, grabbing my cigarettes and the lighter on the table. Just as flame touched paper and I took a long draw, Duncan came in, similarly dressed. The absence of socks and shoes telling me that he too was awaiting his ablutions.

'Morning, Duncan,' I said cheerily; mornings suited me. I had met Duncan only a few times, but I knew him well enough not to say, 'good morning', as he would only ask what was good about it. He had been an actor in New York and while there he had affected a mock persona that was every entertaining. He combined grudging tolerance of all around him with general ennui.

'Is it really? To me it feels like the middle of the night, but it's light. Either I'm in Norway or I had too much malt last night,' drawled Duncan distractedly.

His affectation was meant to make you feel he was thinking of something else like a count thinking of his evening's entertainment whilst talking to his servant about domestic affairs.

Duncan was handsome, in an unkempt sort of way; he was tall and thin, and his hair was always ungroomed. He gave the impression that he couldn't be bothered to eat or comb his hair. The fact that he was waiting for the shower testified to his cleanliness, but he ate the bare minimum in order to sustain life.

'I still feel a bit groggy myself, but it's due more to jet lag than to the malt whisky,' I said sheepishly, remembering that it was only the imbibing of copious amounts of alcohol that had enabled me to pass out in the child's bed on which I slept.

'I believe you,' drawled Duncan. He was the master of irony and sarcasm, he did it to amuse. Anything he said was meant exactly the opposite way than it sounded; he would have made an excellent secondary school teacher, but the world of antiques had beckoned but only after many years of acting.

'I only had two glasses,' I complained like a truculent teenager. I was a teacher and I was going to defend my sobriety; it doesn't take a lot for someone who hardly drinks to fall foul of the soporific qualities of alcohol, particularly after a dehydrating flight to a dehydrating climate.

Of course, he did not believe me.

'With Pip measuring out the glasses that's the equivalent of quarter of a bottle,' he noted.

Duncan was unimpressed with my protestations and generally unimpressed with anything that life might show him. It was all an act; he played to the gallery even when it was empty.

'He's always generous with his Scotch.'

I recalled nights past, staying at his house in Frome. Pip was the most generous host – wine, whisky and fine conversation, a combination that everyone enjoyed, but Sundays were always half-lived. The only extra that was needed was a generous supply of Alka Seltzer or Resolve.

'Is he still in the shower?' Duncan asked peevishly. He was not really upset, he was always acting, it was part of his charm; he entertained you with his words. He was witty, clever, razor sharp and acerbic.

His face wore the expression of someone seriously aggrieved. I knew it was an act and I smiled to myself, this was Duncan's way. He kept everyone in stitches with his act, the aggrieved cynic. I wasn't sure but I thought I heard him tut, but he might just have been clearing his throat. I assumed it was as dry as mine was after all the drink consumed. I was thirsty but I was determined to await the restorative effects of coffee.

'I suppose so, I've only just woken up,' I replied wondering whether Duncan's question was necessary.

There were three of us in the hotel chalet and as both Duncan and I were in the sitting area, it was quite obvious that Pip had to be the one in the shower.

'He must be,' Duncan decided vacantly.

He acted terribly put out, but it was only acting.

I was not feeling too well, and I put it down to over-tiredness and the effects of the drink the previous evening. I was sure that I had not drunk too much alcohol.

It could well have been the effects of the malarial tablets we were taking; Lariam was rumoured to have damaging side effects, but even if they had, those would have been preferable to the fatal strain of malaria that was carried by the mosquitoes in that area.

I later learnt that Duncan would carry on an internal dialogue out loud. It was always entertaining and amusing. So, his question was not addressed to me, he was merely reaffirming that Pip was still in the shower.

'I'm here and the shower's running so it's a pretty safe bet,' I responded in similar character.

I tried to keep any irony out of my voice, but Duncan raised his eyebrow and looked at me quizzically, wondering whether he should challenge my cheekiness.

He decided it wasn't worth the effort.

'He always takes so long,' Duncan complained; he loved to complain, it was his one and only hobby – no sport, just smoking and moaning. He did not really mean it at all; it was part of his dry humour.

'You've only been here two days together,' I pointed out for fairness sake.

'Two long days,' Duncan moaned, sighing loudly for dramatic effect, but his eyes twinkled mischievously as he exaggerated the toll it had taken on him.

'Duncan, I'm surprised at you,' I scolded him.

I, too, could act.

'You haven't heard his snoring,' he spat in mock disgust.

'I shared his room and didn't hear a thing,' I replied.

I knew Duncan was teasing me, but I was still fiercely loyal to Pip at that stage, but it had little influence on Duncan. I would have to admit later that nothing wakes me when I'm asleep.

'I need some coffee, badly,' Duncan complained, rolling his eyes, before negotiating the chair with my clothes on and skirting the steel-framed, glass-topped table in front of the sofa.

The autosuggestion that my smoking provided was too much for him and he too lit a cigarette before flinging himself on to the sofa. Everything he did, he did to amuse, it was subtle and dry but there was not a spoilt or ungrateful bone in his body.

'Pip will be out soon, you can go next,' I offered graciously.

'There's no telephone here, otherwise I'd order some down'. He acted as if he had not heard my kind offer. Maybe he hadn't.

'Did you sleep well?' I tried again.

'Eventually, it was quiet at first, but then I could hear you two snoring all night.'

'I can see mornings are not your ideal time of day.' I joked. There was no hysterical laughter in response.

'Nor are nights, when I actually got a little sleep, it was like being down at the watering hole with the wart hogs.'

'Sorry,' I apologised, there was little else I could say, and I was being sincere.

'I should think so too,' Duncan retorted drolly. Duncan was using his tetchy voice, actor that he was. Duncan drew on his cigarette and looked daggers at me but drew none. I laughed and he smirked but tried to look deadpan and serious.

'I'll get a peg for my nose,' I suggested, trying to make light of the situation and trying to get Duncan to lighten up a little himself. All I did was provide him with more material. Funny people like him need a straight man as a foil to their jokes and I was a willing candidate.

'Good idea and one for Pip, he was hacking away,' he leant forward and flicked his cigarette ash dismissively, staring at me sulkily. All acting, over-acting badly in fact, I could not control my laughter.

'It must be the cigars,' I suggested just as mischievously. I was determined to act in a civil way even if Duncan refused to. My back ached but I was on holiday.

'He's been doing it for the last two nights, just to keep me up,' he noted sardonically. Duncan's petulant expression had set on his face and it looked like nothing would remove it.

'Have you spoken to him today?' I asked lightly. My determination really was admirable given the circumstances. In my stupor, I was able to remain calm and charming.

'Not yet, I heard him go into the shower about an hour ago,' Duncan's mock impatience was evident in his resigned voice.

'He'll be out soon,' I intoned reassuringly.

'That's what I thought twenty minutes ago. I know there's a lot of him, but does he have to take so long in the shower?' he asked incredulously.

He pretended that he found it all too incredible to bear and I couldn't help but laugh at his words. That reaction was greeted by a look of mock disbelief in Duncan's eyes.

There was a glint that told me that he might well be acting all this out. I'm sure Duncan did not feel too good in the mornings, but he exaggerated his feelings for dramatic effect.

Pip came out of the bathroom and went straight into his bedroom to change. Duncan disappeared, leaving me to stub out my cigarette and wonder how long it would take him to have a shower.

As it turned out Duncan took a good twenty minutes, which allowed me to read. I heard the bathroom door open and that was my cue to go in.

Feeling that I would never eat, but too weak to care, I stepped into the bath and under the shower. I turned on the hot tap; the water was warm and invigorating.

The cigarettes that I had smoked while waiting had done the trick, numbing my appetite. The shower spurted and my stomach acids gurgled.

It was bliss to be under the solid torrent of hot water.

It was an old-fashioned shower with a watering can nozzle that spread the water evenly over my head and shoulders. I brushed my teeth as I showered and then dripping on to the bathmat, I carefully shaved my face.

My clothes hung ready on the hook on the back of the door. Once changed, I walked into the lounge area to find Pip sitting at the wooden table, smoking cigar in hand. He was pouring over a large-scale map of the Uganda.

Four open guidebooks at each edge, weighted open by a cigar box, a tumbler, a closed book and a squat candleholder.

He could have been transported to a canvas tent and then he would have looked even more the great white explorer, fighting off malaria to find the true source of the Nile. His dark hair was long at the back and receding at the front, he was jovial and enjoyed life; his brown eyes had a mischievous twinkle in them.

They masked a sharp mind; Pip was a computer expert at home having graduated from Cambridge, and his ceaseless research meant that he had already assessed the opportunities that presented themselves for exploring the country.

More impressive was his mastery of the most important phrases in Mugandan, the language spoken by the Bagandans (endonym: *Baganda*; singular *Muganda*). Traditionally composed of 52 tribes – although since a 1993 survey, only 46 are officially recognised – the Baganda are the largest ethnic group in Uganda, comprising 16.9 per cent of the population. He was forty years old and therefore the senior partner in our small firm of friends.

Duncan, his dark hair still uncombed, sat on the sofa reading Bill Bryson's *Notes from a Small Island*. His long legs crossed, a spent cigarette in the ashtray nestled on the cushion beside him, his pack of cigarettes and lighter fighting for room on the cluttered coffee table.

The atmosphere of a typical bachelor flat pervaded his part of the living space. Magazines and books tossed on the coffee table, whisky tumblers and water glasses, three ashtrays, all full, two mosquito coils, their rings half burnt, leaving ash on the dinner plates below and three candles and two night lights vied for space. They both seemed happy in their respective preoccupation, so I walked quietly across the room and folded myself into the large armchair by the window.

The shutters in this room had remained closed to keep out the insects, not that it was much of a deterrent as the windows were open. There was a general preoccupation with the shutters throughout our rooms, all of them needed to be kept closed day or night, and it seemed as if they might provide an impenetrable barrier to the animal and insect world outside.

Admittedly, lizards might find it hard to squeeze through the horizontal slats, but the flies and mosquitoes could slip through easily. It was our own Maginot Line – it looked good but if you went around it, the line was pointless.

With three grown men and the heat of Africa combined in a small space it was not practical to have the windows shut for too long. I grabbed my Prince and the striking of a match made Pip look up. He took a long draw on his cigar and as our eyes met, he smiled warmly.

'Hello, Mike, how are you?' he asked.

'Fine, and you?' I was glad to be taking part in a polite exchange.

'I can't complain,' Pip never did, unless strictly necessary.

'Did you sleep well?' I was enjoying this exchange.

'I was up until about two looking at the maps and guides and drinking whisky, but I got off to sleep quite well, although I do think that the Anopheles mosquitoes were out in force last night.

Pip was a big man, tall, broad shouldered and long legged, but his love of food over forty years had expanded his waist a lot. He had made, therefore, a promising and irresistible target for the mosquitoes, one of the largest blood banks that they had come across.

Duncan and I were both relatively slim and our blood did not have the same sweet smell as Pip had. Although he had the largest bed, it was nearest the window.

'I think I heard them once or twice,' I admitted. I had woken once to shift position and I had heard them buzzing about the room, lying in my bed, wondering which of us was going to get malaria, but sleep had overcome me. Duncan looked up from his book with an exasperated look on his face.

'Are we going to breakfast or what?' he asked, ever churlish in his demeanour. Subtlety was not his style. I dared not laugh out loud; I internalised the humour.

Pip and I looked at Duncan surprised to find him still there as we had forgotten his presence.

'We could move along, shortly,' Pip answered with good nature and patience.

Duncan was trying to bully us into doing what he wanted, and Pip was having none of it.

'Good, the mosquitoes weren't the only noisy creatures last night!' exclaimed Duncan; he looked from Pip to me and then back at Pip again.

Pip ignored this and closed all of his books stacking them neatly on the desk. He might have found Duncan amusing as I did, but he wasn't going to admit it.

'What have you been trying to find?' I asked, intently interested in Pip's studies both through the night and this morning. It seemed to me that he never relaxed fully, such was his thirst for knowledge and his natural curiosity.

'I thought we'd go on a safari while we're here and I was looking at the various parks.'

'I see.'

'The ones in the far north are too dangerous because of the fighting up there, but there's a possibility that we could go to the source of the Nile and perhaps Murchison Falls.'

'That sounds great,' I ejaculated enthusiastically; I wasn't sure if I would be staying with the group or moving on to Tanzania at that stage.

'You're the king,' Duncan said in his laconic way.

Pip and I looked at him, both of us surprised at his continuous and unconnected outbursts. It was unusual to find him so talkative when he had his nose buried in a book and we expected him to be fairly quiet that morning. At the Speke, on my arrival, Pip had informed or forewarned me that it was best to leave Duncan to his own devices until at least midday.

'Pip or me?' I asked.

'Pip of course,' Duncan said petulantly.

He was still acting.

'Me?' asked Pip, he was almost flattered, but knowing Duncan better than I, he was not sure what he was driving at.

'You're the Don,' Duncan added.

Duncan had an accusing tone in his voice, which made us suspicious. I decided that I would let them continue the conversation on their own. I had a highly developed sixth sense and felt that things were starting to turn decidedly nasty in this surreal exchange. I was right but not in a bad way.

'The Don?' Pip furrowed his brow in thought.

'The Don,' repeated Duncan, looking at Pip as though he thought he was lacking in brainpower.

Pip looked hurt, he was twice as intelligent as the two of us put together and one does not have to strike someone to hurt them. I was confused myself; which don did he mean – a university don, a Spanish noble, or the name given to Italian gangsters in America? The trial of the Dapper Don in New York was still fresh in my mind.

'The don of what?' asked Pip.

'Snoring,' replied Duncan, deadpan.

We both laughed, Duncan kept up the pretence by looking askance. He gave the game away, a small smile played at the edge of his lips.

'Bear in mind I haven't slept properly for two days,' Pip defended himself.

'There's no need to be so noisy about it,' Duncan scolded him like an angry mother at the end of her tether. I smiled; it was Pip's turn to roll his eyes – he internalised a lot.

'I'm sorry,' Pip said humbly. 'I had a late night last night, followed by a twenty-four-hour flight to Kampala beforehand.'

'Earplugs have to be found,' Duncan decided, returning to his book.

'You slept with your blanket on, Mike.' Pip observed.

'I wanted to be covered up from the damn insects,' I replied.

'I slept with a blanket on too, over my ears to block out Pip coughing,' Duncan noted testily.

'I think I've been bitten quite badly on the arms,' Pip protested, he was determined to ignore Duncan's jibes, if he could. The atmosphere was getting tense. Two people in a room can rub along, but once a third party is involved the whole dynamic changes and it was no longer necessary for Duncan to keep his peace.

'The blanket didn't offer me much protection either,' I responded readily to Pip before Duncan hurled another barbed remark. I was as determined as Pip to maintain a cordial atmosphere. Duncan was just being cranky, and we could both forgive him that. If we were pleasant, he might follow our example.

'It didn't work for me either,' Duncan complained, he was going to make a full-scale production of his sleepless night, 'Between you two making more noise than Concorde when it breaks the sound barrier and the mosquitoes biting me to death, it's a miracle that I managed to get any sleep at all. When are we going to eat?'

Duncan was pretending to act like a testy teenager, but this was his humour. It was as dry and as deadpan as you could get, Pip was used to it and I managed to internalise my mirth.

We were a happy band, disparate spirits surviving close proximity.

Neither of us encouraged him but he did not need encouragement.

'Let's go now,' Pip decided. He had wisely judged that it would be better if Duncan drank his coffee and griped on a full stomach.

'I don't know why we can't order coffee down here every morning?' Duncan complained; he was determined to whine a bit more, letting us all know that he was used to a different sort of hotel.

He wanted four-star treatment at a two-star hotel.

'Because by the time it gets here it will be cold,' Pip patiently pointed out.

Duncan couldn't argue with such logic and that was the best way to deal with him. Give him a reason and he was satisfied. He didn't really mean it; he was playing the child to break the monotony.

'We don't even have a phone to order stuff with,' Duncan decided, inadvertently supplying his own reason why we couldn't order coffee sent to the room. He was definitely suffering from too much alcohol, the Lariam perhaps, and lack of sleep, mostly.

'You're not used to the African way yet,' Pip tried to reassure him.

'I'm not used to anything yet, least of all you two snoring,' Duncan declared defiantly; he was tenacious, if nothing else.

We cleared the room in less time than it took for a plague of locusts to strip a maize field in Biblical times. I was looking forward to a filling breakfast on a similarly Biblical scale or something along those lines.

Walking out in the sunshine, Duncan waited on the veranda while Pip locked our apartment door.

Pip led the way up the garden path, his loose cream linen shirt a hackneyed statement of a world traveller; two pockets and cut straight at the tail. His loose cotton trousers in beige gave him an air of seasoned diplomat as he strode confidently ahead, chin forward and back straight, the quintessential intrepid, English gentleman. I admired him for this; he had been to Africa before, he knew there was no uncertainty or fear of the unknown, he had travelled more in the time he was at university than both Duncan and I had in our lifetime.

Duncan would goad him, and I would later tease him, but we both knew that without him, and his only slightly eccentric ways, we were lost. We might have managed but I had a feeling we would not have coped too well without him.

It was his impenetrability and his sound intellect that we were envious of, two urbanites out of our depth in a country we hardly knew with a people we were willing to understand, waiting to listen to and wanting to know, but we didn't have the wherewithal. The picture of us going to breakfast summed up the situation.

Pip wore comfortable and correct clothing, I was dressed for shopping on the King's Road and Duncan was similarly dressed in new jeans and a dark blue shirt appropriate for a nightclub, but not for Equatorial Africa. If we'd been in nightclubs or air-conditioned hotels our clothes might have sufficed. Duncan and I might even have cut dashing figures, each of us, but in the heat and dust of the suburbs of

Kampala we cut a ridiculous and obvious caricature of the innocents abroad.

There was no light in the dining room which we reached by walking past several chalets like our own, each with a small garden veranda with two chairs, a sitting room, a kitchen and a corridor which led to the shower room and both bedrooms. The hotel gardens looked surprisingly lush in the tropical heat due to a sprinkler system.

The lobby with a bar and sitting area was also in darkness and it was only through following Pip's steps up the stairs to the left that the dining room was located.

The sunshine from outside gave the room just enough light to see the five tables set with cutlery and white linen tablecloths. The shutters here were open, as was the only window. Pip took a left and seated himself at the table by the window. I sat next to him and Duncan slipped in on the left of us, he could have learnt his arm on the windowsill if he had so chosen. In front of us were four napkins, which lay elaborately folded over each of the four place settings; we were expected. Within seconds, the waiter had arrived and cleared the fourth place and bid us good morning with a winning smile.

'Would you like bacon and eggs?' he asked politely, the smile remaining on his face, I smiled back, and the others did not.

It seemed a reasonable start to the day to me.

'Just fruit and strong coffee,' Duncan was hungry, but he was not hungry enough to risk eggs and bacon that may not have been refrigerated properly.

It wasn't that any food was kept outside of the refrigerator; it was just that the electrical power was never reliable. The hotel generator was shut off from midnight until dawn and power cuts meant that a reliable source of electricity could not be guaranteed.

Fruit was a safer and healthier alternative.

'Fruit for me and very, very strong coffee, please,' Pip emphasised the adjectives as much as possible.

'Very, very strong for me too,' Duncan added. He was reminded of the need to ask for the strongest brew by Pip's words.

'The same for me, please,' I said. I was determined to fit in and so I ordered the same.

'Thank you,' the waiter said and smiled even more broadly before leaving the table.

'Thank you,' we all chorused, and he disappeared into the darkness.

'The last time we ordered coffee we got a very weak cup, they only have one stove,' Pip explained, 'and you know how much I love my strong coffee.'

'That's why we never order the bacon and eggs. Coffee and fried food that is cooked on one Primus stove defies anyone's ingenuity,' Duncan elucidated further.

I was grateful for their desire to fill me in further. I looked over to where the coffee was being prepared. A shaft of light from the back door illuminating a man crouched over a small gas cylinder, boiling a pot of water, it reminded me of Egypt. Despite the heavy cutlery, linen and the surroundings of an English tearoom, we were in Africa and they did things differently there.

I was reminded of the expression: 'The past is a different place; they do things differently there'.

Chapter 2

Kampala, the Speke or the unspeakable

Our party consisted of four distinct groups: The Major and his wife – the reason we were all there – they had rooms at the Speke Hotel. Lucy and her children, Matilda and Emily, and Hattie, my friend, were staying with a family in an affluent area of Kampala. Anna and her four children, Sam, Aubrey, Ollie and Punch were staying in a house in Aka Bua Road with an ex-pat Italian family. Finally, there was Pip, Anna's husband, Duncan and I; we had the chalet at the Reste Corner, on the road out of Kampala.

We had to take a ten-minute taxi ride into town to see everyone, but equally we had our own privacy and could be bachelors without having to put on airs and graces for our hosts. The least privacy was afforded to the Major and his wife because all their old friends would call, and radio and newspaper journalists wanted interviews all the time.

The journey from Reste Corner to the centre of town could have been walked in half an hour but in the tropical heat we preferred to take a ten-minute taxi. The walk would have only offered Duncan more opportunities to complain about the heat, his aching feet, the coughing and snoring.

The route was lined with shacks of breeze block construction, mostly painted white beige or in a few cases denim blue, somewhere between Mediterranean blue and violet, providing a violent contrast to the other paler buildings.

The shops all shared the same rectangular shape, the same rectangular flat roofs; they looked like Mexican haciendas. Most had a portico that projected out three-quarters of the way up the wall facing the street. These covered porches were held up by equidistant steel columns; some had four, some six, others eight. They were painted red, blue or grey.

Above these protuberances most of the buildings had the company names; either they were grocers, hardware stores, or insurance companies with red and green writing.

The bars had advertisements for products sold within. The signs were fresh and interesting, a testament to the skill of sign writers and a reflection of the need to attract custom. The ground in front of the houses was completely indistinguishable from the tarmac road such was the level of dust.

As we neared town, the buildings rose higher. Kampala was just like any other modern city with its concrete offices and tall, multi-storey buildings, only these had been constructed thirty or forty years ago, in the sixties and seventies. The Sheraton looked like a small version of the United Nations Building in New York and from about the same era, the 1960s or the 70s. There was only one modern hotel, The Imperial, which had been built in the 1980s by the look of it.

The Speke itself was colonial in style, but it had been extended over the years and protruded halfway into the gardens on the corner. The foyer was being refurbished after a bomb blast had ripped apart the telephone kiosks in front of the stairs. We had arrived fairly early that day at the Speke, ten o'clock.

By noon, there was a sea of coffee cups, saucers, beer and Coca-Cola bottles, beer glasses, and tall tumblers on the tabletop. The furniture was cane, the tabletop glass, and the chairs had bright cushions on them, and the veranda of the Speke kept the sun off our faces. Hanging around had made us bored already.

Lucy was on her first gin of the day after gallons of coffee; we had just ordered beer. Still, we waited for news of our imminent audience with the Kabaka, Freddie Mutesa. Apparently for the last two days Pip, Anna, Duncan and Lucy had waited for a summons from the king, the children watching television in their grandparents' room.

Various rumours had surfaced: the king was still in London, he had gone to America to see his fiancée before coming out to Uganda, he was going to invite everyone in the next hour or so to the palace, therefore everyone should stay put.

There was misinformation and rumour; there was no concrete communication one way or the other.

It was the African way, waiting is expected; patience is not so much a virtue as a necessity. We waited for the real Major's sake, he wanted us to make ourselves available and, as he had organised the trip, we were beholden to him.

'I had four things to do today, including going to the bank,' Pip complained bitterly.

As a newcomer, I was unable to share the angst and frustration of my compatriots.

'Number one is: be a geek at the Speke,' Duncan teased.

He was being helpful, as ever, trying to amuse everyone but he was equally bored with hanging around.

'I'm fudged off we've been jerked around and I'm fed up waiting for the lighter to come around,' Pip grabbed the lighter from on top of Duncan's packet and lit a new cigar, giving Duncan a stern look.

'Won't anyone tell you what's going on?' I asked, ever the naive observer.

'It's a need-to-know basis,' Duncan informed us eyeing Pip, waiting for him to put the lighter back on the table.

'And I need to know what's going on,' Pip grunted, placing the lighter firmly next to his cigar box out of Duncan's reach.

'And they're not telling,' I noted despondently. I had my own lighter, which I put back in my jean pocket once I had lit a Prince cigarette.

It was hot on the street, but I had slaked my thirst on coffee and beer; having a cigarette was just another thing to do while we waited.

'That's a pleonasm,' Duncan announced apropos nothing. He sat back in his chair, his long legs crossed, and his right ankle on his left knee, nursing a cold glass of Bell beer in his lap.

'What?' I tried to convey the irritation of his remark in my reply, at the same time looking askance.

The others looked languidly at Duncan; I was not sure of the relevance of this word that I had never heard.

'A redundant expression,' Duncan looked at me accusingly; my lack of knowledge seemed to amaze him.

'I see, thank you.' I was hurt but tried not to show it. Instead I drew on my cigarette and took a gulp of beer from my glass. The props of the company were cigarette in one hand, glass or coffee cup in the other.

'Like most of your expressions.' Duncan had seen the weakness and he went in for the kill, he wasn't the type to take any prisoners, conversationally.

'I thought it was a tautology not a pleonasm,' I tried desperately to counterattack.

'That shows how much you know.' Duncan was keen to show his superior knowledge of English and, in turn, my ignorance.

I, for one, was impressed.

'Well?' I asked keenly, leaning forward to listen better. There were loud conversations going on to drown the sound of passing traffic.

'A tautology is the use of words that say the same thing, like pristine clean or...'

'I don't like my coffee too hot, could you pass the milk?' Pip thankfully interrupted Duncan; he had a habit of going on about nothing for a long time. Pip knew how to diffuse such situations after only two days with Duncan. Lucy passed him the milk.

'Where is everyone?' Duncan asked, taking the hint.

'The king, where is he? My kingdom for a horse, my horsedom for a king,' I said as brightly as I could, I was feeling frivolous and I didn't care who knew it.

'You're shrewd like the Reverend,' Duncan said, nodding his head meaningfully and pointing to an imaginary dog collar at his neck. He had met the Reverend at the airport, and he felt that the priest was a very shrewd man, but he wouldn't tell us why.

'We have to wait until Ronnie is ready,' Pip informed us. We were not as well versed in international politics as he was.

'Why is Ronnie involved in all this politics?' Duncan's thirst for knowledge, generally led to a stream of questioning.

'President Truman said it was best to have enemies inside your tent peeing out then to have them outside peeing in,' Pip noted; we all smiled. We had almost lost interest in meeting the Kabaka because we had been kept waiting so long to see him.

'I had an argument with David, the driver. I must be approaching the time of the month. I'll need plenty of water and coffee.' Lucy noted dreamily to no one in particular.

'He likes to be called *Dae Woo*,' Pip told us. 'On account of his car, his Daewoo.'

'Daewoo and his Toyota?' Duncan squinted into the sun at Pip. 'It's a Toyota not a Daewoo!'

'That's another tautology – aren't they both cars?' he paused for the raucous laughter, but none came. 'Besides he owes me cash, I paid him for the ride here and he asked for extra to get some fuel and I haven't seen it back yet.'

Duncan stared open mouthed, looking towards the spot where Daewoo would park his taxi, a privileged spot on the rank. Duncan's eyes looked as if they were searching for his return, but his face had an incredulous: 'Would you believe it?' look. Both the expressions of pining and being wounded made him look confused and hurt, or just vacant.

'When was that?' Pip asked, flicking ash in the vague direction of the ashtray. He had his elbows on the table, sitting hunched as if ready to leap up at the slightest notification of the Kabaka's arrival.

'Yesterday, when we went to get Mike and Hattie from the airport,' Duncan replied, as if it had nothing to do with Pip when it happened, but that the mere solicitation of some support in the matter was the main thing.

'That's no time, you'll get it back,' Pip was laid back about it all, he had got to know David 'Dae Woo' over the previous few days.

'For sure,' Duncan hissed sarcastically; he was horrified that Pip was not on his side. He didn't trust anyone.

'Stop being the paranoid tourist for one minute,' Pip spoke reassuringly, 'David's our driver for the three weeks, he'll be driving us around town during our stay, he's not going to jeopardise all that work for the sake of a few thousand shillings.'

'He might,' Duncan sounded wounded.

'He won't,' Pip assured him.

'Anyway, the drive back from the airport to collect the others was an experience of horror as he weaved his way along, he drives like he hasn't got a licence to lose,' Duncan warmed to the theme. All attention was on him.

'Have you noticed how the taxis never have any fuel in their tanks,' I began, wanting to be included in the conversation. 'They drive around almost empty, then use the fare to top up the tank.'

'Let's go back to the Reste Corner, I can get some rest.' Duncan ignored me, rudely.

'Last night the sound of generator humming drove me mad, although it might be the Lariam.' I was determined to be included in the conversation, I was new to Africa, but I had a voice, I was not going to be invisible.

'Not another diary of a Lariam eater. I've only heard fifteen thousand people complain of the effects of Mefloquine and half of them haven't been out of Greater Manchester.'

Duncan was as cruel in his damnation as he was over-optimistic in his statistics and I loved that in him.

'The boys have a fever,' Lucy announced; she was to be the fifteen thousand and first.

'Listen, I've been on it for two weeks before we came out here,' Pip interjected; he had held his tongue for too long. He was the seasoned traveller and Duncan's complaining, and whining was becoming too much.

'My point exactly, It might seem like longer before we all wake up,' Duncan said as he snapped open his packet of cigarettes and helped himself to one, leaning over the table to retrieve the lighter from on top of Pip's cigar box.

It was never clear whose lighter it was but they both lay claim to it all the same, a constant to-ing and fro-ing from dawn until dusk.

'It's had hardly any effect on me,' I ventured, the third attempt to get someone – anyone – to listen to me.

It didn't matter whom.

'I'm mildly loquacious,' Duncan muttered after a draw on his cigarette, 'but I'm still listening.'

'Anna's kids have head lice as well,' Lucy sighed; she was a half-hearted reporter, not too fussed about how she broke the news but still feeling she should deliver it.

'That's why I had my head shaved,' I said seriously.

'Really?' Lucy realised as she spoke that I had not meant what I said and the whole table smiled; I really hadn't expected her to be so gullible.

'No, not really, I was kidding,' I admitted sheepishly.

Before I left, I visited the barber and he had persuaded me to have a 'number four', which was a severe hair cut with a small hedge trimmer. I thought it would keep me cool, but in fact it just left my head more exposed than before and I was therefore more open to sun stroke.

'Ha, ha,' she looked daggers at me.

This was the start of my first full day with the family. I had met Lucy briefly before at the Major's house. We had got on well, but already, in Africa, I had made her a potential enemy; the next three weeks could be awkward if I didn't try and make up for her embarrassment.

I had to try harder to win influence and befriend people.

'Will someone please buy Duncan a lighter?' Pip grabbed back his lighter, giving Duncan a withering look, lit his cigar that had extinguished itself, puffed luxuriously and then he smiled to show there were no hard feelings. Lucy and Duncan both wore sunglasses, so it was disconcerting to talk to them, never seeing their eyes.

'You look very South African with your hair cut, Mike, you'll have to watch out, they'll think you're a mercenary,' observed Duncan.

He was ever observant, and he was also good at setting people up for a fall; a joke at someone else's expense was all part of the entertainment. He could be charming and friendly too, so you never knew where you stood.

'You've also got the South African look with those sunglasses,' I noted with a cheeky grin. My observation was greeted with a smile and Duncan folded his sunglasses into the breast pocket of his shirt.

He no longer looked South African, but I could read his eyes, which was the most important thing; his eyes always seemed to narrow before he went for the satirical kill.

'Where are we going to eat lunch?' Lucy asked. 'I've worked my way through this hotel's menu three times, already.' She had been out for a week and already the novelty of the Speke's bar snacks, and pizzas had worn off despite their quality.

'We could try Fang, Fang Chinese restaurant. I saw it on the corner when we drove into town. I haven't eaten Chinese for ages,' I suggested.

I was new in town, but the restaurant looked well established and the name sounded good. We subsequently tried the place and I have to say, it was the best Chinese outside China.

'Fang, Fang, no thanks. If we're going to a Chinese it will have to be a good one,' said Pip.

He drew on his cigar as if he was part of the cognoscenti when I knew that he'd only been in this part of Africa a few more days than I had.

'Fang, Fang does look good, you haven't seen inside. You can't judge it until you've tried the food. Lots of places don't look good from the outside,'

I was slightly upset that he should condemn my choice of restaurants out of hand. I reached for the lighter and lit a cigarette; I hadn't bothered with Duty Free and had bought a local brand in the hotel bar as soon as I arrived.

'Fang, Fang could be good,' I insisted, not unreasonably. I made no attempt to return the lighter to either Pip or Duncan's packs. I left it on the table next to my beer bottle.

'No thanks, not there,' Pip insisted; he could be stubborn.

'But how do you know it's no good?' I wasn't to be fobbed off. If there was a solid reason for his intransigence, I could understand, but it seemed he was just being bloody minded about it, which I couldn't understand.

I couldn't win the argument, but I could take the lighter with me.

I slipped it into my top pocket and envisaged the accusations that would follow my imminent departure to the bank.

'I'd prefer something more African, this isn't Kowloon, or Hong Kong,' Duncan reminded me with the supercilious manner that would become ubiquitous.

'The Ethiopian, then? The one we saw as we drove from the hotel.' I had tried Ethiopian food once before in Washington DC, and I liked it. The Ethiopian was close to the Reste Corner, a traditional hut with a barbecue on the side.

'The one on the road just before the Reste Corner?' Duncan asked.

'Yes, the one set back from the road behind the bamboo fence,' I elaborated. I had pointed out the sign that very morning on the way down and had suggested we visit sometime.

'The one with the thatch roof?' Pip asked. He must have known. He was trying to get a reaction from me.

'Yes,' I was exasperated by their deliberate procrastination.

'Fine, but they have small portions,' Duncan noted, then he half smiled. I hadn't as yet seen his teeth, but they flashed, the bad taste of the joke appealed to his eccentric humour.

'That's in poor taste, I fasted for a week to raise money for the famine in Sudan this year.' I failed to find black humour amusing.

'Fang, Fang it is then,' Duncan decided, he was trying to annoy Pip.

I didn't mind, as long as he left me alone. He was fair, he spread his sarcasm, and banter; it was friendly teasing and I think Pip and I would have felt left out if we had not been included.

'Or the Tai Singh?'

I was always offering options.

'Eat in Tai Singh?'

Pip was dismissive of the idea.

'In Thai Singh – very good, Pip,' Duncan said in a voice that revealed he didn't mean any such thing. Taking another draw on his cigarette, he looked across the road to the gardens of the Sheraton, raising his eyes heavenward.

'It sounds enticing,' I added to cause him further pain.

'I feel like going home, it's the Hampstead of Kampala,' Lucy sighed.

She was not enjoying the conversation, the location, the heat or her condition.

'I went there and there were big black gates,' Duncan added encouragingly; he was pleased to be off the subject of food for five minutes. 'A geezer with a Russian machine gun was outside. "What do you want?" he asked. "Lucy," I replied. "I think they have gone," he told me without checking. I couldn't be bothered to argue.'

'No one bothers to argue with a guy with an AK-47. He'll fill you with lead sooner than you can say "Remington shotgun",' I explained.

I knew a thing or two about guns, both these weapons were designed to kill rather than maim, but the Russian automatic rifle gave the owner more chances to spread his fire. These were deterrent weapons, designed to kill outright; they weren't like a .38 that might give you a chance to survive. You'd have to feel very lucky before you messed with anyone carrying such weapons.

I had fired weapons of this calibre at the Royal Marine Commando training camp at Lympstone: An S.L.R. rifle, the equivalent to a Belgian FN, 7.62mm round, and a Sterling machine gun, basically an updated 9mm round, both made a mess of the target. I had also fired my personal favourite, the 9mm Browning automatic, which is basically the European equivalent of a Colt .45 pistol, favoured by U.S. Marines.

'I'm very reassured by the pump action shotguns with all the news reports in the press,' Lucy noted in her languid fashion.

She gave the impression that nothing much fazed her. She was looking over to the guard who stood near the foyer of the hotel, an automatic pistol in the belt around his waist and a Remington pump action shotgun held in his right hand. Three nights ago, a bomb had gone off opposite reception, a small device that damaged the telephones. No one was hurt and no one claimed responsibility.

'The guards outside the bank help to reassure the anxious traveller.'

Duncan's sarcasm was never far from the surface. His humour eased the tension. It was more than a little unsettling to have so many armed militias around the place; we were not used to it. There was always the danger of being hit in the crossfire.

'I always draw out more money when the guards are about.'

'They're always about; isn't that a pleonasm,' I suggested quietly.

'What?' Duncan sounded as if he'd been dragged from a very important auction to talk to someone insignificant.

'Nothing,' I replied sweetly, I was beginning to get the feeling of 'internalising' my humour for the sake of better relations.

There were more security guards present at certain times of the day, the busy period at lunch time or when a security van drew up outside. I remembered such a delivery of cash that we had seen in the morning, it was like a scene form a Hollywood film.

The bank was only a few metres away from the hotel and there were possibly twenty soldiers with shotguns and rifles that arrived in new Japanese pick-ups to surround the armoured car, which had a turret and machine gun on the top.

Only desperate or crazy bank robbers would dare to mess with such an entourage. Any attempted robbery would be a complete blood bath.

'Where's the old man?' Pip asked.

'He's still being interviewed by the Central Broadcasting Service, they're using a private room and we're not to disturb him,' Lucy said.

She was looking hopefully for a light for her Silk Cut and I gallantly used the shared lighter to put her out of her misery. I subsequently placed the lighter as near to the centre of the table as I could to enable Pip and Duncan to fight over it – ever the considerate one.

'The Major was being interviewed when Hattie and I arrived, yesterday. I only saw him briefly before some friends of his arrived.' I was disappointed that I wouldn't be seeing him either. Trying to gain an audience with either the King or the Major was an equally difficult operation

'That was Mama Rose and her friends, she's an old friend of dad's,' Lucy explained, sipping on a restorative gin and tonic. It seemed to be doing the trick and they used to call gin mother's ruin – how little they knew.

'He was being interviewed by another one of the papers, *The Monitor*, I think,' Duncan mentioned, leaning over and grabbing the lighter although he had no intention of lighting a cigarette.

'Headlines like "Mutesa poisoned, Major confirms", don't exactly win friends,' Pip piped in

He was gently reminding us of the Major's comments in the press regarding the Kabaka's death in London almost thirty years ago under mysterious circumstances.

He hadn't noticed Duncan pocketing the lighter as he was so busy stubbing out the last inch of his cigar in the ashtray.

'He'll have to be careful what else he says,' Lucy warned, clearly worried about her father.

Lucy was understandably concerned about what her father might say and the political or direct consequences of his expressing an opinion or revealing facts that may well be embarrassing to the government.

'That's what Mama Rose and all the visitors say when they come to see him,' Duncan told her. I listened; I had much to learn.

'Dad says that he has to answer any questions frankly and truthfully.' Lucy was torn between admiration and concern.

'I think he'll be all right, most of the Ugandans in Kampala are Mugandan and loyal to the Kabaka,' Pip assured Lucy.

The rebels who were letting off the bombs seemed to have no argument with the Kabaka.

'I hear one of President Museveni's ministers is going to pay a courtesy call,' Duncan added, and I wasn't sure whether that was to reassure Lucy or worry her further.

'Where's Hattie?' I asked, trying to change the subject. I was her guest and I hadn't seen her since our arrival at the Speke.

'Shopping,' they all answered in unison.

Chapter 3

Another Really Stimulating Evening

I lit a Sportsman cigarette as we sat in the lounge of the Reste Corner that evening, Pip was at his usual post pouring over guidebooks and maps on the dining room table, Duncan had taken the couch as his own and I had my usual chair.

Already we had allocated ourselves our own space within the living area without even discussing it. I was amused by the thought that they had been there only a few days longer than I had and yet they said that they never ordered the cooked breakfast, as though they had been in Uganda for weeks.

It was my first proper evening at the chalet, the previous evening we had dined at the Speke before hitting the malt on our return.

We had decided not to eat supper and stay in; rather Pip and Duncan had said they were not hungry, and I was content to let my stomach rumble distantly rather than eat out somewhere on my own.

On the way through from the foyer where we collected our key, I had stopped at the bar and ordered three Bell lagers, taking them down on a tray.

Duncan had fetched glasses from the kitchen along with some chilled water from the fridge. It was hot in the room; the fan disturbed the air but did nothing to cool us down. The darkness fell in an instant at about seven, so we had missed another spectacular sunset again, too engrossed in our books to notice.

Although it was dark outside already, we still had electric power and read and smoked and drank water, beer and Pip's malt under the harsh light of a high wattage central light bulb. A small angle poise lit the operations table and a black steel standard lamp cast light over Duncan's left shoulder, sandwiched between the sofa and the chair that we waited to be occupied by the fourth guest, Anthony, another one of the Major's sons. Outside, the hum of generator and noise of crickets competed for our attention.

Duncan slapped the side of his neck; the mosquitoes were out, despite a third insect repellent coil being lit that evening. The green coils on their black metal stands smoked orange, like fat spiral incense, glowing at the tip, burning in a circular fashion, leaving a trail of ash on the saucers below.

'The insects are attracted by the light. Close the door,' Duncan demanded not moving.

He sat with his legs crossed, ankle on knee as usual, wearing sandals and a short-sleeve shirt, a prime target for the insects, but he had been sensible enough to wear jeans and not a pair of shorts.

I was in shorts and a T-shirt, conserving my more presentable clothes for another more formal occasion, but the insects seemed to find Duncan's blood more to their liking, although if it was as acid as his tongue, I couldn't imagine them finding it sweeter than my own. I had smeared my arms and legs with Deet insect repellent, and it seemed to be working.

'Close the window, then,' I enjoined not wanting to move but feeling I should contribute to this rare outbreak of conversation.

'I can feel them,' Duncan cried, 'they're everywhere.'

'Perhaps they're attracted by the mosquito coils,' I suggested.

'They should repel the mosquitoes not encourage them,' Duncan replied peevishly

'You're in Africa now,' Pip pointed out, looking up from his paperwork with a sigh. He looked every bit the world-weary experienced traveller or journalist, right down to the glass of malt and the smouldering cigar.

'I thought it would be like Bognor Regis, but warmer.' Duncan declared dryly. 'They won't go near you with the smell from those cigars; they're being repelled from you towards me.'

'We should turn off the light, they're attracted to that,' I wanted them to know I was pretty savvy when it comes to insect habits.

'Silent running,' Duncan said seriously.

'Batten down the hatches and splice the main brace,' I continued the nautical theme.

'What are we going to do, Major Bruton?' Duncan asked Pip.

'I'm not a major,' Pip replied testily.

'Captain then,' Duncan insisted before he turned off the light with the switch by his head.

'Get the light on,' Pip demanded as Duncan flicked the main switch as well which plunged the room into almost total darkness.

'Silent running, depth charge threat over, returning to full electrical power, skipper!' Duncan reported.

'I can't read my maps,' Pip complained.

I could see the dark shape of Pip's frame and the three glowing mosquito coils, but little else.

'All right how was I to know that switch controlled all the lights,' Duncan protested as he flicked the switch back on, giving Pip a defiant look.

Our eyes adjusted to the harshness of the light. Pip returned to his books as though nothing had happened, although he squinted at first revealing his need to refocus.

'So, you just wanted to turn off your light so that the mosquitoes would be attracted to us instead, that's not very nice,' I chortled, taking another draw on my cigarette and returning to my book on Uganda. I thought I had got Duncan's measure: no women and children first in his lifeboat, it seemed. Duncan sat down and toyed with the cover of his book, almost reaching for a cigarette and then deciding against doing so.

'What time is it?' Duncan asked ignoring my comment.

Bill Bryson wasn't doing much to alleviate his boredom threshold it seemed by his voice.

'Have you got a clock?' I asked

'Yes, to wash my teeth by when the power goes, it's in the bathroom,' Duncan informed me as though I should know the situation and looking at me accusingly as if to say, don't you wear a watch?

'Well it's no good there, now,' I observed. Casually I sipped on my beer, drew on the cigarette, and shot a dismissive glance in his direction.

'You go and get it,' Duncan stared at me. It was showdown time and he wasn't going to give me an inch.

'You get it, you want to know the time,' I replied testily, looking up from my book and staring back at him but twice as hard.

'It's seven thirty-five,' Pip announced.

At least he could be relied on to wear a watch and to keep the peace.

'That's it I've been bitten again, I'm dead, even with the window closed and curtains drawn, I'm still bitten, I've got malaria!'

Duncan threw his book on the sofa beside him and reached for yet another cigarette. If the mosquitoes didn't kill him, the tar from the cigarettes would, given his current consumption rate. He was just warming up.

'My life's over, three weeks of fever, hot and cold sweats, then a really painful, prolonged death, groovy. Just signed my marriage certificate and just about to have another certificate signed for me.'

'Duncan you're becoming depressing,' I moaned.

My stare softened into a look of sympathy; I hoped he could read my face well enough.

'I'm not depressing,' Duncan was affronted. 'The situation is, I'm not depressing. I want to take council. Pip do you think that I'm depressing?' he appealed to Pip, leaning forward with doe-like eyes, the effect slightly spoilt by the presence of a cigarette in his mouth.

'I'm going to have another whisky is anyone going to join me?' Pip asked, ever the diplomat. Duncan lit his cigarette, accepting his defeat graciously for a change and slumped back on to the sofa, drawing deeply.

'I will, thank you Pip,' I answered thinking that perhaps it was the alcohol fumes that kept the insects away. It seemed like a good excuse, allowing me to get smashed. I might as well be stupefied with alcohol as with boredom. I was smoking a Prince cigarette and they are not the mildest smoke that is known to man. My throat felt dry.

'I will too, once I've shut every door and window in the place,' Duncan danced around the room, closing every window and door that he could find.

'What about some Deet?' Pip suggested, helpfully.

'Deet should do the trick, Susan swears by it,' I added encouragingly

'I prefer whisky, but I'll try drinking anything once.' Duncan flicked his ash into the saucer under the mosquito coil. 'The damn stuff gives me a rash; it's like a roll-on deodorant without the perfume, the smell gets right up my nose.'

'That's all right,' Pip piped in, 'you get right up our noses with your complaining.'

'Exactly!' I agreed.

'Listen, Major, I do the jokes around here. I'll get the ice for the drinks,' Duncan asserted seriously, though his body language betrayed the jest.

He was in the kitchen and back with the ice before we noticed the blissful silence that was produced by his brief absence.

'Shall I close the bedroom windows and doors?' I asked, being absolutely determined to be part of this new activity, Duncan with the ice-tray and Pip standing to twist off the cap from the whisky bottle; I was the only one still seated with my book on my lap. Bill Bryson was still looking dejected on the sofa. He wasn't moving either, but he had an excuse.

'It's too late for that, the power will go off soon and we'll be in candlelight, I'll try and drown a few mossies in my malt,'

Duncan sat down with his glass and finished off his cigarette while Pip passed me the cool glass of malt.

'We shouldn't strictly be adding ice to this stuff,' Pip the malt expert informed us.

'You're in Africa, now,' was Duncan's terse rebuke.

We settled down after that on our first full night alone together, unimpeded by jet lag, swapping stories of travels and traumas. Pip and Duncan had taken the long way to Uganda, a twenty-four-hour flight via Dubai. Pip had travelled out with his four children, ranging in age from two to ten.

Chapter 4

The Trip to Entebbe on Alliance Airways

Before it all happened...

Waking up on a plane is never high up on anyone's list of pleasurable experiences. It is especially true for me, being six foot two and a half and poor.

While the business and first class passengers stretched in their wide seats, cosseted by leather cushioning, I was shoe-horned into a space that even a dog would have difficulty fitting into.

People are getting taller, but the gap between seats gets smaller. The traveller will have to get used to curvature of the spine or perhaps the airlines will have us all standing up like commuters on the subway before too long, if the accountants get their way.

None of this mattered to me, European flights are short, and a brandy and ginger ale can ease the discomfiture. Brandy lowers the blood pressure so it can be counted as a stress buster and relaxant.

There are not enough barrels in Cognac itself to alleviate the contortion and tedium of intercontinental travel. Yet here I was numb from gluteus maximus to Achilles heel, from lumbar region to clavicle and scapula. The reason why I didn't care was that I was going to Africa for the first time.

Admittedly, I had been to Egypt and Tunisia, but this was the real Africa, the Africa of missionaries and the Scramble for Africa that I had studied in history at school. This was the first trip that I had taken that would bring me past the equator; I was joining that special breed, like those who had rounded the Cape of Good Hope in the sixteenth century.

I wasn't a diplomat or returning home, I was a traveller, not a tourist. I was to visit the Pearl of Africa, Winston Churchill's words for Uganda. So why was I feeling like I had been run over by a truck, woken up from a drinking bout, or coming around from an over-zealous anaesthetist?

I couldn't blame it on the air conditioning. It must have been sheer exhaustion. I had been extremely busy in the run-up to the trip. As I struggled to regain both consciousness and feeling in my limbs the thought of Uganda seemed less attractive not more so.

The more I thought about Africa, the more I realised that I had studied only some of central Africa's history: the rush for control of the Gold Coast trade, synonymous with slavery; the struggle for Sudan, focusing on the Mad Mahdi fighting Gordon of Khartoum and, then, the European partition of Africa. Our main focus had been on South Africa: the Boers, Transvaal, the Orange Free State, Cecil Rhodes, the history of a people breaking free from the imperialism that had enabled the British traders, soldiers and finally governments to colonise the cup of Africa's south.

Cape Town was meant to be beautiful in winter, so why was I heading for Uganda in June? I had already tasted the fruits of the vineyards of Stellenbosch, and other areas, found Backsberg Chardonnay, a rival not only to Chablis, but Meursault and at a fraction of the cost even in England. I also knew that *the Rand* was weak; I could have lived like a king in Durban or Jo'burg or any other South African city.

With the money I could have saved on the flight alone, I could have travelled out business class, stretching my legs out. South Africa was, bizarrely, cheaper to fly to than Uganda; it was something about regularity of flights to and from cities, just like New York.

Uganda, what did it mean to me? Idi Amin, a ghastly figure who destroyed the country and was responsible for the expulsion of the Asian community. His rule conjured up death squads and dictatorship, a large, fat, African on the cover of *Sunday Times* supplements when I was seven or eight. There had been references to Idi Amin's career at Sandhurst, the college that trained a despot. That and famous operation in Uganda, immortalized in *Raid on Entebbe*, the details of which are still not entirely clear since I have not read the book or seen the film.

I have subsequently learnt that the film focuses on the basic facts of the rescue of hostages held when hijackers belonging to a splinter group of the PLA (Palestinian Liberation Army or the Popular

Front for the Liberation of Palestine) under the orders of Wadie Haddad, boarded and hijacked an Air France plane. It recounts the events and response of the Israeli government and the controversy that the rescue stirred.

It shows the difficult deliberations held by the cabinet of Israel to decide on a top-secret military raid, on the Sabbath, by commandos to release the hostages held at Entebbe airport.

It was a difficult and daring operation carried out over 2,500 miles –roughly 4,000 kilometres – from Israel and reflected the unwillingness of the Israeli government to give in to terrorist demands.

One commando was killed (the breach unit commander and brother of future Prime Minister Benjamin Netanyahu, Yonatan), as were three of the hostages, and forty-five soldiers under the then dictator of Uganda, Idi Amin. A fourth hostage, Dora Bloch, who had been taken to Mulago Hospital, in Kampala, was allegedly murdered on Amin's order.

I could feel the Alliance Air 747 bank a little; my awareness had not been totally numbed by my confinement. There was one stop-off on our eight-hour flight – eight hours, the time it would take me to be at El Ted's, my favourite Mexican restaurant in New York, give or take three hours in the customs line-up at Newark or JFK immigration.

The more I thought of the venture I was embarking on the more alternatives sprung to mind. I had never been to India or Thailand, Vietnam was meant to be an attractive place, only just opening up to the tourist.

The collapse of the Tiger Economies made Indonesia and the Philippines look like a good bet with their weak currency and cheap living. Even places where the Foreign Office had warned tourists off had a sudden appeal.

While I was at it, I had not been to Florence; July would be a good time perhaps before the August rush.

The Greek islands and sailing was another option as was the Turkish Riviera and sunbathing, or another historical trip to the Amalfi Coast, Positano, perhaps, looking at Pompeii, then on to some Norman churches further down the coast.

The Norman knights had conquered Sicily and Naples, calling it the *Kingdom in the Sun*. Even visiting Libya, by taking a ferry from

Tunisia, seemed to have a rugged appeal. No flights could be found to Tripoli because of the embargo but it didn't mean that travel in the country would be unwise or unsafe. Gallipoli or Tripoli, that was the question; Amalfi or Napoli, in which direction should I go?

The first impression of a country can often be found in the contact that you have with the aircraft staff. No clues were to be had here. Uganda, like many African countries, had handed over control of their routes to South African Airways. The crews were from all over Africa.

The airline leased the corridors and created a Pan-African company with newly painted planes. Alliance Airlines was therefore SAA in a different guise. The crew was courteous but stern. The boy – he looked about fifteen – who was sleeping in the seat next to me was roughly shaken awake by the steward.

'What is it?' he asked sleepily. I half expected him to say, 'Are we there yet?'

'You must eat,' the steward ordered.

Reluctantly, the boy let down his seat-back table for the steward to slip the tray on to and mumbled thanks, seeing the sense in what the older man had said.

There was a matter-of-fact approach to their work, it had to be done and done efficiently. British or American stewards would have let the guy sleep on, but every passenger had a meal allocated and they were going to get it, like it or not.

The ravenous way in which the boy ate the meal was testimony to the practicality of this approach, even if it did seem strict to me.

Hattie played with her food and I ordered a bottle of South African white and red; both of them were delicious, better than French, in my opinion.

The films seemed appealing but so did getting as much sleep as I could, so I settled under a rug and watched the movies through half-closed eyes.

I awoke to pandemonium and orange juice. A plastic sealed beaker of juice was on the lowered table in front of me while I could feel a pressure pulling on my seat back. I could feel the passenger behind hauling themselves out of their seat, using my seat as leverage.

Several people were milling around excitedly, trying to look out of the windows.

The captain's voice spoke to us all: 'There is Mount Kilimanjaro, we'll circle around three times so you can get a good look and take some pictures.'

Many of the passengers on board will be trekking for three days to get to the top. You wouldn't catch me doing all that hard work; I prefer to see it from this angle. I get just the same view without all the effort of climbing a mountain.'

By the time the pilot had admonished the hikers for their foolhardiness, practically every window on the port side had a huddle of passengers around it. The Kilimanjaro fly past was a treat for all passengers and a chance for the pilot to show how well he could circle an extinct volcano.

The first proper camera that I had ever, a Russian Zenit SLR 35mm camera, had fallen apart and I hadn't owned one for five years. Before we left on this trip, I was determined that I would be able to take my own photographs.

Wanting to support the European Community, I had bought a German camera and allowed the shop assistant to get the film for me, a big mistake. As I tried to fit the thirty-five-millimetre Kodak Gold into my Advantix camera, I heard the voice of a German barely able to speak for chortling.

'That is the wrong film for that camera,' he said gleefully.

The struggle out of my seat, aching limbs and tired mind, the venture into the busy thoroughfare, which had been the aisle and the Herculean effort to open the overhead hatch, pull down the right bag and rummage for both film and camera had all been in vain.

I contented myself with leaving my bag on the seat and walking to the emergency exit to peer over the shoulders of several Chinese tourists whose Japanese cameras clicked and wound on with a satisfying reliability that they expected. I knew that I would not be purchasing a German camera with its 'different' film.

The view was stunning looking into the bowl of the volcano, the mass rising out of the searing morning sunshine. The parched earth and the steep slopes whirled slowly below us. Even to this day I can see in my mind's eye the massive mountain, seen from a small window tens of thousands of feet overhead, but I have no documentary evidence of my having been there or seen that.

We were told to return to our seats for landing. Our juice cups were collected.

Hattie woke up, I handed her the juice, and I explained what had happened as she sipped on her orange juice, which I had hidden from the efficient steward in the seat back in front of me. She listened sympathetically to my animated account of dicing with death in order to record the momentous event. Secretly, I think she was a little upset that I had not woken her, but she had seemed so at peace and I was loathe to do so as she was sleeping so deeply.

'You can have my film for the trip if you like, I can't use it. I'll return the camera to the shop when we get back to England,' I added by way of appeasement.

'I'll be the official photographer for the trip then,' she suggested, happily, much to my relief; typically, Hattie, she let me off the hook for not waking her over Kilimanjaro

'That's a great idea, How are you?' I knew that Hattie was an excellent photographer and I could help her to spot good subjects or her compositions

'Sleepy – you?' Hattie whispered, stretching, she had hardly touched her juice, which was precariously balanced on her armrest.

'Tired, I can never sleep on planes,' I replied.

It was a white lie, but she didn't mind. With relief she drank off the carton and spirited it away in her bag before the crew had a chance to make their checks prior to our final approach.

'Wake me when we get to Entebbe,' Hattie mumbled as she tried to make herself as comfortable as possible with the seat back upright. She pulled the airline blanket up to her chin and dozed. I decided that sleep was out of the question, so I watched the landing. Landing at Kilimanjaro was an uncomfortable event. The plane thudded down on the tarmac with three distinct bumps that shook the airframe and jolted my back. We taxied to the apron and the plane stopped with a shudder.

'On-going passengers, please remain in your seats until those disembarking at Kilimanjaro have left the aircraft,' ordered the South African pilot.

Hattie was woken by the bumpy landing and we both stretched out while a throng of passengers like puppets with elastic strings danced in the aisles grabbing their belongings and shuffling patiently to the rays of sunlight at the end of the tunnel, leaving us behind in the metal tube.

A glow of bright luminescence sucked the people out of the cabin.

Against the electric light, the brightness was a beacon and you could imagine the white-hot heat that you might meet there.

Returning to my seat, I huddled under my blanket for warmth; sleep had lowered my body temperature and the air conditioning seemed to be particularly chilly. I'm sure they had turned it up to aerate and cool the cabin with all its human activity, pleasant for those struggling off or on the aircraft, not so hot for those who were prone and trapped.

I tried to doze but my back ached. There seemed no chance to move about with passengers leaving and boarding, so I determined that I would wait until we were airborne again before stretching my legs.

For some unknown reason the South African pilot came and stood in our aisle to talk to us. At first, I thought it was because we had done something wrong. We recognised who he was by his shoulder flashes; I was worried that I was going to be bumped off the flight. Such a scheme would have negated the point of me escorting Hattie on her first trip to Africa.

You cannot be a chivalrous escort and chaperone if you are stuck in another airport. I had been refused entry to Dubai due to a lack of visa on my return from Hong Kong and I had been bumped off lots of flights to Boston, New York, Washington and even Charlottesville, North Carolina.

I was nervous, it was not the best frame of mind to make a good conversationalist. However, I did not want to upset the pilot who was coming towards our seats, the first row still occupied, it was kind of him to come and talk to us.

'Hi, I've come back to stretch my legs and talk to some new faces,' his voice was warm, his accent clipped, his shirt starched, his hair was grey and neatly cut.

He even took off his aviator sunglasses to reveal steely blue eyes. I was glad he was being nice to us; he was well built and seemed fit, and not the sort of person you would want to rile just for the sake of it.

'I'm glad you can stretch your legs,' I whispered, hoping he wouldn't quite catch what I was saying. He failed to register that he had noticed any irony in my voice, either out of politeness or because he couldn't be bothered.

'What did you think of Kilimanjaro?' he asked, slipping on to the armrest of the chair in front of me, folding his sunglasses, pocketing them and placing his hands on his knees.

'Fabulous, you're right about walking up it, I couldn't do it. We came down quite, quickly didn't we?' I was living on the edge by mentioning our hard impact on landing, but I felt he could take it.

'You have to slam the plane down in these mountainous areas, there are too many different currents around,' he smiled – Rothmans smoker, no doubt, tar stains and a gold tooth.

'I see,' I agreed, forgetting my nervousness and I smiled back, gleaming, recently polished teeth – no gold, just diamond white.

'So, you're going on to Entebbe, where are you going on to from there?' he was determined to snap us out of our sleepy state.

'We're staying in Uganda,' I said hoping that he wasn't going to tell us horror stories. Hattie was a worrier and I was quite sensitive too. We had heard that Uganda was safe but there were rebels in the north. You could never tell how safe somewhere was without local info.

'Ach, man, forget Uganda,' he told us, 'Get on a plane to South Africa, Cape Town is beautiful, Table Mountain, the coast, the best sea food. Better still stay on the plane, we'll take you on to Johannesburg and you can visit Durban, best beaches in the world.'

'We call it Jo'burg,' I informed him with a smile, but he was not impressed.

I had also heard about the violence on the streets, drive-by shootings, East L.A. style. I reckoned we were safer in Uganda than most places in Africa.

'What's wrong with Uganda,' Hattie asked, politely.

'Nothing, it's just there's nothing to see there, have you been before?'

'No, but I've been to Kenya which was beautiful,' Hattie asserted her international traveller credentials. 'What about Murchinson Falls and the game parks, the source of the Nile and Lake Victoria?'

'I've never been to those places,' the pilot admitted. 'It's just that Kampala and Entebbe are dull places.'

He was feeling awkward. I felt sorry for him, but I was proud of the fact that Hattie had done her background research thoroughly; otherwise I might have stayed on the plane.

'We're visiting friends of my father,' she explained. She was discreet enough not to mention the Kabaka and the coronation Hattie's family had been invited to attend.

'Oh, I see.'

'They've promised to show us around. They'll look after us.'

'Well, that's different,' he admitted. 'Enjoy your stay.'

'We will,' I asserted, we all smiled again, 'and we'll visit South Africa soon, I've heard it's great.'

'Do that,' he said genuinely, 'I've got to go back now, enjoy the rest of your flight.'

'You should try and see more of Uganda when you can,' Hattie suggested affably.

'Perhaps I should find the time to do so, nice meeting you,' he got up, flashed gold and very white teeth at us again, and putting on his aviator sunglasses, sauntered back to the flight deck. He had a plane to fly. I, subsequently, learnt how difficult the approach to airports near mountains could be and his smooth landing at Entebbe was fantastic.

The onward flight was mercifully short or seemed so once we had breakfast in the air. Hattie was chattier and we talked about her perceptions of Uganda. The trip was an opportunity for her father to see his African friends and for his children and his grandchildren – Hattie's brothers, sisters, nieces and nephews – to see Africa for the first time and perhaps fall in love with its beauty and its wonderfully warm people. I was glad that I was not journeying to Entebbe on my own, I would see Africa, but I would be guided to the right spots.

Chapter 5

Why (or if)?

Hattie was an old friend of mine from London. I had met her while I was living in Battersea with a few old school friends. It was 1980; we had left school that summer. The house was in disrepair, plaster from the ceiling fell into the bath when you were washing and in winter it was like an icebox, but we enjoyed the freedom. I paid five pounds a week to share a two-bedroom, first-floor flat with four people. One of them was seeing a girl who lived in Egerton Gardens and Hattie was a flatmate there. Not only were they our age and living in a smart part of town (compared to our location anyway), they had their own rooms.

We had become good friends and then lost touch for a few years while she worked out of town. On her return, like all old friends, we had met up and picked up where we had left off. Her father had been posted out to Africa while he was in the army and he was going to Uganda for the coronation of the Kabaka of Baganda (or Buganda). In an absent-minded moment he had kindly invited me along.

At first, I thought he was just being polite, as it was the topic of conversation on my visits to see the family. I had dismissed the idea until a letter arrived, inviting me and giving me details of how and where I should book my ticket. It was a 'once-in-a-life-time opportunity' and I couldn't refuse. The Major had been kind enough to invite me and I felt that I should be gracious enough to accept. That was the real reason why I was visiting Uganda; I was flattered that he held me in high enough regard to include me in what was a very special and poignant trip.

Everyone was enthusiastic about the journey; the Asian chemists, who I had known for many years, through picking up prescriptions for my mother, had once lived there. My doctor who was Indian had relatives who had been there on holiday. I was pleased until he gave me my injections; my arm was swollen for ages afterwards. My sister, a former nurse, told me that generally the injection was administered into the gluteus maximus.

He was obviously so envious of my trip that he had stabbed me in the arm. Even the thigh would have been preferable. My bruised arm was tangible proof that he was jealous.

I stayed with the family just outside Bath for the weekend. Hattie, Richard, the real Major, not Pip's sobriquet, and, his wife, Susan were also joined by Duncan who had filled me in before the trip when we met for a kitchen supper at his parents' house in Bath Easton. Hattie, her mother and father had gone to bed and left us with water biscuits, Stilton and port to fuel our conversation:

'So, tell me again, when was Freddie Mutesa murdered?' I asked.

A plate of Stilton and water biscuits lay in front of me. I was sipping a splendid port that had worked its way from the decanter into a glass the shape of a tiny, transparent Wellington boot, which held a surprising amount.

The Aga was giving off cosy warmth adding to my comfort but increasing my thirst and we had – the six of us – polished off two bottles of South African Pinotage that I had brought along. It was difficult to make things clear enough for me.

'On 22nd November 1969,' Duncan breathed exhaling a cloud of cigarette smoke; he was patient and smoking; the others had left for bed two hours ago, at ten; the midnight hour was announced by a gorgeous mantel clock chiming.

'That's the year I was born,' I responded happily.

'You were born in 1962,' Duncan corrected me.

'How did you know that?' I was stunned, we had only met each other a couple of times, and we were friendly but not that friendly.

'Because all year you've been telling us that it's your year in the Chinese calendar, the year of the tiger, it's every twelve years, 1998, 1986, 1974, 1962. I doubt whether you were born in 1974, no matter how young you look,' he soothed charmingly as he drew on his cigarette before continuing. 'I also know that you weren't born in 1950, otherwise all your hair would be gone!'

Duncan smiled as he spoke the last few words. It was a thin, grim, self-satisfied smile, he enjoyed going for the jugular and was perfectly aware of my sensitivity regarding my thinning hair, and he knew me that well. He knew I would appreciate his humour and forgive any insensitivity.

'Thanks, mate,' I acknowledged sarcastically. I was capable of being as sophisticated in my humour, if the wind was in the right direction.

Ultimately, I could not argue with his deduction. 'Tell me more about Freddie.'

'His Highness, Sir Edward Frederick Mutesa II, 35th Kabaka of Baganda and first President of Uganda,' Duncan pronounced each title so that it would sink into my addled brain. 'Freddie wore many hats and he was christened Edward, so I have just focused on his main roles, king and president.'

'That's the one,' I agreed slicing some Stilton off my lump before delicately placing the slither on to a dry biscuit.

'Freddie died aged forty-five, in near penury,' Duncan explained as he blew smoke in my direction just as I lifted the wafer to my mouth, determined to destroy my enjoyment of the subtle cheese.

I sipped some port from the boot, to show him that his ruse had no effect, and nothing could spoil my enjoyment of the meal. As port melted with Stilton on my tongue, Duncan continued his story.

'He was living in a borrowed flat in Bermondsey, in south-east London,' Duncan explained. 'It was the first of my father's refuges,' Duncan said as he sipped some port.

'I am aware of the locality,' I interjected, loftily. My sister had a boyfriend who came from there, but I wasn't going to tell Duncan yet. 'I used to go clubbing there,' I said, desperately trying to sound a hip twenty-four-year-old, rather than a spent thirty-six-year-old.

I wasn't going to mention that we were searched for knives on entering and that I was witness to a few 'bottlings' while I was there. A bottling involves smashing the top off a beer bottle and pushing the fragmented remains into any part of the nearest person's body.

Bermondsey was the equivalent of Marlowe's Rotherhithe and look what happened to him; he was stabbed for being a great playwright and a spy.

We were lucky to get out of that place alive.

'Freddie was just managing to survive on four pounds a week from the Social Security, it was tough for him. All his friends callously abandoned him in his absolute hour of need,' Duncan announced as he dramatically emphasised the details.

'That's terrible,' I complained, I was no longer interested in my cheese or the port.

I lit a cigarette myself as Duncan stubbed out his own. There was no point in trying to eat when Duncan smoked.

'Indeed,' he replied.

He covered the area opposite him in a dense fog.

I was also upset by the fact that Freddie had been left destitute. 'Tell me more.'

'Freddie was educated by British tutors in Uganda until he went to university in Kampala. From there he went on to Cambridge and after getting his degree joined the Brigade of Guards. My father who was in the Coldstream Guards met Freddie in the late 1940s.'

Duncan reported the facts like a history teacher or a television presenter.

'They met in England,' I interrupted; I had always thought that they had met in Uganda.

'Dad went to visit him in Uganda three times and lent Freddie our flat in Bermondsey when he found himself homeless in London,' Duncan explained as he sat back and crossed his legs; I knew that the story had a sad ending, but the details upset me more.

'Was there nothing the army could do for him?' I asked, horrified by his plight.

'Apparently not, the last three years of his life were spent being given the cold shoulder by the British government,' he said sadly.

'The Foreign Office even insisted that the British royal family should not see or speak to Freddie,' Duncan sounded as if he took personal offence at this affront to his father's friend. It did seem cruel.

'Was that because they were supporting Idi Amin?' I asked putting my cigarette in the ashtray in front of us. Depressed by Freddie's plight, I ate some cheese for comfort, pleased that Duncan had not smoked it this time.

'I think so, he was very upset by this abandonment particularly as he had shown such hospitality in Uganda when they had visited him,' Duncan's world-weary tone added weight to his words.

'So, he considered them his friends?' I asked, naively.

'They were, during his early twenties, in England, certainly. He led an immensely and intensely glamorous life, particularly as a Grenadier Officer stationed at Wellington Barracks. Freddie wore Savile Row suits and Lobb shoes, spent long weekends staying with the Duke and Duchess of Hamilton, enjoyed endless nights at the opera and ballet – he was, after all, part of the social set of the time.'

Duncan seemed to wish for a similar life so lavish was his intonation.

'So, what went wrong?' I was confused

'In 1942, aged eighteen, he had been crowned Kabaka and, seven years later at the insistence of the tribal elders and after completion of his university education and training in the Guards, he returned to Uganda to resume his official duties.'

'Go on.'

'He then spent the next seventeen years, with a two-year break in between, being treated as a deity. The two-year blip was in 1953 when the then British Governor, Sir Andrew Cohen, arranged for Freddie to be exiled to London as he was seen as an obstacle standing in the way of the British plan to unite Uganda with Tanzania and Kenya.'

Duncan had carried out extensive research; he knew his history.

'That plan worked,' I mustered all the irony that I could inject into my tone. I was curious to know what the British hoped to achieve by uniting these three vast countries, but it was not the time to ask. 'Where did he live when he left Uganda?'

'During his first exile he lived in Eaton Square, he was still in favour with the government,' he remarked contemptuously.

'They had to look after him at that stage,' I noted, cynically.

'It was on his return to Uganda, at the British government's request, that his problems really began. In 1964 his country was granted independence and he was made its first president.' Duncan's voice was becoming graver.

'That sounds positive, but then Idi Amin arrived on the scene,' I was starting to make connections myself with my scant schoolboy knowledge of international politics.

'Amin was working on the orders of Obote, Freddie's Prime Minister. Tension between the two of them had been mounting for two years.'

'So, Freddie didn't have a loyal Prime Minister, I always thought Amin was the one who organised the coup.'

'It was way back in May 1966 that Obote gave the command to Colonel Idi Amin to storm the Kabaka's palace at midday. Amin was then Commander of the Ugandan army, he didn't become President until 1971.'

Duncan was doing his utmost to explain things clearly, he had done his research, and I had only part of the picture.

'How did Freddie get away?' I couldn't believe that Amin would allow Freddie to escape so easily.

'Freddie managed to escape during a flash storm and hid until he could move on further under cover of night. After three days of avoiding capture in the jungle he made his way into Rwanda and then on to England.'

'So, no one helped him when he arrived in England?'

I was incredulous. Amin would have been considered a terrorist by today's standards, but in the 1950s international politics had its own code of conduct.

'Initially,' Duncan explained. 'On his arrival in England, he had been assigned Special Branch protection by the Home Office and, with the constant presence of his bodyguard, Major Jehoash Katende, who had escaped with him there was an effective security cordon around him.'

'So, he was in real danger?' I had read my share of Fredrick Forsyth and John Le Carré, but this had been balanced by a large dose of cynicism. The world was full of conspiracy theories, but little evidence to back them up.

'As long as he was alive, wherever he was, he held great sway within the potentially combustible world of Ugandan politics and that's why Obote had placed a bounty of £34,000 on the Kabaka's head.'

'I'm surprised he survived any time at all, £34,000 was a lot of money in those days. It must be equivalent to half a million. I'm working on the premise that the average price of a house was £5,000 and the average house price is £100,000 now,' I was doing mental arithmetic, but only vaguely.

Despite the port, I reckoned that property had increased twenty-fold.

Therefore, thirty-four times twenty was six hundred and eighty thousand, well over half a million, allowing for a large margin of error.

'The Home Office was aware of this and, as a result, placed twenty-four hour protection around him for the first eighteen months of his exile.'

Duncan took a cigarette out of the box on the table and tapped it on the arm of his chair as he continued.

'Freddie was very aware of security and went to great lengths to be cautious. He attempted to alter his route whenever he left his flat, using different bus routes and he was very wary, especially at night-time, of standing in a lit window with the curtains drawn back. Even though he was penniless, he had a spyhole installed in his front door.'

Duncan tossed the unlit cigarette that he had used to beat time on to the tablecloth; it rolled to the edge and stopped. He sat back, gripping the arms of the chair as he settled into the seat.

'He was out of the picture so why was he in such serious danger?' I could understand if the Kabaka had been in Africa that he might have posed a threat, but he was in exile in England.

Obote had the presidency and Freddie was living in poverty; surely, he was no danger to the regime, living quietly in Bermondsey.

'As an exiled monarch, there was an obvious threat to the stability of the new regime in Uganda as long as he was alive.' Duncan raised his hands to his chin as if in prayer before carrying on, 'Freddie was a Kabaka, a hereditary tribal king. His kingdom, Baganda, covered roughly a quarter of Uganda's landmass and the loyalty of twenty-five per cent of the population. Baganda encompassed Kampala the capital city, its only international airport at Entebbe and the country's main university, Makerere. This gave the Baganda – and therefore him as leader – huge significance and political power.'

'I see,' I said encouragingly; I felt the unfairness of the situation. 'Basically, he was a prisoner.' I encouraged Duncan to go on, offering him a cigarette which, in his excited state, he refused, holding up his right hand and waving away the temptation in a pantomime gesture.

'In 1969, Freddie mysteriously died. The coroner's verdict was given as alcoholic poisoning, but it was suspected that he was murdered by a government agent sent over from Uganda.'

Duncan let his words hang in the air. I remained silent but took a sip of port to alleviate the tension I felt. 'There is still one man alive who knows whether he was assassinated or not. Idi Amin.'

'He's still living in Jeddah, isn't he?' I knew that much.

'Under house arrest, I believe; he has it is rumoured all he needs to keep him happy,' Duncan smiled for the first time, 'I'm sure he has more freedom than Freddie did.'

'Surely, Amin won't tell anyone anything to incriminate himself still further?' I said, realising the hopelessness of the whole situation.

'Maybe as a final gesture of showmanship, *Dada*, as he likes to be called now, might give a last interview and tell the world that he had arranged to have someone kill Freddie,' Duncan sounded hopeful, he shifted his chair nearer the table, sat forward and reached for the packet of cigarettes.

'That's surreal,' I remarked, sliding the matches across the table. Amin knew and yet he kept his silence, it didn't seem to add up.

'Dadaism?' Duncan asked, taking the matchbox.

I was in no mood for metaphysical argument, nor was I prepared to discuss the merits of Surrealism and Dadaism when I now realised that there could be irrefutable evidence of Freddie's murder.

'No, what surprises me is the fact that Amin hasn't brought it to light already!' I was surprised that Amin had not implicated Obote in the assassination attempt unless he feared reprisals himself.

'It's not really difficult to understand,' Duncan assured me.

His condescending tone might have irked someone else, but not me. As they say in Ireland: '*You can't insult me, I'm ignorant*; Sticks and stones and condescending tones won't break my bones.'

'No one's interests would be served by the revelation. It would only restore Freddie's reputation, almost thirty years on, most people think he drank himself to death,' Duncan elucidated. He finally succumbed to his need for nicotine, lit his cigarette and holding it in one hand, he poured us both a generous measure of port.

My head was spinning slightly, but despite the alcohol intake my mind was surprisingly focused as the grim facts revealed themselves. I was thirsty so I drank more port when water would have been more effective in quenching my thirst and clearing my mind.

I was not able to make it to the sink for fear of breaking Duncan's thread; I sipped on my drink, as Duncan blew smoke over my glass and plate.

'Freddie was a natural aristocrat and he had the common touch. It must have been difficult, arriving in England in the late 1940s, a decade before the initial wave of immigrant boats from the Caribbean arrived, but he mixed in with all the pub landlords and dockers of Bermondsey.' Duncan drew on his cigarette as he paused for breath.

'It made sense for him to befriend the locals from a security point of view, they would let him know if anyone suspicious was around,' I mentioned with erudition.

Duncan was not one who was easily impressed.

'Quite,' he replied, tersely, he had perhaps not thought of that himself. 'Freddie was a sociable and social character.'

'It must have taken him time to adjust to being poor,' I suggested, trying a different tack.

I was being smoked out as surely as if I was a wasp in its nest, so I lit my own cigarette to keep Duncan company and to allow me to blow my cigarette's smoke his way.

I also thought it would be healthier to limit the second-hand cigarette from Duncan's direction by blowing both streams towards him.

'Not at all, he was used to changes in his life,' Duncan said emphatically as he leaned back into his chair. 'He might have mixed with the royal families of Europe, travelling around with Aga Khan, the business mogul, Cecil Beaton, the famous photographer, and Oliver Messel, the stage and film designer. He was in their social circle for four years. Then he returned to Uganda and Freddie was reintroduced to African tribal life; that was the real test of his adaptability,' Duncan summed up. He seemed to have a good understanding of his father's friend.

'Quite a contrast,' I noted for sake of something to say.

'After this he became President and later, he narrowly escaped death at the hands of Amin's soldiers. Having lived such a privileged life for forty-two years, he found himself suddenly on the outside, with no way in. That must have been soul destroying.' Duncan sighed.

He realised that Freddie could adapt to different environments, but he could not be expected to cope with the desertion of those who had once called him friend.

'I can't believe everyone cut him off so completely,' I interjected; I was incensed at Freddie's fair-weather friends and their callousness and yet I may have been unfair to judge them so harshly.

'They most assuredly did, either of their own volition or on the advice of others, perhaps.

'It was a good job that your father could help him.'

'They were friends,' Duncan insisted.

He had inherited his father's ideals.

'Why do you think he was murdered?' I asked. I was feeling that perhaps Freddie had died of alcohol poisoning. I was drinking myself to death that night; I could imagine being depressed and drowning my sorrows in a bottle or three.

'Freddie was hardly drinking at that time, but he received a telegram from Kampala in November 1969 saying that *the girl who wants to harm you is on her way to England,*' he explained, dragging on his cigarette.

'He had good intelligence, then.' It seemed that Freddie had a good spy network in Kampala, considering he had been away from the capital for so long.

'During his twenty-five year reign Freddie had exercised his power with great fairness.' Duncan elucidated. 'It was this, allied to his god-like status as Kabaka that produced such devotion amongst his people, the Baganda.'

'So, he was warned that he was in danger?'

All the pieces were falling into place but as I dragged on my cigarette, I couldn't help thinking that Freddie should have gone into hiding when the death threat came to light.

The smoke in the room made my eyes smart, but I continued to smoke, wiping my eyes with my free hand. I hoped that Duncan didn't think I was crying; blubbing in front of anyone is embarrassing, particularly if the person is a virtual stranger or the brother of an extremely dear friend. Duncan failed to notice, and I felt that I was getting to know him better as he continued his report.

He seemed a skilled orator to me, even if he was a bit impatient with my numerous questions and limited understanding.

'It's not as simple as that; the threat of assassination seemed to have receded. Although the danger still existed, the Special Branch policeman had been dispensed with and Freddie's life returned to relative normality. It turned out that this girl not only existed but was already living in London posing as a student, and that Freddie had met her a couple of weeks beforehand at a dinner party given by an exiled Tanzanian minister. She was even brought to Orchard House by one of Freddie's nieces.'

'So, he met her, why?' I wondered out loud.

I thought it very brave to confront her.

'It was the insistence of his advisers that had made him agree to meet her,' Duncan said.

He finished his cigarette and drank some more port; his voice was strained from talking so much.

'Freddie's daughter appeared that afternoon and she was told by Freddie that there was a telephone message for her which he'd written on a pad by the side of his bed. Sceptical at first, she went into the bedroom and found a note from her father saying: 'Be careful what you say, this is the girl we have been warned about'. It's a bit dramatic, I know, but it does show how seriously the warning had been taken and how real was the threat of kidnap or murder.'

'I suppose there was nothing conclusive to go to the police with,' I suggested, wondering why Freddie stayed if his life was under threat.

Surely Freddie could have gone into hiding somewhere in the countryside or left England altogether, couldn't he?

'The following Saturday was Freddie's birthday party and there was a large party and a church service to organise. The whole saga seemed to be forgotten but the day after the meeting in the flat, a loyal follower working at the decoding office in Kampala intercepted a telegram from Tatu to the then Cabinet Secretary.

'The text said: "The operation is going ahead a planned".

'Then a letter smuggled out of Uganda reported that on the Kabaka's birthday a minister who had been opening a new stretch of road declared in his speech: "We have managed to do it at last. We have managed to poison the Kabaka".

'These two pieces of evidence are difficult to prove but they point to some form of conspiracy.'

'Go back to Freddie, what happened?' I wanted more detail.

'The main celebration was to be a service at St Martin in the Fields, on the Saturday. This was to be followed by a party for which friends from all over the world were flying into London.'

'So, what went wrong?' I asked.

'On the Friday evening before, Katende found Freddie lying unconscious on the sitting room floor at Orchard House. He put him to bed and after failing to wake him, he tried desperately to contact a doctor. Eventually, after being examined by the doctor, in the early hours of Saturday morning three days after his actual forty-fifth birthday, Freddie was officially declared dead.'

'That's dreadful,' I gasped. I felt a sudden wave of sadness wash over me, even though I had never met Freddie. He hadn't even been able to celebrate his birthday.

'It was a shock to everyone, not least Katende,' Duncan whispered, brutally stubbing out his cigarette in disgust.

'Friends rallied round and helped fend off the intense press interest that was beginning to grow around Freddie, specifically, his death. In the chaos after his death there was a growing suspicion about the way he had died, and the fear of a potential Foreign Office cover-up. Harold Wilson's government had, for the last three years, found Freddie's presence in England extremely awkward.'

'Why was that?' I was incensed that justice should be negated by political considerations.

'I believe it was to do with Uganda's role within the Security Council of the United Nations. As Britain was in the process of applying to the UN for sanctions against Rhodesia, the Foreign Office wished to keep on friendly terms with Obote's administration.'

Duncan's points were beginning to gain more credence.

I had been unconvinced until I saw the motivation behind such malevolence.

The pieces of the jigsaw were coming together in my mind; a clearer picture was emerging despite the lateness of the hour and the relaxing influence of the perfect port.

'So, what was the coroner's verdict?' I asked.

I was sure that some evidence would have come to light, I wasn't sure that someone could drink themselves to death with a retinue, however small, looking after them.

'I was coming to that,' Duncan relaxed a bit before going on. 'The verdict brought in by the Coroner was one of alcoholic poisoning.'

'But you told me he had given up alcohol,' I complained.

'The verdict, certainly, surprised those of his friends who had seen him in the days prior to his death, as not one of them had noticed that he was drinking heavily, let alone being so drunk that he was putting his life at risk.'

'So why was the verdict accepted?'

It seemed monstrous that he should be accused of drinking himself to death when his life had been threatened. The proof had been provided, both unwittingly, publicly, by one of Obote's ministers, and also, privately, by the telegram that had implicated the femme fatale.

'It wasn't, that's the point, and it was challenged. Professor Francis Camps, Professor of Forensic Medicine at London University, said openly that Freddie's death was hardly consistent with the coroner's findings or a drunkard's form of death. Plus, Ian Colville, writing for the *Daily Telegraph*, pointed out the inconsistencies of the case and questioned the judgment.'

'What about the police?'

I was curious to know how they could refute such evidence. Their conduct in the case seemed to be ruled by the dictates of both the Foreign Office and the Home Office, both wishing to clear up the scandal as soon as possible. It is little wonder the police have little respect for civil servants, mandarins and politicians; they insult them by calling them *plebs* and they seem to spend inordinate time, over decades, obfuscating the truth.

'Even the Metropolitan Police believed that Freddie's death had not been the result of an excessive alcohol intake,' Duncan sighed before taking up another cigarette.

I wasn't sure if I could take any more Sandeman's Port, smoke any more cigarettes myself or inhale the second-hand smoke from another one of Duncan's cigarettes but I knew I was fascinated by the story.

'Then how did he die?' I was perplexed.

I could accept the poisoning theory only if I had more details. I did, however, believe that Freddie could not have drunk himself to death in such a short time.

'The most obvious idea was that he was poisoned, which was in keeping with the rumours coming out of Uganda.' Duncan drew on his cigarette.

He leant forward to flick his ash and then folded his arms on the dining table. The glowing cigarette in his right hand seemed to be sending off smoke signals that seemed to be saying to me: 'these are the facts, challenge me on them if you dare'.

'It seems pretty conclusive,' I agreed in order to encourage him to give more evidence. I even nonchalantly sipped on the port that I no longer wanted in order to give Duncan the impression that I proved no threat to his theory.

'There's more,' Duncan exclaimed, becoming more animated again. I knew there had to be more. 'A week before his death, Freddie heard the doorbell and looking through his spyhole, he saw a grey-haired Caucasian woman scurrying away. Opening the door, he found that she had left a bag of groceries with no note. Puzzled by this he had called the police and told them of the mysterious sequence of events.'

'Didn't they take it away to be forensically tested?' I had perhaps seen too many detective movies as a child.

'No,' Duncan stated emphatically, he hated to be interrupted, but I hated to remain in silence. A balance was difficult to achieve. 'The police were equally baffled, suggesting that it was a delivery made to the wrong door and that if it wasn't claimed in the next couple of days, Freddie should by all means eat what was there. This he did, along with Katende, and nobody thought any more of it until his death five days later.'

'They both could have been poisoned,' I hissed.

I was conscious that I should not interrupt but equally aware that some comment should be made in response to their cavalier behaviour.

'But they weren't,' Duncan insisted forcibly.

'Really?' I inquired, wondering what the authorities were playing at.

'Despite the very obvious suspicions that existed, the fact that the food had been shared equally amongst the two men, seemed to negate the possibility of poisoning. What seemed to be more likely was that the groceries had been left by a kind-hearted neighbour who knew of Freddie's plight, yet wanted to remain anonymous.'

'But why was no note left?'

I felt like Watson baffled by Sherlock's deductions.

'The groceries could just be a coincidence. What was interesting, though, was that police enquiries had uncovered the fact that the girl who visited Freddie was a Ugandan government agent. The police ignored this and closed the investigation immediately.'

Duncan dismissed my questions at every turn, but this served to increase my questioning.

'How could they ignore such evidence?' I groaned. 'They must have been given the telegram that warned Freddie that his life was in danger, surely?'

At this interruption Duncan shifted his position to lean heavily on his crossed arms as if to emphasise his points that I appeared to be missing. His body language told me that he thought I was hearing what he said but not listening to it properly.

'Apparently, they were satisfied that nothing out of the ordinary had happened, they concluded the Freddie had died from drinking far too much over a sustained period. "He was an alcoholic, drunk every afternoon by teatime", one senior police officer at Scotland Yard was quoted as saying.'

'So that was it?'

There were too many red herrings for my liking, and they were spoiling my enjoyment of the cheese. Something was fishy but there was no way that Duncan would be encouraged to cut to the chase.

'Not quite,' he uttered with the satisfaction with which a detective reveals the true identity of the culprit. Duncan leant his body over his arms and looked at me challengingly as he revealed the last snippet of information that I needed to make everything clear.

'A Ghanaian from Accra and a Ugandan appeared in London with stories that were very interesting. The Ghanaian was the son of a tribal chief who had died in circumstances almost identical to Freddie's; the cause of death had also been given as alcoholic poisoning which had seemed preposterous to the son as his father was almost teetotal.'

'So that was it,' I exclaimed, unable to control myself. Duncan turned his head, sighed and cleared his throat.

Bringing himself back under control, I found myself wilting under his serious gaze. It was not acceptable behaviour to interrupt at this juncture; his eyes told me.

'Driven to his own investigation he discovered the existence of two herbal roots called Bullinbugu and Waliga herbs,' Duncan continued quickly. I dared not say anything. 'These are only found in West Africa, and when ground into powder and mixed together they prove fatal. Once the powder has been digested into the human body it kills instantly and produces the effect of huge alcoholic consumption.

Likewise, Uganda produced the herb called Akalgala which, when digested, had an identical effect.'

'God,' I let slip.

He had paused for dramatic effect and I had thought that he had finished.

'Wait,' Duncan chastised me. 'Where this Akalgala herb differed was that it could lie dormant in the body for weeks until activated by relatively small amounts of alcohol. All three of these herbs were well known within each respective tribal region and had been established forms of assassination for generations.'

'That's incredible.' I was sure Duncan had finished but his bored expression told me that there was yet more.

'Although not known to western medicine, Professor Camps, a doctor and Fellow of the Royal College of Physicians, seemed intrigued by the possibility of analysing these herbs and was in the process of so doing when he died of natural causes.'

'It gets more and more mysterious.' I was fascinated. Duncan was frustrated.

My interjections seemed to course him vexation.

'The discovery of these herbs opened up the possibility of poisoning which the police had rejected, and it could prove that the operation referred to in the cryptic telegram to Obote from the girl had been the assassination of Freddie. It was possible that at some stage during her visit to Orchard House, on the Sunday before Freddie's death, she would have had the opportunity to administer the poison.' He banged the table with his hand and relaxed back into his seat.

Duncan's story was over, so he allowed himself a cigarette. He'd run out of full strength, so I offered my low tar brand. I slid the packet to the edge of the table.

'Amazing,' I said.

'Indeed,' Duncan agreed.

Duncan grabbed the matches that had been used earlier to light the supper candles, and the packet of cigarettes, before slumping back into his chair. He was happy to accept my tobacco products but not my questions. Casually, crossing his ankles, he slipped down so that his shoulders rested on the back of the chair. After lighting the cigarette, he nonchalantly tossed the two boxes on to the table.

'Incredible.'

'How could she do it?'

I found myself morbidly fascinated.

'Various theories have been put forward,' Duncan exclaimed as he exhaled deeply. 'Sprinkling the herb into Freddie's bedside glass of water or on his toothbrush. The herb would have been absorbed over the next twelve hours or so until stimulated later by alcohol. The whole of Baganda, not least Milton Obote, knew it was the Kabaka's birthday, so it would be assumed that a fair quantity of alcohol would be consumed in the days preceding it. When the girl left Orchard House, she was satisfied that her mission was complete which would explain her telegram saying that the operation was going ahead as planned.'

'What happened to her?' I enquired.

'She had intended to go to Paris the following weekend, but because of Freddie's death, had been interviewed by the police and detained in England. Denying everything, she was released due to lack of solid evidence and with no further information.'

I sighed helpfully; it was distressing but required no comment.

'The police could not detain her further. She flew out of the country, going into hiding. She spent the rest of her life as a hunted woman. The Baganda discovered her name and accused her of being Freddie's assassin and hounded her whenever she was found. After years of going in and out of protective custody she apparently confessed that although she hadn't killed the Kabaka herself, she did know who had.'

'Could she have been lying to save herself?' I wondered out loud.

'Who knows, she was a haunted woman, but she would not reveal what happened to anyone. Freddie found a new champion in Alan Lennox Boyd. He had statements from people who swore that the Kabaka hadn't been drunk in the days before his death.'

'That must have helped,' I suggested hopefully, but deep down fearing the worst.

'You would think so. Boyd had been Colonial Secretary at the end of Freddie's first exile and was a good friend. He arranged a meeting with John Walden at New Scotland Yard hoping to convince him to reopen the case.'

'Did he succeed?'

It was okay to ask questions at this stage; Duncan was too weak to care; his soliloquy was over.

'The meeting was a disaster. Commissioner Walden seemed to want to block any further enquiries and he described Freddie as a drunk who was a huge embarrassment to his rich and important friends. It was ridiculous and Boyd questioned him about what he said. Walden just told him that they had a file on the Kabaka.'

'So that was it?' I wished that I had been proved right.

'Not quite,' Duncan had to smile as he offered me another crumb of information, knowing I was on tenterhooks. 'A second enquiry was opened. I think this was more to do with pressure from influential friends than the fact that justice needed to be served.'

'Did the second enquiry reveal anything?'

My throat was dry from my part in the conversation, so I took a sip of port that finished the glass. I could take no more, so I put the glass firmly in the middle of the table.

'The second investigation was headed by a Special Branch Detective, Sergeant Mike Waller; Waller had acted as Freddie's bodyguard on his arrival in England. Over that eighteen-month period a friendship had developed between the two men and Mike Waller had become very sympathetic to the Bagandan cause.' Duncan spoke in a hoarse voice; he didn't sound as though the new investigation was a source for hope.

'Go on,' I urged, gasping encouragingly, on tenterhooks.

'What was surprising,' he croaked, 'Was that the two other men making up the team were officers from Southwark police station who had headed the first investigation and weren't interested in the case. They were unwilling to believe anything other than the Foreign Office edict of a three-day binge and perhaps feared that causing extra trouble could harm their promotion prospects or indeed their careers. So, despite Mike Waller's enthusiasm the investigation eventually petered out, ran out of steam and was closed.'

'Do you think the two local police officers blocked Mike's efforts?'

I was seeing deception and chicanery everywhere.

'I haven't spoken to him, but it seems to me that the might of the Foreign Office had nullified and suppressed any moral responsibility that the police should have had.' Duncan sat up and flicked his ash into the ashtray on the table, revealing his frustration.

'But this case should have been treated properly. It was a case of assassination, not only assassination but assassination of a head of state,' I opined, feeling the anger rise in me. It seemed so unjust. I was totally convinced by now that it was a case of poisoning.

'Instead, because of the political machinations of the time, Freddie's murder was dismissed as death by natural causes,' Duncan waved his cigarette, dismissing the whole tragedy with one movement of his hand.

It was late and we were both exhausted. Duncan was drained from his account and I was saddened by the story. We cleared the table in silence. I had the last of the cheese as I took the plates through, savouring its pure, unadulterated flavour, stacked the dishwasher and left Duncan to have a last cigarette, wishing him goodnight.

Chapter 6

Entebbe

The landing at Entebbe is one of the most spectacular sights that I have seen; I was able to move to a seat by the window on the second leg of the flight. I had a whole row to myself and I took advantage of the increased legroom.

The plane flew over the airport, giving an aerial view of the banks of the lake and a modern airport complex that seemed to rise out of the marshland, a conning tower and a long, flat expanse of tarmac, surrounded by swamp.

There was a private airfield to the west, and a road that snaked towards the capital, Kampala; a discarded Dakota clearly visible beside the road nestled in the green foliage that separated the water from the highway.

We banked slowly around, four of five miles above Lake Victoria and started a slow smooth decent. The expanse of the lake stunned me, more like a sea.

The grey-green mirror spread out beneath us as far as you could see, small islands, black marks that dappled the sheen, like the spots of faded silvering on an old mirror. The landing seemed to last for an age. As we neared the water, it was with relief that I saw the rushes and marsh grass moments before we eased down on to the runway.

There was no jolt when we landed, no mean feat when landing a jumbo jet, and we cruised at landing speed before the brakes were gently applied. Either the pilot had heeded my complaint about coming down hard earlier, or because the approach was over water, the landing could be executed on a smoother trajectory.

Through the window I could see the rectangular building with the conning tower on top, and then the plane taxied left and into a space only a hundred yards from the building itself.

We would be walking through the heat to the terminal. Being there excited Hattie and, although equally excited, I was relieved I could stretch my legs properly.

Hattie, being long-legged and almost as tall as me, was happy to stand up and stretch, too, but we let others gather their belongings and go, before we had organised ourselves enough to leave.

That same white quadrilateral of light sucked us all out into the warmth of the mid-morning sun, the glare making me squint and forcing Hattie to reach for her sunglasses. I led the way down the stairs through the tropical heat. A gentleman always follows a lady up the stairs and leads the way down them in case the lady slips; he will, in that way, break her fall – a true gentleman puts his safety second to his escort's.

We followed the throng towards the glass-fronted customs hall. Two soldiers with Kalashnikov AK-47 rifles stood by a priest; he wore tan trousers and a tweed jacket, dog collar and black shirt, but the heat did not seem to bother him. As I passed him, he spoke to Hattie.

'Excuse me, are you Hattie?' he asked.

'Yes, I am,' Hattie could not hide her surprise.

I had stopped when he had spoken to Hattie. I was immediately put on guard. I was suspicious, holding an Irish passport and having been almost deported from Dubai the previous year for not having a visa. The friend I was visiting insisted a visa was not needed, which is quite true if you hold a British Passport; mine is from the Irish Republic, so I did need one. Fortunately, he knew someone in immigration, and I was not sent back to Hong Kong. I was sure that our paperwork was in order; we had been given painstaking instruction about travel by the Major and had all the travel documentation and vaccination certificates that anyone would need.

'And you are her friend Michael?'

'Yes,' I could not lie, certainly, not to a priest at least.

'Will you follow me, please, we'll be taking you to the Major,' he smiled and touched his clerical collar whether as a nervous affectation or to reassure us, I was not sure.

'And you are?' I asked.

'*The Reverend,*' he replied.

However, he had met us on the tarmac in a secure airport terminal and seemed to be an envoy of the government if not the Kabaka himself.

We had to trust to him.

The two soldiers lead the way, red berets worn smartly, and their khaki uniforms pressed and starched to perfection; only the relaxed way that they held their rifles gave an indication of their nonchalance.

They were used to escorting *The Reverend* around and they were aware of the respect that their semi-automatic rifles afforded them. Hattie and I smiled at each other for reassurance and followed the three men cautiously around the side of the building.

Our entourage climbed the concrete stairs on the outside of the building, stepping through into the VIP lounge. As we entered through the glass double doors, a guard, who was posted at the reception desk, looked up at *The Reverend* and smiled briefly before adopting a stern face.

Carrying his own Kalashnikov in his left hand, he stood up smartly and came around from behind the desk and shook hands with the priest. Both men smiled at each other while the two soldiers who had accompanied us stood by the doorway.

The Reverend ushered us through to the bright seating area. The lounge was a minimalist's dream: a vast rectangle of open space, which was flooded by the light that streamed through the floor-to-ceiling windows. Eight leather sofas were arranged in two squares, one in the shade closest to the far wall and one by the plate glass window overlooking the runway and Lake Victoria.

'Would you like to take a seat?' *The Reverend* asked us warmly, smiling his charming smile.

Hattie and I obediently went and sat down by the window on the sofa facing into the room, stark and Starck, white walls and black-leather furniture. Philippe Starck's influence seemed to have reached Africa.

Hattie's brother, Duncan, came through as *The Reverend* talked to the guards at the entrance. He smiled at Hattie and I, they kissed, and I shook hands with him. He seemed relaxed and rested, as if he had left behind the stress of London long ago, although in truth he had only arrived three days before us. He sat down on the sofa opposite us and asked us about our flight. Wearing jeans and a dark blue Aertex shirt he could have been anywhere in Europe that summer.

Duncan had taken the same air route as us and he was anxious to tell us about the rest of the family and their twenty-two-hour-journey through the Middle East and on to Entebbe.

Our flight at eight hours to Kilimanjaro, followed by two to Entebbe, seemed like a holiday in comparison. *The Reverend* came over and offered us a drink and we gratefully accepted coffee.

'Can I have your tickets with the baggage reclaim? I'm going to send someone to fetch your bags,' he explained, his voice was friendly; he smiled at us warmly and then touched his dog collar. Hattie and I duly complied and thanked *The Reverend* as he left to organise everything.

'Is that the king?' Hattie asked Duncan.

'He's the king all right but only of spiritual matters,' Duncan smiled. 'We haven't met the Kabaka yet. I think, from all reports, he's still in England or New York, but he hasn't sent for us yet, so he's definitely not in Africa.'

Before we had finished our coffee, our suitcases arrived, held by a distinguished looking man in a suit with a friendly smile. *The Reverend* hovered in the background until Duncan decided we should go, and we all got up.

'Shall we go?' he asked *The Reverend*.

'Duncan, can I have a word?' he took Duncan to one side, but within earshot. 'Can you lend me 2,000 shillings to pay the guard?'

'Of course.' Duncan fished out two 1,000-shilling notes, 2,100 being the equivalent of roughly £1.25. *The Reverend* walked over to the guard and slipped the money into his hand, the Kalashnikov was now resting behind the counter, but within easy reach.

The soldier smiled at *The Reverend* and *The Reverend* pretended that they had just shaken hands. We followed the two soldiers down the stairs outside the building to the covered concourse where a red four-wheel-drive Toyota pickup and a silver Toyota taxi waited for us.

The soldiers climbed into the Japanese pickup with our suitcases and Hattie, *The Reverend* and Duncan got into the cab. I sat up front with the uniformed driver in the pickup. These soldiers were part of the king's personal bodyguard and wore a different uniform to the government troops that we came across later in our stay.

It was a bizarre experience being whisked from the airport, as I sip on a glass of Backsberg Chardonnay, in London, in January, reflecting on that hot day; the surreal feel of that first day still comes back to me vividly.

The taxi driver ahead sped along the black tarmac road ignoring all other traffic; Dae Woo, the driver, was a man in hurry, and I could imagine Duncan, Hattie's brother who was pale already getting paler by the second. The pickup driver next to me was determined to keep pace.

The soldiers perched behind, visible in the rear-view and side mirrors, were holding on grimly to the side of the pickup with one hand and their Russian weapons with the other. The dichotomy of African life was summed up by the people we passed and the contrast between our lives in Northern Europe and their lives in the tropics was bought home to me even at that early stage.

Life in Africa has a different pace, the heat prevents people from rushing around, yet the Toyota ahead with its air conditioning and power everything, disregarded the rules.

We had long periods of hanging around; the inactivity was stupefying and yet, when something happened, it happened at a frenetic pace. The convoy proceeded with almost manic acceleration, overtaking slower moving vehicles even on the bends in the road, regardless of what was coming the other way.

Sometimes the traffic on our side moved over on to the dust track that served as a kerb; otherwise Dae Woo created a third lane on the two-lane highway, missing the flow both ways by inches. I am sure that my driver knew the way to the Speke, but he tailgated Dae Woo as if his life depended on not losing him. In fact, the soldiers and their driver were intent on protecting Hattie, *The Reverend* and Duncan at all costs. I was in the escort vehicle, I was expendable, but I was enjoying that, I was where the action would be.

It would not have been so bad if we were late for some high-level meeting on cancelling third world debt or if we were late for tea or a luncheon engagement, but we were dashing to wait, interminably, for news from the palace.

The convoy passed the shacks on the outskirts of Entebbe; the road was a smooth, new blacktop at odds with the rickety houses and the rusting wreck of the Dakota. It was difficult to imagine how the old plane had got into its position in the marsh, but it might have been dragged from the private airfield, which was shrouded behind tropical trees on the following bend.

The outskirts of Kampala had similar wooden shacks, looking like they were part of a favela in Rio, but they gave way quickly to linear rows of concrete bungalows, painted white. Interspersed between these dwellings were shops whose only differing feature was that the front wall had been replaced by a reinforced steel joist with a wooden sign-board attached to it and the floor had been raised a few feet above ground level.

Conversations were being held on the steps and the stock was hidden in the gloom of the interior. The high-speed chase along the Kampala Road provided the only excitement of the day and set the pace for our extraordinary adventure.

Chapter 7

The First Afternoon

With a screech of tyres, Dae Woo delivered the entourage at the hotel and from the pickup our baggage was dropped in reception. We had no change to tip the soldiers. The Speke Hotel with all its history was a very modern looking place. It was there we waited to meet with the king, only to be told he was not yet in the country. It was at the Speke that I met everyone else, Hattie and Duncan's family: the Major, his wife Susan, their daughters Lucy and Anna and their son-in-law, Pip.

Pip was Anna's husband and they were jointly responsible for four boys, Sam, ten, Aubrey, eight, Ollie, five and Punch, three. Lucy, who was a widow, had Matilda, aged twelve and Emily, aged ten. Hattie and I brought the safari up to almost full strength; another brother, Anthony, was due in the next few days, destined to share accommodation with Duncan, Pip and I.

It had been decided to farm the families with children out to willing hosts with children of their own rather than have the whole family in a hotel. Lucy had been found a lovely couple; the husband was in the drinks business and lived in an exclusive part of Kampala. Anna and the boys had been billeted with an Italian entrepreneur in the hills above Kampala where the Italian Consulate and several government buildings were located. Being Italian, they were charming.

After lunch and an endless wait, Dae Woo drove us hurriedly on to the Reste Corner. Hattie remained to be accommodated with the female members of the party. We gave Pip a lift back to the hotel and the first day was gone in a blur of inactivity. In the evening we caught a cab to the Speke and dined there only to return to our hotel at midnight, exhausted by the heat and by doing absolutely nothing all day.

The next morning, we were driven in the CBS minibus. We went from the Speke Hotel to Bagandan parliament building or Bulange to meet the king's secretary, Katende. The building was where the Lukiiko or Bagandan parliament met to, amongst other things, elect a new Kabaka.

It was built in the fifties and resembled many of the town halls built in Britain at that time; the parliament was similar in look to the buildings at the University of London, a style of architecture difficult to describe to anyone outside England: not quite Corbusier, not quite Russian Constructivist.

In the beginning, the Baganda Parliament convened inside one of the Kabaka's palaces and conducted business under the shade of one or more trees. Later, grass-thatched buildings served as the parliament buildings.

Around the beginning of the 20th century, Prime Minister of Baganda, Apollo Kaggwa, contracted an Indian, Alidina Visram, to build a parliament building using bricks; it was known as the Lukiiko Hall. As the kingdom's government grew in size, the need for a large-enough meeting hall forced the construction of the Bulange outside the king's palace for the first time.

While in exile in Scotland in 1953, Ssekabaka Muteesa II, or Major General Sir Edward Frederick William David Walugembe Mutebi Luwangula Muteesa II, or King Freddie, as Duncan called him, admired the construction drawings of a building. He brought those drawings with him on his return from exile in 1955.

He directed that the new Bulange be constructed according to those drawings. Construction began in 1955 and was completed in 1958 at a cost of £5 million, which was paid for by the Bagandan parliament and it replaced the Lukiiko Hall built in 1902.

We swept through the gates of the Mengo Palace, drove up a mile-long drive into a large sandy apron and along the length of a large rectangular building made of concrete or stone with green shutters on each side of its vast windows. It was a stunning site, seeing the imposing building set on its own with no other buildings surrounding it. It was like Wandsworth Town Hall but slightly smaller.

In Kampala or Entebbe, you were used to seeing such large buildings, but in a rural setting where most dwellings are bungalows, the government building stood out on the hill on which it was placed as a towering presence. There were three main floors but that did not take into account the steps up to the building behind which was where the basement archives were stored. The stone steps at the front of the building led up to an impressive set of heavy doors with embossed square panels.

The wood was stained the same colour as the steps, earthy beige, almost like American oak and the wood around the windows and the panelling above and below were painted the most glorious duck egg blue that stood out from the cream-painted plastered exterior walls. The Ugandan one-hundred-shilling note shows the parliament building in all its glory.

The note is cream with blue and turquoise and is issued by the Bank of Uganda. On one side there is an antelope and a crane both of which surround a tribal shield; its emblem is a wavy top third to signify the waters of the lakes and the Nile, a sun and a tribal drum, the motto professing 'For God and My Country'. On the opposite side is the building: concrete slabs and small windows on the ground floor, plaster and arch windows in the middle, large rectangular windows on the top floor, a slopping colonial roof in dark tiling sweeps to the eaves in a gentle slope.

The palace with its three floors, cool interior of polished stone floors, large square steel-framed windows and dark stained wood looked as if it would make a great hotel. In contrast, the Sheraton with its office block appearance would have made a great parliament building of the type favoured in Strasbourg and Brussels: all concrete, glass and stainless steel.

More stone steps led us up on to the first floor and I was surprised how cool the building was despite the approach of noon. All the windows were open and the fact that we were on a hill helped – a cool breeze blew through the building. The Kabaka's secretary, Kagunda, was a thin man who looked smart in formal trousers, a beautifully ironed cream shirt and burgundy tie.

Nothing was too much trouble and he became a firm friend, even on such a brief trip. He spent a long time showing the Major photographs and explaining issues to him. The Major had a keen mind and was desperate to understand what exactly had occurred between the coronation of his friend Freddie and the coronation of Ronnie.

Visiting the chamber where the parliament sat was like visiting an urban committee room in a council chamber. A vast rectangular space with a raised platform, but on this dais, there was a throne instead of a table for head councillors. Benches not unlike the House of Commons ran down each side and high windows flooded the room in light.

The grounds at the back of the building were equally superb. There were two flights of five steps that led down from two terraces. The higher terrace contained pots or tropical flowers and stone benches below the windows; the next terrace had flowerbeds containing beautifully tended roses. Mama Rose and the Reverend introduced the Major to various people while we kept the children entertained with football in a corner of the grounds.

From there we visited the palace from where the Kabaka had fled Idi Amin and the lake across which the king had swum.

The house itself was like a Georgian country house in Wiltshire that had been neglected and ruined by fire; stone columns were charred and the fascias were beige and black along the walls.

Even the metal doors were scarred and rusting, the glass long gone. It was dangerous to walk on the top floor as the roof was damaged and the beams had rotted even in this heat, but we went up there anyhow, all except the children, and we explored the ruin with scant regard for safety.

It was a shame to see the holes in the roof and to notice the boards on the top floor had rotted away. We stepped carefully on the buckboards, which had been placed there by builders. Looking down between the gaps in the rafters we could see in some cases all the way down into the basement. Even the stairs were ruined, so climbing from floor to floor was hazardous.

The Major was standing in a room on the ground floor where he had stayed on a visit to see Freddie. It was difficult to know what he was thinking, the memory of better times must have been strong; the good old days before the world went mad and bad.

Punch was with all the other children outside in the gardens pretending to drive the van. Bizarrely, there was a jazz sax band playing on the circle of lawn in front of the palace. It was lunchtime and after talking to the builders, who hoped to restore the wreck, we returned to the Speke for lunch.

Back at the hotel, the children were collecting the bottle tops of all drinks, so we were encouraged to drink the fabulous local beer,

Bell, brewed in Kampala. The children squealed in delight when the opener wrenched off another crown cork bottle top.

We sat with the Major, we were all gathered around the table; the children had a separate round table for themselves, but it didn't prevent Punch from trying to steal the drinks from the adults' table because his lemon Fanta was the same colour as our beer – almost – in his eyes.

'That's mine,' Punch declared eyeing a glass of beer his father had just poured, despite the froth that topped the drink.

'That's granny's juice,' Lucy told him as he was diverted from Pip's drink.

'I give it,' Punch replied

'Use two hands, Punch,' Lucy insisted. Punch took the glass and almost made it to his grandmother but in his haste, he spilt the drink on Lucy's dress. Lucy rolled her eyes heavenward, her sunglasses perched on her head, so that everyone could see her expression.

'Caca, Lucy's dress,' observed Punch happily.

'What are we doing tonight?' Duncan asked as Lucy patiently wiped down her dress with a napkin.

'We're going to be organised,' Pip said with determination.

'No Fang, Fang, then,' I muttered as Punch knocked the beer bottle out of Pip's hand and it smashed on the floor.

'If you kept it between your legs you wouldn't have had that problem,' Duncan suggested helpfully.

'Are you talking about the bottle or what?' Pip asked.

'Our hostess dumped us this morning like a ton of bricks. I think she's bored of us already and now I have sticky soft drink on my dress,' Lucy was not happy.

'At least no one has nicked your beer.' Pip was trying to console her.

'He actually spilt the drink on me, Mr Grumpy,' Lucy retorted.

'All right, Miss Happy,' Pip replied.

'A mishap that's all it was, a Miss Hap, ha, Miss Happy,' Duncan laughed; he had a habit of guffawing at his own jokes when they were really bad.

'Cigarette, anyone?' I asked, as I had remained silent for too long for my liking.

'Please,' Duncan sighed, taking one and lighting it with the shared lighter while Pip frowned because Duncan had taken the lighter off his cigar box and had failed to return it, but instead placed it on his box of full-strength Marlboro without even a sideways glance at Pip.

'Good, aren't they?' The local tobacco impressed me.

I was experimenting with the local cigarette brand: Prince Light last night, Rex today. I was moving up in the world.

'Four plus two equals five.' Duncan's cryptic answer set me aback, but not for long.

'Let's go dancing tonight at Silk,' I suggested.

'Half-London is meant to be better,' Duncan told me.

'It's more European and less authentic,' I replied.

'It's a Tyre and Exhaust centre for me,' Pip opined.

'What?' I was slow on the uptake.

'I'm heading for the tired and exhausted centre, the hotel, to bed.'

'That's boring.'

'There's no rhyme and reason. It's my favourite ice cream.'

'Rum and raisin,' Duncan explained to me.

'We should head out with Chopin, Liszt.'

'Shopping list,' Duncan translated

'Did you make them up yourself?' I asked archly.

Pip didn't even justify my comment with an answer.

It was early days and yet I could feel the friendship that we had established on previous meetings ebbing away. It is often useful in stressful situations to have a figure that you can focus all your frustration upon, and I had through my existence there become that figure.

I was happy to be, to absorb the atmosphere of Africa, to sit and watch and take in the similarities and differences between our cultures. The whole point of my coming to Africa was to learn about the place and its people however much a cliché that may sound. As I was happy to just 'be', Pip wanted to 'do'; he was a 'doer'.

It was reasonable; after all, he had paid for his four children to come out to Africa and paid for his wife and himself to create memories that they could share forever, and quite right, too. He had come a long way with a lot of people. He owed it to them and himself to show them a marvellous time.

He wanted to see the country and to go on safari, he had worked extremely hard through the years to provide for his family and this holiday was to be a trip of a lifetime. I did not see it as such until contemplating the trip later, but he was quite right to be frustrated by the inactivity and the waiting around.

He was unable to make decisions about excursions because we were waiting for some word from the king and it was incumbent on us to row in with the schedule that might be prepared for us.

Instead of being sympathetic to his plight, Duncan took advantage of Pip's frustration and teased him as much as he could. This amused everyone. I have to share responsibility and also half the guilt by including myself in his shenanigans.

It was really Duncan's lead that I took but he had the good sense to know when to stop; I did not. I could not help myself; I was in effect amusing myself at someone else's expense. Duncan was doing the same, but he was entitled, as he was a brother-in-law.

I was not entitled especially as I was meant to be a friend.

That night we drank from three bottles: Lagavulin, Laphroaig and Balvenie, all supplied by Pip. He was overly generous and kindly to us and this made our teasing a more heinous crime, but, then, we were bored, too, and we dealt with it in a differing way. It was only later in retrospect that we learnt about all this. It was great to spend time with Pip and Duncan, real time, talking about interesting things. Duncan talked about our snoring to wind us up, but the fact that he teased us both gave Pip and I, a certain amount of solidarity. We all swapped more stories and went to bed exhausted.

Anthony arrived late in the evening on Tuesday and we dined together at the Speke our imagination knowing no bounds. We had to go through the morning ritual of Duncan complaining about Pip's hacking and Anthony's snoring the next morning.

'They've both got to go,' Duncan announced to me as we waited for the other two to shower, ever the accommodating pair.

'Can't we put them in the same room?' I asked.

'No, let's just move to another hotel,' suggested Duncan.

'Another town?'

'Entebbe.'

'I'm dying for the loo. I'll have to ask Pip to get out.'

'He has got out, but Anthony's gone in.'

'Any coffee around?'

'It's in the hotel.'

'Can we get it sent down?'

'It's not far, you'll make it.'

'No, I'm afraid I won't.'

'Stretcher-bearers.'

Pip came in at that point, shaved washed and refreshed.

'Pip did you sleep straight away?' Duncan asked innocently.

'I was looking at the map to get my bearings for the trip, why?'

'I was wrecked by the drink; I don't know how you stayed up.'

'I had to regain my composure after the whisky, too,' Pip smiled.

'Composure – is that on the map?' asked Duncan as Anthony entered the room.

'There's no plug in the sink,' he announced.

'That's right,' Duncan looked at him in disbelief.

'How do you shave?' Anthony asked.

'It's going to be a long day, chaps,' Duncan looked at us both.

'The mossies kept on waking me up,' Anthony complained.

'Yeah, my hands are swollen, they feasted on me,' Duncan replied.

'You should use 100 per cent Deet,' I suggested helpfully.

'Susan said that it stings if you put it on neat,' Anthony recalled.

'No, it doesn't,' Pip chortled

Duncan started to sing 'Viva Espana'.

'*We're off to sunny, sunny Spain, e viva Espana…*' he didn't know all the words, so he hummed the rest.

'We know where he wanted to go for his holiday,' Pip chortled, he was astonishingly patient considering the constant provocation.

'*We're off to sunny, sunny Spain eh, Viva Uganda,*' Duncan continued.

'Blame it on sleep deprivation,' Anthony said to me, trying to excuse his brother.

'Do Fio, no worries,' I replied.

I already knew a smattering of the local language, Anthony looked at me askance, feeling perhaps that whilst he felt Duncan was mad, he had not realised that I too might be afflicted in the same way.

'Fruity had a good war,' Duncan said to startle us

'It's Bunny had a damn fine war,' Pip corrected him.

'Is that you, Bunny,' Duncan said. 'It's only the shell shock has affected my hearing, I'm not sure who I am or where I'm going. Is that you, Bunny, after all these years, meeting again on civvy street, I used to tell my sister, Joan, Damn fine war had Bunny.'

'Shall we shog?' I asked.

'We shall shog and get some grog,' Pip replied, he was the only one of the group familiar with Shakespeare and particularly the word of dear Pistol from *Henry V*.

He was not strictly accurate as *GROG* was a much more modern word than shog; King George used to have rum shipped over from Grenada, George Rex Old Grenadine, which is where the acronym came from; not exactly of Elizabethan extraction.

However, he proved that he knew that shog was an Elizabethan expression for 'Let's go'. Pip lead the way strapping on his money belt before we left with all his documents zipped in; it was a plastic waterproof belt with a large pouch, the type favoured by skiers.

'Pip, don't forget to bring your bum bag,' Duncan warned stepping into the room, pretending that he hadn't seen Pip dressing. Pip wore the pouch at the front, a sensible precaution given the change in topographical and cultural climate.

Duncan followed us out, the last to leave; Pip was already halfway up the footpath to the breakfast room. We were halfway between Anthony and Duncan, but we still managed to hear Duncan's comment not at all like a stage whisper.

'He wears that thing like it's a belly bag, not a bum bag,' Duncan hissed. I laughed but Anthony looked shocked. Duncan was right, it looked like a marsupial's pouch, but I was glad Pip could not hear.

Chapter 8

Advice to Travellers

I read *The Monitor,* Wednesday 15th July 1998. There was a taxi strike over new laws that were to be brought in. The taxi drivers' strike led to a football match being cancelled as only the referee turned up. We were unaffected by the strike as the taxis were mini-buses that took passengers from the kerb like buses. Luckily, our relative wealth meant that we used taxi-cabs from a rank or from the fleet of cars Dae Woo kept parked outside the Speke. Another bit of news was that a briefcase at Crested Towers was suspected to contain a bomb.

I had no idea where Crested Towers was, so I was unsure whether I should worry for the people in the vicinity. Nor did I know if I was in the vicinity myself – perhaps I should worry for all of us. The building was, in fact, not far from the Speke Hotel further up Nile Avenue towards the centre of Kampala.

Yoweri Museveni, the President, was trying to intervene in the war between Eritrea and Ethiopia over disputed land. It was probably a war that had, and would, drag on almost as long as the Israeli–Palestinian conflict. It was a grim reminder of how this wonderful continent of amazing mineral riches and warm and friendly good people was destroyed by conflict, corruption or strife.

Another item of news was that Tanzania, Kenya and Uganda had agreed to free up transport across Lake Victoria by allowing each national railway to cover contracts for each other. At least that was positive.

The railways handled transport and cargo tended to pile up while boats were in dry dock or out of commission.

The Kaawa ferry was the only route to Kenya and Tanzania over Lake Victoria, I knew solely because I wanted to get to Zanzibar and the Kaawa ferry was the easiest way next to flying.

I was so bored that I decided to read my advice for the travellers, dated April 9th, 1998, yet another time:

Uganda plans are developing now that the dates and flights are fixed. I'll list here the various other details so that, with luck, nothing will be forgotten and as much as possible will be known.

OUT: Friday July 10th, 1998. Train from Bath (probably 07.57, to be confirmed.)

Heathrow Terminal 3. Report 09.30. Take off 11.30. Arrive Entebbe (via Muscat) 09.30 July 11th.

Flight Nos. GF/004 and GF/713. Met by whom?

The trip was planned with methodical, military precision, but I hadn't expected to be greeted by armed guards and given a ride into town surrounded by bodyguards.

For Pip the price is £455 each return + £21 tax. Children, 67%.

BACK: August 1st. Depart 10.45. Arrive Heathrow (Term 3) 06.40 August 2nd. Flight Nos. GF/714 and GF/009.

OUT: Friday July 10th '98. Train from Bath (probably 1727, to be confirmed). Heathrow Terminal 1 - Report 19.05. Take off 21.05. Arrive Entebbe 07.00 July 11th Flight No Y2/001. Met by whom?

BACK: July 31st 00.30. Arrive Heathrow (Terminal 1) 06.45 August 1st. Flight No. Y2/002

All flight charges go up after July 10th.

If anyone wants to join us, do ask them to ring Ali Padhani on 0181-385 1234 Or 0181-357 0721 to arrange their own flights, linking with ours, or not as they wish.

Please make any plans you like about return dates (and Anthony outwards as well) direct with Ali (tel. above), once you can be definite; the sooner the better he suggests.

I'll subdivide everything else under headings of A, accommodation, B transport, C tours, D health, E general details F security G history, geography and politics, H climate and I quote.

A - First our address and accommodation:

The plan is to rent a house in Kampala for most of us to use as a base. Susan and I will stay at the Speke Hotel nearby and will have use of a grand hotel's (Sheraton or Grand Imperial) swimming pool two minutes away. The pools were to provide a saving grace.

It allowed us to keep the children occupied during the long periods of inactivity.

Hotel room charges are about £50.00 per night double and £40.00 per night single. The house is not yet decided but the likely one will sleep 15 and cost about £200.00 each to cover 21 days, i.e. £10.00 per night per sleeper any age.

As it turned out their hosts warmly received the families and the bachelors in the party were independent; we were booked into the Reste Corner at Muyenga, in a self-contained bungalow in private grounds, saving our hosts the sounds of coughing or hacking, snoring and, of course, Duncan's cutting comments.

B – Transport:

With luck we'll find a car, but advice is to hold hard on making firm commitments too quickly. A minibus costs £71.00 per day to rent, this includes driver and petrol, and there are no self-drive cars to rent.

(In fact, the Central Broadcasting Service or CBS bus was lent to us whenever it was available which was more often than we could hope. Eventually, it provided the transport for many excursions, to the coronation site, to the Parliament building and even to the source of the Nile at Jinja. All we did was pay for the petrol and tip the driver as often as we could).

(David or Dae Woo had his own taxi firm and he would take us, or we could choose from one of his drivers, parked outside The Speke Hotel).

The one time we did take a cab to Aka Bua Road from the street outside the Imperial, we were driven all around Kampala but nowhere near our destination. Even we could tell he was going the wrong way. I asked him to stop at the Speke and Dae Woo dealt with him and organised us another taxi.

C - Tours:

A visit to Ssese Islands is separate and private; Betty Lutaya is organising this.

There is also a possible visit to Toro and the Ruwenzori staying in the 'Mountain of the Moon Hotel'.

Otherwise all tours will be part of organised programmes. They will start and end in Kampala.

On offer are the following:

a) A four-day visit to Queen Elizabeth National (Game Park)

(This was vetoed not so much for the £680 fee, but because of fierce fighting in that area; there was after all some sort of war going on, but no one told us. Equally there was some form of terrorist campaign going on, but no one would admit responsibility, so no one knew who was to blame.)

Another way of looking at this is that it will cost about £170.00 per day all in, including travel, permits, guides and food, while alternatively staying in a posh hotel, doing nothing, would, anyhow, cost about £80.00 a day plus food.

The Major had a valid point.

b) A three-day visit to Murchison Falls National Park, £680.00. I think for transport and return flight plus one night and a game drive, I paid five hundred dollars.

(This was the safari we plumped for.)

c) A six-day gorilla safari, which will cost £1,625 per head, plus $180 Gorilla permit.

If they really wanted to sting you, the price was quoted in dollars in the hope that you might assume that the permit is cheaper.

The price alone was too much for me and I would be surprised if, once travel and accommodation for the next fortnight was stripped away, anyone would have enough money for such a trip, gorgeous as gorillas are – they had priced themselves out of the market.

d) Six-day Highlights of Uganda tour (including three game parks), £1105 per head. A chimpanzee sanctuary visit during this tour is extra.'

(This seemed reasonable, but a detailed map of Uganda would immediately tell you that the distance between safari parks in Uganda is quite simply vast and therefore it was impractical for all of us due to various time constraints imposed by disparate arrival and departure times of different groups and individuals. Our uncoordinated flight planes meant Murchison Falls was the only viable option for us all to enjoy as a large party.)

Quite a few places can be visited easily within a day (such as the source of the Nile at Jinja, the Botanical Gardens in Entebbe and Kasubi Tombs where the Kabakas are buried).

D - Health Advice:

The following vaccinations are recommended: Polio and Tetanus and Yellow Fever – to have had an injection within ten years. Typhoid Fever – either annual oral capsule or an injection that lasts five years. All fine if not; hepatitis gamma globulin provides short-term protection.

Rabies, report it if you had an injection within the last three years.

Also, Yellow Fever certificates are mandatory and should be obtained for peace of mind.

E - General Details:

Insurance: Each individual needs to take out their own cover, (which I neglected to do, which was a mistake).

Travellers' cheques and credit cards are generally both accepted.

Currency and rates of exchange: the national currency is the shilling and the most popular outside currency is the US dollar.

Rates £1.00 = US$ 1.60 = 1,820 Ugandan shillings

Therefore 900 Ug Shs = 50p and 1 dollar = about 75p.

Visas are not required for British passport holders.

Driving licences should be brought in case there is a need to produce and use one.

Clothes: light summer clothes and one tidy lot.

Mosquito nets are not needed in hotels or private houses, but they are used and should be provided in game parks and on safaris.

Time, Uganda time is GMT +3.

Cameras, advice is to take plenty of film with you.

I suggest we use the Speke Hotel as a forwarding address and for messages, telephone calls, etc. It is: The Speke Hotel, Kampala, PO Box 7036, Uganda, East Africa. The telephone and fax number follow.

F – Security:

The FCO (Foreign & Commonwealth Office) recommends avoiding the northern districts of Gulu and Kitgum because of possible roadblocks and the cause of trouble in southern Sudan looks as if it is about to be settled. The other area of rebel activity is in the west linked to the Congo (Zaire) and the Tutsi/Burundi disputes.

In the Karamoja area of eastern Uganda there is banditry and there have been inter-tribal clashes there. They say there is always risk of armed robbery and hijacks, so they advise not to travel after dark and, if stopped by armed men, not to resist. Seasoned African travellers report that it is far safer being in Kampala than in Nairobi or Johannesburg. (Kampala turned out to be extremely safe where we were, just prostitutes offering comfort.)

I, certainly, have never been aware of any of these dangers in Uganda on previous visits but will, of course, go and see the High Commission in Kampala on our arrival and tell them we are there and what our plans are.

Anyhow the FCO's general dictum is, always seek local advice before travelling anywhere of any distance and that must be wise.

G - History, geography and politics:

Baganda is one of the oldest kingdoms in East Africa (which includes Tanzania and Kenya). Various clans at one time occupied the whole area, each with its own clan king.

However, sometime in the early 14th century, Kintu, a wandering priest, who is said to have come from Abyssinia (Ethiopia), entered Baganda from the north-east. Following his arrival, the clans were for the first time united by Kintu into one people under his leadership. Consequently, Kintu is regarded as the first Kabaka of Baganda.

At first it was a small kingdom, but it expanded in all directions, especially from the 17th century and, by the middle of the 19th century, it was the most powerful in the whole of the lake region.

Geographically it is on the northern shore of Lake Nyanza (Bantu for Great Water) and was once called Lake Victoria, through which the White Nile flows. Baganda's boundaries contain the Ugandan cities of Kampala and Entebbe. Uganda, the Swahili word for Baganda, is divided into counties, divisions, provinces and sazas spanning 130,000 square miles.

The terminology becomes confusing: a citizen is a Mugandan and the Bagandan (the whole population) speaks Mugandan. There are five million Baganda amongst the 19 million inhabitants of Uganda.

The Baganda peoples are divided into fifty-four clans and all marriages are cross-clan so there is a wonderfully strong and supportive and cousinly relationship across the whole tribe.

There are other smaller kingdoms: the Toro, Ankole and Bunyoro-Kitara to name just three of the other tribes. Something which we in the UK could well note is how these kingdoms are maintained within a republic.

This republic was established in 1962 when the protecting power, the UK administration based at Entebbe, handed back the Protectorate. The Bagandans had their own parliament buildings, the Bulange, and appointed ministers. When I first visited the country in 1954, the Prime Minister was another, equally esteemed, Mr Kintu. The Protectorate had begun in 1894 for economic and trading reasons with the establishment of the East Africa Company by Cecil Rhodes.

Thereafter, British explorers opened up the area, followed by traders and missionaries with evangelistic and welfare fervour. Different countries scrambling for control of East Africa drew up territorial boundaries. Europeans divided the whole of the continent up. Some of these boundaries were arbitrarily drawn and agreed through treaties brokered in Europe and therefore cut across tribal and traditional areas.

The first President of Uganda, as a whole, was Mutesa II, Freddie, the 35th Kabaka, and the embryonic thought was that the presidential role might be occupied by the four different kings or each, in turn, with five yearly rotations. (The idea of primogeniture does not apply in any Ugandan family and the elders decide succession after the death of the holder.)

This republican plan for leadership, however, never took off, because in 1966, Obote, the then Prime Minister, nullified the Ugandan Constitution and assumed the presidency himself.

Later in the year, Mutesa II, Freddie, was driven from his home, the *Mmengo Palace*, the *Lubiri*, by an armed assault led by Amin, later to hold the Presidency himself for a while, and fled into exile in England. The Bulange complex, at Mmengo, houses the Baganda government and Baganda Parliament or Lukiiko.

Obote went further and abolished the four kingdoms in 1967 and all political parties except his own in 1969.

Not long afterwards his position was usurped by Amin, who expelled all Asians in 1972; some returned twenty years later, and he himself was, after eight years, forced by an uprising to flee.

He was succeeded by three short-term Presidents before the return of Obote.

Yoweri Museveni came to power in 1986, following a popular revolt against Obote.

In 1992 the administration agreed to return all the property belonging to the Baganda government, which Obote had nationalised.

In 1993, the Kabaka and other traditional rulers were recognised under Ugandan law.

Something else we should learn is how a democratic country is run politically with an opposition but without political parties.

Out of 276 members of parliament 214 are elected by universal suffrage and, as do our independent members in England, vote according to their consciences; the remainder are appointed.

There are general elections every five years, when every office including the presidency is voted on. The plan is to have a referendum in 2000 over this issue of a legal opposition and it looks as if parties may be established providing they are broad-based and not tribal.

Context:

The city of Kampala was originally built on seven hills. Today it has expanded to spread over ten hills. The origins of Kampala go back to 1891 when the Kabaka of Baganda had his court on Rubaga and in the Mmengo hills. Historically the Mmengo Palace and its enclosed surrounding area, the Lubiri, have been the centres of Baganda's administration.

The best musicians, dancers, and poets were encouraged to perform there. Conventions of proper etiquette and dress were disseminated from the palace. Clan disputes and other cultural matters were settled there.

In 1966, Prime Minister Milton Obote, with the help of the army led by Idi Amin, *Dada*, stormed and occupied the palace, turning it into a military barracks. Mmengo Palace was occupied by successive government armies until the Uganda People's Defence Forces (UPDF) finally vacated it in December 1997.

On December 19, 1997, President Yoweri Museveni handed back the Mmengo Palace to His Majesty the Kabaka of Baganda, Ronald Muwenda Mutebi II, Ronnie.

The occupying armies left the palace and the rest of the Lubiri grounds in a dilapidated state. Restoration of the Mmengo Palace and its grounds is progressing.

The Mmengo Palace is one of only three existing physical structures that are symbols of Baganda's past power and glory. The two others are the Bulange, the modern administration building of the Baganda Kingdom Parliament, and the Kasubi Tombs.

The economy is based predominantly on agriculture; coffee 60 per cent and cotton 30 per cent making 90 per cent but there is development in the Kilembe copper mines in the west and general expansion of tea plantations.

With two-thirds of the population living in absolute poverty, defined as having an income of less than a dollar a day, there is much need of the international economic aid, nearly $1 billion a year, as well as investment and expansion of the privatisation programme.

Since trade is now mainly with South Africa, there is a plan to switch the main port from Mombasa in Kenya to Tanga in Tanzania and build, with Chinese financial support (Fang, Fang again), a super railway link between Kampala and Johannesburg.

Swahili is the official language, but English is largely used. Forty per cent of the Ugandan population is Bantu, i.e. from south of the Sahara. Bantu is a Zulu word meaning 'people'. Fifty per cent of the Ugandan population is Tuareg, from the Sudan, leaving the rest as either Asians, who came to build the railways in 1900s, or Europeans, who, during the Protectorate, were not allowed to buy land. There are also various other nationalities, but no one is very specific about the others.

About half the population is 'Christian'; forty-five per cent are 'traditionalists' and five per cent 'Muslim'.

H – Climate:

Although an equatorial country, being inland, it is on a high plateau with snow a permanent feature on the highest mountains, the Ruwenzori. Its temperatures are warm and hot 80-90 degrees Fahrenheit or 26-30 degrees Celsius and mainly dry.

There are many rivers and lakes, but the air is not enervating; the forests give way to meadows and savannah around the lakes.

I - Quote from Winston Churchill's autobiography:

'… The kingdom of Uganda is a fairy tale. You climb up a railway rather than a beanstalk, and at the end is a wonderful New World… The scenery is different; the vegetation is different from anything else to be seen in the whole range of Africa, a tropical garden… I asked myself whether there is any other spot in the whole world where… dreams and hopes… have obtained such happy realisation.'

Chapter 9

The Coronation Site at Buddo

I had a restless night; the generators were off so there was no light. I could not sleep and nor could the others. I visited the bathroom three times and each visit, I heard talking. There was no hacking that I can remember to disturb my sleep.

I do, however, recall waking, later that night, to hear the mosquitoes land on Pip. I only knew that they had gone for his flesh by the distant buzz, then silence and a groan from him.

I knew all too well when they got me as I could feel them bite; they were vicious and uncompromising, they wanted blood and they didn't care from whom they got it. Hearing the buzz echo through the room, it was difficult to know which of the two targets they had chosen.

I could only wait and pray that I would hear Pip moan rather than feel that sting and have to slap my arm or leg, knowing that such a delayed reflex was quite unnecessary as the mosquito had already bitten and run. I awoke the next morning drenched in sweat and nursing welts on my skin the size of a large coin.

The sweat I showered off, the itchy mounds I applied cream to, rubbing them with my fingers to make them feel better. It is meant to send good messages to the pain receptors. I had been lucky that I had not been bitten on the face with all the nerves in that area.

We went down to breakfast together, the four of us in good spirits, despite our mauling by mosquitoes; we were to make a trip that day. Pip led the way, followed by Duncan and I – in deference to our new guest – followed at the back, insisting that Anthony, as part of the family, should stick with the family and follow the others.

'The coffee is weak and watery,' I warned. Not that I was one to complain.

'You should have asked for a strong brew,' Duncan told me.

'I don't normally like strong coffee, but this is disgusting, can we change it?' I asked.

The coffee tasted like a very watery instant coffee.

'Just ask for very, very strong – try mine,' Pip offered, letting me taste his lovely cup of *Joe* or *Java*.

I gratefully accepted the stronger brew.

After sipping the more concentrated coffee, I returned the cup. I did not want to get into hot water, which after all was what it was.

'That's much better,' I sighed happily.

We talked of New Zealand as Pip had been there. I adored the wine, but I had never been. An old girlfriend had come from Auckland, but that was all I knew about the place. Duncan was equally curious as his only connection had been with Anchor butter from New Zealand.

Pip had been more places than both of us put together. He was an extremely well-seasoned traveller.

We were just amateurs.

'The taxis have no fuel,' Anthony announced.

'I noticed that,' I replied.

'They fill up each time they take a fare,' Duncan added. 'The last time I got a cab from Kampala to here, the driver had to stop at the petrol station to fill up and I had to give him money to pay for the petrol.'

The security guard was outside when we hailed the taxi; he never seemed to sleep, but was as cheerful as ever, wishing us a good morning and enquiring about our sleep.

'How are you?' I asked. I was here to make friends and as my relationship with the others was deteriorating, I thought I might need someone on my side, particularly as he carried a large machete wherever he went.

'Fine, Saebo,' he replied.

'Aren't you tired?' I couldn't believe that someone could function like him; he had been there when we had come back in the afternoon and he had been up all night and yet he was like man who had just showered.

'No, Saebo, I only sleep for two hours.'

'That's incredible.'

We had all seen this man guarding the compound night and day.

'I'm used to it,' he smiled revealing a single gold tooth where one of his incisors had been replaced.

I was glad he was on my side.

'Have a good day,' I decided to say unsure what it was for him.

It could be day, or it could be night – with so little sleep, who would care? He was fairly tall and stoically built; we had no fears with him wandering around the tended garden in his quasi-military khaki clothes. Very few people would tangle with such an imposing figure especially armed with a machete and a spear.

Outside the compound, the taxi performed a neat three-point turn and we piled in. Anthony, as the newcomer, got to sit in the front seat and pay the bill. Duncan was sandwiched between Pip and I, his knees pressed against the front seats, as much for his own safety as from the length of his legs.

Duncan was now paranoid that any taxi that we took was liable to be hit broadside by another vehicle, so he was happy to let us all have the front or the back windows; we had become his crumple zones, his air bag protection.

'What time are we meeting the others?' he asked.

'Ten, Ugandan time,' Pip answered, he always took care of the details.

'So, eleven thirty, then,' Duncan replied dryly.

'At the earliest,' I continued, similarly grimly, staring out of the open window as the taxi hurtled towards the crossroads where the driver rested his foot momentarily on the brake pedal before pulling out in front of a truck on the near side and a pickup on the far side.

Duncan closed his eyes, so I knew he had seen this too, but even he was speechless.

At the Speke we paid off the taxi driver, it was Duncan's turn and he was happy to pay the fare having arrived in one piece. Clearly, he had decided to let Anthony off.

'Where is everyone?' asked Anthony.

'I don't know,' I replied.

'Perhaps they've followed in Livingstone's footsteps?' Duncan suggested.

'Livingstone's?' I asked.

'There aren't any Livingstones left, they're all "Deading-stones",' Pip observed with a smile.

'He's a very funny man,' Duncan breathed sarcastically.

'What is there here apart from the hotel?' Anthony asked.

'We've been asking ourselves the same question since we arrived,' I quipped in what I hoped was a friendly and world-weary tone if that combination can be adopted at the same time.

'There are some beautiful girls at Crane Bank,' Duncan exclaimed encouragingly.

'They still charged me twenty pounds for changing money,' Pip complained.

'What are we going to do?' Anthony asked.

'Shop,' Duncan suggested.

'You can buy the material for a shirt and they'll make one up for you,' I informed Anthony, having learnt this from Pip earlier on.

'And a suit,' Pip explained; he was keen to let Anthony know that despite the weak coffee at our hotel, Africa had a lot to offer. He had already bought the material for a linen suit and Anna had bought some material to be made up into shirts for her boys, an infinitely sensible idea.

The cloth would be suited to the tropical climate and the cut would be suitably loose and airy to allow for maximum comfort.

There is nothing so potentially volatile as children who are baking in their clothes and overheating in the sun.

'You've got no clothes since they took them to be laundered,' Duncan laughed. He took great glee in pointing this out; Pip was the seasoned traveller and yet he had run out of things to wear.

Soon he would be wearing the Emperor's New Clothes.

It was not his fault, the hotel had promised to return the clothes within two days; four days later, and he was still waiting. He had expected European efficiency; after all, the bedroom was always made up when we returned from town.

It was reasonable to assume that as a laundry service was offered and there were fewer than ten people staying in the Reste Corner, then clothing would be washed and returned fairly quickly.

However, the work was farmed out, just like large organisations lease their vehicles and put their maintenance contracts out to tender, so the Reste Corner left clothes cleaning to outsourced workers.

Their tablecloths were delivered clean and returned to a company to launder, the towels were similarly treated; there was no need to employ someone to wash and iron. This was modern convenience; the epitome of business efficiency only delivers worked on African not Swiss time.

Poor Pip with his rapidly depleted wardrobe had been caught out. Duncan was hardly able to contain his mirth; the old soldier had been caught without powder in his musket.

'It's ridiculous that it's not a next-day service. I have to wait three to four days for my clothes to come back,' Pip complained.

It was a day for complaining, we had little else to do. It did seem unreasonable that he should have to wait so long.

We planned to take a trip to the Ssese Islands, staying with Andrew Lutaya who owned the island. We were to leave on Friday morning and if the laundry took more than three days, then Pip would be going to the island in his swimming trunks and would have little else to wear. There is one thing about the tropical heat that makes it almost bearable and that is being able to put on fresh clothes every day.

There were a few times on the trip that I admit that I had to wear certain items – no need to go into detail here – for two days running and despite Uganda's relatively mild climate, the clothes were still damp and sticky to wear the following day.

'We have to wait for three days for you to finish in the shower, that's what I call ridiculous, if you ask me,' Duncan announced. He never missed a chance to complain, particularly at the expense of another member of the party. The chance to embarrass Pip had proved too excruciating for him to resist.

Unfortunately, Duncan had woken up with a spot on his forehead; the sun tended to dry out all skin types and bring various impurities to the surface.

'You've got stigmata on your forehead,' Pip said to Duncan. Really, Pip was superb at getting his own back, but he waited for the right moment. Had he used his retorts all the time, then they would have missed their edge.

'It's just sunburn.' Duncan was not used to this form of attack; he expected Pip to take all the jibes he gave and accept them quietly.

Pip knew when to defend and when to parry, he was an expert verbal fencer; his thrust went straight for the mark. Duncan was after all vain and he was a man and they say: 'Vanity thy name is man,' and in Duncan's case it most certainly was a case of vanity thy name is this man. He was good-looking after all. The trouble is he knew it more than most people did.

'You need some sun cream,' Anthony pointed out needlessly, knowing full well that spots were not to be cured by the addition of more oils. Duncan had won few allies and Anthony was pinning his colours to Pip's flag.

'I've got loads,' I said.

I wanted to fan the flames and put salt on to the wound rather than pour oil on troubled water or build bridges, without wishing to use clichés. Duncan had been 'hoist with his own petard' and he had 'burnt his bridges', but he was never one to 'cry over spilt milk', he preferred to 'grasp the thorn by the nettle' or rather 'the nettle by the thorn' or 'the bull by the horn'.

On this occasion he was lost for words: a ship without a sail, a rope without an anchor and up the creak without a paddle.

'Great,' Duncan leant forward expectantly. He was still pretending that it was a suntan that was his major problem, rather than the rather large blemish just between his eyebrows.

'Where is it?' Duncan cried anxiously, deliberately hamming up a desperate need for the cream.

He had acted in New York when he was younger. A method actor, he needed to believe that he was merely burnt; if he came to terms with the truth instead, he might not be able to cope. 'Where have you got it? Is it in the bag?'

'It's at the hotel.' I loved to put the knife in a twist the blade.

There was little else to do. I knew Duncan secretly felt that the addition of more cream would burst the pustule and by the time he had left, at the end of the week, his stigmata would have healed over.

'Thanks very much, mate,' Duncan said with true venom. Again, we all knew he was acting; every sarcastic remark or offensive comment was designed to amuse.

If I had been more sensitive the remark might have hurt, but I had become immune.

After almost three full days into the trip and, in his company, I had built up a thick skin; the adults may have called me *Huck Finn*, the children called me *Granny with her gin*, but I had the hide of a rhino, anything they said would go, I had the skin of a hippo; no comment could be too low.

In other words, I took his humour in good sport. Of course, we all played along with Duncan and I pretended to be offended.

'You're a diamond geezer too, I don't care what they say about you,' I hissed.

I, too, could bare my sarcasm on my sleeve; fight hand to hand, take Satan by the paw, grab the fickle finger of fate, put my shoulder to the wheel, my nose to the grindstone and my best foot forward.

'I'm bored already,' Duncan sighed, he tried to cut me dead as ever, but he knew he was flaying and failing dismally on this occasion. It was not a very good retort to my diamond-hard remark, and he knew it, Anthony was aware it and Pip picked up on it.

'Are we going to hang around here all day?' Anthony asked. The newcomer was not yet conversant with the situation and the shopping carrot that had been dangled had not been taken.

'No one understands that we might want to do our own thing,' Pip explained, long-suffering as ever.

I would have been fed up if I had to wait around with all the children in a city where swimming was the highlight of the day. While the pearl of Africa lay all around us, aching to be explored, I could not blame him.

'There's no fixed plan?' Anthony seemed surprised, he was only in Africa for a short time and he had expected an itinerary to keep to and to have a busy time of it.

In reality there was a lot of waiting around; he was right, there was no plan, no itinerary and no escape.

'We have to wait for other people, who are arranging things,' Duncan assured him. He was an expert at studied loitering; he needed just enough energy to light his cigarette which is precisely what he did do, predictable as that was.

Duncan without a cigarette was difficult to contemplate.

'It's understandable, they're all busy and yet they want to show us so much, things are difficult to arrange, and it takes time. Your father is the centre of attention.' Pip was remarkably understanding and tolerant.

'You ought to get your clothes sorted out,' Duncan hissed.

He never missed a chance to rile Pip. He knew only too well that Pip was particular about his apparel and that Pip was worried about his laundry coming back in time.

'One thing that is arranged is a trip to Ssese Islands at the weekend, so that is definite and something to look forward to,' I mentioned.

'I'll need the laundry for Friday as we're staying on the island, and we're moving on from the hotel after that,' Pip informed Anthony and I. Duncan knew the plan and would be gone the day after our return from the island. 'After the island trip we'll all be staying with various families around the place.'

'Thank goodness it's two days until Friday, that will give the laundry enough time to get your clothes back,' I assured Pip.

'Don't worry about it,' Pip assured me in return. 'I'm not concerned, yet.'

'I'm not but I don't want you to worry about it,' I told him in my most reassuring voice.

'There's going to be a murder at Reste Corner,' Duncan laughed loudly as he spoke, watching Pip as he started to blush.

'You know what I'd like to do,' Pip said calmly, surprising us all with his even tone.

'No, please share it with us.' Duncan's malicious curiosity had got the better of him. I think that he expected Pip to describe some horrid torture that he would like to inflict on the laundry people and me.

'I'd like to visit the National Museum,' Pip announced as though he were telling his wife he would like to get crumpets for tea.

'I'll come with you,' Duncan said, willingly.

'Can I come?' I asked, sweetly.

'No!' They chorused in unison.

The others went to the museum and left me to order a beer; they were determined to leave me behind, and I was not going to argue.

I would have loved to have gone. I always enjoyed visiting museums at home in London; my ideal rainy day is one spent at a museum or an art gallery, but they needed space.

Whilst I smoked a Prince cigarette and enjoyed the cool beer, I decided that perhaps I had been too harsh on Pip, winding him up in that fashion. Duncan seemed to start things but knew where to draw the line. It was a fine line and one that I crossed all too often. Pip deserved a peace offering, so I set off to the shops.

It was my first journey on the streets alone and I took in the scene: beggars on the street just like London; the sun was warm and yet the tall buildings of Kampala offered shade if you wanted it.

I was happy to walk in the sunshine and give coins to the destitute, acutely aware that the coins I had were not enough by European standards and despite knowing the exchange rate.

I was not sure what or how much the money would buy locally in Ugandan terms, or how much more the tourist rates should or would be, but every little helps.

I located a shop that sold alcoholic drink on the corner, a block away from the hotel. There was a bottle of malt for 45,000 shillings, which was well worth it to keep the peace and after all, I had been drinking all of Pip's malt.

Other malts were comparatively expensive, brand names and well-advertised products were premium whereas rare malts like the one that I had spied were relatively cheap.

They had whisky galore and malts too at 128,000 shillings. Glenfiddich at 80,000 was on special offer at 68,000 shillings. The malt I wanted was marked at forty-five thousand, so I offered thirty. You drive a hard bargain, I was told, and immediately realised I should have offered 25,000.

The company was called Luisun Enterprises and the threat of terrorism at that time was brought home by the fact that the shop was located at 7B Bomb Road. The name of the location was slightly worrying as a consequence of the bombs that had gone off in various hotels and bars since our arrival.

When I got back everyone was sitting at our two favourite tables waiting for lunch and I had been hoping for a nice quiet repast while reading a book.

I volunteered to get the children from the Sheraton.

They were there with their new temporary part-time nanny, Sommerly. When I brought everyone back, Mama Rose had arrived; Duncan had already nicknamed her Mama Mia. It took a long time for everyone to order their food. The Major and his wife and Mama Rose were picking at some light snacks, chatting amiably about people they knew, the visitors they had, and those that they expected to see. It was a heart-warming sight, old friends reunited.

The children could not make up their minds and the middle generation people were waiting for the children to order first.

'We have to hurry, the Kabaka's waiting to see us later,' Pip told the children. I was on the periphery watching events unfold, waiting to present my present to Pip.

'Put your hands up for fish fingers and hands up for pizza.'

Pip was an expert at getting reluctant children to order at restaurants.

'We can't keep Ronnie waiting,' Duncan told the children. The boys opted for the dish with chips and the girls went for pizza. If pizza and chips had been on the menu, I am sure that all of them would have gone for that.

'Are you eating with us, Duncan?' Lucy asked

'No, I'd just be eating to be polite,' Duncan replied.

'Hattie, do you want pizza?' Pip asked.

'What else do I have?' Hattie asked; she was a creature of habit.

'Mike, will you share half a club sandwich and chips?' Duncan asked me – he knew neither of us was hungry enough to eat a full meal.

'Of course, for you, Duncan,' I agreed, smiling at him. We were friends and caring is sharing and sharing is caring.

'I was thinking you might just like a little something,' Duncan added, he wanted me to feel that I had been forgiven, by him at least.

'You'll come out all right in my diary,' I responded.

Duncan smiled wholeheartedly and ordered.

'Do you want something – seriously?' Pip asked

'No, I was getting the kids from the Sheraton; I was told you would order for me.'

'I'll order you something now, if you like,' Duncan offered.

'Just give me the crumbs left over from your club sandwich and I'll be grateful,' I whispered pathetically, 'That should keep me going for the next few days.'

'I'm on Lariam, I can't take the extra strain,' Duncan groaned and, pretending to be enfeebled by all the ordering, reached slowly for his cigarette packet as he spoke, not wanting to miss the opportunity to have a smoke before the children's meal came.

'Do fio, I can wear you down further,' I promised. 'The Lariam has affected me too, but in a positive way.'

'I'm on the level above,' Lucy informed us.

We both nodded at her remark, understanding her completely.

'How's the red factor,' I asked, noticing that Pip had engaged in conversation with Mama Rose, the Major and Susan.

'The purple haze has descended, you're in immediate and real danger,' Duncan warned me, as he pulled on his cigarette and took a swig of Bell lager.

'Can it get worse?' I asked.

I, too, had earned a half-litre bottle of the delicious brew, some of which I had decanted into a highball glass and watching Pip, Lucy, and Anna and, especially, Duncan smoking, I had to light up one of my local brand cigarettes as well.

The cigarette was too dry without the beer and the beer too wet without the cigarette.

'After purple comes black and you are almost there,' Duncan took great pleasure in telling me how close I was to my demise. 'I can't say I blame him.'

'Oh dear, you will come off badly in my diary after all,' I warned, wanting Duncan to know the depths of my disapproval.

'So, this is Tuesday and what have you done?' Duncan asked Lucy.

Anthony and I hummed the tune from John Lennon's 'So this is Christmas'.

'If it's not Wednesday, I should be in Paris.' Lucy replied cryptically, perhaps referring to the European whistle-stop tours people used to take.

'We should put our egos to bed for two weeks,' Duncan suggested.

'Mine won't sleep,'

I retorted. My ego was an insomniac and got me into a lot of trouble, so my Id told me.

'Why don't you hit it with a hammer?' Duncan had no need to be so aggressive, but that was like him, a sledgehammer to crack a tough nut like me.

'And what about my ego?' I asked.

'This is the level you've found, isn't it,' Lucy spat, disgusted at our continued sniping and our constant innuendo.

It was all far too boyish for her.

'I was in full flow,' I defended myself. The sun was hot, the beer was cool and the nicotine from the cigarette was making me quite lightheaded.

'That is quite wearing,' Anthony suggested.

He too had succumbed to the rows of glowing cigarette and cigar ends and lit one of his extra mild duty free cigarettes.

'Very wearing,' Lucy agreed. She was always on their side never on mine. I wondered why that was, she either loved to hate me or hated to love me or perhaps it was because I was always in the wrong.

'Keep Pip away from Huck Finn,' Duncan warned everyone, 'I do not want there to be bloodshed today at the Speke.'

'I'll keep quiet.' I was resigned; no one appreciated me, my sense of humour, my company, I was just the holiday gopher who collected the children from their sun lounge sofa. I felt quite poetical about it all, but I also knew that pride comes before a fall.

'Promise to say nothing to Pip until sundown,' Duncan urged wanting me to make a deal. I wasn't in the mood for compromise, but Duncan was going to share his sandwich with me.

Really, I had to be fairly nice to him. I attacked another member of the party, much easier than rebuking Duncan and it guaranteed some food at least. I had ordered a pizza before I left; there was no time for an adult one to be cooked so at least I would have some food before we went to see the Kabaka.

'That's Lucy's problem,' I said, taking advantage of the fact that she had been drawn into the conversation with Mama Rose.

'Did Lucy hear that?' Duncan asked

'Say something, Lucy,' Anthony went on

'You've hurt his feelings,' Duncan insisted.

'That's his problem,' I replied.

'How are your notes coming along?' Anthony asked.

'Fine, thank you,' I had been scribing quite a lot during my stay.

'My God you're left-handed,' Duncan noticed – he was quite observant when he wanted to be and if he could be bothered.

'Are you as well?' I asked.

'No, but I'd like to be,' Duncan was very trying at times.

'You'd make a sinister left-hander,' Anthony suggested to Duncan.

'Go back to sleep.' Duncan could be rude to his brother, in fact he was expected to be rude to one and all, he never disappointed.

'So, sir,' Duncan said trying to mimic me. 'Where do you go to drink, sir? Where is the best place to dance, sir, and to eat, sir?'

'Thank you, Duncan, but I want to go where the locals go.'

'That's very *honourable*,' he replied – for some strange reason his favourite expression had become honourable.

'It's just common sense,' I countered.

I knew that local knowledge was invaluable, and I had been taught that time in reconnaissance is never wasted, that was advice from a Commander in the Royal Navy, and it had stood me in good stead in many encounters.

I lit a cigarette satisfied that I was correct in my approach.

'Talking of honourable, I thought it referred to a person not like an MP, the Honourable John Smith Member of Parliament and conservative candidate. "How are you?" someone asks, and you reply, "Fine, honourable." I didn't think to refer to her as MP. Still "I'm honourable" sounds good. In England, I'll say that I'm honourable, from now on then people will know; some might suspect that I am a politician.'

Duncan was off on a tangent and we were happy to leave him like that, it was his choice and he was old enough and ugly enough to choose his own path.

On the other hand, he was in Equatorial Africa for the first time and salt levels can drop dramatically in the tropics, coupled with the fact that he was on Lariam, which was known to have strange side effects; it was easy to excuse his views and his behaviour.

That afternoon we went up to the coronation site at Buddo. There were trees that were thousands of years old and each Kabaka had a tree planted for them. The older trees were so gnarled and disfigured they looked like crippled old men.

Termite hills were knocked down at the coronation but a new one was being constructed next door by the busy termites. It was too hot to see them crawl around, but Duncan had open-toed sandals and no socks. I was pleased that I had chosen to wear my Doctor Marten shoes, long socks and chinos; I had read somewhere that they gave you a nasty nip.

I told Duncan but he was sceptical.

'They do not bite,' he exclaimed, looking down at his exposed toes. 'These trees are so gnarled, like your brain, Mike.'

'The termites will get you,' I warned, 'they think that your brain is a ready-made termitary.'

'There's no such word.'

'I see you're not arguing with the premise that your brain is a series of tunnels.'

'Your mind is a termite hill knocked down and the brain cells have moved next door.'

'Those termitaries were fantastic.'

'I still don't believe that's a word.'

'Look it up, I learnt it at prep school when we were studying Africa,' I knew there was another reason why I had chosen to explore Africa. 'It comes from termitarium.'

It was at Buddo or Naggalabi Buddo that we decided who was who in our strange entourage. Buddo was the official coronation site for all kings of the Baganda Kingdom, the Kabakas, and is located on

Buddo Hill in Busiro County, Wakiso District, just next to the Kampala-Masaka Highway, approximately 14 kilometres by road, south-west of Kampala, Uganda's capital and largest city. It is believed that it was here that Baganda Kingdom was born during the 14th century.

As we trampled over the red-brown earth to the manmade coronation site, I was struck by our images and how others might perceive us.

The manmade site was a series of marble steps as eroded and as decimated as those marble steps you might find in Rome at Caracala, the hot baths near the Circus Maximus or at the Coliseum. The steps contrasted starkly with the crottle-coloured earth and scorched savannah grass that lay around it.

'Duncan, you look like a journalist on his first trip, blue shirt and blue jeans, even your BOAC style airline bag should be for your notebook and Uher tape recorder.'

Uher was brand of reel-to-reel recording equipment favoured by the BBC and war correspondents in the sixties, seventies and eighties. In fact, it was ubiquitous and formed the backbone of news recording whether it was local radio or national news.

'Don't be so rude, I don't have any tropical gear, I don't look like Pip.'

'That's the point you, could be in Cuba covering a story on Fidel Castro.'

'What about Anthony?'

'Anthony has to be an FBI agent or part of the security services. He sits bolt upright, is always turning his head to check the sites and to make sure the cab driver is on the road and you can never see his eyes behind his shades, which he never takes off. All he needs is an earpiece and his finger holding it in place and he would look like one of the President's protection squad.'

'And what about Pip?'

'It's obvious.'

'That fat people don't look thinner in beige?'

'No, Pip is the official food taster.'

'Who are you?'

'You tell me.'

'With that haircut, your green Osh Kosh military shirt and your Gap chinos, you look like a part of the South African security forces. I'd watch out if I were you, the South Africans are not that popular even at home let alone elsewhere in Africa.'

'I'm not very popular within the group already. Anyhow, I tell them that I'm Irish which is true, and the Irish are more popular than the English almost everywhere.'

'I can't see why,' Duncan observed, giving me a withering look.

Chapter 10

Thursday 16th July – Jinja

The Bagandan hosts were generous and thoughtful to the extreme. Sarah ran her own cleaning company, but she took time out from her punishing day to deliver fresh fruit juice in a container every morning once she knew we were there.

She very kindly dropped off the squeezed juice in a plastic container and took the empty away to be refilled at dawn the next morning. We never knew what to expect – orange, pineapple, mango, paw-paw, or pineapple. It was a very sweet gesture from someone who was working all hours but wanted to make us feel welcome.

Whoever was in the lounge would greet Sarah and she was always very concerned that we should be comfortable and happy; I think she interceded in the laundry situation, putting pleasant pressure on the hotel to try and get Pip his clothes back before the appointed time.

It was good to see a friendly face each day and it was a pity she could not stay longer as we only really got to know her slightly as she had to dash off to supervise her staff. We had established a routine for the shower.

I was last because I liked to lie in, but we would all gather in the lounge waiting for Sarah. Pip would be pouring over guidebooks. The rest of us were termed: 'Those who were surplus to requirements'; Anthony would read with avid concentration; Duncan and I, meanwhile, read our books, Bryson the pair of us.

On the odd morning when Sarah didn't arrive, the morning seemed a little flat. On that particular Thursday, Sarah had just left, and we had actually organised an excursion for the second consecutive day, so spirits were high.

'So, this is mango.' Duncan sat on his usual perch, the sofa, and smiled slightly, it was after all before twelve and a grin was considered the height of bad manners. He drained the fluid and set the glass on the table in front of him.

'Duncan's happy now.' I grinned as I spoke just to break the sound barrier; not a bad effort, I thought, for before breakfast. The mango juice tasted delicious and I, too, drained my glass.

'He's like the taxis,' Anthony noted. 'He needs to refuel a little every so often, just enough to get him to the next destination.'

It was good to see that Anthony felt the same way about Duncan as I did, recognising his strengths and weakness.

There was a renewed solidarity between Anthony and I from that moment on.

'The man is fuelled by the juice of many fruits,' I added, smiling at Anthony and ignoring Duncan's hurt and shocked expression, he was acting again

'That about sums up the whole situation, we're always running on empty,' Anthony continued.

'When we visited the school at Buddo, I was sure that we had no fuel, we had been travelling on a red light to the coronation site. When we stalled, I felt sure the car was out of gas and wouldn't restart. It was touch and go,' I told Duncan.

'I was worried, too,' Anthony confessed.

It was not like him to let everyone know that he was concerned, and it was particularly dangerous to mention anything potentially detrimental in front of Duncan, it was then that I knew Anthony was my ally.

'We had a full tank of gas and I was worried we wouldn't make it, even so,' Duncan confided, he had been in the other taxi and he was feigning concern.

He had been with Dae Woo, and he alone never went anywhere without at least half a tank of petrol and he checked his water and oil constantly. Dae Woo was a great driver.

Of all the cars we travelled in, his was the newest and best maintained. He managed to keep his white Toyota spotlessly clean despite the dirt, dust and grime of Kampala and the suburbs.

It was the other taxi drivers that you had to watch.

'You were all right, our driver drove like a maniac,' Anthony complained.

'How are we going to get to Jinja?' Duncan was always the pragmatist.

'The CBS bus, I should imagine,' Pip looked up from his books long enough to answer.

His juice was still untouched but his free hand held a cigar.

'What, all of us?' Anthony was surprised.

'Do fio,' I said, meaning no worries but I had wanted to say something else like: 'how can we all fit into a microbus, are we sardines?' I did not want to spoil a perfect day, though.

'You never worry about anything, Michael, you're just like Huckleberry Finn.' Duncan loved to use the handles that he had given us as often as possible.

'We'll get there,' I insisted.

'I wouldn't be very sure, if I were you, from what I have seen of the driving around here,' Anthony exclaimed, justifiably voicing his opinion.

'I agree,' I added.

'Huck Finn suits you, with your faded jeans and you're always smoking,' Anthony continued.

'Anthony Ant quite suits you, but I'm not asking for you to be called Ant,' Duncan insisted.

Our alliance had faded. Duncan was a mischievous soul, forging alliances and breaking them, he would have made an excellent diplomat in the sixteenth century. I imagined him assisting Torquemada in the Spanish Inquisition.

'Huck Finn sums you up, it's a great name,' Pip interjected. I knew that Duncan referred to Pip as the Pie Man or the Fat Man behind his back, but I wasn't about to offend Pip just to satisfy Duncan.

If I betrayed his confidence, I would be losing a useful ally and I would be playing into his hands by antagonising Pip, which would, in effect, be driving Pip further into Duncan's camp. It was unlikely that Pip would acknowledge that his brother-in-law would create such a cruel nickname. Equally, Pip and Anthony were excited about our trip to Jinja to see the 'reputed' source of the Nile.

It was the first proper trip that we had taken, and I was loathe to spoil their day completely by revealing Duncan's less than charitable caricatures even if they did make me chortle uncontrollably when I reflected on them.

There was even a shadow falling over our trip to the source because Speke, after whom the hotel was named, was out of favour.

Speke had discovered the source but his claim to fame, his claim that he had indeed found the source of the White Nile had been hotly disputed by the National Geographic Society.

Several other lakes feed the lake that to this day is considered the true source. Several streams converge in Jinja, fed by lakes too far away to even think about and from Jinja the river flows in a torrent, so Speke was correct in my books.

However, geographical and historical enquiry moves with the revisionists, but no one who doubted Speke has really satisfied his criteria. Cynics should visit and satisfy themselves or spend time in Kensington with the detractors.

After breakfast we took a taxi down to the Speke Hotel and met the others – all of us were going. That was: Anthony, Anna, Duncan, Lucy, Pip, the six children and the Major and his wife, plus the Kabaka's aide de camp, Katende.

The blue microbus was from the Ugandan CBS – not the American broadcaster. We would have preferred a nice Chevrolet van with air conditioning rather than the Toyota minibus. It had four wheels and a driver, a charming Moslem, called Hussein, so we could not complain, and it fitted us all – just. All we had to do was to pay for the fuel.

It was another generous gesture from the Central Broadcasting Service of Uganda considering all they received in return was a few short interviews and the van was a much-needed tool. Mama Rose came with us that day, looking resplendent in a green dress.

Unlike many of us Europeans, Mama Rose made an immense effort to look her best each time she saw us even when she had injured her hand; most of my friends would use it as an excuse to wear the same clothes for a week.

Despite their clothes being fresh and clean for the trip to Jinja, everyone was looking hot and bedraggled, but not Mama Rose and Katende. They remained immaculate at all times. Quite a feat.

'Our legs are too short,' Duncan said squeezing himself into the van with great difficulty.

He had decided that the older members of the group should be in the front with the driver but that he should be forward of the children. Anthony, not knowing any better, seemed to be in the middle of the sons and daughters. He had not been warned that the children would torment him with questions and pinches and punches.

I waited very cautiously because I knew they would fill up the entire rear seat and then I could be near the door, the best place to be on any trip.

'Too short, too long you mean,' I corrected him, it was my prerogative, he was always correcting other people.

'Whatever,' Duncan could laugh hard and loud at other people's mistakes but his own he took less lightly.

'I pick up on people's malaprops,' I confessed to Duncan, to try and make him feel better but he had already moved on.

'Put me in the front and Pip in the back,' he cried cruelly. 'There's far too little room up here as it is, and I don't want to be stuck with the rug rats.'

'I'm going to have a breakdown,' Anthony exclaimed. 'If I have to sit between all these children on the way there and back, they never stop asking questions.'

'Are we there yet, have you had your breakdown yet, Pip?' Duncan asked jovially, trying to jolly things along.

'*Muyaya* means breakdown,' Pip replied; he had managed to find the word in his trusty phrase book.

'We'll have that with Pip in the back,' Duncan said cruelly, insinuating that Pip's weight might adversely affect the suspension of the van and result in the springs going.

'I'll have a breakdown soon,' I said, trying to deflect thoughts from Duncan's comments.

'Move back, our legs are spilling over.' Duncan warned.

He was seated to the left of Lucy and in a very cramped position. I wasn't sure he'd survive the two-hour journey.

'We need more people,' I cried much to the surprise of passers-by.

'To see the source of Nile you have to be a sardine,' Duncan announced.

We took a detour for Pip to speak to the travel agent as he was looking at options to mount a safari. I took the opportunity to whip into the convenience store next door.

There I tried to get litres of mineral water but ended up with 24 quarter bottles. It was enough to keep dehydration at bay for the trip.

It was oppressively hot in any form of transport but with all our bodies confined in a confined metal space, it was even worse.

On the way to Jinja, Katende pointed out the lavish and lush tea and coffee plantations and the forests of sugar cane. We saw sugar cane trucks powering up the road to the refinery.

Sugar was a valuable resource but in South America, particularly in Brazil, the cane is converted into alcohol to run their cars. Considering the dam near the source of the Nile provided electricity to export and that there was an abundance of sugar cane, it appeared to me that Uganda could be self-sufficient in energy needs.

If the country provided an organised tourist trade, then it would be unbeatable economically. It always surprised me that Africa with its abundance of resources was the poor relation while Europe with its comparable paucity of resources rode on the crest of the wave.

Debt had to be the key and the control of debt kept Africa poor so that it could not be a rival to the poorer resourced Europe.

People talk of the crime of empire builders who brought wealth and problems, but the real crimes have been committed since African countries have achieved independence, either through corrupt or inefficient administrations or through crippling interest payments to 'First World' banks.

Sometimes it was a combination of both but from the oil of Nigeria to the diamonds of Pretoria and from food to minerals, Africa has an incredible wealth, and yet few people in Africa see the money generated from it. Where does it all go?

The local population, who helped with the harvest of the coffee beans, tea bushes and cut the cane, they were also comparatively wealthy but not as wealthy as they should have been.

All of them had livestock in their smallholdings.

Some had chickens or pigs; there were white cows like the type you get in India and, sometimes, one or two Hereford cattle.

What struck me about the drive from Kampala to Jinja was the quality of the roads, but that was not surprising, as this was the route taken by trucks from the local sugar refinery.

What shocked us was to see a dead boy who had been struck by one of the trucks.

The distressed township and distraught driver huddled around a small figure covered in coats.

A dozen people comforted the mother; most of the rest of the village were working in the coffee and tea plantations that the road dissected or at the factory.

The poor child had taken a risk in crossing the road and misjudged the speed of the truck; the driver could not have slowed down even if he had the time to pump the brakes.

Even at forty miles an hour the impact of a ten-ton truck would remove any chance of survival.

Living in London such accidents have a greater potential and yet there is less likelihood of you seeing one. In thirty years in London, from toddler to thirty-something, I have never seen a road accident. Infant mortality is a way of life, if I can say that, in Africa, but there is generally some form of warning: a fever, an illness, some sign of impending doom – some time to accept the loss of a child as he or she slips away.

A violent, sudden death, struck by a truck, that shocking, instant robbing of life like a shooting must be unbearable for any witnesses but particularly for the family. We were all shaken by the event. We were all parents and we had all lost friends who had died suddenly. It was better we did not stop; we would have been encroaching on their grief.

We moved from the site numbed by the event only to enter bandit country, a forest where armed men lay in wait; this gave us something else to think about other than the poor dead child. I wondered if we were facing a clear and present danger, then I remembered we were in the CBS bus so might be safe.

Throughout our stay we conscious of insurgence – the two bombs were the only events which alerted us to any trouble; we knew about rebels fighting in the north-west, but we had not really thought that we were in danger in Kampala.

No group admitted responsibility for the bombs in the city and equally there was no knowledge about these bandits, only that they existed, and they might have chosen us as their next target. Whether they had some or any political affiliation, or if they were armed, or willing to take anyone for financial gain, it was not clear. Kidnap or murder might be our next encounter.

Long shanks Duncan was complaining of lack of legroom in the bus but would have complained more if he had to walk.

Any historical fact that Pip mentioned from his vast knowledge gleaned from all his guidebooks was met by derogatory shrieks of '*Boffin*' from his children, most of all Aubrey who had learnt the expression at school.

Obviously, anyone with intelligence was castigated at his prep school; it did not bode well for the internet generation. On the way up to Jinja, we saw a restaurant called Fang, Fang II; it stood on a roundabout that led three ways: to the dam, to the sugar refinery and Jinja itself.

'I knew it was part of a chain or rather the most important Chinese chain in Uganda, centred at the most crucial sites, Kampala and Jinja,' I announced triumphantly.

In England a chain used not to be a good thing, it conjured up mediocrity and monotony.

Fashionable and trendy people – the Americans, English and French, the New Yorker, Bostonian, Washingtonian, Londoner, Parisian – all seek out something a bit different.

Wherever you are, on the other hand, you know exactly what to expect from a Taco Bell or Burger King. It avoids disappointment, but experimentation should include food that might disappoint.

Behold the tortoise that makes progress by sticking its neck out, it is important to try new things to broaden our perception.

It is a sad situation that we take food so seriously that we will not risk a bad meal; surely the bad meal makes the superb one the more enjoyable. If fear rules our lives our lives become fearful; if adventure rules our lives life becomes an adventure.

A terrible restaurant would not have a sister restaurant was my argument and I voiced it. It was even next to an Agip petrol station – what more could you want. *AGIP* Azienda Generale Italiana Petroli or General Italian Oil Company.

'Why is it on a roundabout, Huck Finn?' Duncan was always stealing my thunder. I wanted Pip to realise that my suggestion of Fang, Fang was reasonable.

'Because it is next to the Agip filling station, that way people can fill up with petrol and fill up with food as well,' Anthony suggested.

'Their tanks will be empty in a few hours and so will their stomachs,' Duncan was always up there with the most formidable of gags.

He was harshly referring to the fact that some people feel hungry again a few hours after a Chinese meal, or so they say; so, and so that he was.

'It's a sequel,' Anthony said.

'It's a chain,' I corrected him.

'Fang, Fang two, the sequel, coming to your neighbourhood soon,' Anthony announced.

'*Fang, Fang,* the movie, petrol-guzzling, Chinese eating, taxi driver goes on the rampage,' Duncan announced in a dramatic tone, sounding like a gravelly American voice-over artist.

He was being more surreal than the circumstances required.

'Talking of taxi drivers and lack of fuel,' Anthony said, knowing that we weren't discussing any such thing and that we had only mentioned the Agip station at the roundabout. 'There are fewer cars per capita than any other capital in the world, yet more accidents.'

Anthony merely wanted to blind us with the statistics that he had at his fingertips. I was sure that I had read the same information in the in-flight brochure.

'You're telling us this as we career towards Jinja in a tin can?' Duncan was incredulous.

'Are we nearly there,' Aubrey asked.

'Shut it,' I replied.

'Is "Jambo", hello in Uganda?' Matilda asked.

'That's Swahili,' Duncan told her.

'In Bagandan, "Jambo" means shut it,' I informed her.

We drove past the refinery discreetly hidden by a bend in the road and tall vegetation. We could just about see the compound, but there were no refinery towers as I had expected.

The roundabout had three exits; we entered on the Kampala road and the sign simply pointed west proclaiming '*Sugar Refinery*' and the right-hand side pointed east for Jinja. There was nowhere else to go but back, so on balance we took the right turn.

The source of the Nile was reached through the town where we spotted a statue of Gandhi in a park outside a street of villas. Gandhi also had a statue at the source and President Bill Clinton had dedicated a memorial on his visit.

Gandhi's statue prompted debate over his involvement in Uganda. Some of his ashes had been scattered into the Ganges and some into the Nile.

It was not clear if his ashes had been scattered elsewhere but it was testament to all the Asians in Africa that he should have deemed it necessary for some of his remains to be sent to a foreign land. Ever the shrewd politician in the best sense of both words, Gandhi had appreciated the global picture rather than the parochial view.

I was reminded of the Asian chemist in Clapham who dispensed my mother's prescriptions before she died. Nitrazepam belongs to a group of medicines called benzodiazepines.

It acts on receptors in the brain and was therefore my mother's favourite; she was a doctor who had chronic osteoporosis from having six children. If the Mogadon or other painkillers had not arrived that day, he would drive up and deliver them himself.

Mr Goy had been in Clapham a long time and had seen the market stallholders and small food stores like Liptons shut, unable to compete with the purpose built supermarkets that had sprung up in the area.

As another bar or restaurant became established, there was less reason for shoppers to come to the street that made up Northcote Market, but still he catered for his local market.

Before I left for Uganda, I had picked up some Lariam and I had mentioned going to Kampala.

His wife told me that she had spent her childhood there and had left at eleven when Amin had expelled the Asian community.

She joked that most of the families of refugees thought they would return and had coins or gold buried in their gardens for their return and that I should take a metal detector with me to find the fortunes buried under the crottle-coloured earth.

Indeed, the owners of the Crane Bank and the Speke Hotel were Asian and the exchange rate at the bank was better than the European banks that had established headquarters there and the Speke was more reasonable than the Sheraton was.

Admittedly, the Speke had no pool, but it didn't have the need to produce profit margins for a headquarters that dealt in US dollars either. Some of the Ugandans resented the Asian businessmen, but more were grateful for the wealth that they created. Any section of the community that does well is resented for their success: the Jews in

Spain under Ferdinand and Isabella, the Jews in Nazi Germany and even in York in the twelfth century.

In contemporary London, there is a resentment of bankers and stockbrokers and yet these are the very people who create wealth and allow for taxes to be cut. It's the same the world over, the wealth creators are always criticised for their greed.

On the other side of the town, we pulled off the road and drove along a dirt track with a diamond-patterned fence, held up by rough-hewn gateposts about three foot high. Where the track led us, there was a rickety two-bar gate that barred our way. Next to the gate there was a smart white wooden hut with windows all around and a sign on the front proclaiming: '*Jinja Game Park*'.

'Jambo,' said the man coming out of the sentry box. He wore a military style uniform, khaki and smart, as was the norm.

'Jumbo,' I replied, hoping that I had got the expression right. It sounded vaguely Swahili and I knew Jumbo meant hello.

We discussed the fee and the others all sat in the van; I knew it was being left to me to pay for our entrance into the park that surrounded Jinja. I did not mind an iota, as this was twelve pounds sterling, the cost of two cinema tickets in London and Jinja was far more spectacular than any film I have seen.

Also, I had got a free ride up the Jinja Road, so it was the least I could do for having the CBS bus at my disposal. All of us contributed to petrol money as and when it was needed and that was very rarely; the bus ran beautifully and seemed to sip petrol, no doubt because it did not have air conditioning. Really, we were very happy with our CBS chariot, taking us everywhere in fine style and in comfort despite our griping.

Jinja was a magical place despite the fencing that went around the perimeter and a large free-standing hoarding overlooking the lake, which was advertising Bell lager as Uganda's heritage.

The actual park was well-tended and tranquil, trees afforded shade, the grass was watered, and tropical shrubs brightened up the slope down to the rapids. Broad stone steps, crottled with dust on a gentle incline, led to the river's edge. There all forms of maintenance ceased, the fence was falling down and the sun scorched the grass. It was a deliberate contrast and then there was the beautiful steel blue of the water and the swirling of the current as the rapids passed a cataract, which sprouted two lush trees, home to a flock of birds.

There were two makeshift stalls set up in the shade of the trees at the bottom of the steps; on the ground patterned blankets lay with different wares spread over the brightly coloured cloth. Hattie went straight to the makeshift stall that sold blankets and trinkets. That table sold African art and watercolours depicting Jinja and other scenes from Uganda. Behind that was another table with more items like wallets and leather goods spread across another brightly coloured cloth, this one was red.

The children had brought their journals with them and were spread out in the shade to cool off after the journey.

'What do I write in my diary?' Aubrey asked.

'Just write, right,' Duncan replied.

'White egrets, blue Nile, green grass, the islands over there, source of all power for Uganda,' I suggested. 'Or just copy down what's on the board.'

The advertising board overlooking Rippon Falls was a triumph of capitalism: a large board supported by two square yellow wooden posts advertised Bell lager.

A yellow border surrounded this information point, on the left the Bell trademark. A gold bell, white and yellow sunrays behind like the red and white of the Japanese rising sun on their flag all in an oval which had Bell in white on a red background and below, reversed out, Lager written in cursive script, red on a white background.

Aubrey proceeded to write down the copy:

'The Nile is 4,000 miles long. The falls that John Hannington Speke saw in 1862, one hundred years before my birth in April 1962, naming them the "Rippon Falls" after the President of the Royal Geographical Society in London, submerged in 1947 on the construction of the Owen Falls Dam.

'The dam, completed in 1954, harnesses the headlong rush of water from the lake to produce hydro-electric power for Uganda and its neighbours. "Omugga Kiyira" is the local name for River Nile (Note, not *the* River Nile). The bay behind this billboard through which the waters of Lake Victoria funnel through, not into, the Nile, is called Napoleon Gulf.'

For a small man Napoleon got around, there are few places I have been where he does not get a mention, Wellington on the other hand, an Irishman who defeated Napoleon, is hardly mentioned outside England and the Iberian Peninsula.

Such is the infamy of the warrior, even on the Nile; archaeologists and soldiers sent by Napoleon had left their graffiti on the temples of the Egypt. On the western bank of the river is an obelisk marking the spot where Speke stood for hours when he saw the source of the River Nile, making it known to the outside world.

It was Holland's control of the spice trade and the rise in pepper prices that encouraged English merchants to trade with Zanzibar and from there the English trade spread to Kenya and Uganda.

It was the search for the source of the Nile that brought explorers to Uganda and they opened up East Africa to the Europeans.

At Khartoum the Blue and White Nile come together, but towards the source cataracts like the one we saw at Jinja and waterfalls made navigation upstream perilous. Ptolemy asserted that the Nile rose in the Mountains of the Moon. It was Major Richard Francis Burton and John Hannington Speke who were given the task, by the Royal Geographical Society, to find the source of the White Nile in 1856.

The methodical Speke and the flamboyant Burton fell out. Speke was shot in a hunting accident before he could defend himself.

July 28th, 1862 was the date of the discovery of the rapids outside Jinja. These rapids were only thirteen feet high, but the width and amount of water passing by convinced him.

Speke wrote that it was 'a sight that attracted one to it for hours, the roar of the waters, the thousands of Passenger Fish leaping at the falls with all their might. Hippopotami and crocodiles lying sleepily on the water., cattle driven down to drink...'

We saw neither one hippopotamus nor one crocodile and there weren't even cattle or fish to be seen. This great scene had been fenced off; it was a park with three plaques and a bust. The first plaque referred to Speke's discovery of the source of the Nile.

The bust and plaque of Gandhi proclaimed in bold gold writing that some of Gandhi's ashes had been scattered in the Nile.

The inscription read: Mahatma Gandhi (2.10.1869 - 30.1.1948) Universal apostle of peace and non-violence whose ashes were immersed in the River Nile in 1948, unveiled by H.E M.R I.K Gujral, the Prime Minister of the Republic of India on 5th October 1997.

The third plaque commemorated Clinton's visit to the site in the 1990s. Like Madame Tussauds where images or personalities that are not current are replaced, I suspect that Speke and Gandhi will remain, heroes of their centuries, but Clinton's plaque may well be replaced by the next president who graces the peaceful shores of this torrential river. The shoppers finished the shopping, the onlookers their gazing, the historians their inspection of the artefacts. We left soon after, heading for the dam to see hydro-electricity generator in action.

As we approached the dam, we saw security guards in beige uniforms wearing purple plastic wellingtons coming towards us when we stopped on the bridge over the dam. We gave them some money, but after they spoke together, they came back to ask for more. They were armed and looked like soldiers; they even had bolt-action rifles, which looked like they were Russian. The driver paid them off and we parked in a lay-by so that everyone could get out and look. It wasn't a very busy road, but it had no pavement on either side.

'Look at the white egrets,' Pip told the children; he pointed excitedly at the birds of prey circling above the dam wall.

'Boffin,' shrieked Aubrey. He managed to be always within earshot and never within swing shot of those he had tormented.

'Thank you, Aubrey,' Pip tried to sound stern, but he found Aubrey as amusing as all of us did for a child of that age.

'Why is there a green grass islands at source of the Blue Nile?' Aubrey asked putting on his perplexed face and you could see both Ollie and Punch trying to work out the answer.

'All the power for Uganda comes from this one spot.' Pip knew that the under-fives would be loosening off a barrage of colour questions, so he changed the subject from ornithology to physics.

'Boffin,' Aubrey screeched, accompanied by Ollie and Punch.

'This supplies all the modern houses and hotels in Kampala,' Pip continued. 'Some of the energy is exported to Kenya.'

'Boffin,' the chant rose to fever pitch and Pip gave up.

'Shall I take a photograph of you and the children,' I asked Lucy.

'No, but you could move your head so I can get a shot of the dam.'

'Good photo opportunity,' Duncan sneered.

'Yes, you're right, did you forget your camera again, Duncan? I shouldn't want to take photographs with Huck Finn's head in way,' Lucy added.

'Lovely head as it is,' Duncan declared and beamed at me as if he were being genuine. I moved closer to Duncan and out of camera shot.

'Not as lovely or as empty as yours,' I replied, smiling back him. Duncan stopped mid draw on his cigarette, momentarily stunned at my rebellion.

'You and Duncan obviously went to the same charm school,' Lucy observed, smiling at us both; she took a shot of us with her camera, handed the camera to Matilda and then fished around for her cigarettes in her handbag. If Duncan was smoking, we should all smoke or so the group theology went.

I offered to take photographs for everyone else and that occupied me while everyone milled about looking at the dam.

Back in the van, we chatted about what we had seen and about going to Ssese Islands. This was to be the highlight.

'What are you going to do after the trip, Huck Finn? Are you going to stay with us or go on to Zanzibar as you planned?' Duncan asked. 'It won't affect me as I'm leaving next week, but I'm just curious.'

'I'm taking Hattie white water rafting, Duncan,' I replied, and Hattie shot me a horrified sideways glance.

'Oh, no, I'm not,' Hattie puffed.

'She thinks she's going to a craft shop,' Duncan teased her.

'Or going to the Sheraton swimming pool,' Lucy suggested.

'I'm not going anywhere near white water rafting and that's for sure,' Hattie insisted. 'The pool's the only water I like and that's only to cool off after sunbathing.'

'Are we nearly there?' Aubrey asked, a small voice from the back of the bus. The travelling in the heat had exhausted the children.

'What, at Fang, Fang?' Duncan asked.

'We're driving to Shanghai,' Pip continued. In fact, we were planning to go to a restaurant called Shanghai one evening on our stay – it had met with Pip's approval – '*The Pip Seal of Approval*' or '*Pip-pip.*'

'I'm hungry,' Ollie whined.

'You want Chinese?' Duncan asked.

'I'd love some Chinese,' Pip replied for Ollie who wasn't quite sure whether he liked it or not.

'But not Fang, Fang,' I challenged

'Don't wind me up,' Pip sighed.

'Is it any good?' Anthony asked.

'We'll never know,' I replied.

'What did you think of Jinja?' Lucy asked.

'I loved the 1960s houses with their red earth driveways,' Duncan declared as if he were reviewing for an architectural radio show. 'The Italianate villas were stunning in their proportions and details.'

'I prefer the 1950s municipal building style myself,' I interrupted; I was only too happy to join in the conversation uninvited. 'The post-modern style is so alive with opportunities and feelings of space and depth.'

'What are you on about? Not at Jinja they weren't, they didn't look at all like the old County Hall.' Duncan was horrified.

'You mean the building adjacent to the Houses of Parliament which is now the hotel and the London Aquarium?' I had him there, the County Hall building had been converted years ago; it undermined his knowledge of architecture, I felt.

'Well there was nothing like that at Jinja,' he insisted.

'Jinja was more continental, you're right,' I was warming to my theme. 'Not like the other towns with their tannin tinged roads, Jinja had proper black top, a tarmac road and did you see the green tiles on the old Italian style villas.'

'No,' Duncan sounded unsure.

'And the intelligent blend of 1930s Corbusier style and colonial houses.' I had been struck by the diversity of architecture and how the differing styles had blended into one organic whole. 'Jinja was an architect's dream, beautiful houses built to exacting standards for wealthy clients by the best in the profession.'

'No. Did we go to the same place?' Duncan quizzed me.

'Judging by your observation skills, probably not!' I said throwing down the gauntlet – all that I had mentioned was there.

All he had seen were the green leaves of the shrubbery and the red gravel of the driveway. He'd missed the essence of the town and focused instead on the colour co-ordination of vegetation and not the buildings' fabrication; never mind, he still enjoyed it.

Chapter 11

Take it Easy at the Speke

i

There were differing views as to the seriousness of terrorism in Uganda and it was the following mid-morning around the cane and glass tables at the Speke that we discussed whether the party was in real danger.

The security guard at the front of the building with his pump action shotgun had not been able to deter a parcel bomber who had left his package in the telephone box of the main foyer.

Indians, Europeans and Africans used the hotel as a meeting point, and we carried bags of differing sizes, but they were never checked. Who was in a position to say that a Western or Soviet bloc power was not trying to destabilise the country through terror?

Pip and Duncan had been two bars away from an explosion. There were no specific targets and there was no one from any of the continents, or any of the surrounding countries, or peoples to point a finger at.

'My lot were terribly concerned about the bomb here and about Richard and Susan's safety,' Anna announced as we all sipped beer or gin and tonic. It was a peculiarity of our group that the men drank beer and the women drank gin. She sat back to catch the sunshine that flooded her part of the veranda and drew on one of her duty free Silk Cut cigarettes.

'There have been no bombs in Kampala according to my lot,' Lucy followed on, lighting up one of her Extra Mild duty frees with an ostentatious flourish of her hand. 'Despite the devastation in foyer, the people I'm staying with deny any bombings and even when I told them about you two being at the bar that night the other bomb exploded, they refused to accept that there was a problem.'

At that point Susan came down to join us; she ordered a Sprite from the ever-attentive waiter who had spotted her approach. She greeted everyone warmly and asked us about our day before eventually sitting down herself.

'How was your meeting with Ronnie?' Duncan asked.

'It went well, I told him about the time he was staying with us and he was surrounded by girls. He was bored one day and cut the heads off the girls' dolls.'

'What did he say?'

'He said he couldn't recall the dolls or chopping off their heads.'

She smiled as she recounted the king's indiscretion when he was a boy. I sympathised, I had cut off the head off my sister's doll and tried to stop her 'Giggles' doll from laughing when you pushed her arms together. I also found the doll that was fed water through a baby's bottle and it went straight through into a nappy abhorrent.

When conversation ceased, we noticed Anthony was absent.

'Where's Anthony?' Anna asked.

'Anthony's become part of the FBI embargo,' Duncan said.

'Like Jamaica in the 1970s,' I said.

'What are you on about now?' Duncan asked.

'Jamaica had a socialist government and the Americans didn't like it, so the CIA and FBI went around telling everyone the island was dangerous and tourist offices were warned off sending clients there, the result was Jamaica was almost bankrupted,' I explained.

'What did you think of Ronnie's mum's tomb?' Duncan asked.

'I thought it was fabulous and you?' Susan wondered.

'I liked the Pepsi shack,' Duncan breathed, leaning forward and lighting a cigarette as if he had said nothing strange at all.

Back at the Reste Corner, we had plunged into the whisky like it was a refillable vat the previous evening.

'What are you reading, Anthony?' Duncan asked.

'Mao Tse Tung,' Anthony answered

'Lousy tongue, more like it,' Duncan responded.

'A fish surfaces,' Pip obscurely added.

Duncan and I carried on our dialogue, ignoring anyone who might try and interfere with our banter. It was an effective way of passing the time, though we could have learned a language.

'The security guard found your "Deading-stone" joke so funny he took his boot off my head and then shot himself in the foot.' Duncan informed us apropos nothing, staring at Pip pointedly.

'I'm taking Hattie white water rafting, Duncan,' I said.

'She thinks she's going to a craft shop,' he replied

'She thinks she's going to the Sheraton swimming pool,' Anthony interjected.

'Hattie, at the source of the Nile, headed straight to a makeshift stall to buy a blanket,' Duncan chortled.

'I liked the table selling water colours,' I announced, writing surreptitiously.

'Just write, right,' Pip retorted, smiling at me.

'Where are we going to eat?'

'Fang, Fang,' I suggested.

'We can try *Shanghai* if you want Chinese,' Pip replied; he had done his research.

'Richard would love Chinese,' Duncan said encouragingly.

'But he wants to go to Fang, Fang,' I continued.

'Don't wind me up, Mike,' Pip interjected.

'Is it good?' Anthony asked.

'That's not the point,' Duncan said.

'Fang, Fang is off the menu,' I added.

Pip excused himself.

'Red alert, Richter Scale 2 to 3 and rising,' Duncan warned.

'Is it the purple period?' I asked

'Fabulous, you'll be buried under your precious crottle-coloured earth next to your blessed termitary.'

'I'm not going to talk anymore I don't want to upset you or any members of the entourage.'

'It was the bad timing of the remark.'

'I know but I couldn't help myself. Have you ever done something when you shouldn't have?'

'Always, but I have seen all the danger colours today: red, violet, purple and black.'

'My stomach feels delicate,' Anthony complained. He was new to the country and had not adjusted to the heat or the different diet.

'Coca-Cola is the best thing,' I told Anthony.

Research has shown that the combination of the sugary contents and the caffeine both help stabilise upset stomachs and, indeed, others have vowed that the soft drink is good for hangovers; however, drinking such a sugary drink regularly is not such a good idea.

I had no Diorylite. My mother used to pack some when I was younger, or, when I was older, press a box of it into my hand a week before I left for holidays. She would have checked I had it, but I had just grabbed my malaria pills from the chemist. The mention of Coke started a discussion about the Coca-Cola and Pepsi war to win worldwide sales. I had heard it all before but listened attentively, just in case I should pick up a new angle or more information – I didn't.

ii

The next day at the Speke Hotel all the children were downstairs. They normally watched cartoons on the satellite television in their grandfather's room before being taken for a swim at the Sheraton if nothing else had been planned.

That day, the Major was being interviewed and his room was the most discreet location for the reporter and for the Major who was now just an old soldier who was still trying to find what happened to his friend, the Kabaka.

'I'm off to the airport.' Anthony announced.

'Off to Entebbe Airways?' Duncan asked.

'I want to change my tickets.'

'So, we'll see you in three hours.'

'If you're lucky,' Anthony said smiling; he was used to African ways already.

Anthony left in the taxi, Pip had gone to sort out our safari and I was left with Duncan and the children.

Meanwhile Hattie, Lucy and Anna went to get material for some shirts and dresses for the boys and girls and to see if they could find a bargain at the market.

Duncan was patient with the children, but he also teased them without mercy.

Matilda was sitting reading her diary before writing some more. She wore a light cotton summer dress and the sun had started to colour her arms, legs and rosy cheeks.

Duncan was nursing a cup of cold coffee watching his nieces and nephews who surrounded him with their drinks and diaries.

'You're so gorgeous,' Duncan said rising from his chair and moving around to where Matilda sat. He put his arms around her shoulders and cuddled her tightly to his chest.

'Let go,' she begged, wincing as he deliberately squeezed her tightly.

Because her arms were pinned against her body, she could not break free from his grasp and Duncan knew it.

'You're so goddamn gorgeous,' Duncan enthused leaning his head on to hers, which drove Matilda even further towards distraction. The way he said it was so insincere that Matilda was incredulous at first, then frustrated that she had allowed him to get so close and to pounce on her. She was like a small animal being crushed by a python; there was nothing she could do about it.

'I hate you,' she hissed.

'But I love you,' Duncan simpered unconvincingly.

'Let me go,' she screamed, but Duncan just tightened his grip on her. She was powerless.

'People walk by and say, hey who was that girl, and you're too gorgeous for your own good. I'm just so lucky to know you,' Duncan continued.

'Stop it, let me down,' Matilda demanded.

'No, No, I can't, you're too gorgeous to let go.'

'Please, give me some money.'

'You should give me money.'

'But adults give money to children.'

'No, that's what children do; they give adults all their birthday money. You should know that. If you give me all your birthday money and promise to hand over all your savings in your account, then I'll let you go.'

'No, get off.'

'Uncle Duncan wants all your money,' Aubrey cried joyously.

While Duncan clung on to Matilda extorting money from his niece, her sister Emily pulled Aubrey's hair as he wrote in his diary. I spotted the vicious and unprovoked attack brought on as much by boredom as Emily wanting to be the centre of attention.

She had suffered many more stomach upsets and she hated Matilda being in the limelight.

Aubrey, not wishing to involve an adult and needing to take revenge, pulled Emily's hair in return.

'Stop that nonsense,' I demanded, playing the schoolteacher, not wishing for the situation to deteriorate further. I was as much *in loco parentis* as Duncan was.

'But Aubrey pulled my hair and it really hurt,' Emily whined.

'She pulled my hair first.' Aubrey defended himself.

'Go on, fight each other,' Duncan suggested.

'She started it,' Aubrey was smiling his usual charming smile, despite being so badly wronged.

Somehow his good-natured stance diminished his case.

'You pulled my hair really hard,' Emily complained. She had been ill, and she wasn't reacting well to either the heat or the Lariam.

'Fight, fight,' Duncan chanted. 'Fight, fight.'

Duncan was enjoying his role as catalyst, but the children were not rising to the bait, they knew they would hurt each other and get into trouble when their respective mothers arrived. Duncan quickly realised the situation and then, simply pointed at me and appealed to Aubrey and Emily.

'Fight him,' he ordered.

'I will if you give me some money.' Emily, ever the mercenary, replied.

'Yeah or a Fanta,' suggested Aubrey.

Emily had priced them out of the market.

'No way, but you can pull his hair – what's left of it since he's had a haircut. We should call him Sean or shorn,' Duncan suggested, sounding like a statesman announcing a new initiative.

'Where's mummy?' Punch asked.

He had been watching all the proceedings with fascination, but now he had finished colouring in a drawing he was aware that his mother was missing.

'She's gone to the craft shop with Hattie.'

'With "*Carrot-Top*"?' Punch asked.

'Yes, Punch, your aunt Hattie, the one with the dyed red hair, "*Carrot-Top*", that's right,' Duncan explained slowly.

Duncan was ever patient with his nephews, in fact he was more likely to appear to be one of them rather than side with the adults. It often made things slightly complicated.

'Where?' Punch asked; he was not one to be put off easily, he wanted details.

'The craft shop to buy Punch a present, is that okay?' Duncan continued; he could lie through his teeth like the best of adults if it meant a quiet life.

'Okay,' Punch was satisfied and Aubrey, the ever-caring brother, gave Punch another drawing to colour in, so a major incident was avoided.

'Duncan, are you going to go to the craft shop?' Emily asked.

'Are you going, Emily?' Duncan asked.

'Yes,' she replied.

'Then I'm not,' said Duncan, taking enormous delight in snubbing his niece; he chuckled to himself.

Punch started fighting with Aubrey, Emily and his *Teletubbies* doll. I excused myself in order to catch the waitress and order a beer. I needed one since I had volunteered to take the children swimming at the Sheraton that afternoon. I needed to swim; the inactivity was beginning to take its toll on my exercise regime.

I went regularly to a gym, three times a week, and already I could feel that everything I ate was piling on the pounds. It's a curious phenomenon that, in theory, sitting around in the heat should make you less hungry; however, the fact is boredom made eating an attractive proposition.

Although my day started well with fruit and coffee, the breakfast at the Speke was too good to turn down. Bacon, eggs, sausage and toast cooked to perfection and I could read my book as I ate. Normally the others were visiting the bank or had not arrived at the hotel. I had cashed three hundred dollars left over from a trip to New York in the spring, so I avoided the tiresome queues at the exchange counter. It wasn't the most secure means of holding money, but I felt safe.

In Europe, I would have had travellers' cheques or used my credit card to pay for items of expenditure.

That evening, before our trip to the island, I took everyone to supper at the Indian restaurant attached to the hotel.

All the adults, that is.

Only Lucy and Anna could not attend as they were looking after the children. It was good value and I dared not risk suggesting that I treated everyone to a meal at Fang, Fang; Pip would not have been able to take that, it would have resulted in a 'Code Black' situation.

Before supper I was speaking to a man who was drinking beer at the table next to me, and he asked me to join him at his table. I found out that he was here with his wife and they were staying at the Sheraton. He said he was meeting two friends for a drink and I told him I was waiting for the rest of my party, preparing as we spoke to go out.

His two friends turned out to be two Rwandan girls, Eve and Juliet, both of whom were stunning; Juliet was almost as tall as I was, and they were beautifully dressed. We chatted for five minutes and then the man made his excuses and left, the rat.

The girls were a little unsettled by his sudden departure as was I since they needed a refill and it was left to me to either sit there or politely offer them a second drink. They were even more put out when I revealed that our man was most probably going to meet his wife.

The 'double-rat' had obviously flirted with these girls at the Sheraton, for that is where they had met and in order to avoid being caught by his wife, he had suggested the Speke as a rendezvous. There were a lot of very attractive girls around as Kampala and the Sheraton was playing host to the annual 'Face of Africa' competition.

My drinking companion had most probably had an attack of remorse and extricated himself from the situation while leaving me to entertain these two girls. Eventually, I made my excuses, feeling sorry for the shoddy way this man had behaved towards them – the triple-A rat – and my sympathies went out to his wife as well.

As we had not eaten since lunchtime, and it was almost eight when we sat down, everyone settled at the table quickly; there's nothing like a good appetite for focusing a varied group attention.

We ordered poppadoms and scanned the menu, which was equal to the finest in London, which surprised me.

Everyone decided before our Kingfishers arrived.

'You'll miss out on "Half London" and "Ange-Noir" when we go to the island. Friday night at the best dance venues in town and you won't be there,' said Duncan with glee.

I had been asking for advice on the best clubs every time we got in a taxi and also asking where to eat and the best bars. I wanted to avoid the tourist places and get an idea of local flavour, but Duncan in his ribald cynicism focused on the nightclubs.

'I'm going there tonight,' I replied.

'No, really?'

'Absolutely.'

'Which one?'

'Both.'

'Really?'

'Yes.'

'Well you are handsome and appealing,' Duncan said deadpan.

'I thought Pip was the funny guy,' I replied acidly.

'Not from where I'm sitting,' Duncan looked to Pip at the head of the table.

'Would you like to come along?'

'I don't do dancing.'

I was lost for words; I loved dancing.

Chapter 12

Ssese Islands

The next day we arrived at the hotel ready for the island trip, all packed and Pip had managed to get his laundry back. We waited from ten until twelve; everyone fed up with having to hang around for ages. It would have been better if we had been told twelve and had a lie-in, but that was not the way things were done.

We were ushered into two Land Rovers: Duncan, Anthony, Pip and the Major in the first 'Landy'; Susan, Matilda, Sam, Ollie, Aubrey and I in the second 'Landy'. We drove down to the lakeside where a new development was being built below some stables.

We drove through the paddock in order to get down to the beach; to the right we could see construction going on. There was an isthmus at the end of the bay, and we followed the dusty dirt track that ran down to the marshy shore.

As we unpacked our light overnight bags, a big black Hummer drove into view. It sped past the stables towards us sounding like a plane; $90,000 worth of metal was being driven towards us at breakneck speed.

This monster, a beautiful piece of engineering that it was, had seen service in the Gulf War and was twice as wide as the Land Rovers. In a cloud of dust, the car drew up and its engines died. We continued about our business as though nothing had happened although everyone was curious to take a closer look.

An old barge formed a pontoon and Andrew's boat was moored alongside. Once the bags were out of the vehicles, we walked over to the barge and made a human chain, hoisting each item on to a thin plank, over the guardrails, across the metal deck of the barge and then over the rails on the other side and from there, finally, into the boat itself – what a palaver.

The ten or so cases took a while to shift and everyone seemed to have a smaller bag, which needed to be taken across, too.

After twenty items had been put in the boat, we realised that the Major and his wife might have difficulty in crossing over to the boat via the pontoon.

The twin Volvo engines were started and the boat full of adults and children motored around the barge to the bank. From thence the Major and his wife were lifted up into the boat.

Duncan and I groaned at this, surely, we could have been saved the palaver of crossing the pontoon if they had moored the boat here originally. Duncan looked at me and raised his eyes as if to say this is typical of the way things are done, I winked back at him.

'Do fio, no worries,' I said.

'Any trouble from you and your overboard,' he said sternly.

'I've got my bodyguard,' I replied looking at Anthony's back as he took his seat next to the driver's.

'You better put your life jacket on just in case,' he warned.

We all wore our life vests, big yellow foam-filled waistcoats which Andrew's wife, Margaret, dished out before returning into the cabin to sit in the shelter with the cook who had been hiding downstairs while we had been busy loading our gear and ourselves – he was a specialist. After wishing us a good morning and handing us our life preservers we didn't see Andrew's wife until we arrived at the island.

The boat was beautiful, a white thirty-eight-foot long pleasure cruiser. A U-shaped bench seat was set into the cabin, behind which was the engine bay, which sloped down to cowling and the housing for what seemed like the propeller shaft.

The Major and his wife sat at the back with Pip to their left and the children sat on the starboard side, Duncan and I on the port.

Anthony sat up at one of the seats next to Andrew, the driver and owner of both the boat and the island. Between them lay the entrance to the galley and the steps that led down into the bowels of the boat where Margaret and the cook were sitting.

We started off slowly, the big engines throbbing as we reversed from our mooring and turned around in the small channel past the pontoon. As we moved out into open water Andrew moved the throttle forward and a gentle breeze brushed our faces.

It was cooling in the heat and as the wind was over water it was colder than we expected. We were all drained by the stultifying heat of Kampala, so this was a refreshing development. I took off my shirt as my skin was clammy with it on.

The engines hummed and then Andrew told us that it would take two hours at forty knots. I guessed we were doing about twelve – we seemed to be moving quite fast in the water – and that was when Andrew moved the handle by his left hand towards its furthest reach.

The engines started to roar, and the front of the boat rose out of the water; within a minute we were doing thirty-eight knots and the cool breeze became a chill wind. You could not hear the conversations going on for the din of the engines.

It was necessary to shout even if the person was directly next to you.

'It's good to see the FBI is up in the front with the pilot,' Duncan shouted at me.

Anthony was a few feet away, but he could not hear. His face was set, his body stiff as though he was, actually, on the lookout for enemy warships. The rest of us wore stiff faces – 38 knots was most uncomfortable as well as fast.

The boat bounced across the calm waters of Lake Victoria, jarring our backs; it wasn't even worth considering the impact that we would have suffered in the open sea. It was the closest you could get to powerboat racing on a lake.

Two-and-a-half-hours later, chilled to the bone, our bones shattered from the vibrations, we arrived at the island.

As we approached the beach, where a jetty stretched out into the lake, Andrew eased the throttle back and we cruised gently into the bay while the sun warmed our cold flesh. We all had goose pimples on our arms. I had started the journey with my shirt off; I arrived with it on.

Two friendly islanders greeted us. They loaded our baggage and then us on to a trailer hitched to an old tractor. Duncan and I decided to walk up and jumped out, following the windy, crottle-coloured road to the house.

The vegetation on either side was quite thick and the thought of snakes or other unfamiliar animals made me stomp my feet in an uncharacteristically exaggerated way.

I managed to convince Duncan that it was to counter the stiffness in my legs after our sea journey, but that was before I noticed that Duncan's usual shuffle had been transformed into a definite stomp.

After a lavish lunch, cooked to perfection, Andrew asked for volunteers to tour the island.

The wrinklies declined preferring to rest, shattered, in more ways than one, by the journey, but the three children, Anthony, Duncan, Pip and I crammed into the back of a short-wheelbase Land Rover. Andrew drove the Land Rover like he did the boat and we were now being bumped along the dirt track that cut through the thick vegetation.

Occasionally, we had to duck to avoid the branches, which had grown across the rutted groove-way that served as a road. In a clearing, there was the local school, empty for the holidays; it was a low bungalow made of local wood with a thatched roof and looked like a hideaway home in Jamaica – Goldeneye, Fleming's place, maybe, but on a smaller scale.

Then we turned off the road in order for Andrew to show us the airstrip. A trained fighter pilot, he was keen on extremes and he drove us up the sixty-degree slope as though we were merely turning on to a tarmac road, the only clue was the roar of the engine as he engaged first and the way everything went from horizontal to vertical.

'Hang on tight,' he said jovially.

We didn't need to be told, our knuckles were already white from the drive down the dirt track, but we managed to grip the metal side panels even tighter as we rose forty-five, then sixty degrees up the slope.

I felt that we were about to be tipped out of the back. He may have taken this slope at speed on his own, and been perfectly safe, but with three adults and three children in the back, the weight ratio had been altered. I wasn't sure if he had taken this into account, determined as I was not to fall out; the bumpy ground threatened to bounce us from the back.

'If you have a problem then blame the designer,' Andrew shouted back to us smiling.

'Who's the designer?' Duncan managed to ask as he leant even further sideways in the direction of the driver.

'Land Rover,' Andrew laughed.

Just as we were about to release our grip and let gravity take its toll, we cleared the brow of the hill, the vehicle righted itself and we were suddenly horizontal driving on to the flat tarmac airstrip wondering why we were gripping hold of various parts of the vehicle so hard. The airfield was in use, but Andrew wanted the runway extended to take international air traffic. He explained his ideas for taking people from Mombasa, Cape Town, or Johannesburg and even Dubai to his glorious island. There were only two main houses, his and his father's where we were staying but other houses could be built cheaply and quickly.

When we reached the end of the airstrip, Aubrey started fighting Sam. Duncan looked at them incredulously; Anthony gave them a piercing stare.

'You'll have to walk home past the snakes if you can't behave yourself,' I told Aubrey.

'That's no problem,' Aubrey assured me.

'You're some type of special moron,' Duncan said grabbing Aubrey.

'Oh yeah,' Aubrey replied defiantly.

'The main thing is that you are special,' Duncan said in a convincing Tennessee accent.

We continued to the western end of the island because Andrew had promised to show us his house before we went back and it was too late to take us to the beach, which would have to wait until the next day.

It was good to stretch our legs and walk around the garden; the contrast between our accommodation and his house was staggering.

Ours was from another time, colonial in style; his house had less character and charm but was spacious and modern, it was like being in Ireland visiting a new house when you were staying at the castle.

There was everything you could want in a modern house including the 40-inch television and satellite dish for internet connection.

Andrew's wife and daughter joined us, and we all played tag in the garden.

Michelle was twelve and she had never played before so when anyone ran towards her to make her 'it', she ran up to the gate or into the pineapple grove, which was two hundred yards from the house.

We tried to make it fair by tagging Sam, Aubrey and Ollie in sequence, but poor Ollie was the smallest, so his brothers always took the soft option by tagging him and he got fed up of always being on. There were tears but Duncan and I were near enough and deliberately slow enough for him to catch us and then it was a choice between the three older children. Michelle was off the list once she had shared up the drive and there was no way we could catch her.

Exhausted, we stopped and looked around in order to get our breath back; it was still warm, and the adults were sweaty, the children flushed. The avocado trees looked amazing. The vegetation was a vegetarian's dream. The sixty-five or so cattle that roamed around the vast acreage satisfied the carnivores.

The eyes were amused by the view to the front of the house, which slopped down into jungle with the lake in the far distance.

Andrew's wife had brought the tractor and trailer, which had been loaded with some fruit from the garden by the driver. Andrew took his family back to the house in his Land Rover while we all went back in the trailer. There was a direct route back to where we were staying, and we were relieved that we didn't have to negotiate the slope near the airstrip.

As we drove off, we saw a Fish Eagle circling in the sky, which the children viewed through Duncan's binoculars, all reminiscent of *Bird Watching* by James Bond.

The children were tired from their running around, so they sat on the wooden bed of the trailer while the adults sat on the metal rim of the sideboards.

Talking to the driver was out of the question as the tractor engine drowned any conversation. I looked at the tired children; travel is exhausting, and the boat ride had been like an eight-hour plane ride.

I put on my best nature programme voice: 'The lesser stripped 'Bruton' making strange noises as night-time falls.'

I was narrating like David Attenborough on one of his wildlife programmes. The children managed to smile weakly.

The sight of a Kingfisher in the trees as we passed silenced any other comment and the beautiful bird was splendidly highlighted against the dark green vegetation. It was a good job the Sea Eagle was too busy fishing to notice us, no one told the bird that the lake was not a sea.

We passed a smallholding with pigs running wild in the garden; there were a dozen piglets that looked like *Babe*.

The children thought they were adorable, but we couldn't stop to watch them, as we had to be back before the sunset.

'I love pigs,' Matilda declared.

'Yeah we know,' Aubrey said baiting her.

'You're going to marry a pig, Matilda, aren't you?' Duncan goaded her still further.

'If he's a big pig like you, I won't,' Matilda countered.

She could 'give as good as she got'; she was an urban child, her school was French, her wit was her self-defence.

With that Ollie sat up on his knees and grabbed Duncan's leg, wrapping his arms around it and would not let go. Ollie remained clamped to Duncan's leg for the rest of the journey.

'I thought he was going to wrestle with me,' Duncan said.

'Maybe he's getting his strength up,' I suggested.

'He's taking his time,' Duncan replied as he looked at his watch to time how long Ollie was in that position.

Duncan was doing his best to ignore the behaviour in the hope that Ollie might desist. There was no chance of that and five minutes later Duncan spoke to Ollie.

'Get off my leg, you don't know where it's been.'

Duncan was bored of the extra attention. There was no response from Ollie; he remained attached like a limpet to Duncan's leg. Duncan just sighed and folded his arms for a further five minutes.

It's difficult to look nonchalant when you have a child, sitting on his haunches, hanging from your leg, but Duncan tried his best and carried it off, looking at the scenery and not once looking down.

'It's not normal,' he suddenly declared.

It was clear he was addressing his remark to no one in particular and then he looked down at Ollie as though he had just noticed an unpleasant smell. Still Ollie hung on.

'We're coming to a bumpy bit,' the driver declared over his shoulder, barely audible.

'Everyone, hold tight,' Anthony ordered shifting his arms and legs to brace himself for the undulating ride.

'And if you are holding on to a leg, hold on with your teeth, bite hard,' I added watching with some satisfaction as Ollie sank his teeth into Duncan's leg.

I've never seen a man squeal like a pig but that was the closest description of Duncan's reaction. He shook his leg, but Ollie just put his head back on Duncan's fibula as though nothing had happened.

'Ollie bit me,' Duncan declared with affront, rubbing the part at the bottom of his femur where I feared Ollie may have drawn blood; at least the jeans that Duncan wore seemed in one piece.

'What did you do?' I asked

'I bit him back,' and so saying Duncan bit Ollie savagely on the shoulder and Ollie released his grip and scuttled over to the relative safety of the other children.

'You screamed like a "peeg",' I said in my best *Scarface* impersonation.

We returned to Andrew's father's house where we had an invigorating cup of tea and a slice of sponge cake before we showered and changed into clean clothes for supper.

It was casual and most of us wore jeans and white cotton poplin shirts, as did Andrew; Richard and Susan wore linen clothes, Susan a dress and Richard a blue linen shirt, which he teamed with chinos.

Everyone sat on the porch with a drink, watching the sunset; again, the boys had beer, the girls had gin and tonic, the children had

Fanta orange as Coca-Cola would have made them even more hyperactive than they were.

I sat back in the cushions of a comfortable chair stroking their dog, a beautiful, healthy-looking golden retriever, who wandered the island throughout the day; there was no question that he would suffer from lack of exercise. The sunset was terrific: a kaleidoscope of colours, flamboyant yellows, opulent oranges and rich reds. It was fabulous to watch the sun sink into the lake waters.

Enjoying my beer in one of the comfortable chairs and watching the landscape change colour while the lake waters lost their sheen as the grass of the front lawn changed from a pale green to black green.

I felt at peace.

All around was darkness; the creatures of the jungle were beyond arm's length. I knew there might be the odd chameleon or lizard somewhere in my room. I knew that once the light was out, they would stay in one place. The thought of snakes or spiders never entered my head, and if it had, I would not have mentioned them in case it frightened the children.

Despite the original resistance to keeping diaries the children had collected bank notes and postcards as well as drawing pictures next to their varied writings. As they lay on the wooden floor of the porch, hunched over their books, lit by hurricane lanterns, they only paused briefly to watch the sunset. As soon as the trees at the end of the clearing were obscured by night, they returned to their writing.

The jungle below the house had afforded us all a view of a family of monkeys flitting from tree to tree as the light faded. Duncan, Anthony, Pip and I sat around the large table; the Major and his wife sat with Andrew and his wife to our left, the children in between.

'This really is night school,' Duncan observed drily. The children ignored him, engrossed in recording the events of the day, especially the boat ride, I suspect they felt the cold out on the lake as much as we did, but the thrill was greater for them.

'You can smell the clean air after Kampala,' Anthony noted.

Matilda and Sam were writing their journals by the light on the porch; Aubrey and Ollie were drawing pictures.

'Aubrey and Ollie are having an art attack,' announced Duncan, again deadpan; I smiled.

'Can I have some bread, please?' Matilda asked.

'You've just eaten,' Duncan couldn't believe Matilda would want more to eat after the huge afternoon tea the children had eaten on our return from our travels.

'Not to eat, to rub out,' she replied.

'Bread as a rubber, I see,' Duncan nodded his head; his face wore an incredulous look as if he thought his niece was mad.

'Are there bats here?' Sam asked our group.

'A bat is a flying rat,' Duncan pointed out.

'Or a flying mouse as they say in Germany,' Pip corrected him.

'Or Vorsprung durch Technik, as they say in Germany,' Duncan replied, testily, lighting the ubiquitous cigarette and looking out into the darkness.

'It's lovely to see the stars,' Anthony noted; he was determined to savour the atmosphere even if Duncan was not quite so awestruck, or so it would seem.

'You can't see them in Kampala because of the light pollution,' Andrew reminded us.

'We never see them where I live in London, although friends of mine managed to see the Hale–Bopp comet when they were in the country,' I informed him.

'Hale–Bopp was great seen from Bukasa,' Andrew assured us, smiling his infectious smile; he really did live in a perfect setting, far from our urban existence.

'I bet,' I replied enviously; I had been impressed by the sunset and, now, more so, by the stars in the big sky.

'We don't have to worry about the traffic or the CBS bus,' Duncan exclaimed, investing the remark with a pent-up resentment of all things urban – he was an Island Man now.

'The tractor is the best open-top transport I have ever been in,' Anthony noted.

'It was quicker for Huck Finn and me to walk,' Duncan said; he did not mention the cannibalistic attack from his nephew or the possibility of being bitten by snakes.

'The rest of the family arrived only a few minutes later in the tractor, we would have beaten you if you had been carrying your heavy baggage.'

'I travelled light,' I defended myself.

'You did,' Pip acknowledged, 'but Duncan packed a suitcase which would have lasted most people six weeks.'

'Pip, did you get stuck in the traffic?'

'Traffic lights!'

'Only one set work in Kampala,' Anthony noted.

'They cost a lot of money,' Andrew told us.

'For one set of lights?' Anthony teased Andrew.

'The other set will come later,' Andrew assured him, not saying when exactly they would materialise, this year, next year, sometime, never. He smiled warmly at Anthony.

'Perhaps the lights have been held up in traffic,' Duncan suggested.

'What did you all think of the source of The Nile?' Andrew asked. He had obviously being talking to Richard about what we had done so Far.

'We're not sure if it is or if Speke was correct,' Pip said, and we all feared he was about to trot out his theory gleaned from the *Royal Geographical society.*

'Either way, Speke and Burton were great explorers,' Andrew soothed and seemed to know more about these British explorers than we did, and he had immense respect for these travellers who had risked all to open up Africa to curious geographers and, of course, explorers, followed by Evangelists, followed by traders and eventually, unwittingly, the Her Majesty's British government.

'They were out grouse shooting and one of them killed himself, so they were better at finding things than they were on the grouse moors,' Duncan explained.

'They both mapped Rwanda, Victoria, Jinja and Lake Albert,' Pip defended the explorers, men who'd fought disease, heat and all manner of difficulties and they had died with their boots on, well one of them had.

'What do you think of the island?' Andrew asked.

'Everything's perfect,' Pip said graciously.

'But nothing is perfect,' Duncan countered.

'That's right nothing is perfect,' Anthony enjoined,' but this is the closest you'll get without offending Allah.'

'We try,' Andrew noted, pleased.

'Matilda says I'm perfect,' Duncan announced.

'If she thinks you're perfect and she's perfect why does she want to marry a pig?' I asked, really wanting to know the truth.

I never got an answer as The Major and his wife joined in our conversation, at the table, while the children took it in turns to bathe. There were incredible smells coming from the kitchen, supper would be soon, and we had worked up an appetite despite the massive and delicious lunch we had tasted on our arrival and our slice of cake at four o'clock, part of the huge afternoon tea that was to serve as the children's supper.

'Everyone should charge their glasses so we can drink to the health of our host and to those who have never been south of The Equator,' The Major suggested.

'Do dreams count?' asked Duncan.

'The children, Anthony, Duncan and I have never been south of The Equator, I hate not to be included,' I said for that reason.

'To those absent, too,' Pip suggested gallantly.

'Anna and Lucy, Hattie, Emily and Punch,' Anthony listed the absentees.

'Not my sisters,' Duncan said with a groan.' Do I really have to drink to my sisters?'

The Major also proposed a toast for Mama Rose who had organised the trip by getting in touch with Andrew.

'Mama Rose refused to come,' Duncan pointed out for no good reason; she had organised the trip not offered to lead it.

'It's too late, the toast is Mama Rose,' Pip raised his glass.

Choruses of *Jabwei* and cheers echoed through the stillness of the night.

Our conversation hummed through supper and Andrew told us about his flying exploits attached to the Israeli Air Force and the United States Air Force, but we always felt he held things back and were never sure whether he saw combat in active service.

We ate wonderful food: local vegetables, meats – goat and pork – and drank delicious wine, talking late into the night.

The island was paradise and the next day we drove down to the beech by the lakeside on the other side of the island. The Land Rover and tractor and trailer provided excellent transport on the dirt tracks to our destination. Our group consisted of Andrew, the children, Duncan, Anthony and me.

At the beach, there was a rectangular steel pontoon. The fierceness of nature was brought home to us by the ants that lived there. They bit us as we walked barefoot from the scrub where the vehicles were parked down to the soft sand of the beech.

The water was warm, and we raced to the floating island and then dived off the pontoon, swimming around in the cool waters further away from the shore.

Andrew spied a young boy of about eleven in a canoe who was fishing and waved him over. He instructed the boy to row us beyond the pontoon and we took it in turns, two at a time to be paddled around the bay.

It was extraordinary how the boat moved through the water at such great speed; it was one of the fastest canoes I had ever been in, slicing through the water and the pilot's smooth measured strokes on alternate sides of the boat ensured speed and accurate navigation. The only problem was getting in and out of the boat.

We almost tipped the boy out of the boat, but he corrected our ham-fisted antics and we allowed him to put the tip of the boat on the sandy beach before gingerly stepping out at the end of the trip. The young boy handled the canoe like a veteran even when he had us as his clumsy cargo.

We had towels provided and we watched him disappear into the distance as we dried ourselves well away from the ants and we made sure Anthony, the bodyguard, who was not swimming, collected our shoes before we went back into the jungle.

'His boat is faster than yours, Andrew,' I joked.

'Almost,' he replied with his good nature and humour-filled smile.

'Butterfly,' one of the children announced as a striking large tropical butterfly danced around the Land Rover.

'Flutter by,' I corrected.

'Funny guy,' Aubrey said.

'Funny guy about the flutterby, butterfly.' I mimicked Aubrey's voice.

'Like all grown-ups he thinks he's funny,' said Aubrey as he appealed to the larger audience, the children for support; they all knew how un-amusing people, especially parents, can be.

'You're so ugly you look like a pig,' Duncan said.

'No, I'm not.' Aubrey protested.

'Yes, you are. In fact, I won't say "Aubrey", I'll just go oink, oink,' Duncan then tried his new form of address. 'Hey, oink, oink, let's get in the Land Rover.'

'I'll tell Mama Sue on you, and then you'll be in a stew,' Aubrey informed him.

Supper that evening took a more serious and adult tone as the children went to bed early and we discussed topics that were less trivial. We had got to know our hosts quite well and we were keen to find out more of their views.

Although Andrew and his wife lived on an island, they had interest in the political situation in the capital across the water. Stability and success for the country would filter through the lake. Being the senior member of our group, the Major kicked off the conversation soon after fruit arrived; polite mealtime conversation had been maintained during the first course despite Duncan's usual efforts.

'The Land Rover drives so fast; didn't it take off at the airstrip?' Margaret asked, picking up on Anthony and Duncan's conversation about earlier the previous day.

'Almost,' Duncan replied.

'If you want to take off you should try our local brew, Waraga.'

'What's that?' Duncan asked, looking horrified as though it was a sexually transmitted disease.

'It's a Ugandan spirit.'

'We'll all try one,' suggested Pip, ever the adventurer, 'Richard?'

'No thank you,' he replied flatly, the Major knew his limitations and was not about to mix his drinks. He had most probably tried it before anyway.

'It's a banana port,' Pip said, knowing his father-in-law's predilection for that spirit.

'Nice try, pass.' The Major had a winning smile, but it equally showed his resolve.

'Two hundred litres of banana make twenty litres, pure distilled,' Andrew told us.

'Two hundred litres of crude make ten litres of aviation fuel,' Duncan was remarkably well informed.

The glasses for the liqueur were brought and the bottle that was used to fill them was left on the table for us to help ourselves. We all tried the sweet concoction and it was delicious. It was tangy and yet there was a definite banana taste followed by the hit of pure alcohol, rather like butterscotch schnapps.

'I may be an ageing ex-soldier but I'm very excited about Uganda, but mindful of its history,' Richard said.

'The past is full of turmoil,' Andrew replied.

'You went to the school in Buddo, Andrew, and you have remained in this country whereas the Kabaka was unable to do so. You are more aware of the situation than I am,' Richard continued, humbly trying to extract Andrew's views on the political situation at the present time.

'Buddo is a very special site,' Andrew would not be drawn on this issue. Instead he wanted to focus on the spiritual significance of the coronation and burial sites.

'We visited the tombs and the hut that was built there,' the Major continued. When we had visited the tombs there was a round low hut with a tall conical roof made of brush or rush or reeds or some such covering; we had come across a lone lady who had sat in the darkness praying, just as a monk would pray.

'That was the first Kabaka of Buganda who invited the English to Uganda,' Andrew knew his history.

'Toro Koli,' Pip interjected.

'Kato Kintu Kakulukuku was the first Kabaka of the Kingdom of Buganda. Kato Kintu is not to be confused with Kintu, the first person on the earth according to Buganda legend. Kato Kintu gave himself the name Kintu, a name that he knew the Baganda associated with the father of all people.'

'I see,' Pip added; he most probably did.

'Muteesa I Mukaabya Walugembe Kayiira wrote a letter to Queen Victoria asking for missions to come and convert the Ugandans to Christianity. As a result: James Grant, John Speke and Henry Stanley, all of them, amazing explorers.

We all agreed.

'The way Kabaka Muteesa handled all the Europeans resulted in Uganda becoming a Protectorate rather than a colony of the British.'

'I thought it was mean of her or rather the Foreign Office to send only a gas lamp, a few other odds and ends, and a bicycle,' I suggested; the Foreign Office appeared to be ever mindful of expenditure, at least in those days.

We had seen these articles at the tomb site, the artefacts from another era, given pride of place on one side. In the darkness, they were set on rattan mats atop of Victorian table.

There was nothing else in the hut apart from the sand that covered the floor on which were spread several brightly coloured striped rattan mats on which those who wished to pray knelt.

A raised wooden plinth contained the traditional throne and a blanket screen shielded the visitors from the remains of the Kabaka.

He had been the first king to invite in the missionaries to Uganda.

He little realised that next would come the traders and after them the military garrison to protect that trade.

Then, after that there was a short step to the imperial army that would merely be protecting British interests in the region, but in reality, exploiting the area as it was too early and too uncomfortable at that time to take on rivals in Europe on European soil.

Anywhere else was considered fair game and had been since Wolf had struggled for dominance in Quebec. After disasters in the Americas, success in the Caribbean and in India, the British knew how to build an empire before anyone else got there first.

A look at a map of 1900 Africa proved that if the British didn't get there first, someone else would. Therefore, as far as the British were concerned, it was necessary to annex large tracts of Africa to prevent the Germans, French, Belgians or Italians from doing the same.

Twenty years before the First World War the mandarins in Whitehall, Berlin, Versailles, Brussels or Rome envisaged any conflict as being played out in this vast area of Africa rather than on mainland Europe.

'It was said that above all else the king could not kill anyone. He was elected for his leadership skills and he was answerable to the management board and the people, shareholders, just like any corporate CEO.'

'Indeed,' Duncan said.

'However, this Kabaka said, "Oh yes, I can," and he did.' Andrew had put the situation in context and although history cannot rely on our putting contemporary values on situations that occurred in a time when different circumstances, values and judgements were in place, he still had a valid point.

'The missionaries that were executed were seen as martyrs in the eyes of church,' Pip pointed out without an axe to grind but merely as a point of information.

'That's interesting, I thought they were Anglican missionaries, the Anglicans being against martyrdom and the cult of saints.' I was not trying to be clever, not much, but it was pleasing that my Reformation history had after proven useful.

Again, I was adding to the debate, even though we were not strictly at liberty to surmise or to judge situations that had occurred over a century before, but we were keen to understand what went on which is the basis of historical enquiry, after all.

'Martyrs they may well have been, but in the eyes of the Kabaka they were rebels,' Andrew said.

Andrew had more of a handle on his country's history; he knew that the missionaries had incited the people to rebel against the authority of the king and that the Kabaka had no choice but to execute the guest who had abused his hospitality so cruelly.

'The missionaries said that there was rape and so they were stoned to death for lying. My grandfather said they were thieves; it's history that knows the truth,' Andrew gently put his point across, he realised that we were trying to understand the situation and were not being judgmental in any way.

Every country's history has some atrocity, justifiable slaughter and indefensible manslaughter.

'There were no crimes like theft or rape?' Pip asked.

'No, people still fear the rule of that time, there is no rape. There were no police at that time of any sort. Even when the police were formed it was not considered the justice of the area; the chief dealt with misdemeanours.'

'He was the law,' I interjected, showing I understood.

'The county district headquarters were on this island and even they would not counter the authority of the chief, nor would they involve the authorities in a judicial enquiry. If there were enough evidence, they would deal with it themselves. In most cases they turned a blind eye, whereas serious cases were thrown in the water.'

'Lake Victoria is a big lake,' Duncan reminded us helpfully.

'All the money goes to the mainland,' Margaret said.

'Court cases are expensive,' Andrew relished the shock value of his statement. 'The people looked after themselves on this remote island, not many people could commit a crime without being observed or later found out; it was after all a small community quite capable of dispensing its own justice as such communities have done so for years. It is the anonymity in the city that allows for crime and the system is complicated by such considerations.'

'People can sue you for arresting them,' Margaret further elucidated.

'It's like Lord Haw-Haw who broadcast during the war; they hung him for a traitor, even though he was in fact a citizen of the Irish Free State. Yet they let the real villains, those in the concentration camps, live out their retirement on a state pension in England.' I added. I thought I'd open up the debate a little.

'So, he was hung although he was American and entitled to fight on either side?' Duncan was fascinated by this new twist, institutional manslaughter. It could of course be argued that Haw-Haw's propaganda broadcasts were provocative and part of the German war effort, but I was not about to let the truth get in the way of a good story.

'It's a long, complicated story,' I endeavoured to explain. The wine was beginning to take hold after the meal, plus, we were trying a local banana liqueur which made me more liquercious, or loquacious. I continued, hoping my voice was not sounding slurred whilst trying to avoid any words, which began, contained or finished in the letter 's', which was not an easy job.

'Ireland had been promised independence for many years and so some activists took control of the General Post Office in Dublin and took on a hunger strike for independence. The English over-reacted, as usual, and blew up the Post Office that they had built.'

Everyone was listening, so I continued.

'There was even a gunboat in the Liffey. Later, they sent convicted criminals over with machine guns; they called them the "Black and Tans".'

'Interesting,' Andrew acknowledged, politely.

'However, many thousands of Irish voted with their consciences and fought in both the First and Second World Wars. Heroes like Paddy Finucane the air ace in World War Two who fought for freedom. Many of those who fought in the First World War did so because they had been promised that it would be a guarantee of independence.'

'Patriotism is the last refuge of a scoundrel, didn't Shaw say?' Pip asked.

'Indeed, he did, but the fight for freedom went back way beyond to the famine, that's where we get the expression boycott, from Captain Boycott who refused to let the Irish keep their share of the harvest as the price was so high for corn and wheat in England. The local people refused to bring in the harvest and ostracised the family,' I continued. 'Being English, troops were brought over to bring in the harvest and Irish people died in their thousands.'

'I read that the government gave more to Battersea Dogs Home than they did to the famine,' Duncan observed.

'Yes, we were savages and we bred too well and deserved to be culled by the potato blight.'

'That was harsh,' Duncan noted.

'Yet our grain fed the mills of the north of England and supplied the flourmills of England. It even goes further back to Cornwall and his scorched earth tactics in Ireland, and Elizabeth's plantations; you'll have to reread some Irish history and I'll have to read some more African history.'

'It all depends on who writes the stuff and which side they are on,' Pip exclaimed. He could see I was in danger of dominating the conversation and becoming a bore.

'Read a lot of sources and you can make up your own mind,' I acknowledged. 'Tell us more about Ssese, Andrew.'

The conversation moved from the island to the lake to Uganda, her neighbours and on to Africa as a continent and then on to Andrew and his time in various air forces.

We talked of his brother and his Hummer desert vehicle.

'It's a monster,' Duncan chortled.

'$100,000 US, and 20 miles to the gallon, if you're lucky,' Andrew smiled. 'It's an expensive car to buy and run.'

'A gallon a wheel spin,' Duncan suggested.

'How far is it to the waterfalls tomorrow,' Anthony asked.

'108 kilometres,' Andrew said deadpan.

'What?' I asked.

'Three kilometres,' Duncan replied with a smile.

'You're all athletic, it won't take long to walk.' Margaret insisted; she was as good as Andrew was at teasing us, the island was small, and the waterfall could not be far away.

We were still trying to get our head around the idea that Lake Victoria was the size of Wales.

'I'm taking the tractor back,' Anthony said.

'How do we get back?' Duncan was worried.

'We'll get you as close as possible by Land Rover, it's a twenty-minute walk from there but the bush is clear, and the track is flat. The view makes it worthwhile.'

'Couldn't you fly us there and drop us in?' I asked.

'Is that with or without parachutes?' Duncan archly responded.

'I could take you there now, but night flying is slower,' Andrew was warming to the idea.

'You have the airfield to take off on,' Duncan seemed quite keen especially as the possibility was remote and he could seem brave.

'But we have no plane on the island,' Andrew seemed sorry about that

'How long have you been flying?' The Major wanted the conversation to return to near normality. With Duncan there it was wishful thinking.

'Twenty-five years, give or take,' Andrew looked much younger than he was.

'Just in Africa?' Pip asked.

'Mainly in America and Israel,' Andrew explained, without being specific.

We knew he had been high up in the air force. My Headmaster Derek Henderson had trained American pilots to fly Supermarine Spitfires in World War Two, was very specific about being posted to Florida to do so.

'Was it an exchange programme with Israel?' Pip wanted to know.

'Not exchange, no,' Andrew admitted; he left an ominous silence.

He had obviously been employed by the Israeli Air Force for his flying ability and it was a moot point that he had seen active service; no one dared to ask him if he had or not. 'My job has taken me to Israel, Texas and to Belgium,' he informed us.

'Belgium?' Pip asked; he could understand the other two countries, but Belgium was not noted for its powerful air force.

'I was working on a simulator,' Andrew explained and smiled; his comment had the desired effect. 'It was to put us through flying in storms. Pip, your flight was uncomfortable.'

'The flight from hell, we were bumping along,' Pip remembered, he drew on his cigar for comfort.

'Bumping along is good, the pilots can see the storms on the radar; it's in colour and red and yellow mean that you are secure,' Andrew explained.

'We were multi-coloured, I was looking decidedly blue. I thought we were going to crash,' Pip exaggerated.

'You were lucky, some storms are at the ceiling of the plane. In that case you have to go around the storm which can be tricky.'

Andrew was bringing back the bad memories for Pip but equally, as a pilot, he was trying to reassure him that flying was extremely safe so he would not be concerned on his return journey.

'We were suffering terrible turbulence,' Pip remembered.

'You need to power through turbulence, that's why it's so uncomfortable.'

'It certainly was that.'

'The danger is an air pocket.'

'How so?'

'You can lose a thousand feet in one second.' Andrew informed us and this information shocked even me – 'how big were these pockets?' I asked myself.

'What about tropical storms,' the Major asked.

'They only last for thirty minutes on the lake, they're very short.'

'What about tornadoes in America?' Duncan asked

'They're not wide, like a hurricane you simply steer to an alternate course.'

'So, storms are not a danger,' Pip was already thinking about his twenty-two-hour return trip.

'Turbulence is just a change of air density.'

'So, it's the vacuum you have to worry about,' Pip offered.

'Air pockets are just that, there's a problem but once out of the pocket you can fly normally.'

'I noticed we had a smooth landing into Entebbe,' I ventured, 'a very long descent. I hardly felt the pressure on my ears.'

'That's because we are fortunate here, we can have a long approach. Most airports or airfields, where there are few winds, that are approached from water allow for a shallow descent,' he explained. 'It's in the built-up areas, near cities, or near mountains, or where there are strong air currents where you have to make a steep descent. You literally have to bang the plane down on the tarmac which can be uncomfortable for commercial passengers.'

We talked on some more about flying but Andrew did not mention the troposphere which is thicker near the equator, which, I learned later, from a pilot friend, held its own dangers.

The conversation moved back to the subject of Africa in general, a continent seeing many changes as newly formed, young countries struggled to establish themselves.

The Major and his wife decided it was time for bed and, excusing themselves, bid us all good night.

'Pip, you're keeper of the keys,' the Major said, referring to the last to go to bed. 'I'm going to turn in, thank you, Andrew and Margaret, for a lovely day and for a fabulous meal.'

We wished them good night and had some more to drink. Five minutes later Pip also left the table.

'I'm going to bed to read,' he announced.

'Why change a habit of a lifetime,' Duncan said with a small smile.

Bedtime came late, at three in the morning, my head reeling from the banana liqueur. My bedroom was cool and inviting; crisp linen sheets awaited my collapse but so did the unwelcome gate crashers of bedroom lizards, big spiders, termites and big biting ants.

Luckily, unlike Reste Corner, there was a mosquito net over the bed, which was a huge relief. I hated the nightly visits of the mosquitoes and I feared even worse insects out in the islands.

I was reminded of the scene in *Doctor No* when Fleming describes the poisonous millipede left in Bond's bed and so I slept with the net curtain draped over my bed. I didn't want creepy crawlies clambering over my naked flesh in the night.

I was aware that outside the lodge, the jungle was alive and quite capable of gaining access into the house. It was strange because I was as vulnerable at Reste Corner, but because of its urban setting I had felt safer.

The sound of the generator woke me the next morning. The room was filled with a grey light, the light of a brewing storm. I showered quickly. I was feeling hungry and dehydrated, and I checked the bathroom for lizards and spiders before luxuriating in the flow of hot water.

The shower was powerful and invigorating; I washed my hair and soaped the sweat from the night before from my body. Returning to the room, I aired the bed and dressed, it was nice to have a room of my own. It was large and had a second bed in it.

The walls were white and opposite the door, on the far wall, was a window that had shutters. The window was open and through it I could smell the dampness of a tropical storm and a myriad mixture of scents from the plants outside and I could hear voices.

On the veranda, there was some excitement, so I dressed and rushed out. Through the four cylindrical pillars, I could see from my position in the wide doorway the view of the lake; it was stunning.

The sky was grey-black. There was an isthmus that swept down at the far end of the bay looking like a grey mass in the gathering mist. The bay was equally grey, but the green of the jungle at the bottom of the garden was still verdant as though the dampness had brought the shining leaves to life.

The lawn looked as manicured as ever.

'Look at those black clouds,' Aubrey exclaimed.

Rolling in from the west were big, ominous cumuli nimbus clouds. The clouds brought with them big blobs of rain.

'Innocent, the cook, said it rains every day to water the plants,' announced Matilda.

As she said that we could see two lightning strikes appear to hit the water of the lake.

'Oh, my Lord,' exclaimed Pip, 'the bathing things are drying on the line.'

As Pip spoke, the two great doors of the lodge slammed shut, caught by the wind, and the keys fell to the floor. I picked up the keys and put them back in the door but left the doors closed.

'Washday blues,' Duncan noted as he watched Pip sprint towards the washing line at the side of the house next to an outbuilding.

'The sky is meshing with the lake water,' I observed, more interested in the scene than in Pip retrieving the swimsuits until I remembered that mine was amongst them and I followed him out helping him to take the swimming trunks off their pegs. 'I'll get your bathers, Duncan, unless you want to come and fetch them yourself.'

'That's very kind of you,' he replied watching Pip and I getting soaked.

'Pleasure,' I shouted back, taking the last of the clothes off the line and pelting after Pip into the shelter of the canopy.

My clean white shirt and fresh pair of black Levi 501s were drenched already. We hung the damp swimming costumes on the wooden rail that fronted the veranda and I shivered. Duncan handed Pip and I towels to dry our hair.

While we dried off, Duncan and the children looked out over the shifting scene; the finger of the Isthmus was gradually being absorbed into the mist.

'I've got to move because of the rain blobs,' Duncan announced, flinging himself onto one of the chairs in a dramatic fashion. Hamming it up was his speciality. He did *ennui* excellently.

'They are blobs aren't they,' I smiled, as I wiped away the rain from my face with the left sleeve of my shirt.

'The sky is still meshing with the lake and the rain is still falling in blobs,' Duncan reported in a bored fashion. 'Blob and Mesh, that's what I'll call these two,' he pointed to Aubrey and Ollie. Sam and Matilda had sat down after him, the younger boys still wanted to stand. '*The Adventures of Blob and Mesh.*'

'There's steam coming from the barbecue,' Pip noted. The embers from last night's cooking were still glowing. We had eaten barbecued fish and chicken, watching the cook who had set up his barbecue just outside the veranda.

'It's a good job that it didn't rain last night, or we would have just had vegetables for supper.' Duncan didn't bother to crane his neck back to look at Pip or the steaming embers. Just then there was a strike of sheet lightning, an electrical flash that seemed to light up the dull grey-black, sky.

The intensity of the brightness faded quickly leaving the landscape duller than before; the land was now a darker green, and the trees' wet green had lost their sheen.

Even the four white pillars, American colonial style, on the stoop seemed to have lost their newly painted look. The furniture we sat on seemed older and darker. It was, however, a beautiful sight.

'Everything is really meshed now,' Duncan announced.

'Or even merged or blurred,' I suggested.

'Every time we talk, we miss the lightning forks,' Matilda announced, sounding slightly peeved by missing the light show.

I noted that the earth of the flower beds was turning to mud. Two terracotta pots on either side of the steps held tropical plants and the soaked earth came splattering out, and I could hear the noise of water gushing from the guttering above. The wind had changed, and the rain was starting to bounce off the wooden floor of the stoop and bouncing off the white plastic tabletop. The swimming costumes were getting wet as well, but no one cared at that stage.

'The line between the lake and sky has gone beyond meshing, it has disappeared,' Pip commented. There was just mist ahead and the finger of the isthmus was shrinking before our eyes.

'No, the sky has mushed,' Duncan remarked, just as a roll of thunder shuddered from the sky.

The clap was so deep and resonant that it seemed to suck the air from around us and I could feel my chest vibrate as if I was close to an explosion or too near high wattage speakers. The sound silenced all of us for a moment as we all counted the gap between the clap and the next bolt of lightning. There was no lightning after fifteen seconds.

'The island is disappearing.' Matilda exclaimed.

'Before you say it, it's almost gone,' Duncan remarked.

'It saw you, Duncan, and you're so ugly, it ran away,' Matilda said with a sweet smile and a glint in her eyes. She was beginning to learn her uncle's technique.

The rain increased, pelting down around our safe refuge. All that could be seen now was the bay and the knuckle of the isthmus. The overflow was oppressively noisy.

Moving the table further away from the end of the porch, out of the way of the rain, we wiped it down for Innocent, the cook, as he went to fetch a tablecloth and announced that breakfast was on its way.

The children set the table. Andrew, Margaret and the Major and his wife were inside talking and would eat later, Innocent told us. The adults dried the seats with towels kindly provided by Innocent.

We talked about the day before as Innocent brought a pile of plates for us to distribute, followed by toast, bacon, eggs and coffee. We were grateful to be able to have such a substantial breakfast after our overindulgence the night before.

'It was nice not to be bothered by mosquitoes,' Pip announced; as their main target, he sounded relieved.

'And snoring,' added Duncan, rolling his eyes in a dramatic way; he was such a great actor.

'And moaning!' growled Pip good-naturedly.

Pip had shown us his welts from the mosquito bites. I was reminded of the buzz of the insects and his moans as they feasted on him.

I remembered the satisfaction in knowing that they hadn't got me, giving delicious pleasure, but that pleasure had been short-lived as I had been bitten so often myself.

'I was worried about poisonous spiders.' Duncan was always trying to frighten the children and he looked at their shocked faces as he spoke.

'Just like the one in James Bond,' Aubrey said.

'In the book it was a black millipede that was poisonous,' I pointed out pedantically.

'In *Dr No*? Was that a book?' Aubrey asked.

'In Ian Fleming's book, it wasn't a spider like in the film, it was a poisonous millipede like you,' I assured him.

'Huck Finn likes to kiss mosquitoes,' Matilda announced.

'Does he?' Duncan arched his eyebrow and reached over for some more toast.

'Yes,' Matilda said before she drank from her orange juice glass and smiled, pleased with her remark.

'I told you not to tell anyone,' I helped myself to some piping hot freshly brewed coffee, giving Matilda a disapproving look.

'Uncle Doodle told us.' Matilda picked up a triangular slice of fried bread and munched the base thoughtfully.

There we were, Duncan and I, uncle and friend of the family, re-christened 'Doodle' and 'Huck Finn'. We could have been on a porch overlooking the Mississippi, plotting to see who we might get to paint the picket fence or planning how we might avoid being caught by the murdering, escaped convict 'Injun Joe'.

'How long does the storm last?' Aubrey was carving up another slice of bacon and dipping the cut piece into his fried egg before putting it slowly into his mouth.

'Three days,' Duncan announced; he looked bored with it all, as he helped himself to another coffee.

It was as though he was waiting to light up another Marlboro Light cigarette and fling himself on to a comfortable chair.

The necessity of eating seemed to interrupt his ennui.

'It's almost done,' Innocent assured us, and he smiled at the children as he placed a plate of fresh toast on the table along with a new jug of juice.

'How long does a storm last?' Ollie asked. He was not about to believe Duncan even if he was only young.

He was having difficulty eating, even though his food had been cut up for him by Pip; he seemed not to want to eat and picked at his food, playing with a piece of toast in his hand.

'How long is a piece of string?' Pip asked, he was enjoying the fact that breakfast allowed him time with his family, as was I – it took the pressure off Duncan and I. Pip helped himself to fresh toast, buttering the slice thickly.

'It's finished when the owner says so,' Duncan elucidated.

'Does it rain in Como?' Matilda asked. She had been promised that the next summer holiday would be in the Italian lakes and she wanted to make sure her days would not be curtailed by bad weather.

'Does it rain on the road to *Dumbville?*' Duncan asked.

'Where's that?' Matilda asked jovially; she knew the answer, but she liked to give her uncle something more to think about and wasn't going to allow him to have the last word as he so often did and expected to do.

'You're riding pillion to *Dumbville,*' Duncan asserted as he finished his coffee, returned to the table and refilled his cup, smiling sweetly at Matilda knowing she had no answer.

'What's a pillion?' she asked, all innocent, but her eyes sparkled with mischief.

'Riding shotgun,' I suggested, trying to be helpful.

The drinking of the previous night had given me a good appetite and I had wanted my two eggs and three strips of bacon, as much as the next person; food was more important than it had been the night before. As Innocent arrived with the food, conversation was suspended while we adults served the children, ensuring they had equal amounts of egg, bacon, fried bread and sausages, sufficient toast and marmalade and full glasses of juice.

Once the children had finally finished eating, Duncan, Pip and I filled our plates with our usual array of fried food.

The previous evening alcohol had heightened the appetite, but after such a large lunch, a light meal would have sufficed. Innocent arrived and we all sat around the table to enjoy wonderfully crisp bacon, grilled to perfection, fried eggs with sun-yellow yolks that were firm yet also runny, beautifully brown sausages and fried bread.

'What's riding shotgun?' Matilda asked as she started on her fried bread before attacking her bacon and eggs that Duncan served to her. She was speaking in between mouthfuls, the polite girl that she was. Aubrey wasn't always so careful to finish what he was eating before he spoke.

'I have a poem for you, Matilda,' I announced. 'Would you like to hear it?'

'Yes, please Granny Finn,' she smiled up at me before attacking the rest of her meal.

From Huck Finn to Granny Finn in a few minutes, some things worked quickly in Africa.

I started to sing the song:

'Oh, queen of the African plain,

Don't be such an awful pain,

Pass me the bread and butter,

And stop acting like a nutter.'

'Exactly, eat your breakfast.' It was unusual to have Duncan back me up. Perhaps it was my lyrical skills that had impressed him. He cut into his food and daintily ate a forkful of egg and bacon, making the most of the necessity.

'Did you know the storm is really Uncle Doodle's farts,' Matilda giggled; she would not be put off, particularly as she had faired rather better at polishing off her plate than Duncan appeared to be doing.

'Same as in the Land Rover,' Aubrey informed us. Duncan looked embarrassed so we decided that we would not be drawn into debate with the children.

'I know how to annoy,' Aubrey had finished his breakfast and now he wanted to play, regardless of, or because, the fact that no one else was done and he would not be able to leave the table.

'Really,' Duncan doubted whether a child would be able to annoy him. His half-finished breakfast awaited a return of strength.

'I know how to annoy you, I know how to annoy you, I know how to annoy you, and I know how to annoy you. I know how to annoy you. I know how to annoy you. I know how to annoy you.'

Aubrey repeated his mantra, over and over, in a highly annoying high-pitched voice. Although it almost made our ears bleed, we ignored him and Anthony, Duncan, Pip and I continued our breakfast as if all we could hear was tropical bird song.

Pip stood up in mock anger, his repast complete, and he walked around Anthony and me to Duncan.

'Stop,' he boomed, 'I have to come to say something private to Duncan, and I need silence. He leaned over and, in a stage, whisper he said, 'I know how to annoy you.' Laughing, he went to the edge of the stoop and lit a cigar.

'I know how to annoy you,' Aubrey took up the chant again.

'I know how to mess your hair,' Duncan informed him with a menacing look.

'What's the number for Childline?' Aubrey cried.

'Got enough food in your mouth?' Duncan asked Matilda.

'I have,' Matilda cleared her throat.

'Good, *Babe,*' Duncan said.

'He keeps calling me *Babe,*' she complained.

'How about *Porgy*?' Duncan asked.

'*Babe*, pig.' Ollie decided to attack Duncan.

'Mental man,' was Duncan's reply.

'You're the mental man,' Ollie replied petulantly.

'Time for a clutch check,' Duncan announced standing and pinching Ollie's arm.

'Pig.'

'You're a special type of moron, but at least you're special,' Duncan smiled.

'You're a moron,' Aubrey countered.

'I'll show you what a moron is; it's someone eating their breakfast with a toothpick.' Duncan was right, Aubrey had cut up his food and he was stabbing it with a toothpick and then eating it.

'Let's play it goes around the table once,' Aubrey said flicking his circle of sausage on to Matilda's plate.

'Right, stop. This is boring,' Pip told them firmly from the stoop.

'Why do they call them boys? They're Samantha, Olivia and Audrey; they call them boys what's that all about?' Duncan shook his head in wonder.

'Shut it,' Aubrey put on a cockney accent.

'Stand clear he's going to wet himself,' Duncan retorted.

'You look troubled,' I turned to Duncan, a frown on my face.

'Of course, I am. I'm on a table with so many ugly people.'

'You're the ugly one,' Aubrey shouted back, giggling as he spoke.

'Hands, work your magic,' Duncan said getting up and squeezing Aubrey's shoulders.

'Dad, he's strangling me.'

'Duncan, I thought you were massaging Aubrey,' Pip chortled.

'FB,' Duncan whispered in Aubrey's ear before letting him go.

'What's that?' Aubrey asked

'Fabio Bozzo, your new nickname.'

The storm was slowly clearing up to right of the porch. We could see the cumuli clouds rolling away from the stoop towards Kampala.

The children cleared their plates and ours, Pip telling them to brush their teeth; we stayed behind to smoke before washing.

Andrew came out as it was safe now that the children had gone.

'How was breakfast?' he asked.

'The cooking has been fab,' Duncan stated, glad to have the nicotine in his system again.

'Delicious,' Pip echoed Duncan's sentiments.

'The food has been delicious, especially the fish last night,' I went further.

'Innocent tells me that there's a lot of night-time fishing because the insects are on the surface, so fish come up,' Pip told us

'Pip, you're the Bill Bryson of the Ugandan Expedition,' Duncan teased him.

'We're going to the waterfall, are you coming?'

'Judging by the weather, the waterfall has come to us,' Duncan remarked. We all laughed despite ourselves.

When the rain stopped, we took the tractor and the Land Rover to a clearing just before the pathway that led through savannah type grass. On either side was dense jungle but at one stage the jungle had been cut back about ten metres on either side of the track. We walked for twenty minutes.

'I'm thirsty,' Aubrey said.

'Are you, I'm hungry, how do you do?' I replied.

'You can drink from the waterfall when we get there,' Duncan suggested helpfully.

The waterfall was spectacular, the path down to it was steep and overgrown but it was well worth it; we swam in the pool nearby before returning to the house for coffee and to talk about our adventure. All too soon, we had to return to Kampala.

On the boat that afternoon it was still cold. We drove at the usual breakneck speed with scant regard for other shipping on the lake. We could see various fishing boats shaped like the canoe that we had travelled in, but some were almost three times as big. Duncan and I sat on the roof, looking out over the gunmetal grey water peering at the overcast sky, a grey-white curtain drawn over the horizon.

'Pirate ship on starboard side,' Aubrey cried.

'Captain Pugwash,' I shouted above the noise of the engine.

'Master Bates hoists the Jolly Roger,' Duncan was warming to the theme as he warmed to any theme. 'Seaman Staines mans the cannon.'

'Where's Tom the cabin boy?'

We broke down at 5.00 pm. The engines just spluttered and stopped, both of those massive Volvo turbo diesels died.

Wearing life jackets, Duncan and I moved up to the front of the boat, right to the metal frame that surrounded the bow, to look out for any passing boats that might offer help and to have a cigarette away from the children.

Andrew was a tall man, six foot two and despite showing evidence that he enjoyed his food, he was fit and strong, but he had difficulty raising the cover of the aft engine compartment. The whole of the rear deck lifted up held by two hydraulic struts. We both stood up and could see the cowling of the two engines.

As Andrew bent down to look into the engine bay, we saw that he had a gun in his trousers. The black metal barrel was stuck into his belted jeans, but the grip and trigger guard were clearly visible. It looked like a Browning nine millimetre; the automatic pistol favoured by European NATO troops. It could have been a Colt .45. It was that sort of weapon, more discreet than a revolver but powerful, nonetheless. Like the Magnum .44, the most powerful handgun in the world, it was a people stopper, it was not designed to wound.

Those who wanted to complain would have to keep their mouths shut, everyone to a man and woman offered help. Innocent who had been sensibly in the cabin with Margaret came up on deck. Andrew asked him to look at the engine and then went down below himself to have a look at the oil pressure and fuel gauges located just inside the cabin by the steps.

It was becoming increasingly clear that this was not going to be a problem solved in minutes and increasingly embarrassing for our captain that the new engines had proved powerful but thirsty brutes. It appeared that we had run out of fuel.

Night came quickly like a blanket and we were robbed of a sunset as the clouds were still low after the storm earlier that day.

Everyone was becoming colder as the temperature dropped. I myself felt pressure on my bladder. Ever conscious of sunstroke after my trip to Egypt the previous year, I had got into the habit of drinking copious amounts of water come rain or shine.

An hour can move pretty fast, especially when you have nothing to do but stare at the butt of a pistol and try not to refer to the predicament you are in. We were still an hour away from Kampala and our two and a half hour journey had just ticked past the fifth hour.

Coldness always affects the body and my desire to expel excess water was becoming unbearable, particularly with Duncan's comments.

We were still at the front of the boat, pretending that it was our job to spot any vessels that might save us. Andrew had brought up his flare pistol from the cabin. Being in the middle of a lake the size of a small country without fuel might pose a problem to lesser mortals, but Duncan seemed to take it in his stride.

We still had electrical power and so our navigation lights were still alight, and Andrew scanned the water for a fishing boat with the big searchlight mounted on the bridge.

Miraculously or maybe fatally, a small canoe with a fisherman was spotted and Andrew called him over. An exchange in Bagandan and some rolled notes pressed into the fisherman's hand had secured his services.

Poor Innocent who had been cooking and cleaning up all weekend was dispatched into the canoe with the fuel tanks. Only a man of Andrew's fame could have brought about this satisfactory conclusion and everyone was grateful for the 'God sent' courier.

My bladder was not so pleased, but I hoped that I could hold out a little longer. The patience of the other members of our crew was staggering. The children seemed quite undisturbed by the whole series of events. They were storing stories that would hold their friends in awe when they returned from the holiday, if they ever did.

Events like this certainly beat the usual: '*I went to the south of France and stayed in a gite*'.

'No comments about Andrew running out of fuel or we're dead,' whispered Duncan as he sat with his knees up smoking a cigarette; as long as they lasted, he would be in good humour.

I wondered absently how many he had in his pack; I only had ten left and by that time he had smoked half. That would leave five, which would keep us going for an hour at the most.

From what we could tell, the island was an hour away, 'round-trip', in a canoe. The boat if it had been working would have taken us there in ten minutes.

'I know a thing or two about those Brownings, they have nine shells, and how many of us are there in the party?'

I confidently and authoritatively announced that I had shot several at Lympstone when I was considering joining the Royal Marines and went for training with the Commandoes.

'Pip, Anthony, Aubrey, Sam, Ollie, Matilda, the Major, Susan, you and me,' Duncan understood exactly what I was driving at. There was a bullet for each of us and the lake was deep and wide.

'It's a good job that it's dark and we're away from everyone else.'

'So, who takes the ninth bullet? I've only just got married.'

'Fair enough, but I have a family at home.'

'Don't worry; I assure you they won't miss you.'

'If we distract him, he might miss.'

'The man's a fighting machine, highly trained. I suggest you take the fall.'

'You're thinner than me, he might miss you, and so you should be the diversion.'

'Anthony's a tough guy; he might have to use two shells to take him out.'

'Nine millimetre bullets, I don't think so. He could line us all up and put one through all nine of us.'

'Just be nice and pretend we find the whole thing amusing.'

'You want me to laugh, you're joking, he'll go for me first and we're both at the front of the boat he might just miss me and get you.'

'Okay, internalise the humour but keep your teeth gritted,' Duncan suggested.

'That's like trying not to laugh in church.'

'Exactly, don't worry. If I know Anthony, he'll say something to upset Andrew, then the pressure is off and we're safe.'

'I hope Pip doesn't say anything.'

'He's far too sensible for that,' observed Duncan.

'You're right.'

'The children are very well behaved.'

'I think they saw the gun as well. Besides would you complain if you were their size? Andrew is a man mountain, children respect that.'

'I respect him, you could fit three of me into his jumpers and trousers,' Duncan observed,

'Please don't make me laugh, I'm dying to go to the loo. It's becoming excruciating.'

'I'm dying for a drink and my supper and bed at the Reste Corner, but you don't find me complaining,' Duncan grinned, looking at me with a glint in his eye.

'Thanks, Duncan.'

We watched as the canoe with Innocent – sat uncomfortably in the front on top of the fishing nets – headed for land. No sooner had the boat disappeared to the nearest island than we saw the hulk of a large ship approaching. The ship turned out to be the Kaawa ferry that links Kenya with Uganda. There was only one way for goods to avoid circumnavigating the lake and that was it. The Kaawa ferry takes people, provisions, containers and railway carriages all bound for Kenya.

'I hope they stop.' I was aware that they might not see us even though we were lit up like a visiting Royal Navy cruiser.

'I hope they've got some cigarettes on board,' Duncan added.

'The cigarettes are imported from Kenya, the boat's going the wrong way.'

'Not as far as Andrew's concerned.'

The Kaawa ferry made most ferries look like toys, it was vast. Despite that fact the skipper brought the boat to a stop within metres of us. The bow loomed over us and, in a blink of an eye, we were alongside, and ropes were thrown from above. Duncan caught one and Anthony had caught the one thrown to the stern; he was at ease with ropes and boats, it was good to have him on board.

Andrew leapt up on to the platform that had been lowered for him and climbed the steps of the metal walkway to talk to the captain. He looked confident and athletic as if he were a visiting army officer making a courtesy call in mufti.

'Thank God,' Duncan gasped. 'Talk about the luck of the Irish.'

'Duncan, ferries run on diesel, I'm not sure whether these engines are petrol or not. Hopefully they might have some kerosene, or they can siphon the tanks of several cars, perhaps.'

'We're diesel, I checked,' Duncan assured me.

'Well, they might well have a loo on board,' I decided, and I followed Andrew up the steel steps that clanged as I ran up, holding on to the handrail. I did not want to stumble as I rose up the huge hull of the ferry; there had been enough humiliation that day. The members of the crew were smiling at me in a welcoming way; it was a break from the routine and a bit of excitement in a normally uneventful crossing.

I said hello to as many as I could and asked for directions to the toilet. They all laughed and pointed me to the end of the starboard bow. The whole incident was highly amusing; they did not normally assist stranded powerboats in the middle of the lake.

After several wrong doors, I finally found relief. The steel doors reminded me of a submarine. The first door that I opened was a storeroom for ropes and fenders. The second contained six bunk beds, three high on each side of a narrow room, the crew's sleeping quarters; these reminded me of sailing with the Royal Navy down in Portsmouth where we slept on a supply ship, HMS *Rame Head* when I was considering a career in Her Majesty's navy.

The third room contained 'Heads' – a standard stainless steel maritime bowl and a stainless steel handle for the flush. For me, at that time, it was paradise on earth. I dropped my trousers and underpants and sat down as my sisters had trained me to do from an early age. Then I finally relaxed. It was a huge relief.

Within minutes of my returning to the boat and taking up position at the bow, Andrew and one of the ferry's crew came down with the fuel. Anthony followed the crew member up to collect a third on Andrew's instructions. I returned to the steps to carry the third twenty-five-litre jerrican. We passed them to Andrew, who emptied them and Anthony, Pip and I helped bring the jerricans cans back up to the deck and return them to the crew members.

Once we were started the crew waved us off and we could feel the throb of their engines accompanying the vibration of our own. We waved heartily as both boats sailed off in different directions. We were soon out of the beam of their searchlights and motoring through the blackness to Kampala.

Chapter 13

Discussions

Transport was waiting for us at the other end. Dae Woo had organised everything as usual; he was amazing. Two hours later than scheduled, we unloaded quickly. Supper at the Speke seemed like a good idea and we were all relieved to be back. Anna, Lucy and Hattie, 'the others', greeted us.

Punch and Ollie, the two youngest children were tucked up in bed, the lucky blighters, the rest of us had drinks. When Anna came back, we filled in 'the others'. We drank beer and gin, ate pizza and burgers and wished for Innocent's wonderful cooking.

At the Speke the next day, we discussed the island. It was back to the old habits; we had discussed going elsewhere for a coffee and a chat, but the Speke was easy.

'Wasn't it brilliant that Sam noticed that the Kaawa ferry was the boat on the five thousand shilling note,' Pip enthused. 'I told him he'd go far and gave him a note saying there would be more where that came from if he continued to be so observant.'

'The only real shame was there was no fan inside those mosquito nets and that would have been bliss,' Anthony noted.

'If you have a problem just watch it or I'll get Andrew on to you,' Duncan warned; he thought the whole drama highly amusing. 'Margaret the control freak stopped them filling up the tanks before we left, she thought there wasn't time.'

'They could have siphoned the second engine to give enough fuel to the first,' Pip explained; he had been keeping a better eye on things than most of us, particularly Duncan and I, up front.

'Both were too dry.' Anthony seemed to have a grasp of the technical matters. We had in fact returned at only twenty knots, running on only one engine. I felt sorry for Andrew and Margaret. We have all run out of petrol at some time, I know I have, frequently. Plus, he and his wife had to make the return journey that night.'

'What about Michelle, she must have been worried about her parents?' Anthony suggested.

'I don't think their daughter was too worried as they would have got Innocent to call and explain the situation, but then again, I'm not sure that they had a telephone on the island. Our weekend had been booked on one of Andrew's trips to the city.'

'I am sure she would have been fine, she looked like she was mature enough to look after herself,' I noted.

'She would have been in bed though, at her age. She was very independent and intelligent, just not pampered like our children,' Pip added.

'Do you remember the laughing pilot on the ferry; he'll be dining out on that story for years to come, rescuing Andrew,' Pip added. As usual, he had hit the nail on the head.

Andrew's embarrassment would turn to mortification. The bush telegraph would ensure that all of the islanders, most of Kampala and even Kenyans at the port, who did not know about Andrew, would hear the story; we all felt very sorry for him.

'Andrew had checked the fuel gauge, it was half full, fifty litres, I was with him when he did it. The gauges were faulty,' Anthony announced.

'That was on the way out.' Pip had been there too.

'He added 20 litres before we left the island.' Anthony was a staunch ally to Andrew and rightly so, we had had a superb time, he was an interesting and amusing host, generous and kind and on top of all that we had had an adventure to write home about.

'It was a new engine, so he didn't even know the mpg at the time of our departure,' said Duncan.

He had decided it was time to get all technical, but I remembered he was not willing to move from the bow to assist with the repair or restarting of the engine.

'It's actually knots per gallon?' Pip chortled as he corrected Duncan.

He had after all sailed around most of the world and he knew Duncan had once taken a cross channel ferry but that was the extent of his maritime experience. He was not like Pip who had crewed on a ship that had sailed around the Cape of Good Hope.

'Whatever, nautical miles, blah, blah.'

Duncan never found other people's humour as amusing as his own and was sounding just a tad tetchy. It was interesting because he had spent all his time trying to make Pip prickly.

He teased mercilessly but he could not take being teased in return.

It made Pip's acerbic remarks even more amusing. Duncan never came back with a retort if he was challenged but he was challenged rarely as his remarks made us laugh.

'One thousand dollars for ten should soften the blow,' Pip noted.

It doesn't sound a lot but once converted to Ugandan shillings it represented a sizeable sum, but what price could you put on staying on a private island with such fantastic food and such stimulating company.

'I wish I could remember a tenth of what we discussed. As it happens, a fifth is all I can manage,' I exclaimed.

'Andrew was a Lieutenant Colonel in the army, an air force pilot and the head of anti-corruption.' Anthony explained.

'I thought it was anti-smuggling not anti-corruption,' Duncan replied.

'It was both,' Pip settled things.

'*Big Bear* was in the air force, but I felt he was not telling us all,' Duncan announced, nodding his head knowingly.

He loved the mystery and giving people characters. Anyone, who was not as slender as he, became a big bear in his books.

'He grinned and put on a veil of silence,' Pip continued; he lit a cigar as though he was so satisfied with that remark, he would reward himself with a cigar.

'Interesting metaphor for a bear,' Duncan noted; he was determined to avenge the fact Pip had corrected his nautical terminology. 'Bears and veils?'

'Andrew is retired and can run the island for the rest of his days,' I noted wanting to break into Harry Belafonte's song, 'Island in the Sun'.

'There, he is chief of the clan,' Anthony commented, 'he'd have successful security if ever there was someone with an old score to settle.'

'A bit melodramatic,' Duncan protested; he liked to control the macabre and mysterious turns of conversation.

'He did say that he knew who was on the island and when,' Pip stated incisively. He was locked on to Duncan and anything he said brought a comment like a cruise missile always hitting the mark

'He's dependent on his people,' Duncan complained, snapping open his cigarette pack, he was under pressure and no one could help him.

It was yet another tense day at the Speke.

'The islanders tell him everything,' Pip admitted condescendingly; he felt Duncan was deliberately misunderstanding him.

'They're paid for the information,' Duncan asserted, though it was clear that he was not sure of this remark, after all they had a responsibility to Andrew as their leader as he had a responsibility for them. Both parties were far more loyal the Prime Ministers and politicians. 'We all know that!'

Duncan was putting the wrong values on these people, just as in history contemporary values cloud people's views of the true situation of the time.

We were part of a different society but insisted on putting our cynical perception of events on to theirs.

'They're loyal to Andrew without being paid,' Pip remarked, flicking his cigar ash on to Duncan's cigarette ash. The ashtray was a metaphor for their argument.

'Tricky artist,' sighed Duncan. He didn't make it clear whether he was referring to Pip or Andrew, but we all suspected that it was Pip.

'Tricky kid,' Pip replied and, again, we were unsure of the reference.

Our deduction skills led us to believe that it was Duncan who was subject of the comment. African politics had nothing on the events around the table at the Speke.

'Burundi was beautiful,' I announced, hoping to steer the conversation on to less controversial topics.

'So was she,' Anthony interjected. He had spotted yet another attractive woman walking by. People-watching had become a hobby for us all, but Anthony specialised in the fairer sex.

'What?' Duncan asked; he sounded incredulous, he was hoping to redress the balance of argument and found himself interrupted. It would be difficult to return to the subject.

'A lovely girl did you see her?' Anthony revealed as he appealed to me. The other two were married and should not be looking.

'Just.' I had in fact just seen a good body disappear with beautifully dressed hair. I had not seen the gorgeous face that Anthony had claimed to see.

'I love it here,' Anthony sat back, put his hands behind his head and crossed his legs. The girls in Kampala certainly seemed to be the best-looking girls around but all cities are honey-pots for the gorgeous.

'If you can't control yourself you should get married,' Duncan suggested, he was still reeling from his defeat at the hands of his brother-in-law and he was determined to keep his brother in check if he could.

'You don't have to agree,' Anthony smiled.

'Follow the yellow brick road,' Duncan advised cryptically.

'She was the wide-mouthed frog,' Anthony sighed.

'What?' we all chorused.

'You don't get many of them round here,' Anthony chortled.

'What does he mean?' Duncan asked, appealing to Pip and I for some sanity.

'What do you mean by follow the yellow brick road?' I asked; I was interested.

'Never you mind,' Duncan said; clearly, he was not.

'What is a wide-mouth frog?' Pip was interested.

'Shall I tell them?' I asked Anthony.

'If you like,' Anthony agreed; he was on the lookout for more frogs, so he didn't want to be distracted. He brought his right hand down to lower his sunglasses on to his nose so that he could get an even better, unobscured view of the street.

'There's a tadpole and he's swimming around eating all the plankton or whatever in the pond.'

'How long does this take; we leave in two weeks' time?' Duncan inquired, ever the helpful audience member.

'Not too long if you don't interrupt,' I warned Duncan, giving him my death stare, the filthiest look that I could muster, but it was too hot and had no effect. 'Then he metamorphoses into a frog, but he has become separated from the rest of the pond life.'

'Just like Anthony, staring at the girls,' Duncan interjected, 'he's pond life separated from the rest.'

'Whoa, tiger, steady, this joke could take all week at this rate,' I complained before Duncan could warm to the theme. 'Anyway, he decides to go to the animals in the jungle to ask for advice. 'Excuse me Mr Giraffe what do you eat?''

'I know this!' boasted Duncan.

'Please, you don't. The giraffe says: "The leaves off the trees of course." The frog replies: "I don't fancy that much, and I can't hop that high." Then he meets a zebra and he asks him: "Excuse me Mr Zebra, what do you eat?" The zebra replies: "I eat the savannah grass of course." The frog tells him: 'I don't fancy that much, thank you, Mr Zebra." Then, he goes to see the king of the jungle, thinking that he of all the animals would know the answer: "Excuse me, Mr Lion, what do you eat?" The lion replies: "I eat wide-mouthed frogs." The frog sucks in his cheeks until his mouth is as narrow as a needle and says: "You don't get many of them around here, do you?"'

'Pathetic,' Duncan commented dryly.

'You do better,' I challenged him.

'Why did the Mexican throw his wife off the cliff?' Duncan asked.

'Why?' Pip threw caution to the wind.

'Tequila,' Duncan announced.

'That's funny.' I didn't get it.

'To kill her; in Spanish: "to keel ha", tequila. Also, tequila, he threw her over the cliff by accident because he had drunk too much tequila.'

Chapter 14

The Crash

i

Anthony and I left that evening before any of the others; the charm of the Speke had worn thin after five hours of sitting around. We weren't keen on eating and so we thought we'd try the bar at the Reste Corner and turn in early to read.

Anthony was fascinated by the statistics he had read about car accidents in Uganda. It was strange that, of all the African countries, the one we were staying in had more accidents than elsewhere.

We were sitting in the taxi, having just stopped at the petrol station so that we could make it back to our hotel without running out of fuel, when a car overtook us at breakneck speed in the path of five or so cars.

'Do you have many road accidents?' Anthony asked innocently, pretending that he was unaware of the research he had read.

'No,' the driver replied concentrating hard on the unlit road ahead. The light from the odd shop or scattered bars gave a vague idea of where the road was.

On either side of the flattop was a dusty dirt track so when you left the tarmac the tyres rumbled; our driver seemed to be concentrating on the white lines in the middle of the road despite the glare of oncoming traffic.

'I've been here two weeks,' Anthony went on, 'and I've seen two people knocked down and a truck and a car in a collision.'

'That is not common,' the driver reassured us.

Twenty yards in front the car that had overtaken us had been in a collision, head on, with another vehicle.

'That's not an accident is it?' Anthony noted dryly.

'No,' replied the driver dead pan, 'an accident is a car crash in which someone is seriously injured or dies.'

'I see the distinction, now' Anthony replied.

We paid off the taxi driver and sat in the lounge of the Reste Corner. I bought a couple of beer and we settled into the comfortable armchairs that had been covered in plastic. Fortunately, the fans above our heads were on high speed so we did not stick to the furniture. I poured my beer slowly into the glass while Anthony lit a cigarette. I had to jump up and get an ashtray from the bar and put it on the table that rested between us. Seeing him light up made me want to smoke too; auto-suggestion, boredom and habit, that is all the smoker needs to join in, generally. I've never been parsimonious either but the fact that a packet cost fifty pence or one dollar certainly encouraged me to indulge.

'I can't get over the taxi driver saying there was no problem with accidents and then we see one five seconds later,' I started.

'Andrew told me about the driving test,' Anthony smiled cruelly.

'An unfortunate term,' I smirked

'More like a crash programme, if you crash you fail and if you can get the car to move forward you pass.'

'Did he tell you that people try and bribe officials to get the test?'

'Yes, he did.'

'Then it's a cash test.'

I went to the bar and paid 5,000 for two more beers, each beer was 2,000 so I waited for my change.

'How much are the beers?' I asked.

'Four thousand each, Saebo,' the bar man replied.

'Two thousand each?'

'Yes.'

'Do you have any change?'

'No.'

'You might have some later?'

'Oh yes, maybe later.'

'Maybe.'

'Sure, you'll get your change.'

'Do fio.'

'Do fio.'

'Oh, and a packet of Marlboro, please.'

'Of course, Saebo.'

'How much is that?'

'Six thousand.'

'Well I owe you 1,000. I'll pay you later, maybe.'

'Maybe.' We both laughed.

I settled down to drink and chat and then someone remembered we didn't have any mineral water for the night, so I volunteered to get some at the bar.

'Can I have some mineral water, please?'

'How many bottles, Saebo?'

'Two bottles.'

'Two bottles is 4,000.'

'I owe you 1,000, there's five. We're quits.'

'Do you want them now?'

'I'll get them, maybe, later.'

'Maybe, later,' he smiled.

'Waybalay – thank you.'

'Waybalay, thank you.'

Later, the four of us sat and watched the television; even Pip was getting into the film when the power failed. The television died, the fan stopped spinning and the lights went off.

The generator had stopped for the night. Such was the penalty for staying in a cheap hotel on the outskirts of town. There was nothing we could do. The staff lit candles and I imagined all the ice melting in the freezers and chill cabinets only to come to life the next morning when the generator came back on at eight thirty.

Considering there was a HEP station at Rippon Falls above Murchinson Falls, which leads along the Kafue River to Lake Albert, as well as the HEP station at Jinja, yet there was little electricity to be had in Uganda; most of it was being exported, which was a wise way of getting foreign currency but a nuisance for us.

The currency was complicated but unlike the dollar each note had a different colour, but some had similar shades to each other: 50 shillings, *Shilingi Hamsini*, showing Entebbe Airport, was the same beige-brown as the 5,000 but the smaller denomination note was smaller in size so easily distinguishable; later notes were pink.

The 500 or *Mia Tano* was predominantly green with an elephant on the back and the Bagandan parliament on the front. The one thousand, *Elfu Moja*, note was similar to the 500 even in size but it depicted a cane cutter on one side and the sugar cane factory on the other.

The five thousand (*Elfu Tano*) depicted the Kaawa ferry on one side and Lake Bunyonyi and terraces on the other. I never got to see the terraced fields and the lake, but I saw a postcard and marked it down as another reason to return. All very interesting but you should know the Lugandan for: one, five, fifty, one hundred and a thousand.

You could walk into a bar with 10,000 and come out with one 5,000, one 1,000 and an annoying amount of, 50s, 100s and 500s. Your wallet might be bulging with notes, but they wouldn't buy a tourist much. It was best to wait at your table to check the bill and then pay rather than fumble around at the till. Sorting the shillings became almost a game. How I yearned for the dollar, greenbacks where you checked if it was ten, twenty, fifty or a hundred bucks; it was like dealing with Turkish Lira.

The next morning, we met all the children at the Speke Hotel; they were hoping to go to the Sheraton for a swim and one rebel suggested we go to the Imperial. That was vetoed as the pool was not as big to start with and there was no paddling section for Ollie and Punch to enjoy themselves. We therefore decided to go to the Sheraton, so the routine was not broken. We thought me might be seeing the Kabaka, so we had to wait until we had word from him; it was easy to get a message to the children at the hotel across the road from the Major's hotel.

'Granny Finn, would you like some shortbread at tea?' Matilda asked me.

'Yes, please. Granny Finn loves shortbread and tea. Twinning's tea from Piccadilly and cucumber sandwiches.'

'I love those too,' Matilda said enthusiastically.

'Cucumber sandwiches with the crusts cut off. Granny's teeth aren't her own,' I informed her.

'Cucumber with the crusts cut off.'

'And shortbread and tea from Piccadilly.'

'Granny prefers her Harrods tea after a big day at the pool. Irish Breakfast tea in the morning and a darling Darjeeling in the afternoon, it perks Granny up.'

Without me knowing the children had ordered some tea. It arrived in a plastic hot water container with tea bags, milk and sugar, in a stainless steel jug, and pot. I would have preferred coffee at this stage, but I drank it graciously anyway, making sure that I kept my little finger crooked daintily away from the handle.

'Would you like us to sing to you, Granny Finn?' Emily asked; her face was the epitome of a child pleading for food on the streets of Victorian London, a Covent Garden street urchin.

'Granny Finn would love to hear you sing but she'd rather wait until it gets late and she can have some gin. Bombay Sapphire to help her suffer.'

I looked pleadingly at Matilda, hoping she would agree.

'Please can we sing, Granny Finn,' Matilda's face was the epitome of a child who was pleading just like Emily's but older and more heart wrenching; my son was her age at the time.

'Very well, you can sing for Granny Finn, but don't make too much of a din,' I groaned.

I was too weak to resist their request, a fault in parents but an admirable failing in a family friend. I could afford to condescend to capitulate, parents are not allowed such a luxury since irresponsible parenthood has been succeeded by 'tough love'.

'Coca-Cola came to town,

Pepsi Coal shot him down,

Dr Pepper sewed him up,

Now they drink Seven Up,' the children sang quite splendidly.

'Short and sweet, how lovely,' I was relieved.

'Here's more,' Matilda insisted

'More, more,' I broke into my best Dickensian indignation, equal to any Victorian thespian. 'You want more, nothing from Oliver please.'

'I saw a bird with a yellow bill,

It landed on my windowsill,

I coaxed it in with a piece of cheese,

Then I smashed him on his knees.'

Matilda sang with relish, particularly the brutal and cheesy parts.

'How brutal you children are, street urchins the lot of you,' I insisted in Victorian mode. 'A bunch of gutter snipe, that's what you are.'

'I saw a bird with a yellow bill,

It landed on my windowsill,

I coaxed it in with a bowl of spaghetti,

Then I cut him up with my machete,' Sam sang.

'How very unpleasant,' I complained. I was quite intuitive when I had to be; it was a horrid song designed to appeal to horrid boys and girls.

'It's your turn, Granny Finn,' Matilda cried.

She was persuasive and I agreed.

Fortunately, I had already had time during the past performances to formulate my reply if I was asked for it. I cleared my throat and sat up to make sure that I had an open chest and that my diaphragm could move with impunity.

Then I sang.

'I saw a bird with a yellow bill,

It landed on my windowsill,

I coaxed him in with a glass of Gordon's gin.

That was no old bird; it was Granny Finn.'

'That doesn't make sense,' Ollie said, disappointed with my non-violent ending.

'I've got one for Matilda, especially.' I sang to the tune of 'Dancing Queen' by Abba.

'Drama Queen,

Young and mean,

Thinks she's seventeen,

Oh, what a scream,

She's ever so mean,

Oh, witch of the African plain,

Don't start to moan again,

It can be such a pain,

Some of the time,

Or from time to time,

The verses don't rhyme,

Oh, queen of the East,

You can be such a beast,

Oh, East African witch,

You make us all twitch,

Some would say you're a,

Queen of the African plain,

But I now you're just a pain.'

I was quite pleased with my imaginative lyrics and the cadence of my rhyme.

'That's pathetic,' Matilda, the critic, cried. She was most pleased with the fact that she had her own song, no matter how awful; any other palled in comparison.

'Children, I think that you have worked up a thirst with all your singing. We'll get you some Coca-Cola with straws – that should keep you quiet. We'll plug you in and we won't hear another word with any luck.'

'I want a big one,' Punch declared

'Oh, a big one, you are a fuss pot.'

'I want a big one.' Punch reasserted his desire; he was young and determined.

'Very well,' I acquiesced.

I ordered the Cokes and we talked about swimming again; the conversation never varied very much as, the children were hot, and they wanted to be cool by the pool.

'Me do it,' Punch declared when the drinks arrived, and he made a meal out of taking the wrapping off the straw.

'Anything for a quiet life,' I reflected.

'Where the dut pin?' Punch asked.

'The dust bin is over there,' I said pointing to a can in the corner

'I want Miranda orange,' Ollie declared.

'Fusspot.' I knew that most children would prefer Coca-Cola if they were allowed it. I also knew that Miranda contained no caffeine and probably less sugar, hopefully, but, knowing the drinks industry, it was most probably a Coca-Cola brand, Fanta with another name.

'Me too,' Punch echoed; at two, he was easily influenced.

'Teapot.' I thought that would confuse him, though he was definitely the biggest fusspot in the group.

'I want Miranda,' Punch reasserted, after blinking at me, open mouthed, for a few seconds.

'Be nice to me or I won't buy you any more drinks,' I threatened. I knew every one of those rascals had been taught to say: 'please'.

'Miranda,' Ollie declared swinging his foot into my leg.

'Don't kick me, please,' I said firmly.

I remembered my manners if they did not; despite being taught to be polite at all times.

'I will.'

'Okay, don't bite me then.'

'I will.'

'Right that's it; I'm going to drink your drink.'

I had been loose head prop forward at prep school; at around Aubrey's age, give or take a year, at eight, I was grinding my jaw into the opposite team's hooker's head. At the Oratory I was lock forward; these kids did not know with whom they were messing, and no one had warned them.

'No, no, I'm sorry.' he begged, pleaded; I thought he was going to cry. I handed back his drink, begrudgingly; it looked good. I had dealt with Ollie; I could turn my attention to Punch.

'Do you want your dummy, Punch?'

'Yus, pliz,'

'Ollie, you behave yourself you little rug rat.'

'You're a rug rat,' Ollie complained.

'We're going to have lunch in a minute on the dable,' Punch decided. He was not yet able to differentiate between meals like most very small children.

'We are not having lunch on the table it's only ten thirty,' I told Punch in no uncertain terms, I hated to ruin his day, but I knew he had just eaten.

'Who's got me a drink?' Hattie was standing at my side; the children all looked as if they had been behaving immaculately.

'What would you like?' I asked.

'A Stoney please.' Hattie looked like she could do with something stronger.

'A Sparletta, Stoney, Tangawizi, please?' I asked the waiter who had seen Hattie coming and had come to greet her as he always did. He smiled at us and we returned his genuine warm smile.

'A Stoney,' he confirmed before disappearing as unobtrusively as before.

'Carrot-Top, look,' Punch was pointing at his drink pleased as Punch. The brown Stoney bottle arrived. Punch was intrigued by the different colours. The labelling interested the others; the bottles were 300ml. There was no label, just printing on to the bottle, in white writing and a yellow scroll above saying, Stoney.

'I'm chilly,' Miranda rubbed her arms.

'Right, we'll call you Jilly from now on.'

'I mean that I'm cold.'

'Well you won't want to go into the cold water at the pool.'

'It's sunny there.'

'Are you coming, Hattie?' I asked.

'I have to shop,' she replied.

'So, I'm babysitting, again.'

'I feel sick,' said Matilda.

'You'll be all right at the pool,' I assured her.

It was difficult to leave the bar and Ristorante La Fenice at the Speke Hotel and cross Nile Avenue to the gardens of the Sheraton; it was like leaving home for the first time.

I suspected there would be tears, theirs or mine. We had got used to the place; we knew all the prices; the club sandwiches were

4,500 shillings; a beer was 2,000 shillings; tea was 1,800 shillings, as were soft drinks; it was very much more expensive than the Speke and Reste Corner, but we were paying for the pool and the rarefied atmosphere. There was literally no one there at any time we were, ever. It was extraordinary. It was our pool exclusively. I suspected the children frightened away any interlopers or maybe residents were exploring elsewhere.

I much preferred the Speke and its more realistic prices; it felt as if you were getting value for money there. We were not all aid workers on huge salaries used to American inflated prices. We were tourists, we expected to pay above the going rate; that is the duty of the adventurer, explorer and traveller but there was a limit to which you feel a bit sullied by the cheek of the place charging you an inflated and outrageous price just because they can, regardless of what is fair.

After all, at the Speke, a full English breakfast – which was huge – came in at 7,500 shillings. They even did pizza, which I never tried, but looked good on people's plates. To give you some idea of the value, the Crane Bank changed US$200 travellers cheques I had left over from an earlier trip to New York at a rate of 1,215 which gave me 243,000 shillings: a lot of beer, breakfasts and cigarettes.

When I changed $100 cash, I got a rate of 1,250 and 121,000 shillings. The Sheraton Kampala was a lovely hotel and we paid 30,000 for five us of us to use the pool, roughly four pounds, but lunch cost me 106,800 Uganda Shillings which was about ninety pounds, European pricing. I preferred the friendlier prices at the Speke, but the children could have precisely what they wanted, and fish fingers travel a long way from Iceland. I was clearly paying their transport costs; I think they must have driven there in their fish-finger Ford Focuses.

The Sheraton, with children, was a breeze; I allowed them to go up to the bar to get drinks and reminded them that they could order from the poolside menu. Therefore, I could relax in the sunshine, trying not to get burnt. Of course, I had to keep a weather eye out for Ollie and Punch, but the older children just splashed about, swam and played pool games. I had to inhibit their running in case any of them slipped but once the ground rules were established, they were fine. Fortunately, they were good enough to see the sense in the no running rule and instead practised a strange hybrid action, half-running, half-walking; a high-speed shuffling, like a Geisha girl late for a tea ceremony.

On our return to the Speke we found Duncan reading and smoking with a bottle of beer and some boiled sweets on the table in front of him.

'Can we go and watch TV, upstairs?' Matilda asked Duncan.

'No, g-pap and granny want to have a rest from everyone,' Duncan replied.

'Granny Finn wants a rest too. Punch and Ollie are exhausting!'

My comment brought broad grins filled with pride from the two youngest children.

'Can I have a sweet?' Matilda asked Duncan.

'No,' he answered. He looked and sounded bored by the question.

'Please,' she pleaded.

'Your lips are moving but I can't hear you.'

'But I'm hungry,' Matilda complained.

'Me too,' Aubrey joined in, 'I haven't eaten for days.'

'You both look healthy and tubby, to me,' Duncan replied.

'Have you read the paper today?' I asked.

'There was an interesting article about a man wanted by the police. Anyone with information should report not to police station, but Fang, Fang restaurant,' Duncan announced. He clearly thought this highly amusing, I could tell by his small smile.

'Unbelievable, we should get Lucy to marry someone who owns a chain of Fang, Fang restaurants, she'd be made,' I replied.

The Major came down to have a cup of tea. He looked tired but he also seemed as relaxed as ever, despite the constant demands to hold court for old friends and to speak to journalists. We exchanged pleasantries and talked about the latest local news while waiting for the waiter. When the waiter arrived and he was giving his order, Hattie returned from the market and she ordered a Coke and sat down to join us.

'Interesting things there?' the Major asked.

'Lots of lovely things,' Hattie was not prepared to elucidate.

'It's Tuesday, are you going to any night clubs, Mike?' Duncan asked.

'It's Granny Finn,' Matilda corrected him. 'You invented the name. You should stick to it!'

Matilda had annoying habit of being logical – most unattractive in one so young.

'No, Granny Finn is not going to those noisy dipsos,' I deliberately emphasised the malapropism, not wishing to be misunderstood.

'Discos,' Matilda corrected me, as I knew she would.

'They're full of dipsomaniacs,' I replied.

'What is that?' Matilda asked.

'Who are they?' Duncan corrected her.

'What are they?' she was persistent.

'What are they?' I asked

'Who, not, what, to whom are you referring?' Duncan insisted, he was rather good with grammar and I was the English teacher.

'To whom are you referring?' Matilda shot Duncan an icy look.

'All in good time, Matilda,' I was not to be drawn.

'You're all talk and no action, encouraging us to go to Ethiopian bars and local nightclubs. Then when we're keen you suddenly don't like the idea,' Duncan rather cruelly observed.

'You ask today? I'm too tired,' I replied, feigning a swoon. I, too, could do high drama.

Pip arrived and broke up our conversation, thankfully. Duncan was putting me on the spot, and I wasn't sure whether I liked it.

'Good morning, strong black coffee, please,' he said when the waiter delivered the drinks for the Major and Hattie.

Did you sort out the trip?' Duncan asked.

'I certainly did,' Pip replied, looking justifiably pleased with himself. Getting anything done was a trial. 'The Safari is going to cost about 320,000 shillings each.'

We talked some more about the details and afterwards I went to the bank to change £500.00 sterling. Unbeknownst to me, some of the others decided to join me; we queued at the bank having established that Barclays were giving the most competitive rate for cash that day. I was chatting to the teller as she processed my money exchange and I heard a noise behind me. Without my knowing, Lucy had also arrived at the bank.

'Hurry up,' Lucy hissed behind me.

The teller told me that she wanted to start a union and organise the bank work force as 'black staff' were not allowed to move from branch to branch and were forced to stay put while 'white staff' were allowed to move more freely.

She had managed to get two people to join her union, so far.

'The management sacked two people for trying to start a union, they were looked upon as troublemakers, so we have to be careful,' she whispered. I found this both disturbing and fascinating.

'Hurry up,' Lucy hissed, again, 'we haven't got all day.'

I thought this most unfair and was tempted to say so.

During our conversation, the lady teller had worked quickly and confidently, much more efficiently than anyone in any bank I have been to visit throughout the world. It was not her fault that it was a busy day at the Bureau du Change. I was sympathetic to her plight, it seemed unfair to treat staff differently; I encouraged her while counselling caution.

'Thank you for all your help,' I exclaimed loudly, smiled at her, and pointedly turned around to look at Lucy with a suitably withering look, or so I hoped, but she just walked around me in high dudgeon.

'Enjoy your stay,' said my newfound friend whom I hope was able to establish equality for all staff at the bank.

Lucy smiled sweetly again at me when she was processed as swiftly as me but at that stage, I did not feel like smiling back.

I went to the post office to buy some stamps and postcards for two people I had forgotten to write to so far. The man at the counter looked upset when I proffered a 2,000-shilling note. He proceeded to give me my 1,000-shilling change in grubby, torn fifty-shillings notes. I waited patiently as he slowly counted out the twenty notes. They were in such a delicate state that I thought they were artefacts from the 12th century.

A two-minute transaction was slowly becoming a fifteen-minute ordeal and the post office was not the coolest place in town at midday. I longed for a beer, but I needed the change to pay for it. At least I could dump most of the change at the bar or I could keep it all for dishing out to beggars as this was the expected rate.

I thought it seemed a bit mean, but I guess twenty people giving fifty shillings would get the poor guy a third of the way to a beer. Then I remembered there were local prices for everything, and five hundred shillings could buy a decent meal at local rates, whereas tourists might only get an apple for that price.

For that reason, we always went shopping with one of the drivers and that allowed us to get an idea of the different rates that we were charged. Locals got the best rate, locals with a foreigner got a reduced rate and a kick-back from the stalls and Europeans on their own would get ripped off good and proper. It's very much the same the world over. Try getting service in a restaurant in Rome full of Italians or a French restaurant in London full of Parisians. People, the world over, rip off visitors to their countries.

If it's not the taxi driver, then it's the hot dog seller or ice cream man; if it is not higher prices for the same goods, it's ignoring people who are not from your set and giving priority to countrymen over the foreigners.

It's tough if you're the majority of honest drivers and purveyors of food because the one guy who takes advantage spoils it for the rest, a short-term gain for him a long-term loss for all because, human nature being what it is, tales of woe make for better recounts than those in a positive light. If countries want tourists, they have to be fair to their visitors. Outside the markets and with the exception of one taxi driver who took us around the block four times, we were treated more fairly in Uganda than anywhere else I had been, with the exception of South China.

Chapter 15

The Safari

Two clean, shiny minibuses arrived outside the Speke Hotel at eleven o'clock: a Toyota in metallic brown and a Mitsubishi in beige, which the brochure would probably describe as Sahara sandstone. We had all breakfasted – Anthony, Duncan, Pip and I at the Reste Corner, Lucy, Anna and their children at their respective houses. Hattie had a room at the hotel.

The Major and his wife were sitting with us in order to see us off. They had been to Murchinson Falls years before and needed time to rest after their hectic schedule. The family had many friends in Uganda whom they wanted to see, and reporters were keen to get interviews resulting in a constant stream of visitors from ten until ten each day.

The trip to the island was meant to have been a respite, but it merely replaced mental exhaustion with physical exhaustion. I had been excited about the trip but hanging around drinking coffee had dampened my enthusiasm.

We were meant to leave at 9 am and it was a five-hour trip. My heart sank at the news that one of the minibuses would be collecting Anna from Aka Boa Road, a half-hour round trip. Lucy had been dropped at nine with her baggage – that is the bags and her children – but Anna's family could not manage so many people in the transport they had.

To fill the time, we helped the drivers to load the suitcases into the vans. To my surprise, Anna arrived just as we finished with her children and luggage; we would be off only two hours late, after all. It was a huge relief. The vans were to travel in convoy.

The children, and as many adults as we could fit in on top, were crammed into the newer Toyota that boasted four-wheel drive and air conditioning. It was a brown monster with leather reclining seats. The mothers and children were allocated the more luxurious vehicle, naturally.

Our one had coarse brown cloth seats and windows that slid open.

Our van was air-conditioned by opening the windows, but the seats moved back a little. They all faced forward, the ones in the other van rotated. Only two hours late, we set off for the lodge at the falls. I had a good view of the back of our driver's head. His name was Mohammed and he drove us smoothly and along a very good road out of Kampala. The traffic was heavy, but I was from London and had seen worse.

Our late departure meant we had missed the brunt of the rush-hour, but people were still struggling to work, queuing for the minibus taxis or walking along the dusty pavements.

I was always impressed by how clean and smart everyone's clothes were; European cities are full of people with torn jeans and some of the most appalling mismatched clothing you have ever seen. In Kampala, they all looked super smart, no Euro-grunge, thank goodness.

We were heading for Paraa via the town of Masindi, which was meant to be a five-hour drive, or three hundred kilometres. Along the way to Masindi was the Ziwa Rhino Sanctuary – home to the only wild rhinos in Uganda; we were not stopping there though. If we were going to see wild animals, it was going to be on safari.

After a few hours, we stopped at *The Masindi Hotel* to refuel. The journey had been 220 kilometres and was meant to take three hours but traffic in Kampala and on the road had slowed our speed and added an extra two hours to our journey time.

Luckily, the petrol station was located next to the hotel, so we seized our chance to stretch our legs while the two buses refuelled.

Our driver, Mohammed, refused coffee, but we needed something to slake our thirst. The coffee was fresh, the best that I had tried in Uganda and the hotel looked like a colonial mansion which it probably had been. I would have liked to have stayed there, if I could.

Despite the fact that it looked like it had been deserted, a hotel out of season, the people there could not have been more helpful. There was hardly any wait before someone came to see us, seated as we were on the terrace in the sunshine, and they looked after us well, refilling our cups without being asked.

We sat out on the terrace; the orange tiles had been dusted with sand blown in from the dry roadside.

The chairs and tables were metal with brightly coloured plastic banding for the seats, which we had dusted down before sitting on and the coffee was most delicious and welcome.

Lucy noted that every time we asked the drivers when we would be stopping, he would repeat the mantra, three-quarters of an hour. We were never given a straight answer, just the one – it was suspected – that we wanted to hear. If the fuel hadn't been so low, we would have carried on and the drivers did not seem sympathetic to stopping for coffee breaks or chances to use the loo.

They were on a mission to deliver us to the lodge before nightfall and they would not fail.

I was glad to have the break as I had tried to sleep, but I was too uncomfortable despite the reclining seats. Finishing our coffee and going to the bathroom gave us a half-hour respite and a chance to stretch out our legs. It was pleasant to sit in the sun and feel its warmth until Pip pointed out that we were only a quarter of the way to our destination. He had all the information; we had been told random figures by our driver/

The journey was meant to take five hours and instead it took eight. It might have taken longer but the five o'clock Parra ferry was late departing and we managed to get on it just in time. It was lucky there was space as the next ferry was at seven o'clock.

The ferryman was persuaded to wait while we were loaded much to the bemusement and I'm sure frustration of the Europeans with their Land Rover Discoveries and Range Rovers who had perhaps underestimated the length of time it takes to drive such vast distances. We had been equally innocent.

As we neared the hotel, we saw a boat straight out of *The African Queen*. It was a low shallow-bottomed boat made of steel, painted green. It was a double-decker steam ship that had a flat roof, on which a floor had been installed, railings added and benches, made of wooden slats attached for an uninterrupted view of the scenery.

Like the old trams that you see at transport museums, the backs of the seats could be pushed forward and the seats made to face the opposite direction. Downstairs was a similar arrangement, but the bench backs were fixed and curved backwards like Victorian park benches. There was beer available, kept in a chiller cabinet by the captain's cabin and a loo, too – luxury.

We had to cross our legs on the minibus. I regretted having the coffee at our pit stop.

Pip asked the driver to pull up by the boat, which was filling rapidly, and about to depart. He established that the next tour was at sunset and it was decided the children would benefit from the coolness of being close to the water, so we asked the drivers to wait for us while we took advantage of boarding the current sailing.

They did not mind a bit.

There were only three tours a day, a morning sailing at about ten, a two-thirty trip and this sunset voyage. Not only could we tick off another experience from our agenda but also, we could start our safari early, and keep the children occupied until it was time for their supper.

Sommerly had informed us at the ferry that she had never been on a boat before and had vowed that she never would because she could not swim, but having taken a ferry already that day, she gamely agreed to come along. We boarded last and sat downstairs, the roof offering us shade from the heat.

The fittings of the boat were all white-painted metal and the deck was a dark stained wood. Although the boat was made in 1970 in Cowes on the Isle of Wight, it seemed as if it had been built to a Victorian design.

You could imagine boats like these taking day-trippers along the Thames in Edwardian times from Boulter's Lock to Henley. It was very much shades of *Three Men in a Boat* on a sultry summer's day.

The murky grey-green waters weren't anything like the Thames, though and the wildlife that teamed in its depths was a good deal more frightening. I have never seen so many crocodiles and hippos; hundreds of them surrounded us.

The river was wide and wild, the size of an estuary. Mud banks on either side sprouted tall grass or reeds. If you looked carefully you could see crocodiles basking in the sun and the heads of the poor indigenous hippopotamuses lying next to them.

Obviously, the skull of the hippo makes poor fare. As we motored towards the falls a crocodile with a hippo's flank in its mouth slithered off the bank and under the water. The crocodile likes to wedge its meat under a rock below the surface and this tenderises the meat.

We were travelling over one of the largest larders in the world. The cool waters provided a fridge for the crocodile, or a pantry, should the hippos prove to be too difficult to catch. It must have been disconcerting for the hippos to know they were swimming over parts of their families' carcasses, so it was no wonder that they kept a low profile. They mainly grouped together – safety in numbers – their snouts and Mickey Mouse ears protruding from the water.

They were used to the boat and it was difficult not to jump up and point to the well-fed crocodiles on the beach behind and say 'he's behind you' in a loud pantomime voice. Alas, they would not understand. It only occurred to me afterwards that we were in as much peril as the hippos; a steel-hulled boat that sprung a leak would provide a smorgasbord for the crocodiles.

As the round trip was three hours, I bought us all a drink. Sommerly and the children had lemon Fanta and the rest of us had beer.

They were well organised. A steel rectangular cabinet, painted green of course, was filled with ice, and drinks were stashed between the cubes. All our drinks were beautifully chilled. The cabinet would have housed ropes or anchors, originally, and I suppose the need for so many of them was deemed surplus to requirements on such a calm river.

Truthfully, there was no tide to speak of and the ropes for mooring did not need to be protected from the elements. An anchor was superfluous with the engine providing a brake or force against the current when it was needed. I am sure they had several small anchors; they were just not in this particular cabinet.

There was so much to see; shoebill storks, cruising crocodiles, hippos and antelope coming down to drink by the water.

'Some friends of mine were in a game park in Tanzania,' Lucy announced. 'They went to swim in the local river and the game wardens said it was safe. Three girls went down to the pool and only two came back. A crocodile took one of them and all the others could do was to sit and watch. The crocodile was so quick that they didn't have time to do anything.'

'That's horrible,' I said.

'You could have told us after the trip,' Pip added, chuckling.

'Punch, be careful of your dummy,' Anna warned the little boy as he hung his comforter over the side.

'I've lost my dummy,' Punch announced seconds later.

In no time at all we could see the rock outcrop that denoted the base of Murchinson Falls. We could hear the rush of the water well before we could see the falls clearly.

It was striking to have sailed along the river basin, seen flat land for miles around and then suddenly we were faced by this huge escarpment. The bush beside the river had looked sparse and parched; at the waterfall it looked as lush as the vegetation on Ssese Island.

We could see the steep rise of the rock to our port bow and hear the cascading water, then we rounded a bend in the river, and we were in another world.

In front of us was a vast pool and above us the falls. The water around us was swirling wildly and I thought we were going to be sucked into the waterfall itself.

In front of us was a rock out crop that rose out of the river; a tree fought for its existence on the side, clinging precariously to the slope. It was all very much like a safari; it was wonderful to see so much wilderness surrounding us.

The crew warned us that we were going to go alongside the island and asked us all to move to the back of the boat. Everyone did as they were told, having complete faith in the crew. Beside the island was a smaller piece of rock that rose like the summit of Kilimanjaro itself, the tip of an iceberg.

The crew drove the boat at the gap between the two rocky islands and we slid on to rocks beaching the bow of the boat on the rocks themselves.

People were encouraged to move forward and the boat became wedged in its anchorage.

Securely made fast by the weight of everyone moving to the bow, we became beached on the rock and it was time for a photo opportunity.

Several people climbed out and on to the rock, their telephoto lenses making it an awkward scramble on to the island.

Mostly, timid people took photographs from the safety of the sheltered deck; a few went upstairs to the sun deck for their photographs.

We were a good one hundred yards from the falls itself, but we could still feel the spray and the sound of water had become a roar. The thud of the diesel engines ticking over had become drowned out and for one worrying moment, I thought the engine had been cut.

Torrents of water fell from a hundred feet above, looking clear and clean; the mud disturbed in the plunge pool swirled around us, giving the water a beige tint. I asked who was going to plant a flag for the Bruton family and despite the fact that there were no volunteers forthcoming, discretion dictated that I myself should not hog the limelight either, so I stayed put, not setting foot on the rock, which I later regretted.

The brave photographers clambered back on board and we all moved to the back of the boat again when the boat seemed to drift off the rock. On the way back we saw more shoebill storks and decided that they were big black ugly birds. We were on the lookout for those brave little birds that floss the crocodile's teeth, but the crocodiles were keeping their mouths firmly closed and that was fine by us.

The drivers were waiting by the van, smoking and they started up their engines before we had fully disembarked. The air conditioning in the four-wheel drive was on for the children; our van was like a furnace, but we managed to get a breeze going through once we were moving by sliding open every window possible to flush out the heat retained by the van, which had been sitting out in the sun for three hours.

It was a thoughtful gesture to have the fans on in the vans, but our fan merely stirred the hot air around the cabin. Fortunately, the hotel was a five-minute drive away and the children were dispatched to look at the pool while we helped the drivers with the luggage and waited for the sunset, which we had been promised would be spectacular,

A friendly girl, Florence, greeted us in the lobby. She was dressed in a beige safari suit, wearing a two-pocket beige cotton shirt and a beige knee-length skirt and she was beautiful, too.

We put our bags down at reception, checked in and then Florence offered us a glass of chilled guava juice, which stood on a table by the staircase. Everyone gratefully took the drinks offered.

'This is my sister from church,' Sommerly said smiling at her friend.

It was quite a coincidence, Sommerly meeting an old friend on safari.

We drank our juice and chatted before deciding to go upstairs and unpack and watch the sunset that we had been promised would amaze us, over a drink on the veranda. The rooms upstairs were comfortable and spacious.

I was to share a twin room with Anthony and eyed the shower with longing as we both moved into the room. White towels were stacked on stainless steel shelves and there was a bath, which I knew I would have to wallow in before supper. Our beds were enormous – well, compared to our experience thus far they were. They looked comfortable and in between a standard single and double; it looked like they could accommodate my six-foot-two and a half frame with ease.

At the foot of our beds were slatted leather-covered stools for our suitcases, cable television in the corner on a chest of drawers and two chairs. Each bed had a mosquito net over it, hanging from the ceiling and looking like a medieval tent of muslin. In the centre of the ceiling was a brown fan with drawstring speed controls; pull once on the cord for slow, twice for fast and thrice for tornado. Through the mosquito nets we could see brown furry blankets folded neatly at the foot of the bed, which was covered in pristine white starched sheets. The walls were white making the room seems both cool and clean.

There was time for a quick shower before our swim, so I took the opportunity. The pool was inviting and the pool bar in the centre was even more tempting. I lay in the sun to dry off and then, when I was feeling hot. I eased into the cool water and swam to the submerged barstool to order a beer. This was luxury and I liked it and of all my experiences in Uganda this was the most decadent except Innocent's cooking.

I was living in the style to which I would like to become accustomed. The barman informed anyone who listened that the hippos would come up from the river and have a swim in the pool at night.

No one believed him, but who was to say that this was not the case as the steps were terraced and one could imagine such an event. We ate some of the best food I have ever had that night and Lucy said how good Sommerly was over dinner.

'She eats with the children and makes sure that they finish most of their food – it's bliss,' Lucy said.

She told us that she used that time to have a gin and a well-earned cigarette.

'It's bloody noisy,' Duncan complained, just for a change.

There was a cacophony of sounds from various wildlife in the darkness beyond the veranda where we ate our supper.

'That's the jungle for you,' I added helpfully.

'The food is fantastic here,' Anthony commented. He worked in the hotel business, so he was entitled to be food critic, although I had seen some of the meals he had eaten.

'Johnson said if you're tired of food you're tired of life,' Duncan misquoted.

'Correction, London,' Pip was still in competitive mood.

'Who was the French philosopher of food?' Lucy asked

'Descartes?' I suggested.

'Eat to live…' Duncan helped me out.

'Or live to eat,' Lucy interrupted him.

'Richelieu? He had a good appetite for power,' Pip joked.

'No, it sounds like a cheese,' Lucy was sure.

'*Chèvre? Brie? Camembert?*' Duncan was not being helpful by naming every cheese that he knew, but that was his nature.

'*Gevrey Chambertin*,' Lucy guessed widely.

'That's a Burgundy.' I knew that much after a year in the London wine trade.

'Red or white?' Duncan asked.

'Often white,' Pip guessed.

'Actually, it's a rather nice red,' I raised my glass to Duncan.

We were enjoying a delicious South African Pinotage, distant cousin of the main grape of Burgundy, Pinot Noir.

'I give up!' Lucy wailed.

'What's wrong?' Duncan asked.

'It was a simple question,' Lucy replied.

'Was it?' Duncan arched his eyebrow.

'Wasn't it?' Lucy appealed to us all.

'Obviously not,' Duncan decided as he took a slug of wine and fiddled with his fork.

It was almost time for his next nicotine boost; Duncan was fuelled by little food and cigarettes.

'It was the French philosopher of gastronomy, Brillat-Savarin, the man who called Swiss wines "fresh and clear as a mountain stream" I believe,' announced Pip. It was good of him to finally put Lucy out of her misery.

'Thank you,' Lucy sighed, her relief was obvious.

'Who was he?' I knew Sade and Sartre but there was no Savarin in the 's' section of my dictionary of famous French people.

'Brillat-Savarin wrote a tome on the philosophy of eating,' Pip explained; he could be relied on to clear the picture for most people.

'The journey here was hellish,' Anna added, in the hope of steering the conversation on to other topics, it sounded like she was as bored as we were with the conversation. French food philosophy was just not worth the effort.

'The Yellow Brick Road,' Duncan sighed, 'the one we had to follow.'

He seemed to be obsessed with *The Wizard of Oz*.

'We were told that the journey would be more or less an hour from where we stopped for coffee,' Lucy complained, she was already fed up with the misinformation we had received.

'Never tell the truth,' Duncan advised.

His comments showed a deep philosophical understanding of the world, but no one was sure whether this was a general comment or not, whether it referred solely and specifically to Africa, and our time there, or to life in general.

'It hurts!' I said.

I was trying to be as deep as Duncan was being but even as I spoke, I realised that my audience weren't interested in philosophical or metaphysical arguments.

'From the hotel to ferry, we were told it would take an hour,' Anthony interjected, wanting to take the pressure off me, and my totally crass remark.

He smiled then drank some wine; he knew the score.

'Three hours later, we weren't even in the game park,' Pip humbly acknowledged; he had known all along how long the trip might take and had probably computed that it would take another hour at least to reach the ferry, but he had kept quiet.

'Our sump was busted, we were lucky to get here at all,' Lucy explained. She always saw the bright side and there was always some worse-case scenario.

'What did you do?' I asked, hoping we would be able to smoke soon, not for myself but for Duncan's sake, he was getting very twitchy.

'We gave him a handkerchief,' Lucy answered, looking at me as though this was the only viable solution.

'Our mother's hanky,' Anthony said. He knew, so why didn't I?

There was not the exchange of information that I had imagined.

'I knew it would come in useful,' Lucy said, smiling.

It was good thinking, I would have thrown in the towel, but she just gave her handkerchief to the driver expecting him to make the repairs.

'Sommerly knew someone here from the Pentecostal church,' Pip said. He had left them to it in the lobby, allowing them to catch up while he organised the rest of us.

'It's a small world,' Duncan mused; his philosophy knew no bounds but equally his sarcasm knew no limits, unfortunately.

'Yes, but meeting a friend at the Murchinson Falls Savora Park Lodge is a bit bizarre,' Pip exclaimed.

He was right again, a point not lost on Duncan.

'I was just thankful to get here,' Duncan sighed, knowing that the remark would sting Pip as he had organised the trip.

Duncan could be as effective as I could at ending conversation; he became particularly prickly without his cigarettes.

'The Toyota was great, so comfortable,' Anna remarked.

'The Mitsubushi van had a temperature gauge, it was 33 degrees inside and 35 degrees outside,' I had been thankful for the breeze but jealous of the air conditioning in the other bus.

Chapter 16

The Game Drive

The next morning there was some confusion as to where we should all be meeting. There was a compound for staff at the bottom of the hill and Sommerly had not yet been seen. We brought the larger bags downstairs while the children had a last swim and showered. Pip oversaw the loading; Anthony and I only had one small bag each.

The majority of items belonged to the children, Anna, Duncan, Lucy and Pip, and they were loaded into the air-conditioned van. They were going on a longer safari than us, so they deserved more comfort. Thankfully, in the cooler morning air, our bus was comfortable to sit in at first.

Anthony and I smoked while we waited. Pip introduced us to our guide, Charles, who wore green fatigues and beige wellingtons; he didn't smoke but seemed content to chat to Mohammed as he puffed away on his cigarette.

'Where's Sommerly?' Pip asked after we had loaded our luggage. The plan was to take a game drive, pay the bill at midday and separate. Anthony and I would take one van and go to the airfield to catch our flight to Kampala and the others would go on to a tented camp for another night. They would split into the two buses for the drive back to the Speke.

'She is waiting for us at the compound,' Mohammed informed us as he smiled a sly smile; he knew what was going on and he was not about to tell us. He enjoyed his games.

'We told her to meet us here,' Pip explained – he showed remarkable restraint.

Mohammed had obviously told her to stay put and she had not been confident enough to explain that she had been asked to meet at the lodge.

'In Africa the ladies are always slow,' Mohammed announced helpfully, clearly pleased to be causing mischief; he obviously wanted to make the dull trip more exciting.

'We were waiting for her,' Pip added; he knew that it was useless to try and point out to Mohammed that he should have brought her up with him in the van. Mohammed knew that was the case, but he had not been directly asked.

'She is waiting for us,' he said flatly.

For Mohammed that was good enough; we were tourists and he was in charge of the transport and he wanted us to know it. We had believed him when he had exaggerated the length of time that it would take us to get ready.

'You know, but you did not tell us,' I said.

Mohammed laughed at this.

'You're not being very helpful,' Duncan noted.

'Sommerly was trying to get here and you left her behind,' Pip added accusingly.

'Yes,' he replied; it was simple as far as Mohammed was concerned.

'You just want one job that you can do well, don't you?' Pip asked

'Yes,' he affirmed, looking innocent but still smiling; Mohammed's smile was becoming irksome.

'Drive, we'll organise the rest, okay,' Pip insisted; he was now ready for his first cigar of the day. He deserved it for remaining so cool.

It was decided that as I had checked out already, I would go and collect Sommerly with Mohammed and return to the lodge. I left the three of them standing by the other bus, smoking and chatting to Charles. The road down to the servant's compound was curved and steep.

It was mean of Mohammed to have driven off without Sommerly and to expect her to walk up through the orange crottled clay made wet by the rain.

He drove down in first gear, the tyres skidding on the damp mud; it had rained overnight but I had not been aware of it until then, so deep was my sleep. Fenced in by a tall picket fence, there were about six huts with a thatch roof on each.

Mohammed knew exactly where Sommerly was and I waited by the gates in the van, smoking a cigarette through the open window.

By the time I'd finished my cigarette five minutes later, Sommerly was through the gate. I noticed she was struggling with her bag and Mohammed was walking ahead, threading the fingers of one hand through worry beads.

I rushed to help her, and he opened the side door for her, which was his concession at being gallant. He slammed the door after her and came around to the driver's side; he seemed 'put-out' that he should fetch her. We drove cautiously up the hill, the van sliding sideways when the tyres could not get a proper grip.

As we approached the lodge, the children came down the steps with their overnight bags escorted by Anna and Lucy. Pip allocated vehicles; Lucy, Anthony, Aubrey, Emily, Punch, Sommerly and I in one van and the others in the air-conditioned four-wheel drive. I always seemed to be in the boiling blue van loaned by CBS in Kampala or the white Toyota with its comparatively less effective fan system.

We had Charles with us; he carried an AK-47, or Kalashnikov assault rifle, yet he looked like he should still be at school.

He smiled broadly to reveal the most perfect teeth I have ever seen outside a dentist's office. He wore a brown beret at a jaunty angle and a green camouflage combat jacket and trousers, belted at the waist. He looked like a soldier but for the bizarre beige wellington boots that he wore.

If he had been born in Rwanda, he'd be a front-line soldier. As it was, we hoped that his AK-47 would frighten off poachers or rebel units that were rumoured to be around the area at that time. I only hoped that he knew how to use the gun properly. If the rebels had similar armaments, we would be a pretty soft target for them.

Charles hopped into the back and sat by the door next to the children who seemed unperturbed by our armed escort – except Punch who stared open mouthed. He loved to see real guns, and this was the closest he had been to one.

As we drove off in our respective vehicles I sat in the front, a pack of Prince in my top pocket ready for any eventuality. The cigar lighter popped out of the dashboard and fell to the floor as we went over a rut in the road. I picked it up and put it into the ashtray under radio.

Mohammed tried to put it back into its allotted space as he steered the van down the hill; it was necessary for him to change gear and I wasn't sure how he would manage it, so I took it from his tenuous grasp.

'I'll do it,' I said taking it off him.

I put the lighter back in its socket knowing it would vibrate out again on our tour. He concentrated on his driving and I tapped him on the shoulder when he was on the straight.

'Okay?' I asked, smiling.

'Thank you,' he said, smiling back.

'Pleasure,' I responded. I knew we would get along.

'The road's pretty bumpy,' Lucy remarked; she wore a sun hat as if she was off to Henley for the afternoon or taking tea on the lawn in summer, an English rose in the African *veld*.

'The rain washes it away,' Charles remarked confidently.

'That's erosion,' I told Aubrey.

'I know, I'm not thick you know,' came his sulky reply.

'Ask Charles how many shells are in his gun?' I said trying to appease him.

'You ask him.'

'Thirty in each magazine,' said Charles.

He wore a canvas-webbing belt with his extra magazine and radio, so he had to sit forward on his seat legs open, holding the rifle vertically between his two hands, left hand clasping the metal barrel, right hand clutching the wooden grip. From his wellingtons upward he looked as if he was off to war, but the boots spoiled the effect; beige was not a bellicose colour, certainly not the wishy-washy shade of Charles's boots, almost a cream colour.

'I feel safe,' Lucy announced apropos nothing, and she smiled sweetly. I was not sure whether she was being ironic or not, but Charles smiled back warmly.

He clutched the rifle between his two hands throughout our trip. Charles looked like an American paratrooper in a Dakota about to make his first real parachute jump. However, he did seem at ease with us and with the gun, so much so that we almost forgot it was there.

'You needn't worry, there are UPDF everywhere,' Charles assured her further. 'We are safe.'

'Just like the crocodiles in Tanzania,' Lucy said, for my benefit. I think that she was trying to frighten me, or at least help me to empathise with her; Tanzania was where the three people she knew went down to have a swim in the water, which was 'safe' and only two came back. They had been told there were no crocodiles in the water there.

'The government's troops are everywhere, so it's safe,' Charles repeated reassuringly as if Lucy didn't understand what he was saying.

In truth none of us knew what UPDF stood for and it could have been a warning about the rebels for all we knew. UPDF, actually, stands for Uganda People's Defence Force.

'Have you used the gun?' Lucy asked. I think she meant ever but Charles missed the irony in her voice, and she was smiling her most charming smile.

'I still have thirty rounds in,' Charles announced proudly. That should take out a few of the endangered species in the reserve, but could we rely on him to hit anyone who might have it in for us.

The ominous black clouds that had been hanging over the lodge and reserve suddenly opened up and we could see large dollops of rain splattering the dust track.

'One day to see the sights and it rains,' Anthony announced smiling; he appreciated the irony of the situation.

'Stay in the van, it's wet,' Charles told us as if we were going to hurl ourselves out of the moving vehicle – he really didn't trust us.

'Tsetse fly,' Aubrey said when he saw a fly that had flown in.

'Close the windows,' Lucy suggested calmly.

'It doesn't carry disease,' Charles assured us.

'Just sleeping sickness,' Anthony retorted.

'Not tsetse, Sessy fly, it just bites,' Charles explained, laughing; he obviously found the confusion amusing.

'Like a horse fly?' Anthony asked.

'Horse fly, don't they kick?' Aubrey asked askance.

We were not sure if he meant it or he was trying to be funny, but I remembered the painful bite from horse flies at my prep school poolside. The bites were never very amusing unless they happened to someone else who was sitting on the side of the pool waiting for the picnic lunch to digest before plunging in.

'No, they bite like a horse,' Anthony corrected him.

'That makes it much clearer; a fly that bites like a horse, how thick is that?' Aubrey complained.

He was of sound logical mind but having been bitten by a horse and a horse fly, I could vouch for their being little difference, except for the area covered, obviously.

'Ever been bitten by a horse?' Anthony asked Aubrey.

'No,' Aubrey answered amazed; he could hardly believe that a horse would bite anyone, and he jiggled his head and let his mouth drop as though he thought Anthony was completely mad.

'It feels like this,' Anthony assured him as he pinched Aubrey's arm hard, which made him squeal. Aubrey was about to punch or kick Anthony back but a ruthless stare from behind Anthony's sunglasses made him realise that discretion was the better part of valour.

'Silly,' Aubrey responded lazily. He could be wound up as effectively with words as he could with blows and Anthony smiled cruelly to prove the effect of such an epitaph.

'There's no danger of sleeping sickness here,' Charles assured us; he sounded authoritarian, the only way he could handle the battle between Anthony and Aubrey.

'I've been sleepy all my life,' I added laconically.

'Lazy,' Lucy corrected me.

Her smile was so sweet it made the remark more painful than it strictly needed to be, I had been after all trying to diffuse a potential family feud. If Ollie had been there, he might well have bitten Anthony's ankles, which might have been equally effective at deflecting attention from the dispute.

'Low blood pressure,' I defended myself.

'Not heart disease, then,' Lucy replied acidly.

She seemed disappointed.

The bond between us grew, I knew that the ruder she became, the closer we became: 'It was all just a game', or so I told myself.

'Hello, Joshua,' a voice crackled from Charles's walkie-talkie. Charles unclipped his radio and spoke into it.

'It's Charles here, over,' he said; he used correct radio procedure. I suddenly felt safer still.

We could not quite hear what was being said as the reception was bad, but Charles seemed to understand what he was being told. After a few minutes he put his radio on the seat next to him. Looking worried but it was clear he was not going to share his anxiety with us.

'What's up, Charles?' Anthony asked, convinced that he was receiving bad news about our flight; he worried incessantly and with reason.

'That was another guide,' Charles responded.

'Where from?' Lucy asked, ever the curious one.

'From here, Joshua, he has some Germans in a jeep that he's taking on a game drive,' Charles complained.

Charles seemed very upset by this news.

'The Suzuki jeep?' I asked.

Throughout the previous day, we had spotted the white Suzuki jeep at the ferry, by the riverboat to the falls and at the lodge.

We had even seen the adventurous German couple drive off the ferry in the morning slightly before us.

'He's not happy.' Charles was clearly upset by one of his gamekeeper colleagues having problems and not pleasing his clients.

'Why?' Anthony asked.

'I don't know but their guide is being told off for jamming up the radio frequency,' Charles explained, 'so I can't talk to him.'

'Can you ask the German driver what his problem is?' Lucy saw through all problems with an incisive logic. If Charles could establish what was wrong, he might be able to rendezvous and help.

'He's German, they are never happy,' Anthony added, helpfully. He was, of course, joking; his dry humour would not let him ignore racial stereotypes.

Charles's disappointment was short lived as we passed the Suzuki coming the other way. After a short exchange, Charles seemed to have sorted out the problem.

All too soon, the game drive was over. We spotted giraffe and deer of all sorts, but no lions, thankfully.

We drove back to the hotel to pay our bill and depart for the airport. As well as being totally self-sufficient for water, the hotel's energy requirements were served by solar panels set into the lawn at the front of the hotel.

The only communication that we had with the outside world was a satellite dish; there were no phones.

We paid our bills by credit cards and the system seemed to accept the payment. Pip was fascinated by this system as most of the checking of limits and validity was done through cable networks and satellite dishes, state of the art in the African savannah – it was amazing.

The Lodge was a technical island in one of the largest animal reserves in Africa. Despite no phone lines, Pip was able to pay for his bill from his cheque account by card. It was equally easy for me, though a similar transaction in Kos had not been so simple or smooth.

The Lodge had been in communication with the airstrip and they were expecting us, which was a relief. We had been unable to raise the airfield with our small walkie-talkie but the radio in reception looked impressive. It was practically the size of a catering oven.

'I'm glad the lodge knows what's going on,' I said as much to assure Anthony as to make conversation.

'I can't believe the hassle factor involved in all this,' Anthony replied. 'We just want to talk to the airfield.'

He still wore his sunglasses, so it was difficult to read his expression, but his face tightened. He was exasperated. It was testament to the efforts he had made to establish contact with the airfield. We could reach our banks thousands of miles away, but we could not talk to the airfield less than two kilometres away. It was frustrating, particularly as we had learnt the importance of confirming everything. He had a flight to catch and work back in England, it was vital he caught the flight from Entebbe.

'No wonder organised trips are so much more expensive,' Pip sighed.

He was trying to help Anthony to relax, but he had a flight out of Entebbe the next day so while Pip only had to get to the tented camp that night, Anthony had to get home and to work.

Pip was called over by one of the men behind the desk. With resignation, he went over to sort out yet another problem; the man had the patience of a saint. He had organised all our individual travel and accommodation.

'We have just had a communication from the airline that says they have no record of your travelling with them,' the radio operator informed Pip. He sat behind the concierge at a massive map table that supported the bulk of the radio.

'But this was organised last week in Kampala,' Pip explained.

'This problem has not been foreseen,' replied the concierge, stepping in for the radio operator.

'What do we do?' Pip asked.

'You could radio us at 12.50 to find out more,' suggested the concierge.

'You want us to radio at one for a three o'clock flight?

'One o'clock or one thirty,' the other man confirmed.

'Can you contact the plane?' Pip asked.

'We cannot locate the plane,' the other man explained.

'They might not even land at the airstrip, but continue on to Entebbe,' the concierge told him.

'What do we do then?' Pip asked.

'You will have to pay redirection costs,' the concierge announced.

'Excuse me,' said Pip. He left the desk with remarkable restraint and approached Anthony and I to explain the situation.

'What should we do?' Anthony asked; he was calm now, resigned to the way things were done. There was nothing he could do, and he was relying on Pip to sort out the problem.

'I was there when the telex was sent, we should go to the airfield as planned and get them to confirm the flight and talk to the plane when it comes into radio contact and then work from there,' Pip suggested, ever the calm and reasoned thinker.

Anthony and I agreed to this plan, it was highly unlikely that our booking would be missed and if that were the case it would be the airline and not the Lodge that would sort out the problem. We could gain nothing from staying and talking to the hotel staff. We set off again westward to see more animals.

'This is just like Jurassic Park,' Lucy and said I together.

We were bonding.

We stopped to look at some giraffes.

'Drive on,' Charles commanded from the back.

'I can't see,' the children chorused.

'The driver's not moving until we see the giraffes,' Lucy responded patiently.

'That one's pregnant,' Charles exclaimed excitedly, he could not argue with Lucy, so he gave us the proper tour.

'How long do they carry their young for?' Emily asked.

'Twenty-two months,' Charles replied.

'My goodness,' Lucy balked at the idea. Nine months was bad enough seemed to be her view.

'They are the tallest animals here, they walk at five miles per hour, but they can run at up to fifteen miles per hour.' Charles knew a thing or two about these tall animals.

'Look,' Aubrey cried; he had spotted something.

'Buffalo,' Charles said as he pointed them out to us.

'How long are they pregnant?' Lucy asked

'They have an 18-month pregnancy,' Charles informed us.

'It's a tough world in the jungle,' I noted.

'How fast?' the children were into speed.

'Five miles per hour walking and ten miles per hour running,' Charles told them.

We drove down a winding path.

'Stop,' Charles said.

'Stop, Mohammed,' Lucy commanded, 'Charles is the guide.'

'Do Fio,' Mohammed replied, as if it was no problem. We wondered why he was behaving that way, ignoring us and doing his own thing.

'Stop means stop,' Lucy reminded him.

They weren't going to be firm friends; something made me feel Lucy lacked male bonding skills where this particular individual was concerned.

'You're quite right,' I agreed, anxious to keep her on my side, so verbal support and a stern look at Mohammed, I found, were the best ways to show solidarity.

'I'm getting out,' Lucy announced.

She leant over from her bench seat, grabbed the door handle, pulled back the door and stepped out. She hadn't had a cigarette and the heat of the van was beginning to get oppressive again.

'She has no fear,' Mohammed sighed. He felt real respect for her tough spirit and so did I. She wasn't one to suffer fools gladly or to be trifled with and Mohammed was slowly learning this.

'I know,' I agreed.

I reasoned that I could be sympathetic to poor Mohammed and support Lucy at the same time. This peace-keeping role was becoming exhausting, yet it was enjoyable in a macabre way. I wondered idly if my skills could be used to good effect in Cyprus or somewhere equally safe, nowhere that challenging.

'I fear them,' Mohammed added, it was his first heartfelt and genuine comment; it was directed at the buffalo.

'Don't fear the animals, fear her,' I enjoined.

Mohammed laughed again at this, he really was responding and bonding. I knew I would miss my appreciative audience once I flew back to Entebbe.

I was going to add that the animals could be dealt with by Charles's Kalashnikov, but Lucy was a different kettle of fish. We all got out, leaving Charles to entertain the children while we smoked. Mohammed gratefully accepted a cigarette from me, and Lucy puffed away standing to one side of the rear of the sliding door. We stood between the headlights.

Mohammed stopped whenever told to do so and drove like a saint from then on. It was as if he was under Lucy's spell. The next time we stopped to take a view outside the van, I took the opportunity to tell Lucy about our conversation and she laughed too, obviously not as wholeheartedly. Perhaps a career as a stand-up was not beyond my reach.

'Oh, what's that orange flying object,' Lucy asked Charles.

'Red-headed weaver bird,' Charles exclaimed; he knew his stuff and he was rightly proud of his knowledge.

We drove on to where a herd of buffalo were supposed to be grazing. As we drove on, we saw some African antelope skipping by.

'Stop,' Lucy commanded as the children craned their necks to see the prancing creatures.

Bambi was somewhere amongst that group, a less fallow variety but she was there.

Mohammed stopped on a dime. I saw that and winked at Lucy.

Although Mohammed had stopped right away, Charles was anxious to move on.

'Would you like to see some more buffalo?' he asked, deliberately appealing to the children. Cute deer or ugly beasts that chew the cud and twitch their ears like flapping wings against the insects that pestered them constantly; it was a tough call for the kids.

'They are cruel animals,' Mohammed warned, he was anxious to get the game drive over – whether it was to say his prayers or because he wanted to sleep a little longer at the next destination.

'Next to the lion, they are the fiercest,' Charles elucidated.

Again, he tried to appeal to the children's love of vicious creatures but as they had not seen any lions and there were still scampering deer to be viewed – they were not interested.

In truth Charles and Mohammed were the only ones who realised the extent of their cruelty and were the only ones who wanted to see the beasts.

'If you see one,' Mohammed continued, 'you better make sure it is dead.'

'If you find a girl buffalo make sure she's wed,' Charles joked, he was referring to the Buffalo Tribe; different clans chose an animal or plant as their symbol.

We parked by a tree while Charles got out to look and see if he could spot the famous buffalo.

'They have moved on,' he announced gloomily.

'Charles, let's get going,' Lucy suggested kindly.

She was anxious to catch up with the deer. Charles looked disappointed but jumped back in, shut the door and sat down in his seat.

'We have time, we will see plenty more,' Charles smiled.

'Oribi,' Mohammed said.

'Too far away, save your film for a close-up,' Charles demanded.

'They're only forty feet away,' Lucy said.

'We're spoilt,' Anthony announced, his acerbic tongue had come back and he smiled behind glasses.

'My camera is no good since Punch put it in the mud when we went to look at the termite hill,' Aubrey complained, sounding slightly peeved.

'That termite hill was disgusting,' Ollie announced.

'They call it a termitary,' I stated.

I was determined to indoctrinate the children.

I had gained the knowledge at about eight when we had studied Africa at prep school. Not only could I spell it and knew the word existed, the picture that I drew was one of the tallest and muddiest ant hills that you are likely to see. It was much better than the picture of the elephant swallowing a snake in the book *The Little Prince*.

'Termites give a nasty bite,' Anthony pointed out, chuckling as he did so.

'What, like the horse fly, like this?' Aubrey asked, but he was not quick enough, and had spoilt the surprise, allowing Anthony to shift across and on to an empty chair to avoid Aubrey's clutches and the painful pinch.

'Oribi are small impala,' Charles pointed out.

The mention of impala reminded me of New York because all the Chevrolet Caprice cars that were converted for and built as taxis were called Impalas.

One late night, we spent ten minutes trying to hail occupied cabs by shouting 'Impala' as they sped by. Eventually, an Impala for hire came our way, sweeping to a halt at the kerb like in the movies. In our joyous state, the word Impala became highly amusing and we referred to taking a cab as 'roping an impala' from that night onwards.

'Thomson gazelle,' Charles cried as he pointed excitedly at the big deer that bounded past us through the bush; perhaps the buffalo had frightened it. He was a soft-spoken man and we did not expect him to raise his voice so much.

'That is my clan,' Sommerly announced proudly.

She had been quiet all morning, preferring to stay in the van when we viewed animals or sit and watch Punch; she was not too diligent, I suppose, otherwise he would have been thwarted when he had his hands around Aubrey's camera and went to investigate the rain-soaked road. If she had been paying better attention, she would have stopped Punch dragging the camera through the mud and over the termite hill.

We felt bad about the way Mohammed had treated her earlier in the day. We had forgotten about her, assuming she was catching up on her sleep and that was why she sat at the back.

She was awake now, and she seemed to be flirting with Charles and we were glad to see she was coming out of her shell. They had a quick chat about their tribes, and we felt they may well be seeing each other in the future.

Our joy at being cupid for these two young people was interrupted by our driver.

'On the left oribi, antelope,' Mohammed exclaimed, as a group of antelope were grazing towards us and came into view; even he was getting into the game drive.

Despite his insistence that he had worked in reserves in Kenya, he was always in awe of the animals; whatever his real story, he seemed impressed by the wildlife outside his windscreen.

Lucy was satisfied so we drove on.

'Ugandan kob,' Charles said.

'Heartbeat antelope, aren't they?' Anthony tenuously suggested; he had obviously been studying Pip's books on wildlife as well, the cunning chap that he was.

'They are all of the group that is oribi,' Charles replied.

'So, what's the difference?' Anthony asked.

'Very little,' I suggested.

'Sausage tree,' Charles whispered, pointing again.

'That's what we had for breakfast,' Aubrey commented.

Charles was right and Aubrey was mistaken. Kigelia Africana is an African tree, easily recognised due to the large sausage-shaped fruits hanging from its branches. The generic name Kigelia comes from the Mozambican name for sausage tree, 'kigeli-keia'.

'*Habibi*, Heartbeat,' I breathed.

It was my turn to point, Mohammed laughed at this as the Arabic for darling, or baby, is *Habibi*.

'Heart Bete,' Charles repeated and spelt it out slowly for us, thinking we were ignorant and missing my Pan-Arabic-African joke, the truly international comedian that I was. I was appealing for the Arabic laugh and dear Mohammed did not disappoint.

If you drove all day like him, you might find it funny too.

'Heaf bite,' Anthony said cryptically; it sound like love bite, so we ignored it for the sake of the children. I am sure he meant to make a joke combining bite and the Heaf test.

'Heart Bete,' Charles repeated.

Anthony spotted some wildlife himself.

'Two Thomson gazelle,' he exclaimed.

'Oribi,' I corrected him, not really knowing but wanting to take the wind out of his sails.

'You're both wrong.' Charles informed us.

'Only partially,' I countered, I was in a correcting mood, 'after all they are all antelope.'

'I haven't read my *Guide to Wildlife of East Africa*,' Anthony apologised.

'Don't worry, I haven't brought my *W H Smith Guide to Safaris*, either,' I assured him.

Poor Charles was mystified, but determined to alleviate us of our ignorance.

'They're Uganda kob.'

'I see,' I said, not really being able to tell the difference.

'The male has horns, the female has no horns,' Charles elucidated.

'The men do all the fighting,' I said grimly; it was like the real world out there after all.

'That's because we females can communicate verbally,' Lucy exclaimed; she was pleased to unravel this conundrum, but we knew that she fought with her tongue and she was as quick as a whip.

'Giraffe,' Aubrey shouted. He was excited at sighting something that was not an antelope and proving how observant he was compared to the bickering, or bantering, adults.

'It looks like a tree,' I declared, teasing him, 'Are you sure it's not a mirage?'

'I'm not thick you know,' he replied, Aubrey was always conspicuous in his standard reply.

'Gazelle to the left,' Anthony announced.

'Impala,' Charles corrected him.

'It looks like a kob,' I insisted.

'Or a heat beat,' Anthony deliberately mispronounced the name.

'Hear Bete,' Charles reminded him.

'Or an Acre Deere,' I suggested, I was convinced it was a possibility; after all, we had seen every other antelope under the sun and still further sightings of buffalo evaded us. I began to wonder who was frightened of who at this stage of the game drive.

After the rain there were big puddles on the dirt track road, so we were not so keen to stop; Mohammed was happy as he could keep driving without interference. He did like to keep going at all costs. We were happy because we didn't want to get muddy except poor Punch, but he was not going to get a chance to have his way in this democracy.

'The lions feed on kobs,' Charles was now addressing Sommerly rather than us and she thoroughly enjoyed it

'Do they eat the antelope?' Sommerly asked, knowing that they did, but pleading ignorance so Charles could demonstrate his knowledge and encouraging him to engage with her.

'They devour the antelope,' Charles growled; he was flirting with the girl now, big time.

She seemed more than satisfied with his reply.

It was a big game on a small game drive; most exciting and they had very little time.

'You have hyena here?' Sommerly asked.

'Yes,' Charles said with a glint in the eye, which said: we have everything you want here and more. You think it's wild out there; you wait and see. It was uncomfortable to watch as it brought back all our youth and I thought I saw a tear of remembrance slide down Mohammed's cheek, but it might just have been an insect in his eye.

'I'd like to see it,' Sommerly said seductively. We knew that hyenas were a pack animal so it should strictly be 'them'. Perhaps her slip of the tongue had been deliberate, it was possible.

'What do they eat?' Lucy asked.

She was determined that, as customers, we would all be included on this game drive.

'All animals,' Charles replied.

'The giraffe?' she asked.

'No,' Charles replied unsure.

'Then not all animals?' Lucy seethed. 'Only some of them.'

She was getting increasingly annoyed by the constant misinformation that she was supplied with each day; it was becoming too much.

'No,' Charles admitted.

'Then what do they eat?' Lucy asked, insisting on an honest and comprehensive answer.

'The highland lion, which comes out at night,' Charles replied lacking his previous confidence.

Lucy and I looked at each other. Both of us had remarked the previous evening about this strange trait we had come across, frustrating questions that needed to be asked and frustrating answers.

'Your answers bear no resemblance to the questions,' Lucy told Charles honestly.

At least she was being straightforward.

'Look, gazelle,' Charles declared, ignoring her.

'Show Mohammed,' Lucy said, she was clearly not impressed.

'Where's the gazelle?' Aubrey asked.

'They taste good,' Anthony said making a noise from *Silence of the Lambs* when the Chianti is tasted in Hannibal's imagination; it was the sound of someone noisily aerating a mouthful of wine. Then, Anthony rubbed his stomach and licked his lips. All the children and Charles looked horrified.

'Yeah,' Aubrey said sarcastically, realising that it was just a joke.

'Do you have elephants?' Anthony asked.

'No, we haven't seen them yet,' Charles replied.

'No, do you have elephants here? Lucy insisted.

'Yes,' Charles decided, he sounded even less confident. Lucy frightened him.

'Will we see them?' she asked.

'Not yet,' Charles decided.

'They've been eaten by lions,' Anthony suggested.

'Kob are eaten by lions,' Charles insisted, he was becoming confused.

'Look at the Ugandan kb,' Aubrey commanded; he pointed out of his window, being a boffin.

'Do they taste good?' Anthony asked.

'You can't eat them,' Charles pointed out.

He meant it was illegal to eat them.

'You have your gun, we can have a barbecue,' Anthony suggested, teasing him.

'People do eat deer, kob and buffalo,' Sommerly insisted, thankfully taking Charles off the hook.

'Biltong is dried buffalo and they sometimes use zebra,' I added. I was able to demonstrate my knowledge at certain times.

I felt Charles and Sommerly should be free to continue their flirting and we should allow their relationship to blossom.

'Smoked?' Anthony inquired.

'Actually, dried, then cured and seasoned,' I replied. I was not sure with what seasoning they were treated but they tasted delicious. A Zimbabwean girlfriend introduced me to the delicacy, at one time only sold at a single butcher's shop in Richmond.

'I have the recipe,' Lucy announced, helping out.

'Good, all we need is the main ingredient,' I replied.

'Black-beak stork,' Charles exclaimed; he was determined to keep up his naturalist commentary despite the unruly recipients of his knowledge.

'Ugly bird,' I said.

It was, but Lucy gave me a defensive, offended look all the same, as if I had been addressing her.

'You find more in the grass,' Charles offered.

'What do lions not eat, to get back to it?' Lucy asked.

She would not be put off her enquiry. She had asked Charles to give her information and she expected concrete, diamond-hard feedback, not vague answers given to mollify her.

'They don't eat giraffe or buffalo,' Charles offered.

He was being as specific as he could or as specific as he thought he could get away with. Perhaps Mohammed had given him the lead by not being open and honest with us in the first place.

'Larger animals, then?' Lucy wondered.

She had been just been interested to know, to start off with, but the less information that she got, the more the whole question had become like a challenge to her, and she had to get the full story.

'The hyena is poisonous,' Charles admitted.

You could almost hear Lucy's gasp of triumph, so lions weren't too keen on some smaller animals then.

'The hyena is safe,' said Mohammed. He too was involved in the conversation now, although I preferred it when he stuck to just driving.

He was not interested in Sommerly or Charles or in their blossoming relationship.

'Yes, but the liver is poisonous,' Charles insisted.

He was very patient answering Lucy's questions but his answer to the driver was terse; he wasn't going to have everyone ganging up on him.

'So, it's safe apart from his organs?'

Lucy was wondering, as we all were, whether lions were picky about what they ate, you don't get to be king of the jungle without knowing that you shouldn't eat hyena liver.

'That's offal,' I interjected, trying to inject some humour into the events but my timing was off.

I was hoping to defuse the tension, but my comment left all the adults unmoved.

I remembered a friend's American wife telling me that she wouldn't eat her husband's favourite breakfast, fried kidney and liver, saying she didn't eat organs, which when you look at it, lion or not, makes sense when you consider they are the body's filter system. However, Mark's breakfasts with black pudding, kidney and liver with eggs and bacon, were delicious.

'Four lions will eat a buffalo, but not just one,' Charles added.

He was giving us more information than we needed and confusing the hell out of me.

'It takes four lions to kill just one buffalo?' Lucy asked, looking for confirmation. She was still obsessed and fascinated by this information; we were led to believe that a lone male did the killing for the pride.

'They kill hippos in pairs,' Charles expanded; he was becoming quite authoritarian.

He had studied for many years and he was right to share the information.

Previous groups had not pressed him so hard and he was shy, but he seemed more confident when he was showing us his expertise.

'Hippos can be quite tough,' I hypothesized. I had never eaten one, but I imagined they were fairly thick skinned.

'Crocodiles kill lions when they come down to the water's edge,' Charles informed us.

'Don't their jaws get locked?' Lucy asked.

'The crocodiles can distort the lions head,' Charles explained.

'The crock's jaw locks,' Aubrey added, he had seen a few wildlife documentaries in his time and was keen to show his awareness.

'They turn their prey around until the legs fall off!' Charles insisted.

Charles was charmingly descriptive. I could not imagine it myself, nor would I want to imagine such a sight.

'Or the head falls off,' Aubrey expanded; he quite liked the idea.

Charles had meant to say that the body and arms and legs are severed from the head by the crocodile jaws.

'That sounds gruesome,' I ventured.

'It's called the crocodile spin,' Aubrey concluded, he was proving that he had been paying attention.

'No, the crocodile rotates round very slowly, it is called a "crocodile roll",' Charles insisted.

He had obviously seen this for himself, but I could not imagine animals falling apart as they are rotated slowly – where would our spit roasts be in that case?

'In Zaire they feed cows to the crocodiles,' Lucy added.

She had heard it through the safari grapevine or bush telegraph as it used to be known as, but Bush was also a manufacturer of radios and televisions.

'Alive?' Aubrey asked askance. He was surprised and wanted to know the gory details.

He just could not conceal his macabre fascination with nature and its cruelty, the more grotesque, the better. It was good to see he was a normal child, after all and not a boffin.

'No, they slaughter them and then they feed them to the crocodiles,' Lucy stipulated, she was matter of fact in her reportage, as she expected Charles to be.

'They kill shoebill stork, too' Charles informed us.

He was warming to the subject of crocodiles; he wanted to make sure he gave all the information this time. He was confident, but I was not sure whether it was his knowledge or his need to impress Sommerly that increased his verbosity.

'And small fish,' Aubrey added.

'They are forced to eat such things,' Charles replied.

'We saw two crocodiles on the river yesterday next to the body of a hippo,' Aubrey informed Charles.

'They took a piece of hippo for their larder,' I further elucidated.

'Mohammed, could you stop, please?' Lucy asked.

Mohammed ignored her. I wasn't sure whether he was slightly deaf or whether he was just bloody-minded.

'We're almost where the giraffe are,' Charles announced to everyone; he understood her.

Mohammed could hear her, I'm sure, but he drove on.

'Stop!' Lucy shouted.

'Can we stop here Mohammed, please?' I asked.

Mohammed braked sharply and stopped.

'What's wrong with him?' Lucy asked in a loud voice from behind Mohammed's ear.

'He must have misheard you,' I suggested, turning in the front passenger seat and facing her, smiling.

I was willing her not to antagonise him, which I should not have done. It was not my war.

'Stop means stop, you can't mishear that,' Lucy stated forcibly. She rolled her eyes.

She was quite right. I thought that I noticed Mohammed flush as she brought his stubbornness to everyone's attention. It was perhaps his last stab at defying her.

His Moslem roots made him look upon women in a different way than most other people do, perhaps. His Egyptian roots made him look upon women in a different way, too, perhaps.

We stopped and had a look for some wildlife; I was keeping an eye out for any life whether it was animals, Ugandan military or rebels. I took our stop as an opportunity to smoke and to check on the others in our convoy.

Lucy and Anthony took the children on to a mound to have a better look and became frightened once they discovered it was an anthill. Ants had bitten them all at some stage in their travels and they were wearing short socks. Ants have an ability to travel unnoticed in most people's clothes.

'You're back soon,' I said. I had only smoked half of my second cigarette.

'We were frightened on the ant hill,' Lucy explained.

They still stood in front of our lead van. I took another drag on my cigarette and threw the butt into the dust, eco-traveller that I was. Climbing in next to Mohammed, I watched the rest of the group.

'What's up?' Mohammed asked.

'They got frightened on an ant hill,' I told Mohammed, offering him a cigarette. He shook his head and pointed to his pack under the dashboard to his right, next to the hand brake.

I forced him and we both smoked with the window open and the heat rising in the van

'She frightens me,' I announced, making my voice deliberately quake.

From then on whenever Lucy asked Mohammed to stop, he did it immediately; it was very effective psychology.

Chapter 17

The Flight from Murchinson Falls

Anthony and I were part of the American tour: quick pick-up, whirlwind safari, whistle-stop tour and quick drop; we had paid for one night and one game drive, transfer to the lodge by minibus, and a flight from the lodge to Entebbe so we would be returning to Kampala that afternoon.

Both of us were anxious not to miss the daily flight back into Entebbe. It would be a short flight and infinitely more preferable than travelling back in the bus. The others were going on to a tented camp and I could not afford the extra night, unfortunately. Charles had a radio strapped to his belt to keep in contact with the airfield. His call sign was William Tell, but I would have thought Robin Hood would have been more appropriate, such a band of merry men were we.

'This is the way to the airport?' I asked as Pip's map had shown a location much further to the west of Murchinson Falls.

'Yes,' our erstwhile driver assured me. Even the way Mohammed had confirmed that fact had filled me with suspicion. He had an unnerving way of making his answers seem ironic.

'The airfield is in the opposite direction,' I assured him.

'Yes, we're going the other way and then coming back,' he finally informed me. It was like being told a deadly secret.

So that was what he was up to; as tourists and foreigners we were treated as completely unable to palate the truth.

All the information was on a need-to-know basis and should be delivered at the last possible moment in order to keep us happy. There was not even an inkling that we required to be kept informed of our progress and if we were, then we should be supplied with misinformation.

'I trust you,' I replied, my words sounding hollow even to myself. I wasn't sure how I was going to convince him that I believed him.

'Good,' Mohammed declared.

He showed me the second flash of his teeth that I had seen on that trip. I did not trust him, but I had to try and convince him that I did. The amount of gold in his mouth made him more valuable dead than he was alive. Like the rhinoceros horn and the elephant tusks, game bandits would find value in his carcass. I could sense that Charles could navigate, and a plot was forming in my mind.

'Don't worry,' Mohammed announced.

His assurance was doubly worrying and missing the plane seemed an increasingly likely event, particularly as I had been watching the petrol gauge drop alarmingly throughout the morning.

'Do fio,' I replied and smiled back.

Mohammed roared with laughter, we were really bonding, now, laughing and joking like old friends but I hadn't tried all that hard.

'Where did you lean that?' Mohammed's laugh was interrupted by a guttural cough, which halted the hilarity.

'Calling, Michael Zebra, do you receive me, over,' Charles said with seriousness into his radio.

He repeated this mantra several times, looking more concerned each time there was no reply. Eventually, he furrowed his brow and he was clearly deciding which one of us he should speak to about the problem. He knew Anthony and I were due to take the flight back to Entebbe and Anthony would be flying on back to London.

Charles could hardly bear to address Anthony and tell him the news that he had even though he was sitting in the same row as him, so he talked to the back of my head instead.

'The airstrip is shut,' he announced.

'Did you say the airstrip is shut?' I asked incredulous, turning to the messenger who might be about to be shot. We could wrestle the AK-47 from him and do the necessary.

He had to be spokesperson for the group as Anthony stared ahead of him willing his vocal chords to vibrate. I saw his mouth moving as though he were taking small deep breaths.

I wasn't sure if it was stress management or if he was imitating a carp feeding on plankton as part of his meditation process.

Perhaps, he was trying to find the words to express his horror.

Silence prevailed.

'Yes,' Charles confessed.

Charles could not bear to face either of us.

'Thanks, Charles, I feel better,' I admitted.

It was refreshing to be told the truth, the whole truth without hyperbole or embellishment.

'That's more information than I need,' Anthony managed to stammer

'Can I have a rule? I want to be treated on a need-to-know basis. Anything that will make me cry, I don't want to know,' I begged.

'I am sorry,' said Charles.

As we meandered along the track, it became clear that there was just too much involved in the whole operation.

Charles was to provide the game drive; Mohammed was to get us to the airfield and link up with the others later.

The other van was to take Pip, Hattie, Lucy, Anna and the other children to the tented camp.

We had left at ten am, returned to the hotel at eleven forty and now we were trying to extend the game drive to fill up time.

Our flight was not until one o'clock and the others wanted to make the most of the day and the area, the tented camp would not be ready for them so soon in the day. They were expected in the late afternoon, or early evening, they had nowhere to go, quite literally.

'Look,' Charles cried, more excited than ever.

He had us back on track, we would miss our flight, Anthony would miss his intercontinental connection the next day, but Charles would show us all the wildlife we could and perhaps could not see.

'Where?' Aubrey asked.

'Stop, please Mohammed or we'll miss them,' Charles begged the driver.

He was ever the polite and kind guide.

Mohammed was pleased to stop; he no longer saw it as so many people giving him orders but as a chance to see some wildlife. He had been quite blasé about the whole thing at first, but Charles had won him over.

'Four kob, one baby, two female and one male,' he whispered conspiratorially in case they heard.

'There they are,' Aubrey announced happily.

He was pleased to have spotted them and even Ollie craned his neck to get a better look. Anthony hoisted him on to his lap so he could see out of the window. They preferred the docile animals: antelope, kob and giraffes; they did not mind not seeing buffaloes and lions, the big bullies of the savannah.

'Six in the morning or between four and seven in the evening is the best time to see the wildlife – it's cooler,' Charles assured us.

'I suppose that's why we left for our drive at ten o'clock this morning,' Anthony said dryly.

I laughed but I couldn't envisage the whole of our party rising at five to greet the dawn just to see some animals, but I did see Anthony's point that we could have seen the game the previous evening. The suggestion was not put forward, perhaps, because the lodge doubted that we would arrive in time and that the last thing we would want to do would be to stay in our buses for another two hours. They knew the situation, we did not, they were in the sunshine of knowledge; we were in the dark.

At eleven fifty we hit disaster. The temperature was rising in our van. The reading for outside temperature on the savannah was twenty-six degrees centigrade. Inside the truck, it was thirty-one degrees. Those five degrees made a difference. Despite every window being open, we were approaching the hottest part of day and yet – irony of ironies – one of the vans got stuck in the mud.

As luck would have it, Anthony being 'Mr Fortune', it was our truck that got stuck. With the track record that Anthony had, I wasn't sure our flight would make actually make it to Kampala in one piece.

His 'lucky streak' made me want to actually wave him off from the tarmac at the airfield and take the next available flight. That was if the airfield was actually open. I doubted it was closed, it was part of the disinformation. The only certain truth was flying with him was pushing my luck.

We all piled out of the van, including the children and jumped gingerly on to the grass of the safari park. We stepped carefully over the muddy earth; there may well have been snakes in the grass.

All four wheels of the van were immersed up to the axle in a huge puddle.

I was unsure how Mohammed had missed such a large expanse of water, but then I recalled that he had accelerated wildly before we had stopped.

The mud was such that there was no way that the tyres would get a grip; we were lucky not to sink even further into the quagmire. There was no way we could rock the truck out of its pond, nor could we push it although we tried.

In front of the van were more puddles with clods of earth jutting out. The tyre ruts of so many journeys were brim-filled with water.

It looked hopeless; even if we could get our van out of the puddle the ruts may not support the van and we would again be plunged into sludgy mud.

Charles, to give him his due, leapt out with his AK-47 and radio. The green uniform, the shirt a shade lighter than the green trousers, made him look like some desperate paramilitary mounting a coup, but his beige Wellington boots, standard rubber issue, practical as they were, did not inspire confidence; unfortunately, they made him look like a gardener.

The stock of the AK-47 would have made a handy paddle but I failed to see how anything save the radio could help us in our current predicament.

Rebels hiding in the bushes might well have been scared off by such show of arms, but I doubted that they could be hiding where buffalo and sleeping lions would be somewhere in the undergrowth.

They would of course travel in the cooler part of the day and, as romantic a sight as sunset over the savannah might have sounded to Anthony, it got dark very quickly and our chances of encountering bandits would be greatly increased.

'How far is the airstrip?' Anthony asked

'Four kilometres,' Mohammed replied.

We all stepped out and transferred to the other bus. With a lighter load Mohammed might be able to rock the van out.

Charlie stood beside the van talking into the radio. 'Do you read,' he repeated every so often.

Then he climbed up on to the step of the van to get a better reception.

'Will you walk us there, Charles?' I asked.

'Not me,' Charles replied horrified.

Mohammed tried to shift the vehicle from the mud, but the dark brown ground beneath the tyres was too slippery.

The savannah grassland around us offered us a chance to pack vegetation under the wheels.

However, all this would have taken time and would mean standing in puddles to do it; even then it might not work, but at least we had the four-wheel drive to nudge our vehicle on to the grass mat that we could create.

The last time I had been stuck in a car was in a wadi in Oman. It took us five hours to travel three kilometres in a Land Rover Discovery. The little blue van looked like it was nesting in the mud. If we could reach the lodge help might be got but Mohammed was determined to get his van out of the mud.

'I hope the airfield is not like this,' Anthony said as though he imagined we had a chance of getting there. A quagmire at the airfield did not bear thinking about.

'I'm sure it's tarmac,' I said with jollity, not believing my answer.

A rope was found and attached but it broke.

'The sump guard will slide on the ruts and break again if we're not careful,' Lucy pointed out.

I was surprised by her technical know-how; I shouldn't have been as she was the one who had supplied the handkerchief tourniquet in the first place. She was an engineer.

Being ignorant , I had assumed that she would know nothing about mechanics, which was my error. When the rope was reattached, both the vehicles were slipping and sliding in mud.

'Good fun, isn't it Mohammed?' Anthony said.

'Yes,' he agreed and smiled but behind that smile was a worried man.

The other minibus arrived.

'We'll never get the other van through here,' Pip noted.

After some conferring, it was decided to tie a rope around the tow bar of the Toyota and hope that the four-wheel drive Mitsubishi would drag it out. Mohammed executed a complicated series of manoeuvres. He was determined he did not want to remain in the stranded vehicle and, as he was senior driver, he had taken over the rescue operation. We could drag the van out of the puddle backwards but then we would be on the wrong side of the water. We eventually had no choice. How Mohammed got the truck off the track on to the grassland and back down the other side of the puddle, where the truck was stuck, was an object lesson in how to handle cross-country driving.

We were all impressed with his handling of the vehicle. He couldn't have learnt that on the roads of Luxor or in the sands around Cairo; desert driving is a different skill altogether. Our admiration turned to dismay when the rope that Charles had attached snapped. The Toyota was determined not to play the game.

Anthony was anxious about the flight now as it was leaving at one o'clock and we had no idea how far the airfield actually was. We had received so much misinformation on our trip, we were unable to believe anything. It was out of sight and the low ground gave quite a clear view, so we knew it was some distance away. We could not ascertain if it was the 4km they had promised or how far along the 4km we were.

Appeals to Mohammed for information about how far away the airfield was by road had been met with the standard 'ten minutes' reply, which we knew could signify anything from fifteen minutes to five hours. A second attempt, with a shortened rope, had dragged our transport from the mire. We stopped at a fork on a hillock just five minutes along the winding path.

This was where the others would continue their game drive and we would head to the airport. All children and Lucy were evacuated from our van and Anthony, Charles, Mohammed and I were to carry on to meet the plane… hopefully.

It was an emotional moment; the children had got used to us both and the girls hugged us as tightly as leaving us with some breath left allowed. The boys shifted on their feet, looking down at the ground, giving us a most perfunctory handshake, which shielded their sadness.

I thought I detected a tear in all their eyes; we were different to their parents and they would miss that unique bond that we had forged. I felt the same and Anthony, I was sure, was sad to leave his nieces and nephews, but behind his sunglasses you could not read his eyes and he was not one for allowing expression to crowd his face.

'You keep Charles and the radio, we'll head on,' Pip said and shook my hand and smiled warmly; it had been an adventure.

'Thanks,' I grinned, almost saying 'sir'. It was like saying goodbye to a commanding officer when you were going off on a mission to occupied France or saying goodbye to your housemaster when going to play for the county in a regional rugby tournament.

'Good luck, you'll need it.' Pip laughed; he was still chortling when he said goodbye to Anthony who managed a thin smile in return.

They shook hands warmly as good brothers-in-law should.

'Bye, Granny Finn,' Matilda called from inside the bus.

I waved madly back; her enthusiastic waving was infectious.

I was glad we were keeping Charles, but I thought the others might need the radio.

'Are you leaving everyone behind?' I asked Mohammed as we drove off.

'Yes,' Mohammed replied.

'Stop,' I wanted to see if it worked.

He stopped

'Thank you.'

'Do fio,' he replied. He was happier in the company of men and he even smiled at me.

'Well done, Mohammed, give me five!'

We slapped hands above our heads.

I went to check if the others wanted to take the radio. Pip was sitting in the passenger seat, the window open, even their fan system was superior to ours.

'Are you sure you don't want the radio?' I asked him.

'We've got four-wheel drive and we're not stopping off at the lodge. Mohammed will take Charles back once you've left and he'll meet us this evening at the tented camp.'

'Is it really that far?'

I thought it was an hour away. It was in fact three hours' drive according to Mohammed; that therefore could have been anywhere from five minutes away to two days away.

'We'll be there in ten minutes,' Pip chortled, he never missed a chance for devilment.

I ran back to the van, climbed in and we drove off gingerly through the mud. We had the whole van to ourselves; that is, we had no tourists asking constant questions. Mohammed, stuck in second gear, reached for a box of Rex, which was a popular brand of cigarettes.

'Have one of mine,' I said to my new brother. '*Rex*.'

'Rex?' he was surprised at my choice of generic brand.

He had obviously assumed he had been smoking a European brand when I offered him cigarettes previously.

'Of course,' I replied.

'Thank you,' he said, he took the cigarette and I lit it for him to save any trouble that we might have with the van's cigar lighter. It had managed to stay in place, and I didn't want things spoilt by Mohammed dropping it on to his lap or the floor.

'I didn't know you smoked, or I would have offered you one earlier.' He had been very good not smoking in front of the children and Lucy. 'Anthony, do you want one?'

'No, thanks, I'll stick to Silk Cut.' Anthony was sitting on the bench seat behind Mohammed.

Charles was at his usual post on the jump seat by the door, clutching his *AK*. I offered him a cigarette, suspecting that he didn't smoke and for once I was right. I also felt that we would make the flight and I hoped that I would be right about that.

We climbed up the hill out of the dip in the road where we had been stuck and the terrain improved. The mud was beige-brown like sand and remarkably this was flecked with peach dust on the brow of the hill.

It was difficult to understand why this part of the road should be dusty still. The grass that grew from the rise in the centre of the road brushed our sump guard, but I did not voice my concern to Anthony that our sump might rupture.

'So, Mohammed, have you enjoyed yourself?' I asked, trying to make conversation.

'I have worked in Kenya and I prefer it,' he responded. He had, obviously, worked his way south from Egypt.

'Why?' Anthony asked.

'They pay better,' he replied.

'Not better scenery then?' I suggested.

'More wildlife,' Mohammed explained, he seemed to miss that aspect, but surely that was before he met Charles.

He saw a lot more wildlife with Charles's help.

'How much do you earn?' Anthony asked.

'One hundred thousand per month,' Mohammed could not have sounded gloomier even if he had tried.

'One hundred seems fair,' Anthony noted. He knew Mohammed was complaining, but he also knew how much, in the real world, ten thousand buys when you're not paying tourist rates.

'Before, in Kenya, it was one hundred and eighty-five thousand,' our driver continued. Mohammed was forgetting how expensive Kenya was compared to Uganda.

'That's good,' I said encouragingly. I wondered why he'd taken this job, but dared not ask.

'Plus, a travel allowance of thirty thousand.'

'Don't you get that now?'

Anthony was as surprised as I was.

I had to admit that a drop of two hundred and fifteen thousand to half that was quite a reduction for anyone.

'Our expenses are met, but we get no allowance,' Mohammed continued; he seemed to be going for the sympathy vote.

I felt it was more misinformation.

We were nearing the end of our trip and he would be expecting a tip.

'The hotel was twenty-five thousand a night,' Anthony said; he was calculating that Mohammed would be able to afford four nights, but Mohammed was calculating that he might get that from both of us as a tip. I was calculating if we would pay him that much; he would be tipped by the others on their return to Kampala at the end of the trip.

'We are here,' Mohammed announced.

'It looks like a village,' Anthony gasped.

He was being facetious. Was this our drivers' trademark misinformation? If we were there, then why was there no airstrip.

'The village is not in the airfield,' Mohammed sighed pointedly – he had thought Anthony was serious. 'The runway is behind the huts.'

'Are you ready for this?' I asked Anthony.

'Definitely,' Anthony replied, and he actually smiled, again showing his teeth.

'Great!' I laughed, out of relief more than anything else.

We were both immensely relieved that we had completed the journey thus far without further incidents. All we had to do was hope that the plane would land here and not head straight for Entebbe, leaving us stranded in the savannah.

As Mohammed reached to turn off the radio, he accidentally hit the horn switch on the indicator stalk, and he cursed under his breath.

'That's a ten thousand shilling fine,' Charles said smiling.

'I heard nothing,' I said conspiratorially.

'Ten thousand just for blowing the horn? That sounds absolutely insane,' Anthony complained angrily, he was incensed.

'That's right,' Charles agreed, wagging his finger at Mohammed, 'a ten thousand shilling fine.'

'Poor Mohammed,' I soothed, I smiled sympathetically; even I could work out that it was ten per cent of his monthly earnings.

'That's the law here in the reserve,' Charles insisted.

He was terribly pleased to relay this piece of information. I could see Mohammed scowling at Charles in his rear view mirror. We turned sharp left and drove down a short track.

'You heard nothing?' Anthony asked.

He liked baiting Mohammed, who took another sharp left, more vicious than the first and he braked sharply in a cloud of dust. I think Anthony was exacting revenge for the way Mohammed had treated his sister, Lucy, but perhaps he just wanted to entertain Charles and I.

'My hearing is bad,' I decided and beamed.

Mohammed was pleased with this explanation.

'Not as bad as Mohammed's when he thinks he's going to get a ten thousand fine,' Anthony chortled uncontrollably.

I was just relieved that he didn't hoot the horn at the beginning of our journey otherwise he would have been in a funk and sulking the whole game drive.

We decamped at the ranch building. It literally looked like a building from a Western: the waiting room was a wooden shack; the control room was part of the building and there was a wooden veranda.

There was a clearing, crottle-coloured earth, with no tarmac strip.

This was an Australian 'outback' landing field. I expected to see a kangaroo hopping into the bush nearby and someone stepping out of the building to tell us the flying doctor was on his way. My mother had wanted to be a flying doctor in Tasmania but that is another story.

Charles introduced us to the station manager and his assistant, two men who looked like they knew what they were doing. Like Charles they wore green military uniforms, which also helped to inspire confidence. They had proper soldiers' boots on; they were extremely highly-polished black leather, covering their calves with black laces. They made Charles seem even more eccentric in his rubber footwear.

'So, what news of the flight?' Anthony asked.

'We've had a problem with radio monitor,' explained the station manager.

'Is it working now?' Anthony asked, looking worried.

'Oh yes, we've been in touch with Pakuba airport,' he assured Anthony, smiling.

'Are we booked on the flight?' Anthony asked.

'They're sending a plane especially for you.'

'You will avoid two stops,' his assistant interjected, reassuringly. He too smiled; it was good to feel that we had found a competent crew after all our misadventures.

'We might be able to contact the plane,' the manager suggested in order to put Anthony more at ease.

I was in no hurry to get back to Kampala.

We followed the manager into the radio room; a map of the locality was on the far wall, and opposite were posters of government regulations. Between each wall was a clean, clear window with metal frames making up eight squares. The wall opposite this was painted a grey dull matt; the other walls were whitewashed. The anonymous office had only two distinguishing features: two large wooden desks, on one of which was a gigantic grey metal radio similar to the one at the lodge. So, this was where ex-military hardware ended up in Uganda: safari lodges and savannah airfields.

'Alpha, Lima, Papa, fiver, threer, threer, zero,' the radio operator repeated into the microphone.

Even I figured out that the plane's registration was ALP A5330.

'What time is it due?' Anthony knew the right questions to ask.

'Fourteen hundred hours,' the senior officer replied.

'You will be part of the flight from the medical centre,' his assistant informed us.

'They thought they were coming for you the next day,' the senior officer informed us; he thought this highly amusing.

'That's when I fly back to the UK,' Anthony told him.

'They said you had not paid, so they could not show up,' the assistant announced, and he laughed.

We were rapidly becoming the focus of mass hilarity.

'Wait until I tell them about Mohammed hooting his horn, that would kill them,' I thought.

'But we had booked it ages ago,' Anthony explained.

He was on the defensive, understandably.

'We know, Pakuba Airport found your reservation,' the officer said, smiling.

They all loved to tease the tourist.

I needed to go to the loo; it was a shed the other side of the track on which we had entered, and it was a dunny. I was unsure of what creatures might lurk there and what type of facilities it might have. I could see that the door only came down to six inches above the ground; so, all manner of creatures could get in and out at random. I was just about to return, deciding that I could wait when the assistant came out after me with a wad of tissues for me. I refused them, but thanked him anyway.

I couldn't bring myself to urinate outside the appointed building; it was impolite, so I clicked the latch. It was stiflingly hot in that small space; the heat of the day had baked the air and the roof had absorbed all the heat. Just for the short time that I was there, it seemed to be like visiting a sauna. It did not smell too bad; I have smelt far worse in gentlemen's loos in lots of places in London. These guys kept everything clean and functioning efficiently.

We were told to wait, and Charles and Mohammed waited with us.

Mohammed stayed inside talking to the airport manager and his assistant, which should have made us suspicious.

We spoke to Charles as we bided our time. We all sat on the stoop and Charles kept his rifle in the usual position between his legs. He talked to us about his work and his life. We found out that Charles's father was blind and that his mother was dead and that he had to pay for his brother's education.

Everywhere we went there were similar such stories, some true some not, it was always difficult to tell. There was a lot of hardship, suffering and poverty; tourism would help but the rest of the world paying proper prices for African goods and taking down trade barriers would help far more.

At half past two, we were still waiting for confirmation of our two o'clock flight. I was put in mind of Gatwick or Heathrow on a summer's day, the only difference was the lack of people in a similar situation, lying on airport lounge furniture.

It was hot in the sun, but we had mineral water. We shared our packed lunch from the hotel with Mohammed and Charles. We had intended to save our food for the flight, but neither of us had much of an appetite and Charles and Mohammed seemed hungry.

The airport manager beckoned me into his office. On his desk was a pad, which I had not noticed before. He offered me a chair and I sat down.

'When is the flight due?' I asked to break the silence.

'We are still awaiting confirmation,' he informed me truthfully and I was grateful for that; the officer was used to appeasing Europeans; the plane would be here when we saw it.

I was thankful that Anthony was flying out the next day. If he had wanted to connect with a flight that evening, he would have been lost.

'I see,' I replied.

The heat in the office drained me of any will to argue and the fact that Anthony was calm made me worry less than I might have done.

'You will have to pay a departure tax of thirty thousand shillings.' The senior officer was now an airport manager.

He looked me in the eye as I asked him to repeat the sum, which he did without blinking or flinching.

I could not understand that he had not asked us for this 'tax' when we first arrived – that would be normal. Thirty thousand was steep and no mention of taxes had been made by anyone. As far as I was concerned, we had paid for everything. I had about twenty-five thousand on me, but I wasn't going to let him know that.

'For both of us?' I wanted to be quite clear what was involved here.

'Each,' he said.

In one sentence he had blown it – for both of us. Thirty was steep, sixty thousand was absolutely outrageous. I was not sure, but I suspected this had the hallmark of a scheme dreamt up with our driver.

'We have no money, we gave it all to Mohammed's company,' I lied. I thought that I should fight fire with fire; I was getting used to the way of doing things in the reserve, pass the buck, fib, procrastinate but never be straight.

'You will have to pay the departure tax, I will give you a receipt, I can accept dollars if you wish,' he assured me.

He wanted me to think he was being so generous.

'Mohammed will pay,' I insisted.

I stood up and walked out into the sunshine. Oblivious to my Machiavellian negotiations, Anthony was talking to Mohammed and Charles.

'Anthony, I think you should know that we have to pay departure tax,' I announced.

I sat down next to the three of them, still not quite sure how deeply the other two were involved in this.

The two of them had been talking quite a lot to the airport staff, we had been naive enough to think that it had been about our flight or a general chat about nothing much.

Maybe they had been plotting this 'sting' together. I was becoming paranoid.

'Trust no one' was becoming my motto. It was like being back in Warsaw in 1983, the communist armed forces on every street corner and everyone mistrusting everyone else.

'How much?' Anthony asked; he was used to the idea that you paid, and you paid and paid again.

'Thirty thousand,' I replied, but before I had finished the first syllable of the second word, Anthony let out a grunt, half shock-horror and half laughter.

'Let's go and see the man,' he suggested ominously. Al Pacino himself could not have put it more threateningly than Anthony had.

Before we had got up, the airport manager came out on to the veranda.

'I know nothing about any departure tax,' Anthony exclaimed, addressing his remark directly at the approaching figure. Anthony looked menacing in his sunglasses. In fact, he looked like a mercenary on leave. Even I was scared, and he was on my side.

'Regulations state that you have to pay 3,000 shillings per head departure tax, I can show you the documentation,' he explained innocently.

The airport manager seemed to have changed the amount, dividing by ten; thirty thousand and three thousand do not even sound similar, but I admired his ability to cover his mendacity.

'Did you mishear him, Mike?' Anthony asked; he was finding the whole situation as bizarre as I was.

They would have happily taken sixty thousand off us, paid six thousand for the tax and split the remaining fifty-four thousand four ways; a tidy sum of almost fourteen thousand, just for making conversation. Considering Mohammed earned one hundred thousand per month, that was 3,333 per day; he would clear four days' cash give or take a few thousand. .

'Mohammed, I have no money,' I said in order to strengthen our negotiating position. It was like chess but not a pleasurable match.

'I have no money, I have to go to the bank in Kampala,' Anthony announced immediately afterwards. He was shrewd enough to play along with me; if we did not have the cash, we could not pay it.

'I only have ten thousand and that is for the lodge tonight, I need it,' Mohammed protested.

I doubted whether this was true. I was sure he had been given petrol money and we had already had to pay for that. I would have been surprised if he kept so little on him. I was going to suggest that he sold some of the gold from his teeth, but I was sure that the airport manager would give an unfavourable rate.

'That will do, you'll still have four thousand,' Anthony assured him. His serious face stopped Mohammed from asking him if he was joking, which he was.

'Mohammed will pay,' I announced confidently, looking at the airport manager with a poker face.

I wanted to ask him what he would charge in dollars just to see how outrageous he could be, but I was enjoying seeing Mohammed squirm. It was payback time for all the misinformation he had given us throughout the journey and for his mistreatment of Sommerly and his disrespect for, and stubbornness with, Lucy.

We were tourists but we were not completely stupid either.

The assumption that foreigners have more money than sense is why Africa has never been a top tourist destination. From Tunisia to Tanzania you have a feeling that you are a walking wallet, a target for every scam that they can pull. No wonder people go elsewhere; the Africans never realise that people have a choice of holiday destinations. They are genuinely surprised that so few people visit their country.

We waited outside for two hours, talking to our hosts, explaining why more people did not visit Uganda. It was not the troubles in the north or in Rwanda on the border, we explained, but the trouble in the country; tourists felt they had been taken advantage of in so many different ways. Also, we pointed out the cost of getting to Entebbe.

For half the price you could get to New York or to Florida. For the same money you could get to South Africa where the weak rand helped, or Thailand where the baht was weak too.

To get to Uganda was expensive and prices were on a par with Europe, not Asia. To be hit twice was difficult since tourists had a choice; they liked the fact that an expensive fare could be compensated for by low prices at the destination if they headed east. They had generally cheap flights if they headed west for North America whereas heading south beyond Saharan Africa, you were hit both ways: the flight and expenses were both exorbitant. Only those who needed to go to East Africa were willing to pay; the area could not compete with other destinations. I am afraid we depressed them all with our honest interpretation of the situation. By the end of our talk, I was feeling very sorry for them, they hoped tourism would be their salvation.

Of all the continents, Africa had suffered most from exploitation by its leaders and governments. Tourism would have helped individuals. These were lovely, warm people who you could never forget. Their country desperately needed foreign currency and tourism would be the key, but they just could not compete.

'The flight will arrive at three thirty,' the senior officer announced as he arrived on the veranda.

'We could have taken the game drive offered at one o'clock and two o'clock,' noted Anthony wryly.

'At this rate, we could have taken the one at three,' I added. I, too, was able to be cynical if I wanted to be and I doubted the flight would arrive at the appointed hour.

'It will be a miracle if the flight arrives on time,' Anthony exclaimed.

'We are on African time,' I suggested grimly.

'That's another reason why Europeans stay away from East Africa,' Anthony explained. I was sure I saw Anthony give Mohammed a cold stare from behind his sunglasses. 'You never get a straight answer or a correct time for any event. Europeans want to know where they stand.'

Mohammed was too disillusioned at this point to protest or perhaps the penny dropped, finally. Whatever it was, it was highly unusual for him to make no comment at all. He normally had some form of answer or comeback.

'Mohammed, you better pay the airport tax,' I exclaimed, patting him kindly on the shoulder.

I was going to have one more luxuriant moment of seeing Mohammed sweat. I liked the guy; we had bonded, Muslim and Christian, just as it should be, but still he was not doing his job if he expected us to pay. Sixty thousand was a problem but six thousand I could handle and with pleasure.

'But I will have no money left,' he complained, appealing to us both, not sure, now, who his ally was or whether he had one.

Anthony grunted at this.

'You'll be like us, then.' Anthony consoled him; he was not going to be taken for a ride.

'Come on, Mohammed, I'll come with you,' I exclaimed.

I could at least share his suffering. I got up and walked to the office with the airport manager and the radio operator. Mohammed reluctantly followed, although it was only the sound of his footsteps on the wooden boards that assured me that he was following behind.

The radio operator took up position by his set and spoke into the microphone

'This is Aurora Eagle, Angel Four do you read me?' this time there was a crackling response from the speaker. 'Angel Four, say again, can you repeat, please, over.'

'We will reach you in fifteen minutes, over,' the pilot answered.

His voice was as clear as an office extension but there was a slight crackle at the beginning and end of the message.

'Fifteen minutes until arrival, received, thank you Angel Four, out.' He repeated the message back, which was the correct radio procedure.

He would have made a great driver instead of Mohammed. I was glad that he was in earshot. Mohammed and I sat down opposite the desk with the white pad on it while the radio operator went outside to tell Anthony and Charles the good news.

'Two passengers at three thousand each, that's six thousand,' I said firmly.

The airport manager sat back in his chair, elbow and hands resting on the arms of the chair. It was like sitting opposite a bank manager.

'That's correct,' he assured me.

As he spoke, he fixed me with the same stare he had used when he had asked me for ten times as much.

It was uncanny.

'I thought you said it was sixty,' I replied; I was determined to draw the process out, either to embarrass the guy opposite, or more so, to make Mohammed feel uncomfortable.

'I made a mistake,' he explained.

His stare was unflinching. Putting an extra zero on the price was obviously standard practice.

'Have you got the money, Mohammed?' I asked our honest driver.

'Yes, but it is for my room tonight,' he pleaded.

I liked the situation.

'You can sleep in the van?' I suggested.

'If I have to,' he admitted.

He seemed resigned to his fate and sure that we had resolved not to give any ground in this tug of war.

'I'll tell you what, I think that I might have six thousand on me,' I announced, looking him in the eye.

There was a fifty–fifty chance that he might actually have to sleep in the van and I definitely did not want that on my conscience under any circumstances; I had made him suffer enough for his behaviour.

'You do?' asked Mohammed; he was pleased.

'I might,' I agreed cagily; I couldn't resist a last stab at being mischievous.

'Good,' he seemed relieved.

I was not sure whether he was in on the game or if the airport manager had really made an error, somehow, I doubted it. A departure tax was payable at Entebbe, but that was an international flight.

Six thousand was a small price to pay for Anthony's peace of mind and to get him on his flight home.

'Here is five thousand and one thousand,' I exclaimed as I counted out the two notes, trying desperately to shield the others in my wallet.

'I will write you a receipt,' announced the airport manager.

He took the money, opened a desk drawer, and, extracting an old, battered, grey metal cash box, put the notes in and locked it with a small silver key.

'Thank you,' I sighed graciously, putting my wallet firmly back into my trouser pocket.

I was relieved that everyone seemed happy and that I had not been asked to pay money that I didn't have. I had wondered before the trip how much money one needs in a game reserve.

I knew I could charge expenses at the lodge to my credit card, so I had brought just enough for drinks and incidentals beyond the confines of the lodge. I had figured on buying a round or two of drinks and some coffees and some food along the way; I had not banked on having to pay thirty thousand or, even worse, sixty thousand.

The plane, when it arrived, was a sixteen-seater turbo prop with two pilots. We could see the plane getting nearer and as we watched it landed on the sand. Water rose up from beneath its wheels, splashing the wings.

I had forgotten that it had rained so hard the previous evening and in the morning; the sun had shone so brightly that by that very same afternoon, it seemed as if it had always been that way. The landing was not a textbook affair, as the plane aquaplaned on the runway, but it was a small skid and the pilots eased the plane through it.

Anthony was a nervous flyer and such a demonstration did not fill him with confidence.

The pilots got out to stretch their legs and to greet the ground team; they knew each other well and exchanged pleasantries. Bidding farewell to Mohammed and Charles, I couldn't help thrusting some money into their hands despite Anthony's obvious disapproval.

We had taken their addresses and promised to write. Just like people who say, 'let's do lunch', we fully intended to write, but once back in Entebbe the compunction was lost.

We would never be going back to Africa and we would never see these people again.

I suppose we all knew that, yet the ambience that we had achieved made us wish for different circumstances.

I often wonder how Charles and Mohammed are doing, but as I have long since lost their addresses, I will never know.

I hope Charles is still sharing his knowledge with visitors to the lodge and I hope Mohammed is being more direct with those he drives. The former I suspect is the case, the latter, I doubt.

Chapter 18

The Storm

We climbed aboard the plane at the back; concertina steps had been unfurled from the floor of the cabin. Two Norwegian aid workers sat behind the port wing, the pilot's wife sat at the front with her son and daughter and then there was just us.

I found a seat next to the starboard wing. It appeared that the passengers were going to make the flight as well balanced as possible. Anthony sat the opposite side of the aisle becoming more and more ashen with the realisation that this small craft was expected to fly. I tried to engage him in conversation.

'It's a relief to get on the plane.' I sighed dramatically to enhance the comment.

'It will be a relief when we are back in Kampala,' Anthony hissed through gritted teeth. His sunglasses looked over at me; their hard-man connotations were slightly spoilt by the quivering bottom lip, which tried to encourage the dry mouth to utter the words.

'These twin engine props are the safest planes in the air,' I assured him, hoping that the mention of four engines would keep him calm in some way. We could cope with one or even two, or perhaps three engines breaking down.

I had flown with my sister once she had got her private pilot's licence or PPL and she had been rigorous in her pre-flight checks, as I was sure our pilot had been.

'How old is the plane?' Anthony asked.

He was not worried about the engines but the sub-frame shaking apart or the under carriage giving way below us, or the tyres puncturing. It was clear he would not be placated until we taxied off the runway at Entebbe.

'Not old. Less than fifteen years,' I guessed wildly, desperate to reassure my nervous flyer friend.

Personally, I would have dated the plane's manufacture at around 1975 but that would have made it vintage in Anthony's eyes. The cloth for the seats looked worn and the nylon material reminded me of the designs and patterns that were popular in aircraft in the early 1960s.

'That's old.' I wasn't sure whether he said, 'that old?' but it came down to the same thing.

'What time are we due in Entebbe?'

'In fifty minutes, 'bout four o'clock.'

'Just in time for tea.'

We took off, shaking along the short runway. Out of the window I could see our four friends waving wildly, they would miss us, and I would miss them. I waved back madly. To see them out of the port window, I had to crane my neck around Anthony's head. I noticed that he was sitting bolt upright and staring fixedly at the back of the seat in front.

I could have sworn he was counting the stitches on the weave of the white polyester napkin on the headrest in front; perhaps he was just praying. I never asked but both options were likely, anything to take his mind off the flight. We flew over the lodge, our luxury hotel in the midst of the wilderness; it looked like a Bond villain's lair.

'Look, Anthony, the hotel looks great from here,' I enthused, moving my head back so he could see, too. If Anthony was looking, he could have easily seen the rectangle of the lodge and the wonderful swimming pool and the slope down to the river. Anthony pretended not to hear me. 'It's difficult to imagine we were swimming there yesterday.'

There was no response, so I just enjoyed the view a couple of hundred feet below. We climbed some more and banked, flying over the Murchinson Falls; the pilot was keen to show his family the spectacular drop into the flood plain.

I cursed the fact that I did not have a camera; the view was stunning, as if watching water fall off the edge of the world.

The sun was shining; the plane was soaring, and life was good. The vibration and noise were greater than on a commercial scheduled flight, but it was not deafening.

I had taken similar twin-engined flights from Dublin to Knock or Shannon, in the past.

It was only later on in the flight that we ran into a storm and we were all buffeted about a bit by the tropical winds.

I craned around and saw the pilot's view of sweeping rain and dense grey cloud. The windscreen wipers did nothing to increase visibility, but the co-pilot was doing things by the book, scanning the horizon for breaks in the cloud or signs of other aircraft.

I watched in increasing fascination and admiration as his head moved constantly from side to side, scanning the horizon or looking at the instrument panel as the pilot stared steadfastly through the windscreen battling with the elements to keep the plane trim.

We went through a few pockets where we dropped slightly, a couple of hundred feet each time, and I felt sorry for Anthony.

The clouds obscured my view so I attempted to sleep, reclining the seat back as far as it would go.

The legroom was good, so I was comfortable, but the noise of engine was too obtrusive, so I stood up and moved to the back opposite the aid workers who gave me a suspicious look. They wondered what I was doing on their flight. Their look of disdain was hardly hidden.

I rolled up my jacket and used one of the pillows on the seat to dull the vibration from the fuselage. I dozed rather than slept, which was just as well as the trip took one hour and twenty minutes instead of the fifty; something to do with the storm we went through and the head winds the pilot explained as we came into land.

The head wind we were battling against added a full half-hour to our trip. The weather as we approached Entebbe was clear and we took the same trajectory as the Boeing on which we had first arrived.

I moved back to the spot opposite Anthony as soon as the pilot warned us that we were on our approach to the airport. It was stunning to see the late afternoon sun glinting on the water and to see the landing from the pilot's perspective: sea, shore and runway coming up as we slipped down on to our tyres.

The landing was smooth until the engines were reversed, and as there was another flight coming in, the pilot was keen to clear the tarmac and used his breaks rather forcibly.

They locked up with the damp, so he eased off a bit at first so that we did not skid like last time, before applying them sharply again and taxiing carefully to the holding area before the plane behind landed.

Slowly motoring to the arrivals hall, I thought back to our welcome off the plane from England and how wonderfully surprising and warm it was; this arrival was like the weather outside the window, a bit of a damp squib.

Anthony undid his seatbelt like a man given a last-minute reprieve from death row. It was as if he really couldn't believe that we had made it in one piece. I internalised my humour and let him gather himself. I waited until he grabbed his bag and walked out before following him.

As we left the plane by the door at the rear, I noticed the wife and son of the pilot move forward into the cockpit and I wondered whether it was their first flight with him and whether it could have been his first flight, too. It had been as if the co-pilot was looking after the pilot, checking his instruments and visibility ahead while the pilot wrestled with the controls of the aircraft.

However, as I reflected on the warm walk to the arrivals hall, I thought about the way they both handled the aircraft; they treated this as a train driver might treat a run from station to station, and dismissed the idea.

Anthony was relieved that we had landed, but there was the problem of getting into town. I offered to share our cab with the Norwegian aid workers, but they declined. It turned out that they had a lift organised and rather snootily declined to reveal which agency they worked for or where they'd been.

They said they worked for a 'Christian' aid agency, but their Christianity didn't extend to offering us a ride into town. I know Norway is a cold country, but I have rarely met anyone as cold as that particular pair.

Of course, there was the added reason for them to feel above us; they were worthy, we were not, they worked for an nongovernmental organisation and that made us the unclean. They realised that we were tourists; they would not share with us – not the air-conditioned seven-seat four by four, complete with driver. Charities are businesses, like any other these days; these were well paid executives, they would not want to mix with lowly teachers. Christianity and behaving in a charitable way was saved for the chosen and needy.

We were neither so they did not know what to do, poor lost lambs that they were.

We walked out across the air-conditioned arrivals hall and I noticed I had been sweating profusely; I could not wait to get home and shower. The sky was overcast but it was still tropically warm as we stepped out into the drop-off zone outside the airport. There was a taxi rank and we had managed to be the first in line.

'How much to Kampala?' Anthony asked the first cabby.

'Thirty-five for Kampala,' the taxi driver replied.

'Twenty,' Anthony insisted

'Thirty-five,' the driver responded, not wanting to budge on price – he wasn't going to be put off.

He knew another flight was coming in and he could be guaranteed the fare he had asked. Entebbe was forty miles from Kampala, and it was meant to be $35.00 to the capital, but we found that 35,000 shillings was the going rate. It's funny that no matter where you travel in the world it's between thirty-five and forty to get into the centre of town in dollars or pounds, one of the axioms of international travel.

Chapter 19

Preparations

On Saturday Dae Woo kindly agreed to take me shopping. I had been ensconced in the Italian house on my return to Kampala. I wanted to make sure there was food in the house when the others arrived back from their tented safari.

The idea was that you paid your driver to spend time with you in the market. He would make sure that you paid the local price for your purchases and not the tourist price. I could not have wished for a better guide and protector.

The traffic was terrible, almost grid-lock; an ambulatory taxi ride through the markets made me feel that perhaps we should both be running around with our shirt tails hanging out, taking it in turns at tugging each other's shirts and saying, 'drive on', or 'left here'.

As children, my brother and I used to be either train drivers or wagon drivers in this fashion, sometimes for days at a time.

It would have been simpler to give Dae Woo a list and then ask him to get the goods for me. I knew the local price that I would get would not be as good as the local price that he would get.

There was a two-tier system because there was a local African price and a local European price.

In a way it made sense that the Europeans were charged more; they were paid more and could afford more.

It was a sort of wealth tax and the Europeans and Africans knew the prices in the shops and hotels, therefore market traders could gauge how much the European would be prepared to pay.

The pink flustered tourist on the other hand could be fleeced without mercy. If they could afford the flight they could afford to pay heavily for their fruit and for the atmosphere of the market. Let us face facts; we tourists or travellers love to be exploited.

I remember being on a cruise in Egypt along the Nile, where tourists happily bought saffron and other exotic spices at three or four times the price that they would pay for the same spice at their local supermarket.

No one minded at all as it was *holiday money*.

That *holiday money*, which we took with us, had already been saved in order to be spent freely in the local economy. My girlfriend at the time refused to pay so much for the produce but bought some jewellery instead.

I had already experienced the exorbitant prices of hotels, which made the African market trader's attempts at fleecing visitors seem charming in comparison. Admittedly, they tried to get the best price they could. The hotels tried to take the shirt off your back.

It is a strange axiom that, in the safety of the hotels, around the world, people tell of their horrendous experience of being taken for a ride by a taxi driver or ripped off by a shopkeeper while drinking expensive drinks. They happily pay top dollar for the flight and for an expensive hotel room when the girl next to them has paid half the price for a flight and the guy behind gets a forty per cent reduction on that chain because he uses it regularly for business.

I had nothing better to do. Anthony had gone back to England that morning and the others would be arriving in the afternoon. The Major had another couple of interviews with Uganda's CBS radio and *The New Vision* newspaper reporter, so I thought I'd take in the sights and sounds and smells of Kampala.

I wanted to see what the market was like, but I also wanted to get food for the house that I would be staying in that evening and for the rest of my stay. It was the house in which Anna had been staying all the time and was situated in Aka Bua Road. The impressive house was owned by a family of Italians; they had generously offered it to our party as they were travelling in Europe for the weeks that we were there.

By bringing Dae Woo I could buy more for my money and I knew that he would know the best stalls. Duncan had sent him off to get some fruit for Mama Rose and was still waiting for his change, but I suspect Duncan just gave him the money for the fruit and not for the carriage. Duncan tended to forget that he was not dealing with UPS or Fed Ex.

I was planning to buy a decent amount of food and drink; Dae Woo could ferry me to the house with the load, and it was a perfect plan. The holiday was full of such misunderstandings. 'Duncan had asked Duncan' is confusing enough, both visitor and host shared the same name; both constantly responded to the others name. We called Duncan the taxi driver Dae Woo to avoid confusion.

Everyone knew his car was Japanese and a Toyota; it was beautiful, clean and comfortable, but he ended up with his nickname because his name began with a 'D'. It made even less sense since Daewoo is a Korean firm.

Duncan therefore asked Dae Woo how much it would be to get some pineapples, meaning how much would it cost for *Dae Woo* to go and collect them and bring them back. Dae Woo Duncan gave him a price for the pineapples and therefore Duncan was expecting change when in fact our guide had rightly added on his fare on top, after all he was fetching the fruit.

We could have been clearer in our requests; a common language does not necessarily guarantee common communication. 'Get' means the same as buy but if you do not add the fare to get it, people can get confused, especially if they are called Duncan and their thoughts are on more ethereal things than distribution and transport.

Equally, it was difficult outside the confines of a bar or hotel. The price of beer was pretty constant wherever you went; a bar was cheapest, local hotels doubled the price and international hotels doubled the price again, it was your choice.

Personally, I preferred the bars, but I was also happy to pay for the attentive staff and air conditioning in the Sheraton or Imperial. We had not been out on the town as much as I would have liked so I was anticipating seeing the market.

Dae Woo picked me up from the veranda at the Speke in his new-looking, pristine, gleaming white *Toyota*; I wondered how he managed to keep it so clean in such a dusty city.

We drove from the Speke and took a right, heading down towards the financial sector, the street where all the banks and the post office were located. We passed all the modern offices and moved towards the bungalows and low-level shops of the market.

This was as much a 'booze cruise' as a shopping trip so at the next junction we bought three crates of beer and two crates of orange pop for the children. I would worry about getting sherry and wine for the ladies at another shop; this was purely a deposit-bottle shop.

The shop was a dark rectangle and crate upon crate had been piled against each available wall, the empties filled the wooden stoop and lined the steps that led down on to street level. Dae Woo had reversed into the only available parking space.

He offered to help me source full crates of drinks, but I refused his offer, he was my guide and driver only. The shop owner was an old lady not capable of lifting anything and her deliverymen were out in the truck.

As a result, I was on my own. I climbed up on the crates and found some containers with a complete set of two-dozen full bottles. It was like being back in the days when I worked as a drayman for a brewery, clambering over plastic cases and hauling them down to deliver to city pubs.

I paid the deposit on the bottles and what seemed like an extremely cheap price for the beers. We had been paying hotel prices during our stay and this was my first wholesale transaction since I had bought Pip Bruton the bottle of Scotch.

I would not let Dae Woo help me with loading the cases. I needed the exercise, but in the heat going up five steps and into the shop just five times plus loading the cases into the boot made me feel quite hot. I did not want him working up a sweat when he was dressed in such a startling white shirt and well-pressed navy chinos.

It was early still, and I couldn't imagine having to work all day in that heat, especially doing something strenuous like cutting cane or working on a building site.

I collapsed into the passenger seat next to Dae Woo and was relieved when he started the motor and the air conditioning cut in. The deposit for the bottles and crates was more than the cost of the goods, so I folded the receipt carefully and put it in my shirt pocket.

I have terrible habits but one of the least unpleasant is wearing a shopping shirt; this is green cotton with long sleeves, a button-down collar and two button-down breast pockets, bought in Hong Kong with an Osh Gosh label.

The change went in the left pocket and the notes in the right pocket. Not much protection from a mugger but a convenient way of avoiding pickpockets.

We drove another two blocks past similar shack shops to the one I had visited. All of them had a different purpose; there were soft drinks stores, electrical stores, radio shacks, hardware stores and grocery shops.

We could have got all we wanted from these places without visiting the market, but then, by the time you passed all the shops that you didn't want to buy from, it would have taken an hour to get a few items. The market had the best fruit and vegetables for miles around and it provided a good choice.

We drove left into a side road and all around the shops and houses disappeared from view as an expanse of space spread before us. There was a dusty floor surrounded by bungalow shops, the larger buildings rising up behind them.

I was surprised at how similar it looked to market towns in England except the ground was sand. It looked like a development site just before the big block goes up.

The site was clear but surrounded by real estate. On this dusty floor were parked vans of every size make and description in every possible colour in every available free space surrounding the covered market; the market itself was a rectangular building taking pride of place in the gap in this city within a city.

The tin corrugated roof of the market was painted red and rose to an apex. From the centre, stalls spread underneath, protected from the sun but some stalls spilled out of the market and on to the dust of the car park and competed for space with the parked vans.

We drove around and I looked at the activity, everyone hustling and bustling: older women in bright striped clothes pressed and pristine clean, younger women in figure-hugging earthy coloured skirts with brilliant white starched blouses.

There were also men in pressed jeans or black trousers with similarly starched white shirts or polo shirts; everyone was moving with purpose.

There was much to do.

Duncan drove around to the right and after passing the fish stalls, he took another right and he parked his car at forty-five degrees to the pavement at the bottom end of the market square.

We were opposite a pharmacy and I bought some new blades for my razor and as I came out, I could smell the citrus fruit on the stalls opposite. There was a gentle ripple of conversation and some laughter.

It was far more relaxed than North African or Chinese markets and I looked forward to having a look around; it reminded me of the gentleness of Dubai's fish market. Everyone knew they would sell what they had and if they didn't, they wouldn't have done badly. They were not obsessed with selling like some people.

Far Eastern, Turkish and Egyptian markets tend to have stallholders reach and grab you. Duncan shadowed me through the stalls like a bodyguard and when I stopped at a stall, he would step forward and ask the price; it helped with my learning the language.

Duncan had already taught me what to say to local girls to impress them and it obviously seemed to work from the giggling response I received and the shy smiles after. I just hoped that Duncan, with his highly developed sense of humour, had not actually taught me a rude phrase.

He found the whole thing that I was attempting to communicate in the dialect almost hysterically funny. Still there was little to laugh about in the news, so I was doing him a favour, I guess.

It was a pleasant stroll and the produce was tempting but I was on a budget since so much cash had gone on the deposit for the bottles and I could not get to a bank before Monday. Remember, I had paid the departure tax to get to Entebbe, so a large part of my hard cash had gone.

I bought some pineapples, mangoes and bananas as the children all loved those and I was hoping that by eating those too, I would be healthier. The daily bacon rashers and eggs at the Speke and the larger safari breakfast that I had enjoyed recently were taking their toll and I was expanding rapidly.

I bought some slimming vegetables and a rather sorry looking chicken that looked as though being in a refrigerator might revive him, but he was a scrawny specimen, so I bought another to keep him company in the back of the car.

Everyone was pleasant except when we left; Duncan stopped to talk to the stallholder and passed a young guy who started shouting at me when I refused to buy something from him. I have lived in rough parts of New York and London, but I was shocked by the suddenness of the tirade.

Then I twigged that he actually hoped to embarrass me and in order to keep him quiet he expected me to buy his goods. When I realised that it was a show, I too started to enjoy it as much as the other Africans.

I wasn't about to shrink from someone who was accusing me of imperialism and racism. I was Irish and Ireland has never been imperialist, and I have never been racist, but I could imagine a more sensitive soul paying him off merely to keep him quiet. I listened attentively, as did everyone else. I informed him I was Irish, and he stomped off to loud applause. I wondered whether he played the same spot every day.

Duncan explained that a lot of younger Africans menace the customers and the stallholders in the market. They bring some tourist to the stall, explain what good produce it is and then bump up the price by five hundred or a thousand. They come back later with some friends to ask for the difference in their price and the real price, plus commission on the sale, 1,000 or 1,500. It was bullyboy tactics that frightened the older generation. The angry man had offered me something that I had already bought, and he was charging me three times the price.

I had refused politely and then he had become abusive.

Perhaps he was part of those gangs and he resented my being accompanied by Duncan or he might have been miffed that I was a target for extortion that had slipped through his fingers.

Chapter 20

Walking the Aka Bua Road

i

Dae Woo took me back to the house in Aka Bua Road. The guard opened the sheet-metal gate that protected the compound from the outside world, an eight-foot-high, nine-foot-wide rectangle, painted a tired, faded scarlet. We drove down the drive between palms and pineapple trees to the back of the house. Dae Woo knew the place well. Like any well-appointed Italian country house there were two wooden doors. I rapped on them and one of them opened.

A slim 'house girl' with a welcoming smile opened the door. She was about nineteen and she wore a white vest-like T-shirt and a short denim skirt that covered some of her thighs.

Her name was Mary she told me, and she informed me that she was also a committed Christian. I suspect she added that because she did not want any trouble from me; I obviously looked like the predatory type. She was impressed with our efforts at shopping simply because she would not have to go to market this side of the weekend; I had bought enough food to last us at least until Wednesday and drinks for all of us.

I insisted Dae Woo and Mary have a drink and we toasted one another.

'Nayabo,' Duncan said to Mary, the charmer, as he raised his Stoney bottle.

'Saebo,' Mary raised her Fanta bottle.

'Nayabo, Saebo,' I said as I slightly guiltily raised a large bottle of Bell lager to my lips, toasting miss and sir with the slight movement of my brown bottle beforehand in a respectful salute.

'Yagala casolao ungala mere,' Dae Woo added.

Mary giggled so much she had to cover her mouth to shield her teeth, which were white and strong.

I can't possibly tell you what Duncan said to Mary, you will have to travel to Africa in order to find out. A Bagandan who is not easily embarrassed might tell you what it means.

Despite my shopping before the weekend, I was despatched to get more food on Sunday evening. Clearly, the household thought well in advance and Mary was planning supper on Wednesday in case there should be shortages of items between now and then. I was sent with a shopping list written in clear writing in blue pen. Mary had prepared a comprehensive list, which included the expected prices that I should pay. I was not sure whether she was paying local prices or if she computed her costs in European tariffs in order to play the game.

It didn't matter which it was because I had money to pay for it and that was the main thing. I relished a walk to the more local market, and I knew that the stallholders would help me out, stranger that I was. I looked at my list; Chicken 5,000; Fish 2kg, 12,000 or 8,000 for tilapia.

The vegetables were on another stall: six potatoes, 6,400; French beans and lettuce 3,750 and 2,000. She required mangoes, ripe, 2,000; sugar, white 2,400; custard, one tin 3,000; bread 1,400. Altogether, with a few other items, it was 30,700 and Mary had recommended paying a porter at the market 1,000 to help me carry everything, but I would first have to recognise the porters.

I contemplated the situation in Uganda as I passed an open-back truck with about twenty policemen, all wearing blue paramilitary uniforms with black berets and machine guns.

It seemed to me that Uganda was a country surrounded by insurmountable opportunities.

I have never been a politician and my bank manager will testify to my inability to be thought of as an economist, but I kept abreast of current affairs in the newspapers and had a fair idea of how the economies around the world seemed to function.

I had witnessed economic and political upheaval.

It seemed to me that the Buganda's relative wealth was a source of tension in the country and I got the distinct impression that Museveni's government wanted to divide the land owned by Bagandans between all Ugandans. It was obvious from our travels within Uganda that the Bagandans' method of handing down land from generation to generation was a source of envy for those who did not own land and that such ownership was considered to be detrimental to the prosperity of Uganda.

Yet I saw good use being made of the land and wondered if having larger farms and plantations throughout the area would bring its own problems. If the government nationalised all land and was put in charge of its cultivation, then efficiency might improve but there would be the usual drawbacks associated with government control even if corruption were minimised.

Museveni was aware of the loyalty to the Kabaka, a loyalty that would not be diminished by their land being taken away. However, there was a lot of popular support from those who resented the advantage that Bagandans had. Bagandans were loyal to both the Kabaka and Museveni, but pressure was on the president to make sure that his people only had one master.

The Bagandans owned fertile land and Kampala and Entebbe were Bagandan areas. Asian businessmen or international companies owned most of the banks or hotels but the spin-off in services to these organisations was immense.

Kampala was a relatively wealthy city and Entebbe was fast becoming more than just an international airport.

Naturally the Bagandans felt anxious because they felt spiritual loyalty to the Kabaka, yet could not ask him to guarantee their independence and they felt legally loyal to the president and yet they were not sure that Museveni's government would treat them fairly.

On Sunday, we went to the Anglican cathedral service and afterwards to visit a relation of Kabaka who was a friend of the Major's. She lived in a fine bungalow house, set in lush tropical grounds. I waited outside with the driver and Duncan; we smoked and talked.

I looked around me and realised that it really was true that if you dropped a seed it would grow; the garden had avocado, banana and mango trees; the lawn was a vivid green.

The climate in the hills above Kampala was about 29 degrees, much cooler than elsewhere due to the hills and close proximity to the lake, a marvellous microclimate in equatorial tropical Africa.

I had made it to the craft market the Saturday before we went back to England. I accompanied the others to buy presents and saw the obvious appeal to Hattie; the place was great for gifts.

The stalls were all covered, and their displays spilled on to tables set up on the grass. The building itself consisted of an 'L' shape linear collection of shops, each one about the size of a large stable.

The shops opened up on to a rectangular field of dry grass, too bumpy to play football on. It was an empty plot and I envisaged a hotel standing on the site before too long. The vendors sold all manner of African craft work and everything you could need in electrical or plumbing goods. The tourist sites tended to be nearer the entrance and the practical shops were at the far end.

I bought a 'Lucky Dube' tape. Hattie had introduced me to the Reggae star from South Africa. His music was Kingston, Jamaica, meets Soweto, Africa. There was also an excellent selection of small drums; clever chairs that consisted of a spiral concave cane seat, like a bowl, set on three crossed wooden legs – mere shaved branches nailed together and extremely comfortable to sit on and very sturdy. There were wooden bottle openers with a screw driven into the head to rip off the crown cork from any bottle.

Aubrey brought me a small drum and I was overwhelmed by his generosity to me, his brothers and his cousins, Matilda and Emily; he bought presents for all the party and I was touched by his obvious pleasure in giving and in his consideration – he chose each individual present with care.

I knew he had his eye on an animal-hair cushion decorated with a colourful map of Africa, but he could not afford it, so I bought it for him. I saw it in the drawing room the next time I visited.

The animal hair was most probably cow or goat hide; it could have been horse.

All I knew was that it was a chestnut colour and the hair was short, but the colourful, beautifully embroidered map of Africa really made it and, perhaps, helped the children to keep Uganda in their minds.

I bought napkin rings of carved wood in the shape of African animals that were hand painted; the gifts reflected my lack of imagination, the twelve presents I had to get, as well as how little money I had at the end of the three weeks.

I had lived liked a king, and I had spent time with the king, albeit an afternoon with him as part of a tea party, I had spent my money royally like a king; plus, any holiday of that length was bound to leave a dent in anyone's budget, not least a budget constricted by a teacher's salary.

Chapter 21

At Home

In the autumn we had some happy news that the Kabaka was to get engaged. It was one Sunday in October in Anna and Pip's spacious kitchen; we were all drinking red wine and trying to get close to the Aga.

All of the family had an Aga. Hattie, Duncan and I had been invited for lunch; I had been staying with the Major and Susan in Bath Easton and Hattie had driven Duncan and I over in her convertible Italian sports car.

'Mama Rose is coming over,' Pip told me.

'She never rang me,' I replied.

'I expect she lost your number,' Pip suggested.

'We'd all like to do that,' Duncan added.

'How's her arm?' I asked, ignoring him.

'She's a sprightly one that one,' Pip informed me.

'A sprightly lady, full of spunk,' Duncan added.

'Indeed,' I agreed, hoping my comment had nipped him in the bud, or so I hoped.

Hattie came to my rescue by asking Duncan for a light.

'I saw Lucy the other day, Mike, she says hello,' Hattie announced affably.

Hattie was living between London and Bath, so she saw Lucy in London.

'Talking of sisters, my sister has just moved to Nice,' I exclaimed. I had wanted to change the subject; my sister's move from Toulon to Nice had provided a means.

I had tried to get on with Lucy and she had tried to get on with me but alas we did not succeed.

'That's nice,' Hattie replied, she was always keen on warm places. 'Is she near the sea, I bet there's a lovely outdoor pool near her flat.'

'Shall I book you in?' I asked.

'I'm getting cheap flights to Ibiza next year, I can't wait,' Hattie admitted; she was a true sun-worshipper.

'What about you, Huck Finn?' Anna asked.

'Sailing is the only adventure for me next year, if I can organise it. I'd like to go to Kerala,' I announced. I liked the idea of travelling on water.

'What about Goa or Sri Lanka?' she asked.

'To just lie on the beach?' I replied. I knew how adventurous Hattie's holidays were.

'We could go to Africa and visit Ronnie,' I suggested.

'There was an article about Freddie and Ronnie in *The Telegraph*,' Duncan announced.

'Which telegraph,' Pip asked. All of us knew that he meant – today or yesterday – he was too busy to read the papers as the project he had on was huge.

'Bush telegraph,' I suggested.

Duncan rolled his eyes, Anna tilted her head, Hattie smiled indulgently, and Pip sighed, the sigh of a patient saint.

'Don't wind me up, Finn,' Pip said impatiently.

Then a smile spread to his lips and to my immense relief all the remaining members of the safari laughed heartily.

I went to get *The Telegraph*.

THE END

Other Books

We hope you have enjoyed the story. You might like to consider the following books by the same author:

The Taint Gallery is the story of two normal people who allow passion to destroy their peace and tranquillity. This is an explicit portrayal of sexual attraction and deteriorating relationships.

Switch is a dark thriller; Chandler meets *Fifty Shades of Grey* – a nightmare comes true!

Waterwitch, a sailing adventure: two brothers sailing a boat around the Mediterranean during the Falklands War, resulting in disastrous consequences.

Innocent Proven Guilty is a thriller on the lines of *The 39 Steps*. A teacher discovers his brother dead in a pool of blood; he wants to find the murderer, but he has left his footprints behind.

Seveny Seven is a 'Punk Portrait' The story of growing up in London during the punk era, a whimsical autobiography that explodes the myth that 'Punk' was an angry working-class movement.

Carom is a thriller about an art theft and drug smuggling. Finn McHugh and his team pursue Didier Pourchaire, a vicious art thief. The action moves between London, Paris, Helsinki and St Petersburg. Everyone wants to catch the villain resulting in a messy bagatelle. Carom is an Indian board game.

One also called *Ad Bec* is a dish best eaten cold; a schoolboy takes revenge on a bully. Stephen is a late arrival at a prep school in the depths of Shropshire. He is challenged to do a 'tunnel dare' by the school bully.

When the tunnel collapses on the bully, Stephen has to solve the dilemma: tell no one and be free or rescue the bully.

The story is set in a seventies progressive preparatory school.

Remember the Fifth is the true story of Guy Fawkes; it shows how Robert Cecil tried to destroy all opposition to his power and make himself the hero of the hour.

2029 is an adventure and love story, set in a dystopian England on the anniversary of the Wall Street Crash where England has suffered from a virulent virus, a recession and smugglers have taken over much of England. Aubrey East goes for a swim with Freddie Lawless and when he drowns, Aubrey is accused of his murder. He must fight to win his love but first he must fight to clear his name.

The Clapham Common Caper, set in 1959, is the story of a courageous doctor, Nora Josephine Murphy who discovers a suicide was in fact murder. With the help of Richard Regan, she fights to destroy the gang behind this and other heinous crimes.

Karoly's Hungarian Tragedy is Michael's first departure into historical biography. This is the story of Karoly Ellenbacher taken into captivity and used as a human shield by Romanian soldiers during the war; arrested during the communist era and sent down a coal mine, he escaped to England in 1956. His story of survival is barely credible.

Michael Fitzalan has written four plays:

Veni, Vidi, Vicky: a story of a failed love affair.

George and the Dragon: a painter discovers a cache of bonds and sovereigns in a cellar, not knowing that it belongs to a vicious gang. Thankfully his niece's friend is a star lawyer and can help him return the money before it is too late… or can she?

Symposium for Severine is a modern version of Plato's *Symposium* but with women the philosophers instead of men.

Superstar is a play that sees Thomas Dowting meeting Jesus in the temple, travelling to Angel to meet his girlfriend Gabrielle. They convince Thomas to volunteer for work abroad. Three weeks later J C Goodman takes over Thomas's job and moves in with Gabrielle.

Switch and *Major Bruton's Safari* have been turned into scripts.

Michael is working on a script, which he may turn into a novel: *M.O.D.*, Mark O'Dwyer, Master of Disguise – a private detective agency, Francis Barber Investigators, is retained to find out why a model was defenestrated from a Bond Street building.

Printed in Great Britain
by Amazon